Keith Waterhouse, born in 1929, is a man of many literary parts. Besides having published nine novels, the most recent of which was *Thinks* (1984), he writes a twice-weekly column for the *Daily Mirror*, is a regular contributor to *Punch*, and has produced a wide range of work for television, cinema and the theatre.

By the same author

KEITH WATERHOUSE

Office Life

GRAFTON BOOKS

A Division of the Collins Publishing Group

LONDON GLASGOW
TORONTO SYDNEY AUCKLAND

Grafton Books
A Division of the Collins Publishing Group
8 Grafton Street, London W1X 3LA

Published by Grafton Books 1986

First published in Great Britain by
Michael Joseph Ltd 1978

ISBN 0-586-06650-0

Printed and bound in Great Britain by
Collins, Glasgow

Set in Times

1

'Mr Graph-paper, Mr Seeds, Miss Divorce, Mrs Rashman, Mr Ah Dah, Mr Beastly, Mr Charles Penney, Mr New Penny, Mr Hakim.'

Catching one name in three, Clement Gryce shook hands with such of his new colleagues as were near enough to touch, and nodded to those who were out of reach behind their desks.

Most of them said a word or two: 'How d'y'do.' 'Glad to have you aboard.' 'Welcome to the madhouse.' They seemed a nice enough lot taken all round, though Gryce put question marks over the heads of two of them, Beastly and Graph-paper, who could very easily have shaken hands if they'd bothered to stand up and lean forward a bit. Graph-paper, he already knew from his interview with Copeland who had mentioned a Mr Grant-hyphen-something or other, was Copeland's deputy. Beastly looked as if he might be next in the chain of command.

'Not forgetting Thelma who looks after us all.' Copeland, who put Gryce in mind of the actor Mervyn Johns, waved an arm towards the dumpy office girl, a recent school-leaver by the look of her. She bore a passing resemblance to the girl who had played Judy Garland's room-mate in an old film recently repeated on television. Gryce gave her a brief smile and permitted his glance, as it swivelled back to Copeland, to take a short detour via the other two females present.

Mrs Rashman must have been about fifty, or ten years older than himself. That didn't necessarily rule her out.

5

Some of these homely-looking ones really knew how to let their hair down once they'd watered the pot plants and left the office for the day, so it was rumoured. But the younger one – thirtyish? thirty-fiveish? – was probably the likelier of the two, so long as her real name proved to be something less provocative than Miss Divorce. That was definitely the once-over she had given him when the commissionaire had shown him in. She reminded Gryce of a well-known news reader. Gryce watched TV a lot and nearly everyone he met reminded him of some celebrity or character actor, though he could not always put a name to the face.

'Now, where are we going to park you?' Copeland went on. 'As I think I told you, the whole department is to be reorganized quite soon so I'd rather not move in a new desk just yet. Who's on holiday?' he asked the man he had introduced as Mr Seeds. 'Isn't Fart still away?'

'I believe till next Monday.'

'Let us consult the holy writ.' Taking Gryce's arm, Copeland steered him across to the staff notice-board.

The office was open-plan, so there were no interior walls except the waist-high metal partitions that marked out the corridors between the three departments occupying the seventh floor. Putting up a notice-board that could be consulted without descending to one's knees had therefore presented a problem, which had been solved by a small team from Design and Maintenance after some experiment. First they had hung a sheet of cork on chains from the ceiling, only to find that it swung erratically backwards and forwards with a tendency to bat employees in the face as they walked past it. A heavier board was substituted, resulting in no marked modification except that some of the injuries sustained were now quite serious. The chains were stabilized with strong wooden battens, but the weight of these buckled the composition ceiling tiles. Finally a free-standing blackboard affair, on the lines of those to be seen in railway stations with regrets about late trains in chalked copperplate, had been devised. This method, pioneered in the department which Gryce had just joined, was now standard throughout the building.

The notice-board was dominated by a large sheet of card divided into columns. This, Gryce saw, was the holiday roster: he would have to see that he got his name down before all the best weeks were taken. While Copeland studied the list he was able to do some deciphering. The likelier of the two women, the one whose name he had heard as Miss Divorce, must be Mrs Fawce. (So she was married, then. Best thing in the long run, so long as they were discreet enough. From all he'd heard, the single ones finished up nagging to be taken out at weekends.) Ah Dah was Ardagh, that was an easy one, but who was New Penny? There was a C. Penney and an H. Penney, both taking the same week in June and the same two weeks in September, they must be brothers. Of course: *Hugh* Penney. Graph-paper, he remembered the name now, was Mr Grant-Peignton.

'Yes, here we are. Fart.' The holiday roster mentioned Vaart. Dutch extraction: South African, most likely. 'I should take his desk for this week, and then I see Mr Hakim won't be here the following week, so you'll have somewhere to sit for the time being.'

Wondering idly how the self-effacing Mr Hakim got along with Mr Vaart, whom he pictured as a red-necked Afrikaaner, Gryce took his place at the vacant desk. The desks were in rows of three and he found himself sitting between Beastly and Seeds. Beastly's real name, it would turn out, was Beazley. Seeds, to Gryce's surprise, was called Seeds. Both men looked like Jeremy Thorpe, MP – Seeds more so.

'Ron Seeds, in case you didn't catch the name in all that welter of introductions.' Seeds half-rose and shook hands again as Gryce sat down. Beazley, who was flicking rapidly and endlessly through a revolving card-index as if conducting an experiment in administrative perpetual motion, did not look up. He might have nodded, Gryce thought. But Seeds seemed ready to be friendly.

'Do you prefer coffee-flavoured dishwater or tea-flavoured dishwater?'

The familiar office joke made Gryce feel quite at home. 'Coffee-flavoured, I usually have.' He smiled again at the overweight junior who, with a good deal of clattering, was extracting a number of beakers from a filing cabinet and arranging them in a wire tray.

'Don't worry, we're not offending Thelma,' said Seeds. 'She doesn't brew it herself, it's all untouched by 'uman 'ands.'

'Ah, an infernal machine.'

'The wonders of modern technology. If you press the button marked tea it pours forth a liquid resembling coffee . . .'

'. . . whereas the button marked coffee produces a frothy substance that could be mistaken for tea, yes,' completed Gryce. Thelma was now clomping flat-footedly from desk to desk with her tray of beakers. This was obviously a morning routine: she collected the money for the vending machine, at the same time jotting down individual requirements on a scrap of cardboard – three coffees, one tea and one 7-Up so far, Gryce noted as Thelma reached his desk – and then did the rounds again dispensing the completed orders. It seemed inefficient: two journeys instead of one. In Gryce's last billet, the office girl had kept a little book and they had settled up weekly; but he could quite see that given the need to

8

feed the vending machine with tenpenny pieces, Thelma would have to find a daily supply of coins.

Raising his right buttock slightly he felt among the coins in his pocket for the milled edge of a tenpenny piece, but Seeds had beaten him to it. 'My treat, as you're a new boy.' He mustn't forget to reciprocate in the afternoon tea break. When he had a desk of his own, after the departmental reorganization that Copeland had spoken about, he could see this becoming a little daily custom, always supposing that he was still sitting next to Seeds or in his near vicinity. Seeds would stand him coffee in the mornings and he would stand Seeds tea, or whatever he preferred, in the afternoons. Since all drinks seemed to cost the same, Gryce had no objection to arrangements of this kind. They were what made the wheels go round, in his opinion.

The beverages arrived. The 7-Up drinker turned out to be Mr Hakim. That was easy to pin down because the 7-Up was served to him in a disposable plastic cup. Gryce expected the vending machine dispensed these cups and that it would be possible to have one's coffee or tea served in them. But the staff had probably found that they were difficult to hold when hot, or that their waxen texture caused an unpleasant taste. Perhaps there had been days when the vending machine had run out of plastic cups, and they had had to forgo their coffee break. At any rate they had clearly discussed it among themselves and decided to buy mugs or beakers or fetch them from home. The beaker Gryce had been given was a souvenir one from Cornwall; it was his guess that it belonged to the absent Vaart. He would have to bring one of his own – or perhaps it would be less trouble if he gave some money to Thelma and she could buy one during her lunch hour.

He took a tentative sip of coffee and seeing that Seeds

was looking at him in anticipation of a humorous reaction he thought of making the standard grimace of disgust, but decided instead upon raising his eyebrows and cocking his head slightly, at the same time arranging his mouth in the judicious pout of one who is prepared to concede a point in an argument.

'I've tasted worse. I don't known when, mark you, but I have definitely tasted worse.'

'Wait till you try what passes for tea,' said Seeds.

'Oh, I thought this *was* tea!' That should have been the end of the litany but Seeds seemed to expect more, so he added: 'It's certainly an improvement on the witches' brew they used to dispense at my last billet.'

'Where was that, without being nosy?'

'I served three years before the mast at Comform, if that name means anything to you. Office supplies, filing systems, you name it.'

'Oh, yes. Hammersmith somewhere, aren't they?'

'We-e-ll. Technically Hammersmith. Possibly just inside the Hammersmith border, though I wouldn't swear to it.'

'Long, two-or-three-storey building, white-fronted. Near Chiswick flyover.'

'No, no, I'll tell you what you're thinking of, you're thinking of what used to be the bottling plant. Lemonade, soft drinks, what were they called now?'

'Berry's.'

'Berry's. "You can taste the berries in Berry's." Since taken over by – it was either Watney's or Bass-Charrington, one of the big brewery giants anyway. No, no. *Very similar building*, admittedly, but we were much further out.'

'Towards Richmond, Twickenham, that way?'

They discussed the location of Gryce's last billet until Seeds had it placed to his satisfaction. Gryce had been given no work to do by Copeland, he expected he would be allowed to get the feel of the place for a day or two, and Seeds' duties seemed to leave him plenty of time for conversation. There was a sheaf of documents in front of him, multi-carbon affairs – order vouchers by the look of them – and occasionally he would run a pencil over the various columns and boxes and then rubber-stamp the top copy. This he placed in a folder, while the five or six flimsies were dispersed in a stacking arrangement of wire trays. The folder of top copies was kept in a separate wooden out-tray, so if they were order vouchers as Gryce supposed, they would obviously be collected or handed in at the end of the day for processing. It was much the same system as he had been used to in his last billet, except that Seeds' order vouchers, if that was what they were, would be internal ones and they were uniform in size and style, whereas at Comform he had had to cope with a variety of printed forms, Xeroxed pro-formas and even letters. Regular customers were sent blank order vouchers with every invoice but they refused to use them, so he had had the job of transferring their orders to the standard form before the work such as Seeds was doing now could even begin. He could see that he was going to have an easier time of it here.

'Not wishing to be personal, what prompted you to transfer your allegiance to Perfidious Albion?' asked Seeds when the question of Comform's whereabouts on the map had been settled. 'Perfidious Albion,' Gryce was to learn, was Seeds' wryly humorous appellation for the company they worked for. Others called it 'the factory', 'the madhouse', 'the labour camp' and suchlike, but Seeds' contribution in Gryce's view was the most original. It was genuinely witty. The real name of the firm was the British Albion Group.

'Why does one ever switch jobs?' he replied with the

world-weary shrug that the question seemed to call for. 'Apart from the seven-year itch, or three-year itch in my particular case, I used to dread fighting my way back to Forest Hill every evening. Getting there wasn't so bad.'

'It's a long way,' said Seeds sympathetically.

'It's a *very* long way.'

'Right across London, just about.'

'Not just about, it *is* right across London. Discounting the City.'

'I mean,' said Seeds ingratiatingly, seemingly anxious to patch up this little difference of opinion, 'imagining you were leaving here every rush hour, and travelling the same distance, you'd have to be living out in – where? Bromley? Sidcup?'

'Well, perhaps not so far out as that but pretty far out all the same. Croydon, say. Whereas here, I can get off the train at London Bridge and it's – what, by bus? Five minutes it took me this morning.'

'Yes, you were *rather lucky* there. Unless the service has very much improved.'

Seeds too, it transpired, had once travelled to and from London Bridge, when living for a time at Honor Oak Park. He now lived at Turnham Green, where he had the choice of tube or bus. After some discussion of Seeds' travelling arrangements, Gryce felt he had known him all his life.

Presently Copeland came up to Seeds' desk to ask after the whereabouts of, if Gryce had overheard correctly, the clockwork insect. Copeland, although enquiry would show that he was only two years Gryce's senior, looked older. The likeness to Mervyn Johns was only a facial one: structurally, he was well on the way to resembling Alfred Hitchcock. Signs of an unsuitable diet there – widower, very possibly. The lapels of his suit, a good one but of an old-fashioned cut, were flecked with dandruff, the trousers bagged. He would have been happier, thought Gryce, in a tweed sports coat and flannels. There seemed to be no office policy on clothes, not that you expected one in this day and age. Ardagh and Grant-Peignton wore sports jackets in conservative colours, Seeds, like Gryce himself, a dark suit from Montague Burton's. Hakim wore a lightweight suit in pale fawn, too flashy by far for office wear. The Penney brothers wore navy blue blazers. Gryce, who called himself observant, saw for the first time that they must be identical twins. 'The Penney's dropped!' he told himself: he would share the joke when he knew them better.

The industrious Beazley, surprisingly, was the only man in the office to work in his shirt sleeves; a heavyish mohair jacket hung over the back of his chair. Mrs Rashman plainly owned a large wardrobe of unremarkable dresses bought at chain-stores: turning his gaze away from her, Gryce was immediately unable to remember whether today's pattern was floral, striped or what. Mrs Fawce, or Miss Divorce as he still called her to himself, looked as if she sometimes came to the office in trousers, but today she was wearing a straight bottle-green skirt and a lime-green top thing. Good legs, not that he would be expecting the kind of relationship that legs came into. Gryce's eyes travelled up from them and she smiled at him briefly, reminding him as she did so of Diana Rigg.

The stockbook index, not clockwork insect, that Copeland was looking for was quickly found in the wire-basket arrangement but he remained at Seeds' desk to discuss the illness of someone they both seemed to know called Norwich Terrier. Gryce, for all that Copeland had not given him any work, began to feel embarrassed at sitting there doing nothing. His temporary desk offered no distractions: Vaart's filing trays and other bits and pieces

13

had evidently been locked away. It was bare except for its telephone receiver.

It was a commonplace-enough desk, in dull-finish grey metal. Black composition top, panel sides, front courtesy panel, three left-hand drawers locking, right-hand filing drawer also locking, the kind of thing his last billet had sold in thousands, catalogue number B4A/00621. It could, come to think of it, very well be a Comform desk at that. He slid his chair back a little and ducked his head to see if he could find the trademark beneath the rim of the desk top. Yes, it was there all right: the gold transfer pretty well worn off by now but it was definitely a Comform desk.

'Curious,' he said to Beazley on his right. He would have to talk to the man sooner or later, no time like the present.

Beazley, holding the leaves of his revolving card-index open with a ballpoint pen so as not to lose his place, looked up. Not impatiently, but certainly not as if he had all the time in the world like Seeds.

'I was saying,' Gryce went on. 'Curious about these desks. I was telling our friend here, for my sins I served three years before the mast at Comform.'

'Comform,' repeated Beazley. He had a barking voice. He sounded as if he were accustomed to giving orders, or would like to become so accustomed.

'I was just noticing, all the desks here are Comform. So I suspect are the chairs.'

'They should make you feel quite at home.'

'*Sha!*' That was how Gryce laughed. 'Can't get away from the place, eh?' He was glad they had found a little joke to share. It broke the ice. Certainly it meant that Beazley could not be as unfriendly as he looked. Perhaps he was shy with strangers, as gruff people sometimes were. Encouraged, Gryce continued quickly before Beazley could turn back to his work:

'The curious thing is, I don't *think* British Albion had a contract with Comform. In fact I'd swear to it. Bear in mind, I *was* in furniture sales for three years.'

'Probably before your time,' said Beazley.

'Probably. This particular desk has certainly seen better days.'

He wondered if he'd perhaps gone too far there. Criticizing the office furniture on your first day was not really on. He rehearsed an apologetic rider, he could say there was a good few years' life in the old desks yet: but Beazley, with a curious glance at him, had already turned back to his revolving card-index. Copeland was still talking to Seeds but Gryce was pretty sure he must have overheard the remark about Vaart's desk having seen better days. Again he felt embarrassed.

He rose with the object of crossing to the windows and looking out to see if there were any likely restaurants or sandwich bars he had missed on an earlier recce of the district – he would have to establish pretty soon what his colleagues usually did about lunch. But his path took him past Hakim's desk and Hakim seemed to think he was looking for the lavatory.

'Yes! The geography!' Hakim didn't have the sing-song accent you would have expected, he must have been in the country a long time, perhaps even born here. 'Down the central aisle; all the way through Traffic Control, then turn right and the door is staring you in the face.'

'Thank you. Thank you.' Gryce found he was not only repeating himself effusively but also executing an unnatural wriggling bow, to show Mr Hakim that he had no colour prejudice of any kind whatsoever. Hakim had risen and had extended his right arm slightly. Gryce thought he meant to shake hands again and so he put out

15

his own hand, just as Hakim retracted his. Hakim smiled, showing white teeth, and produced his hand again; but by now Gryce had deflected his own gesture to make it look as if he was adjusting the strap of his wrist-watch. The performance continued with variations: it finished with the two men grazing knuckles rather than actually shaking hands.

'Whoops,' said Hakim, unexpectedly.

'Sha!'

Gryce backed away nodding vigorously, as if to indicate that he and Hakim had just had a stimulating exchange which they must take up again. 'Would you like me to show you the way?' asked Hakim.

'No, that's more than kind of you, I'll find it. Through Traffic Control, then right?'

'And it's straight ahead.'

'Many thanks indeed.'

Traffic Control was the biggest of the three departments on the seventh floor. The section where Gryce had come to work, Stationery Supplies – 'the dreaded SS' as Seeds had dubbed it – was the smallest. It had its rows of desks on one side of the central aisle, and Copeland's partitioned-off space plus some banks of filing cabinets on the other, and that was it. The actual supplies the section handled were held, Gryce had been told, in the Stationery Stores Department in basement two. But if you included the space down in basement two as belonging to Stationery Supplies, which arguably it did, then the department was not smaller than Traffic Control, but bigger.

Traffic Control was laid out on the same lines as Stationery Supplies – rows of desks (but twice as many) on one side of the aisle and filing cabinets on the other, with the addition of a photo-copying machine. Traffic Control was responsible for the smooth running of the building and for reorganizations such as Copeland had promised for the near future, so there was often a need to run off copies of ground-plans or wiring-circuit diagrams. Two office girls, an English one with an Afro hair-do and an African-looking one with her hair cropped short, were working at the machine. The English one was gathering up the photostats of some graph or other and passing them to the African-looking one, who stacked them neatly by shuffling them together than rapping them smartly upon the surface of the copying machine. It was a job that either girl could easily have done on her own. It reminded Gryce very much of his last billet.

Beyond Traffic Control, at the far end of the seventh floor, was the internal post department or In-house Mail as it preferred to call itself. In appearance it was more or less a replica of Stationery Supplies. This too was only the administrative wing of the department, dealing with such matters as co-ordinating delivery times and re-routing letters to people who had changed their offices. The actual mail was sorted in basement one.

Reaching the boundary of Traffic Control and In-house Mail, Gryce turned right as instructed and went into the Gents'. It was a better appointed place than the one he had been used to, with tiled walls, mirrors with shaving points and a choice between paper towels and a hand-drying machine. One of the stalls was occupied by ex-President Nixon and they made the necessary exchanges.

'This is what comes of having orange juice for breakfast.'

'Sha!'

'Ahhhh, that's better.'

Gryce had no real need to urinate but he made the effort until his companion had gone. He rinsed his hands, drying them on a paper towel rather than at the hot-air machine which had a push button instead of a properly hygienic foot pedal. He went back out to the office and retraced his steps through Traffic Control.

The noises were all familiar ones to him: the low background hum of the air-conditioning, the fast rhythmic clattering of typewriters being used by properly trained girls and the sporadic pecking of machines being handled by men or novices, the murmur of private conversations and the louder voices of those who were talking business – 'Have you finished with the book of words, Amanda light of my heart?' Clerks who were crossing the central aisle to the filing cabinets or back again felt obliged as they did so to sing snatches of dated songs. The male ones, that was: the women did not sing, but they added to the medley by sliding back the drawers of the filing cabinets with unnecessary force, as women in Gryce's experience always did. (One or two of them, though, were quite presentable – something to bear in mind if there was nothing doing with Miss Divorce.)

There was one sound missing, he knew that but he could not place it. Individually all the small noises were recognizable almost as old friends but they were not quite weaving together into that acoustic curtain which, in all the offices he had ever worked for, had become as innocuous as the floor covering. He was noticing all the component sounds and that was how he knew there was an ingredient missing.

Back in Stationery Supplies, Mrs Rashman was speaking into her telephone. A personal call it was, something to do with her need to buy a packet of Ritz crackers in the lunch hour, an errand that would make her a minute or two late for a previously arranged appointment in a wine bar.

If Mrs Rashman was meeting men friends in wine bars, and it did seem to be a man friend by the tone of her voice, then that ruled her out positively. Gryce wondered if Miss Divorce met men friends in wine bars.

It was an outgoing call Mrs Rashman was making, because had she been taking an incoming one he would have heard the telephone ring. It was unlikely to have rung while he was in the lavatory, for she had only commenced to speak as he returned to his desk. 'Oh, hello, it's me,' she had said. She could, of course, have been waiting for her caller to be put on the line by his secretary, but Gryce ruled that possibility out too.

There was a telephone on every desk, and there would be – what? say between sixty and eighty desks on the seventh floor. So between sixty and eighty telephones: but although he had by now been in the offfice for an hour and a half or so, he had not yet heard one of them ringing.

2

What Gryce had told Seeds about his reasons for leaving his last billet was not substantially the truth. The transport difficulties he had mentioned were real enough, and the comparative proximity of British Albion to London Bridge had certainly influenced him when applying for his new post. But when Seeds had asked, 'What prompted you to transfer your allegiance to Perfidious Albion?' the question had implicitly incorporated another one, 'Why did you leave Comform?' and the fact was that he had been made redundant.

Gryce knew that redundancy was nothing to be ashamed of these days and among his ex-colleagues he had made light of it. 'So. On the scrap heap at forty-one,' he had said mock-bitterly, putting a tragic fist to his forehead in case anyone took him seriously. Then, more soberly, he had added in the relieved tones of one who is glad to be off the treadmill: 'Frankly it couldn't have come at a better time. I've been thinking of making a change for months but I suppose I needed a push.'

'You can't say you haven't got the push now, he said heartlessly,' someone joked.

'Sha!'

Gryce's three fellow-victims, like himself casualties of a rationalization programme, adopted much the same philosophical attitude. 'Look at it this way,' they said. 'Your redundancy pay is capital. Imagine how much you'd have to earn to have that money in the bank, tax paid.' They spoke of not being in too much of a rush to find new jobs, of looking around for a while, perhaps a complete change of vocation. One of them, a man named Parsloe, thought that by selling his house and taking a flat over a shop, he might make a good living selling do-it-yourself materials.

Gryce had no way of knowing whether they felt the same chill in the stomach that he himself was experiencing. But he noticed that one of them was affecting a sudden interest in racing, to give him the excuse of buying the early edition of the evening paper with its columns of situations vacant. 'For Gawd's sake, don't let me put my redundancy money on Red Rum. Hold me back, I beg of you.' The second of the three took to making social telephone calls to friends in other companies, suggesting drinks on the way home from work. Parsloe seemed in earnest about his do-it-yourself project and spent a lot of his time ringing timber merchants and asking about the price of soft woods and dowelling. For himself, Gryce thought of the official unemployment figures and of the stories he had read in the *Daily Mail* about men of his own age who had been 'shaken out' of their desk jobs and couldn't get further work. He found he was needing to go to the lavatory quite frequently.

He wasn't too worried about the security aspect. With his savings and the lump sum he would get from Com-form, he could keep up his present standard of living for twenty months – call it two years with a few economies, or, allowing for inflation, eighteen months to be on the safe side. His wife Peggy earned a few pounds as a part-time cashier in a betting shop, something he didn't broadcast to all and sundry, so there would always be that coming in. Then the little house in Forest Hill had been left to him by his mother, which meant there was no mortgage to worry about, only the rates. He had no hire purchase commitments to speak of, and he didn't have a car to maintain – although that was a mixed blessing, because it would have been something to sell if the money ran short. But surely something would turn up before the money did run short.

It was having nowhere to go between nine and five, even for only a few weeks, that Gryce dreaded. Working in offices, he had come to realize soon after his honeymoon many years ago, was his whole life. He supposed that he must have become institutionalized without knowing it – what prisoners called stir-happy.

He had worked in offices since leaving school at sixteen: first at the Prudential in Holborn where he had stayed for two years; then conscription, when he had been a filing clerk in the RAF Records Office at Gloucester ('Home from home!' he had written in his postcards to All In Small Claims); then the Docks and Inland Waterways where he had met Peggy; then four, no five billets with various commercial companies, and finally – but not finally, as things now turned out – Comform. He supposed that as 'a mere pen-pusher' – that was how he introduced himself to strangers – he ought to have plumped for local government, where you had your security and an index-linked pension. But if he had signed on before the mast in the planning department of Lewisham Town Hall, which he had once been tempted to do, he would have been there for life. Gryce always told himself that he had a gypsy instinct: he liked to change billets every three years or so.

He tended to move on when promotion prospects were in sight. He didn't want to finish up as a departmental manager, he was quite happy as a senior clerk. He liked the routine – not of the work he had to do, which was usually repetitive and always undemanding, but of the office itself. Once he had found his way about and familiarized himself with the stock jokes and catchphrases and the little daily rituals, it was as pleasant a way of passing the days as any he could think of. If he looked forward to his annual holiday, it was only because of the opportunity a few days in Tenerife opened up for smalltalk. Clicking the button of his Instamatic on a terrace two thousand miles away from home, he could hear himself saying: 'Oh, and this is the German restaurant I was telling you about, where they served twenty-three different kinds of steak, *which of course* turned out to be steak prepared in twenty-three different ways. That rather blurred figure is either my thumb or Otto, our waiter. What a character he turned out to be.'

If he had taken that billet at Lewisham Town Hall all those years ago he would know every nook and cranny of the building by now. On August the sixteenth he would have been sipping his coffee at a trestle table while a chain-gang of fellow-clerks passed his holiday snaps from hand to hand. As things stood, he had better call in at the travel agent's and recover his deposit.

'*Dear Sir,*' he pecked out on the office girl's typewriter while she was at lunch, '*I wish to apply for the post of Responsible Investment Clerk advertised in today's* Daily Telegraph. *I am 41 years of age, with the following experience.*' But although he despatched two dozen such letters, he got no replies. Gryce began to develop an unpleasant digestive ailment, which he diagnosed rightly as a symptom of panic. He was not properly qualified for most of the posts advertised: either they wanted skills with computers or other machinery, which he didn't possess, or they were clearly looking for women – Girl Fridays or Personality Plus Girls, as they used to call them – but couldn't say so because of the Sex Discrimination Act. The two dozen jobs he had applied for during a week of combing the classified columns represented not the cream but the full quota of what was available in his particular bracket. This was the first time he had ever changed billets without having the pick of at least a hundred vacancies.

'*Dear Sir, I was a clerk in your employ from March 1968 until 1971, resigning in August of that year to take up a position with Messrs Hardacre and Prentice in order to be nearer my home, and subsequently obtaining a position as Senior Sales Clerk with Messrs Comform. Reference may be made to your Mr Cottingley, to whom I spoke telephonically this morning and who informs me that a vacancy might shortly occur in the Contracts Dept . . .*'

He had never been in a Labour Exchange in his life, regarding such institutions with the same mixture of disdain and horror as Victorian clerks secure in their counting-houses must have viewed the parish workhouse. Even though he understood they were now called employment exchanges and that you no longer had to join a shuffling queue in an olive-green painted corridor, he felt dispirited and degraded at having to consider this approach. He was a little vague about what the drill was and feared that once he had signed up they might have the power to direct him into a factory.

He was relieved to find that his local employment exchange had enjoyed yet another transformation and was now called a Job Centre, with attractive premises in the main shopping street that could well have been taken for an Electricity Board showroom or one of those commercial temps bureaux for audio-typists. Instead of being questioned by a severe-looking person at a lin-oleum-covered counter or worse still behind a grille of some kind, he was directed by an air hostess type of girl to a kind of wall newspaper with pages of orange painted pegboard, where jobs were advertised on pieces of white card. There seemed to be opportunities in plenty for senior clerks, but as there were other men studying the advertisements, all of whom had to be considered as

24

potential rivals, Gryce allowed himself no time for browsing. He memorized the reference number of the first senior clerk's vacancy on which his eyes focussed – *The British Albion Group requires senior clerical personnel with experience in voucher-processing and/or card-filing systems* – and crossed to the reception desk where another air hostess type punched some buttons on an electronic scanner, gave him a questionnaire to fill out, and told him to report for an interview at 11.30 on Friday week.

British Albion was in Gravechurch Street, one of the main thoroughfares leading west out of the City. Gryce got there an hour early and sat on a low circular wall surrounding a largish area of recently-laid grass sods where some old commercial building must have been at one time. It served to set off Albion House opposite, and to give light to its lower storeys. He could imagine that the British Albion typists sunbathed out here in the summer. If they did, it might be pleasant to start bringing sandwiches to work, he'd never felt inclined to do that in his previous billets because there had never been anywhere to sit. That would be one advantage.

Albion House did not seem to make the best use of the space available to it. Although it was twelve storeys high it was a very thin-looking building, with the same area again squandered on a pebbledash forecourt boundaried by a low chain fence. Not that Gryce himself was a motorist, but he called that a waste of a good car-park. Again, the potential breadth of the glass tower was truncated by a kind of annexe affair jutting out of the second and third floors and supported on concrete stilts. The managerial suite, he supposed. That would be where he would be interviewed.

Gryce looked at his watch. He had fifty minutes to waste. Perhaps he could go and have a drink or a cup of tea while killing time – more likely a cup of tea, since he wouldn't want to go in smelling of beer. But pottering around the area for a quarter of an hour or so he could find nowhere – a distinct inconvenience, he called it. There were some temporary-looking shops on a demolition site – a health food bar, a greetings card shop, and that was about it.

He had known these streets when he was an office boy in his first billet, but of course there had been wholesale redevelopment since those days. He seemed to remember a sandwich bar on this corner, and a pub on that, and an ABC teashop, and some little back street cafés where you could get bacon and eggs style of thing. All those buildings had been pulled down now. There were new office blocks in plenty but the commercial bustle of the area had gone completely. The offices were prestige affairs these days, no longer served by labyrinths of workshops and warehouses in lanes and alleys behind their impressive frontages. No trade counter round the back of any of these places, he would like to bet. No loading bays with parcels bouncing along noisy metal rollers. No fleet of vans in the cobbled yard: no cobbled yards. If you wanted two gross of whatever it was they sold, it would be a question of telexing a brick-built despatch centre out in the fields of Essex. Dispersement, they called it. Not that he disapproved of that kind of policy, it meant more paperwork all round.

Gryce wandered on. The tall office blocks gave way to older buildings: sets of Victorian chambers with the plastic fascias of secretarial agencies and photo-copying bureaux slung across their vaulted doorways; old-established banks and insurance companies with bright new logotypes, boxed in illuminated glass, to supplement their chaste brass plates; and the warehouses that Gryce remembered from his younger days. Although they were warehouses no longer in the classic sense – they had mostly been broken up into warrens of small stock-rooms for the kind of goods like soft toys and dressing-table sets you would expect to see on market stalls, and one of them was converted into a wine bar called the Pressings – it made Gryce feel quite nostalgic to see them.

He remembered his days at the Docks and Inland Waterways, when the smell of coffee and spices wafted in from the bonded warehouses nearby. It was a very happy billet. His duties were light and he had got into the habit of sauntering about the building each afternoon exchanging a word with particular colleagues. One of them always wanted help with his *Daily Mirror* crossword, another was taking driving lessons and liked to be tested on the Highway Code. That was always an occasion for joshing. Peggy worked in the typing pool and he always contrived to arrive there at tea-time. He was in his early twenties and the world had seemed full of promise.

Fearful of being late, Gryce retraced his steps to the low wall opposite British Albion. Apart from the Pressings wine bar, not the kind of place he would want to use on a regular basis, he had found nowhere to eat or drink in the event that he got the job and didn't bring sandwiches. He would have to find out if there was a staff canteen. There must be, in a place that size.

Gryce passed through the revolving doors of Albion House at twenty-six minutes past eleven. The reception area took up the entire ground floor, which was usual enough in many of the offices he had worked in: but where you would expect some display of the company's products – a cross-section of some industrial machinery, say, on a revolving plinth – and probably an occasional table with a selection of the firm's promotional literature, British Albion offered only an artificial rock pool and some plants in tubs. This was a prestige office right enough.

Three uniformed commissionaires manned the long reception counter. Gryce approached the nearest of them, a man with one arm, and stated his name and business.

'Gryce,' repeated the commissionaire. 'You got a Gryce there, Douglas?'

The second commissionaire, who also had one arm, did not immediately react in any way. He was gazing towards the revolving doors in an intense manner and could conceivably have been counting the pale blue tiles of the wall that framed them. After some time he picked up a card and examined it through spectacles the thickness of bottle-glass. Distorting his mouth and breathing out heavily, as if expelling Woodbine smoke, he confirmed that Gryce had an appointment with Personnel.

'He'll see to you,' said the first commissionaire, who then lost interest in his visitor and referred himself back to a periodical called *The Puzzler*.

Gryce moved along the counter. The second commissionaire was still looking at the card, holding it at arm's length and plainly reluctant to take its contents at face value, even though he had rashly endorsed Gryce's right to be on the premises. Gryce waited patiently, and presently the second commissionaire focussed his thick lenses on him with what seemed like deep loathing.

'Bee five two?'

'Sorry?'

'I'm requiring your B.52. Your appointment card. Part two of this.'

'Sorry, I'm not quite clear what, er.'

The commissionaire put the card he had been studying on the counter and indicated its serial number with a bone-white forefinger.

'See, this is part one, and this perforation is where part two has been detached at the Job Centre. You did make contact with the Job Centre before applying here?'

'Oh, certainly, yes. Last Wednesday.'

'Wednesday. *Wednesday*.' The commissionaire consulted a wall-calendar behind him as if to confirm that such a day existed. 'Not,' he added, 'that anyone's doubting your word, because otherwise we wouldn't have possession of a Part One. But see, they should have given you possession of a Part Two. Down the Job Centre.'

'I'm very very sorry but they didn't.' Gryce had started to think that this slip-up might cost him the job. Even if he succeeded in getting over the unexpected obstacle, the digital clock above the lift doors was clicking up from 11:31 to 11:32. Unpunctuality was not going to make a good impression on Personnel.

'So we'll have to take it you haven't got a B.52.' The second commissionaire spoke very slowly, a mental space-bar tapping out a pause between each word.

'No, I didn't even know I was supposed to, er.'

'Part Two of this, we're talking about. This is Part One, and you should have been issued with Part Two.'

'No. Sorry.'

The second commissionaire repeated his Woodbine-smoke performance, then turned – his whole body moving, like a clockwork toy on the verge of running down – to his colleague at the far end of the counter. The third commissionaire, Gryce now saw, was one-armed like the other two. Like the second commissionaire before him, he was staring fixedly at some object ahead, but in his case he appeared to be doing mental arithmetic, for his lips were moving.

'Barney. Gennelman hasn't got documentation.'

The third commissionaire digested this information without switching his gaze from the wall opposite. When he spoke, his lips ceased to move.

'What's he on, then? Interview appointment, has he got?'

'Ar par eleven, Personnel. Mr Lucas.'

'He wants a B.52, then.'

'Yeh, but what I'm saying is they haven't given him one, see. They've sent us the Part One, they've completed that all right, but they've failed to give him a Part Two.'

The third commissionaire now shifted his glance, which involved swivelling his head, to study Gryce. Then, with the measured tread of a policeman on his beat, he moved along the counter and picked up the card, examining it on both sides. Gryce noted that the time was now three minutes after half-past eleven.

At four minutes after half-past eleven, the third commissionaire said, with an air of deliberation, 'Can't understand that. *At all.*'

'I can't understand it neither,' said the first commissionaire. 'Why should they want to make out a Part One, then they don't make out a Part Two?'

The first commissionaire came back into the conversation. 'What they'll have done,' he said, 'they'll have made the card out and processed the Part One, but they'll have forgotten to give him his Part Two.'

'Well,' said Gryce, feeling that he ought to make a contribution, 'I'm not sure what I should, er.'

'They'll still have it down there. Down the Job Centre.'

'What you think, Barney?' asked the second commissionaire.

The third commissionaire remained deep in thought, then looked at Gryce with what was possibly shrewdness, perhaps weighing up his character. Eventually he said, '*Gar*' which to Gryce sounded as if he wished to wash his hands of the whole business. To the second commissionaire, however, the expression evidently meant something else for he said to Gryce: 'He'll take you up.'

He was escorted, not to the annexe affair on stilts which he had assumed to be the managerial suite, but to the third floor. Most of the office floors, Gryce was to learn, were laid out on the same open-plan principle, with three departments to each floor. Personnel occupied a space exactly equivalent to Stationery Supplies four storeys above it. The directory sign in the third floor foyer indicated cryptically that the other two departments were known as Services A and B.

He was taken by the one-armed commissionaire through Services A, where several clerks were enjoying their coffee break, and directed into a reception area, furnished with low-slung armchairs and a glass-covered table strewn with magazines. From the discreet thicket of large potted plants affording it some protection from the public gaze, he judged that this would be where the interview would take place.

Gryce sat down and picked up a magazine with shiny pages. It was to do with management techniques and was incomprehensible to him, so he put it down again. The other literature covered roughly the same field and was equally unpromising. He straightened his tie and smoothed back his hair, though neither adjustment was necessary.

The desks of the Personnel department could not be seen through the greenery, but the heads of the one or two people standing about drinking coffee were just about visible. Gryce saw that the commissionaire had approached a man who put him in mind very strongly of the Opposition spokesman for agriculture, whom he had seen often enough on television but whose name he could never remember.

The commissionaire had made some attempt to modulate his barrack-square voice, but without much success. '. . . Turned up at the main door without a Part Two . . .' Gryce heard him saying. '. . . Been booked in . . . become necessary to book him out . . . Notify us when

31

the gennelman's leaving the building . . .' Gryce thought all this precaution rather overdone: it wasn't, after all, as if he'd been turned loose in the Ministry of Defence.

The Opposition spokesman for agriculture was looking in his direction and presently their eyes met, imposing upon them an obligation to exchange stiff nods across the foliage. This small social contact, rather than any move by the commissionaire to wind up his admonitions and get back to his post, provided the impetus for the interview to begin. The Opposition came forward and introduced himself as Mr Lucas of Personnel. His standing with that department was not gone into.

'Found us all right?' Gryce recognized the jingle of conversational small change and was at once less anxious in his mind.

'Oh, yes. Leastways I found Gravechurch Street all right. Tracking down Albion House was a leetle more difficult.'

'They are much of a muchness nowadays, all these office blocks, aren't they? I sometimes wonder if our present breed of architects didn't have too many rows of dominoes to play with as children.'

'*Sha!* A new application of the domino theory!'

'*Shock!*' Lucas responded to Gryce's laugh with his own staccato sound of mirth, and signalled that the pleasantries were over by opening a cardboard file and consulting a thin sheaf of documents, the uppermost being the missing Part Two which had caused the commissionaires so much concern.

'How this comes to be here we shall never know,' sighed Lucas as he removed, and placed carefully in an ash-tray, the paper clip attaching the perforated card to the lengthy questionnaire which Gryce had filled out at the Job Centre. 'If you'll hand it to one of the commissionaires on your way out, I'm sure it'll be an occasion for rejoicing.'

'I'm sure it will. There was rather a song and dance about its elusiveness, I must say.'

'Yes. We go very much by the book here, as you may have gathered. You've no rooted objection to bumph as a way of life?'

Gryce contrived an amused but vigorous twitch of the head to convey at once a blind acceptance of the rules of the game and a rueful bewilderment at their complexity.

'*Very much used to it* by now.'

'Let's see what you've told us about yourself. Born so-and-so so-and-so, educated blah blah blah, married very good, previous employment all present and correct, and for the last three years until quite recently you've been with Comform.'

'I have indeed.'

On its journey to Albion House his questionnaire had been folded in three, so that although straightened out again it did not quite lie flush, and Gryce was able to glimpse the papers underneath. Beneath what looked like an inter-office slip giving details of the vacancy under discussion, there was a closely-typed letter on a Comform billhead. So they'd taken up references. What most of the other documents were Gryce could not surmise, but he was sure he recognized the distinctive pale-brown quarto sheet jutting marginally out at the bottom of the pile. It was from the Cardinal Building Society, a billet he'd left nine years ago. Going very much by the book was one thing, but this was thoroughness gone mad in his view.

'Glowing references, you'll be relieved to hear,' said Lucas, observing that Gryce was trying to read his file upside-down. 'Comform was rather a departure for you, I gather?'

Gryce didn't know what to make of this. One office was much like another in his experience.

'I mean,' Lucas pursued, 'you seem mainly to have worked for what I suppose one would call institutions – Docks and Inland Waterways, insurance, building societies, cetera. No manufacturing process involved. I see under armed forces, details of any service in, you've put Clerk/GD in the RAF Records Office. You weren't brought into contact with aircraft in any way.'

'That's true enough. Fact, I didn't set eyes on a plane in all my two years. Except flying overhead, of course.'

'What I'm getting at is that Comform is the only appointment you've had where there's been so to speak an end product. I'm saying it was rather a departure.'

'I get your drift now. Yes and no, if the truth be known. You see the actual factory was, still is if it comes to that, down in the West Country. My end of it was very much offices and showrooms. I never saw anything actually being made.'

That, on instant playback, seemed a pretty negative reply to have given. But it appeared to be the one Lucas wanted.

'Then you've no particular objection to being merely a link in the chain – even if you can't see how the chain connects with the various cogs and wheels?'

Gryce sensed this time that Lucas was definitely asking a leading question, albeit an excessively fanciful one. An answer in the order of 'Oh good heavens, no!' seemed to be called for. He plumped for this line, but decided to embellish it a little.

'Oh good heavens, no! I've always found that whatever job I'm doing is in itself an end product. That is, you do what's required of you to the best of your ability, and someone else picks up his own process from there.'

Lucas appeared well satisfied. Gryce was glad, on

balance, that he had not over-egged the pudding by adding, 'No man can ask for more.'

'I'm pleased you said that. It's really just the attitude we're looking for as regards this particular vacancy. It's an in-house post as you know, Stationery Supplies, serving all the other departments in the building, and a certain type of personality might feel cut off from the mainstream. Far from the madding crowd.'

'Oh good heavens, no!' The job was his. It was in the bag.

'I'd say you shouldn't find the work unfamiliar. It's largely various aspects of invoice-processing – much the same as you've been doing, except that all the transactions are internal so you've no cash columns to worry about.'

'And no iniquitous VAT! *Sha!*'

'*Shock!*'

'The department doesn't buy in, then, at all?' Gryce asked the question not particularly because he wanted to know, but because he thought a point in the relationship had been reached where technical jargon like 'buy in' should be offered, to match the flavour of 'in-house' which Lucas had just used. It would put the interview on more of a man-to-man footing.

He was surprised at Lucas's reaction, not so much by what he said as the way he said it. 'No, that wouldn't be your concern at all.' It was offered in a stepping-out-of-line, watch-your-step, let's-change-the-subject tone. And he'd said 'wouldn't' not 'won't'. Perhaps the job wasn't in the bag after all. Lucas's line of questioning, Gryce was beginning to think, was trickier than he'd at first given credit for. More in-depth. Perhaps he'd taken a course on staff psychology.

The next bit was easier. Lucas read out from his inter-office slip-looking thing the details of starting salary, annual increments, holidays, graduated pension scheme and the rest of it. All Gryce had to do was nod judiciously and murmur from time to time that it seemed quite satisfactory.

'It's what we call a Grade C position within the organization, that's to say one down from sub-managerial which is Grade B. You wouldn't be expecting promotion at all?'

Another leading question, and his verbs still retained their hypothetical edges.

'No executive ambitions of any shape or kind,' said Gryce firmly.

'That's good. We do like to recruit for the appropriate grade. It saves any amount of back-biting if managerial vacancies are filled from outside.'

'I do so agree.' Perhaps Gryce shouldn't have said that. Not only was he unfamiliar with such a policy, thus unqualified to offer an opinion one way or the other, but the observation was well outside the bounds of his Grade C status.

Lucas, however, didn't seem to mind. 'The post will be permanent,' he said, reverting to the in-the-bag form of speech. 'But there's one thing we'd ask of you. I imagine there'll be further redundancies at Comform in the sweet by-and-by?'

'I shouldn't be at all surprised.'

'It's not thought advisable for word to get about that we're in the market for recruits. When vacancies do arise, through retirement or whatever, we do like to pick and choose.'

Though gratified at having been picked and chosen himself, Gryce couldn't help feeling mystified. Putting up zonking great advertisements in the Job Centre could hardly be called the first step in a careful screening process. You would have thought, if they were so fussy, that they would have gone to one of the prestige personnel selection agencies in New Bond Street or wherever.

Or perhaps Lucas, having taken that course on staff psychology, was allowed very much to form his own judgement. If so, Gryce was flattered.

He gave the appropriate assurance, and Lucas scribbled something at the foot of the questionnaire and closed his file of papers, suggesting that it was all over bar the shouting. He must have timed the interview to the second, because even as he glanced at his watch, Copeland appeared through the shrubbery and was introduced as Gryce's future superior. Or rather, Copeland introduced himself, giving his name as Goat-plan. Beyond mentioning that British Albion was a happy ship, Copeland had little to say and Gryce gathered that while he might control Stationery Supplies, appointments to the department were not within his living. This impression was borne out when Lucas said: 'I think we can confirm the appointment, Mr Copeland, unless our friend has any queries?'

Gryce could think of none. Only after he had been duly booked out by the three one-armed commissionaires and he was out in the street again and wondering where he might get a snack lunch, did he remember that he hadn't asked about the staff canteen. There was something else he hadn't asked about too, but it escaped him for the moment.

3

Staff canteen, it emerged, would have been rather a derogatory misnomer. It was a staff restaurant more like, housed in the protruding bit on stilts which Gryce had taken for the executive suite. It even had a restaurant-sounding name: the Buttery. It reminded Gryce of all the hotel private-function rooms, most of them called the Churchill Suite, where his various billets had held their Christmas lunches.

Seemingly the Buttery was a fairly recent addendum to the main building, costed originally at £120,000 but in the end devouring the best part of a quarter of a million, thanks mainly to an architectural cock-up which had rendered it inaccessible except via the fire-escape. The restaurant was circular and it was supposed to revolve to catch the sun, but when the supposition had been put to the test it had done one three-quarter turn and then jammed, leaving the dining area in semi-darkness until four o'clock each afternoon, Greenwich mean time.

'If you like salady things, cold roast beef, ham and egg pie, the Salad Bowl *isn't half bad*,' advised Seeds as they travelled up the stainless steel escalator from the first floor. To get to the first floor they had had to take the lift from the seventh floor to the second, then walk down the stairs. Or they could have gone to the ground floor and walked up. The lift was no longer programmed to stop at the first floor – a throwback to an electricity economy campaign during some long-forgotten fuel crisis. The Buttery was at third floor level, but it could not be reached from the second floor because of an obstruction caused by the plant that was supposed to work the revolving mechanism, nor from the third floor itself because of a ventilation shaft that had been installed to deal with excessive condensation in the kitchens. These difficulties had been surmounted by a considerable engineering feat involving re-siting the fire-escape and routing a covered escalator up the outer wall of the main building and into the Buttery. It was the only spiral escalator in Europe and, according to Seeds, had cost more than the original estimate for the entire restaurant annexe.

'But be warned against the Dish of the Day, probably some veal concoction. Sad to say our chef's imagination stretches farther than his capabilities.'

It was very kind of Seeds to invite Gryce to lunch, or he supposed more accurately to accompany him to lunch, by way, it was to be presumed, of showing him the ropes. It would be embarrassing if it turned out to be an invitation in the literal sense. He would have to reciprocate tomorrow and that might commit them to an arrangement that neither would relish. Buying tea or coffee turn and turn about was one thing, but having to stand each other lunch would put a strain on what ought to be an easy-going acquaintanceship.

The Buttery was full, for all that lunch hours at British Albion were staggered and there were in effect three sittings. Peering into the Arctic gloom induced by the faulty revolving machinery, Gryce was able to recognize several faces from Stationery Supplies: but not, to his disappointment, Miss Divorce, not Mrs Rashman who would be keeping that appointment in the wine bar, and not Copeland. The managers had their own restaurant on the twelfth floor, called the Cockpit.

In the centre of the room was a buffet arrangement featuring the salady things recommended by Seeds. If you wanted the unrecommended veal concoction, or any

39

other hot dish, you joined the queue at a cafeteria-looking counter.

'If you'd like to dive in, I'll see if I can grab a table,' said Seeds obligingly. Gryce attached himself to the throng of mainly women, he supposed they were all slimming, who were helping themselves at the Salad Bowl. He had garnished his plate with some potato salad and one or two radishes cut in the shape of tulips when he saw Miss Divorce, or Mrs Fawce as he had better start calling her, stepping off the escalator which after its convolutions fetched up a few feet from the Salad Bowl.

Hovering between the cold roast beef and the ham and egg pie, Gryce decided to hold his horses until Mrs Fawce, undoubtedly a salady things person, was on hand to advise him on the best choice. She would then, if there was a God in heaven, join him and Seeds for lunch as if it were the most natural thing in the world.

Not a salady things person after all. To his surprise Mrs Fawce was aiming towards the hot meals counter. Well, then: she probably took her main nourishment at lunch-time and made do with a light snack in the evening. With no substantial dinner to prepare, that might give her the leisure for a glass or two of wine on the way home.

They would have to be discreet, though. It only needed Mrs Rashman to stumble across them one evening and it would be all round the office.

Carrying his plate of potato salad and radishes, to which he had added a portion of sliced tomato while contemplating the next move, Gryce crossed to the hot meals counter, acquired a tray, and by sliding it along the rail affair and nudging Mrs Fawce gently in the buttocks with it, managed to draw attention to himself.

The smile was encouraging enough.

'We didn't meet properly. Pamela Fawce. Pam, to most people.'

'Clement Gryce. Abbreviated alas to Clem, which makes me sound like a former Prime Minister.' He wondered if he reminded her of, strangely enough, the late Hugh Gaitskell.

After establishing that he was finding his way around all right and agreeing that one's first few days in a new billet were always strange, by which time they were at the head of the queue, Pam Fawce ordered herself shepherd's pie and then raised a query about his plate of salad.

'Couldn't you face the cold beef, then?'

'It wasn't that, it looked delicious. But then I was enticed over here by the tempting aroma of shepherd's pie.'

'Make that two,' said Pam Fawce to one of the serving women. There were five of them, all coloured, plus another two on duty at the Salad Bowl with no clear function, since it was a serve-yourself affair. Then there were at least three women clearing the tables, and a fourth in charge of a slowly-perambulating trolley dispensing coffee to those who required it. No shortage of staff in this establishment.

'The only thing is,' continued Pam Fawce, still on the plate of salad question, 'I'm *not sure* how she's going to charge you for it. You see normally you'd either have a complete salad, roast beef, something like that, *or* whatever you want from the hot counter. Then she tears off the ticket for what you've had and you pay on your way out.'

'Oh dear. Tears off what ticket?'

'You haven't been given one of these? Typical.'

Gryce now saw that Mrs Fawce – Pam – was clutching what looked like a wartime ration book. The pages were perforated into squares, each square bearing some such annotation as 'Main Dish', 'Dish of Day', 'Cheese & Biscuits', 'Salad Bowl' and so on. Some squares, another ration book touch, carried the words 'Not For Use'. He also saw that the woman he had taken to be a cashier at the end of the counter was not a cashier at all, but merely a functionary whose duty was to tear off the relevant coupons. Presumably there would be someone in the vicinity of the Salad Bowl performing the same task, while the woman who pushed round the percolator-trolley would be empowered to remove the coupon marked 'Coffee/Beverage'. You then, he imagined, would present your book at that booth affair by the escalators, where they would take possession of the uppermost page and work out the damage according to how many coupons had been detached. All the surrendered coupons would be collated and sorted, and they would have to correspond in value to the cash received. It seemed an unnecessarily cumbersome system.

Gryce seemed to have two problems: the presence on his tray of an incomplete salad in addition to his shepherd's pie, and the absence of a pad of meal vouchers as he supposed they were called. No harm could come of placing himself thoroughly in the hands of Pam Fawce. Not only would she sort out his difficulties, but her doing so would forge a positive link between them. It would be a talking point for many an evening in the wine bar. 'What are you smiling at?' he would ask – 'I was remembering your look of absolute desperation when it suddenly dawned on you that you'd strayed into the Buttery without your meal vouchers.'

Pam commenced negotiations with the ticket-collecting woman, who quickly assessed the situation as outside her brief and pressed a bell-push to summon someone in authority. Standing to one side with his simulated mahogany tray, Gryce noted that Seeds had commandeered a vacant table and, with outstretched arms, was cradling two chairs in the expectation of Gryce and Pam relieving him so that he could come up for his own meal. He seemed to be growing impatient but there was nothing Gryce could do about that. He could hardly leave Pam to handle the situation on her own, since his plate of salad and rapidly cooling shepherd's pie were evidence in the case, and besides, he wouldn't want to risk her wandering off and joining Grant-Peignton, Beazley and Co. at another table.

A senior-looking woman, wearing a suit in contrast to the lilac smocks of the serving staff, appeared on the scene and listened to Pam's explanations. After briefly examining Gryce she ruled that in the unusual circumstances, and on this occasion only, the potato salad and accompanying radishes and sliced tomato would be classed as vegetables, for which there was no extra charge, but that his shepherd's pie would have to be accounted for by a Main Dish ticket from Pam's own book.

This suited Gryce admirably. It would mean that he owed Pam a lunch. That was an altogether different ball game from owing Seeds a lunch. He thanked the heavens above that the Buttery had been full, so that Seeds had opted to wait for a free table instead of accompanying him to the counter and having to assume responsibility for his food.

'Typical,' said Pam again as they joined Seeds and took up the seats he had been reserving, one on either side of him. '*Not only* have they not given him his SSTs *or* told him where to get them, the poor man didn't even know anything about them!'

SSTs, then, not meal vouchers. 'Supplementary Subsistence Tickets,' Pam explained. More jargon to remember.

43

There was so much to learn in this place, it was like one's first day at school all over again.

'Typical,' agreed Seeds, adding '*Coh!*' as he rose and headed for the Salad Bowl. It could either have been an exclamation of disgust or his means of expressing laughter, on the lines of Gryce's own '*Sha!*' and that Personnel fellow's, Lucas's, '*Shock!*' Time would tell, when they had exchanged an office joke or two.

It came as a surprise to Gryce that Seeds hadn't said 'Let the dog see the rabbit' when he went up for his lunch.

This left him without anything to say to Pam by way of small talk. If Seeds had said 'Let the dog see the rabbit' he could have riposted ' – or the ham and egg pie, as the case may be' and taken it from there. They could have talked about the food.

But Gryce need not have worried about keeping up a conversation. The theme of the SSTs, and the breakdown in communications that had led to the hold-up at the hot meals counter, kept Pam in full flow. It seemed there was a guidelines leaflet, listing all the hundred and one things a new employee ought to know, that should rightly have been placed in Gryce's hands by Lucas of Personnel. But it was likely that the leaflet had been withdrawn for emendations and additions, as happened from time to time. In that event it fell to Grant-Peignton, who as Copeland's number two was responsible for departmental welfare, to show him the ropes, tell him where the first-aid room was for instance, and *particularly* clue him up on the Supplementary Subsistence Tickets.

They were called supplementary, Gryce was intrigued to learn, because they were originally an optional alternative to the conventional luncheon vouchers which could be used in any café or cheap restaurant. But that particular choice was being phased out because the Buttery, which was heavily subsidized, had been losing too much money. Under the old system you had signed for your supplementary tickets or luncheon vouchers up in the Welfare Office on a certain day of the month according to where your surname initial fell in the alphabet. But Pam believed that the Buttery's own administration office, she thought it was on the tenth or twelfth floor, was taking over the chore of issuing SSTs. She would have to find out soon enough on her own account, since she had only a four or five days' supply left. If Gryce liked she could let him know what the new arrangement was.

Gryce could think of nothing he would like more. There was a lot more to learn about the SSTs and the time passed very amiably, with no awkward pauses, before Seeds returned to the table with a plate piled high with tongue and cold chicken.

'One thing worth bearing in mind,' said Seeds, picking up the conversational thread from Pam, 'is that when you surrender a Main Meal ticket you're laying yourself open to paying nearly half as much again as if you'd surrendered a Salad Bowl ticket. Even though the portions are smaller.'

'Which reminds me,' said Pam. 'One shepherd's pie. If you've got twenty-four pee handy?'

'Twenty-four pee? Is that all?'

'That's assuming you'll want coffee. The Main Meal's only twenty pee. Don't forget we're subsidized.'

'And your shepherd's pie's subsidizing my tongue and cold chicken into the bargain,' said Seeds. 'This little lot came to only fifteen pee.'

Gryce's gratified surprise at the cost of the meal, dirt cheap he called it, had the edge taken off it somewhat by Pam's obvious, though quite understandable, keenness to keep the books straight. It meant he wouldn't owe her a lunch after all. But a thought struck him as he put down his knife and fork and meticulously counted out some coins, despite her protest that it would do later.

'But what about the Main Meal ticket you gave up for my lunch? Doesn't that throw you out?'

'Oh, you can owe me that.' So the door was still open. He would be able to say, 'Methinks I'm indebted to you for a Main Meal, or more precisely an SST for same,' and she would have to accompany him to the Buttery. That was assuming the tickets were not valid unless detached by an authorized person, as was probably the case.

'Don't forget,' said Seeds, 'that when you apply for your SSTs, you'll want them back-dated as from today. Otherwise when you refund Pam's ticket you'll find yourself one short at the end of the issuing period, and you'll be wondering where it's got to.'

'That way madness lies,' agreed Gryce.

He liked all this talk about SSTs very much indeed. It reminded him of his Air Force days when there had often been similar detailed discussion of late-meal chitties, issuable to those who had been on guard duty.

The conversation became general, within the parameters of office affairs as they applied to the newcomer. Seeds confirmed what Pam had said about the guidelines leaflet being withdrawn for emendations and additions, but the pair of them, speaking in turn, were able to reconstruct its contents as they could best remember them. Gryce learned about the late-arrivals book that was kept by the three one-armed commissionaires, the drill for collecting his salary on the first Thursday of each month, the holiday roster, the concession whereby he could take up to six separate (but not consecutive) days' compassionate leave a year without producing documentation; and much else. The compassionate leave concession, unheard of in any of his previous billets,

46

interested him a lot. He could see the time coming when he and Pam would scoot off to Brighton for the day, catching the nine-something down and the four-something back. What his wife didn't know about she wouldn't grieve over.

'Any social activities at all?' he asked as Seeds waved his arm ineffectually to summon the coffee trolley. Gryce and Pam had elected not to have a pudding, but Seeds, not having selected his main course from the hot meals counter where the puddings were in evidence, had left the question open. Gryce had hoped to snatch another moment or two alone with Pam by mentioning that the chilled rhubarb fool looked well worth queuing for, but Seeds, beyond murmuring, 'Rhubarb fool, shall I or shan't I?' had taken no action in the matter. Pam might at least have encouraged him by urging, 'Go on, be a devil.' A pity, when they were getting on so famously.

'Depends entirely what you mean by social activities. *Coh!*' So it was a laugh after all. 'The principal recreation at this establishment is to be observed by feasting one's eyes on the next table.'

As directed, Gryce switched his glance discreetly. A middle-aged man and a middle-aged woman, their food untouched, were deep in an important-seeming discussion. From the woman's miserable expression and the man's haggard one, Gryce deduced a long-running affair that was going sour. That was where a casual glass of wine could lead you if you weren't too careful.

'Love's young dream,' said Pam softly.

'The long-suffering Cargill from Salary Accounts,' murmured Seeds. 'The lady, on the other hand, is definitely not Mrs Cargill, much though her ambitions might lie in that direction.'

'A certain obstacle in the shape of the present Mrs

Cargill?' sniggered Gryce. It was good to be privy to office gossip so soon.

'The very substantial shape, from all I gather. Mark you, we can offer you rather more shall we say above-board examples of true love running smooth.'

'Don't be bitchy!' Pam chided, enjoying herself.

'I was thinking of the widow Rashman and a certain gentleman. I gather a date has been set.'

'Twenty-fifth of this month,' Pam confirmed. And for Gryce's benefit: 'You know Mrs Rashman, at least you've met her. At long last she's marrying her admirer from Stationery Stores. Honestly, this place gets more like a matrimonial bureau every day!'

'Exactly the same in my last billet,' said Gryce. A wine-bar romance had blossomed, then: a happy contrast to the sad example at the next table. 'We had four, no five office weddings last year. All colleagues, or former colleagues.'

'And someone coming round with a collecting tin on each occasion,' Seeds said.

'Oh, every time!' He wondered if he'd be asked to poppy up for Mrs Rashman. It would be a cheek if he were. 'And if it wasn't weddings it was retirements, and if it wasn't retirements it was someone leaving.' Which reminded Gryce that Comform had been the first billet he'd left where there'd been no presentation ceremony. Hardly feasible, he supposed, considering it had been not so much a leave-taking as a mass exodus.

'That's one thing you're unlikely to be stung for here,' said Seeds. 'People leaving, that is. Once you've signed on with British Albion you're generally regarded as being here for life.'

'Mrs Rashman's leaving, for one,' said Pam – blurted, almost, and at once looked as if she wished she hadn't.

'Exception proves the rule,' responded Seeds quickly,

and quietly. He and Pam exchanged a curious sort of glance. If the subject hadn't been so innocuous, Gryce would have thought he had detected a warning given, and a warning acknowledged. Perhaps there was some skeleton in the cupboard apropos Mrs Rashman and her admirer from Stationery Stores.

It certainly looked that way, for Seeds laboriously changed the subject.

'But you were asking about social activities. There's various clubs of one kind or another. Chess.'

Gryce confessed that he could not play chess and Seeds and Pam admitted that they couldn't either. There followed an over-animated discussion about their failure to understand the game and how, when playing with young nephews or nieces, they had been trounced.

'What else can we offer you?' mused Seeds, looking more relaxed now. 'Squash. Swimming. Tennis. We're affiliated to the City and Guilds Sports Centre out at Acton, so you can get free membership. Or so I'm reliably informed. My own sporting activities are limited to walking to Turnham Green tube station every day.'

'That makes two of us.' Forest Hill Southern Region station in Gryce's case, but Seeds would know what he meant. What a pleasant lunch hour it had turned out to be. The coffee had arrived at long last and the conversation was going with such a swing that there was no opportunity to remark even briefly on how passable it was.

'There's always the Albion Players,' said Pam, with what seemed like diffidence, although what she had to be diffident about Gryce could not guess.

She'd said something out of the ordinary, though, for the effect on Seeds was very odd. 'The membership's closed!' he retorted, as rudely as he dare allow himself in front of a guest. Again Gryce caught the warning glance, now tinged with anger; but this time it was not acknowledged, or anyway it was not conceded.

'I *know* the membership's closed, ducky, I *do happen* to be the membership secretary,' said Pam through bared teeth. 'But if we don't find out who's interested and who isn't, we'll never get new blood when we need it, will we?'

Evidence of a temper there, for future reference.

'If Albion Players implies amateur dramatics – ' began Gryce in a throat-clearing voice, with the object of pouring oil on troubled waters. Some internecine warfare here, clearly: some committee squabble that had been left to smoulder by an unwise chairman.

To his surprise Seeds did not so much cut him short as simply talk through his attempted interjection, leaving him to tail off foolishly.

'You know the rules as well as I do, Pamela. *All* approaches are made *after* consultation with the full – '

'You can't tell me anything about the rules, Ron, I helped to frame them.'

' – with the full *committee*, Pamela. *After* consultation and not before.'

If Seeds could sail blithely on after an interruption, then so could Gryce.

'*If* we're discussing amateur dramatics, and I *could* just be allowed a word in edgeways – ' This time he chose a joshing voice, and felt even more foolish than before, for he was ignored.

'I'm sorry, Ron, but there is such a thing as being constructive. If I'm not even allowed to sound someone out we might just as well shut up shop.'

'By all means sound him out. By all means sound him out. I'm only trying to remind you – '

' – that the membership is closed. I know that without

50

you telling me. All I was going to say, if you'd let me, was he seems like a suitable candidate.'

'Oh, eminently. I don't doubt that at all. All other things being equal.'

Gryce thought seriously about taking offence at being discussed in his own presence like this. On the other hand, it wasn't as if he were hearing no good of himself: Pam had said that he seemed a suitable candidate for the Albion Players and Seeds had endorsed her approval, all other things being equal, by which he presumably meant when the membership list was open again. They both seemed to be making heavy weather of a trivial issue, but doubtless the protocol of the Albion Players was not trivial to them. Gryce was glad now that they had not allowed him to finish his sentence, which would have been to the effect that amateur dramatics were not in his line. If Pam thought he seemed a suitable candidate, it would be folly not to keep his options open.

He was searching for some innocuous way of insinuating a word to this effect when Pam lightly, and rather deliciously in his opinion, touched his sleeve.

'He must think we're terribly rude.'

'Don't mind me in the least,' said Gryce with hearty gallantry. He would forgive her for apologizing in the third person, it was only a mannerism. 'All I was going to say – '

'I'm afraid passions run high when it comes to the Albion Players,' said Seeds, cutting in again. Gryce did hope this wasn't a habit of his: there were mannerisms and mannerisms. 'As you've probably gathered the bone of contention is that once people have joined they've joined, so we can't be too careful. Nothing personal.'

'Oh, no offence taken, rest assured. In any case I was just going to say that amateur dramatics aren't quite my cup of tea.' Although that wasn't what he had just been going to say at all, pride seemed to demand it. He could wait for some suitable moment to ask Pam why she'd thought him a suitable candidate, and then allow her to win him over.

'Then we've inflicted an argument on you over nothing,' said Seeds, the snappishness in his voice aimed at Pam.

Gryce was inclined to agree with him. They drank their coffee in silence. Gryce furtively glanced at his watch: it was ten minutes to two, so allowing three minutes to get back to their desks they had seven minutes to kill. Neither Pam nor Seeds struck him as keen types who would get back to work a second before they had to.

It would be a shame if a stimulating lunch should fizzle out in this way.

Ingratiatingly he asked: 'What production are the Albion Players embarked on this year, as a matter of interest?'

'It hasn't been decided. *An Inspector Calls* if I have my way, which I probably won't,' said Pam sulkily. So that was one door closed.

Gryce essayed one or two complimentary remarks about the Buttery, its range of food, its cleanliness and the acceptability of its coffee as against the witches' brew served from the machine upstairs. These comments were well, but taciturnly, received. Talking of the Buttery reminded him of the two questions he had meant to ask Lucas of Personnel when he came for his interview. The first one, concerning the existence of a staff canteen, had been somewhat overtaken by events. But the other one, the one that had slipped completely from his mind until now, would seem to have some mileage in it.

'Tell me, what exactly is it we do here?'

Again Gryce caught that curious look from Seeds: but this time it was directed at him personally.

'Hasn't Copeland explained the vital role of Stationery Supplies? No, he wouldn't, knowing Copeland.'

Seeds launched on a description of the department's function which was a fair summary of what Gryce had already heard from Copeland. It took them very nicely to three minutes to two. As they rose he thought he might as well throw in the supplementary question he had been holding in reserve.

'Yes, I understand all that. What I meant was, what does the company do? What is British Albion in aid of?'

'Well may you ask,' said Pam. Another of what Gryce was beginning to think of as Seeds' famous glances was shot at her. There was no mistaking it. It said, quite plainly, '*Shut up!*'

To Gryce, Seeds said in an airy, casual tone that was clearly costing him some effort: 'What is it not in aid of, that's more the question? When you finally get your guidelines leaflet, if that happy day ever comes, you'll find a list of all the firms for which Perfidious Albion is the holding company. None of them household names, but we do have our fingers in a large number of pies.'

They had reached the cash-desk by the spiral escalator, where Pam went into a lengthy reprise of her earlier negotiations with the supervisor on the unorthodox use of her SSTs. As they waited behind her, Seeds added unnecessarily: 'Does that answer your question?'

Gryce confirmed that it did. He felt no curiosity at all about what British Albion did or didn't do. What did strike him as intriguing, though, was the way these two had been behaving, particularly Seeds.

4

The settling-in period was always enjoyable for Gryce. It was what he most looked forward to when changing billets.

He acquired his own beaker, a Silver Jubilee remnant which young Thelma found for him in a nearby Oxfam shop. He learned that as well as the paper towels and hot-air machine in the men's room, there was a further option in the way of personal hand towels which were changed each Wednesday. He would wait until he had his own desk before signing for a personal hand towel.

He got to know something about his colleagues and their little foibles. Grant-Peignton picked his nose with his little finger. Seeds jingled change. Beazley, Mrs Rashman and Pam took saccharins in their coffee. Ardagh often brushed back the lock of hair that, together with his small moustache, made him look like Hitler.

The work of the department, it came as no surprise to Gryce, could easily have been done by four people or two at a push. Most of it seemed to fall, and none too heavily, on the shoulders of Seeds, Beazley and Grant-Peignton, with Copeland supervising. The others, apart from an hour or so's chores which they spread out over the day, were left pretty well to their own devices.

They wrote letters and filled in crosswords. After lunch each day a small group composed of Pam, Ardagh and the Penney twins did the *Evening Standard* word game on a competitive basis, the loser to buy the next day's paper. The Penney twins were also the departmental representatives of the seventh floor football pools syndicate, another example of over-manning if you wanted Gryce's opinion, since the operation for the entire floor could easily have been handled by one person. The Penney twins collected the football pool money on Tuesday mornings. They took Gryce aside and explained that while it would not be fair on the others to ask him to join the syndicate in the middle of the season, an invitation would certainly be extended to him at the appropriate time. Gryce quite understood this.

On the Thursday, to Gryce's astonishment, the industrious Beazley sold him a raffle ticket for a small sum. This too was evidently a weekly event – 'Beazley's Benefit' Seeds called it as he shelled out his five pence, but from what Gryce gathered from Beazley's mumbled explanation it was in aid of a new gymnasium for a boys' club in which he was interested. Several of the staff had on occasion won prizes, so it was not money thrown into the wind.

On the Friday, a stir was caused by the fact of Mr Hakim arriving for work with two carrier bags laden with fancy boxes of chocolates, boiled sweets and after-dinner mints. For a few minutes the office took on the appearance of a street market as most of the staff, including even Copeland, clustered around Hakim's desk to collect their pre-paid orders. It seemed that Mr Hakim had a brother who was a wholesale confectioner, so that anything in that line could be got at a discount. It was as well to put your requirements in by Wednesday evening, with cash in advance to avoid misunderstandings.

So the week had a pleasing shape. Monday, so far as Gryce could judge, was a fairly dead day. On Tuesday, the Penney brothers collected for the pools syndicate which he would be joining in due course, presumably at the beginning of the Australian season. On Wednesday a woman came round with the replacement hand towels. Thursday was Beazley's Benefit day, with the potential excitement of someone holding a winning ticket from the previous week. On Friday there was the highlight of Mr Hakim's makeshift sweetstall. (Gryce would have to think seriously about that. Although he and his wife shared a sweet tooth – it was one of the few things they could be said to have in common – it could be something of an embarrassment to be trundling a two-pound box of liquorice allsorts about in the event that he established any pattern of meeting Pam for a glass of wine on Friday evenings. Probably because of the discount margin involved, Hakim did not seem to deal in smaller sizes.)

As if this calendar of events were not enough, there were other regular diversions such as the mirth which each afternoon greeted Ardagh's efforts in the word game contest: one gathered that spelling was not his strong subject; he had tried, for example, to extract the word 'grill' from 'girlishness' by spelling it with one l. That had led to some good-natured ribbing. After the word game, Pam took it upon herself each day to read out the *Evening Standard* horoscopes for those who were interested in such things – Mr Hakim (Sagittarius), the Penney twins (Leo), Mrs Rashman (Cancer) and herself (Aquarius). (She did not, to Gryce's disappointment even though he did not believe in astrology, ask him for his birthsign.) It could be said, all in all, that newspaper-reading was quite a feature of the office. Young Thelma was an avid follower of a strip cartoon in the *Daily Express* and she would regularly clomp up to one or other member of the staff and ask shyly if they had seen that day's instalment.

Gryce registered, without having any prurient interest in the matter, the times at which his colleagues went to the lavatory each morning, and the number of minutes spent where no man could reach them. The record, he thought initially, was held by Grant-Peignton who regularly at ten minutes to eleven disappeared for upwards of half an hour with a bundle of papers under his arm. Not until the Thursday, when Gryce himself had to answer a call of nature at about this time, did he discover that Grant-Peignton was in fact stationed at the photo-copying machine in Traffic Control next door, where he was running off some plans of a new greenhouse for which planning permission was needed. They had quite a chat about greenhouses and coldframes, although Gryce was no authority on the subject. Contrary to his first impression Grant-Peignton seemed a nice chap, not stand-offish at all.

Another visitor to the photo-copying machine, which he could see was quite the little social centre – rather like the water-cooler one saw in old American films – was Beazley, who was copying some private documents, probably the minutes of his precious boys' club. They exchanged pleasantries about a threatened miners' strike, Beazley gruffly advising Gryce to stock up on coal or coke. Although Gryce had installed gas-fired central heating with the insurance money accruing from his mother's death some years ago, he was grateful to Beazley. He had been right in thinking that the brusque manner was a mask for shyness.

One way or another, Gryce had conversations with everyone in Stationery Supplies before his first week was out, including even young Thelma who could be quite a chatterbox when you drew her out. She was keen on amateur dramatics, having once played the third witch in a school production of *Macbeth*, and was anxious to join the Albion Players as soon as there was a vacancy.

Mrs Rashman, Gryce was to learn, spoke of little but groceries: the nuisance it was that a particular brand of water biscuit was no longer stocked by most supermarkets, or the fact that small tins of corned beef were expensive, taken weight for weight with similar products. Her impending marriage to her gentleman friend from Stationery Stores, being a private matter, was never touched on. Not that Gryce had much curiosity about it, beyond still wondering if anyone would have the nerve to sting him for a contribution to her leaving present. He made no effort to picture Mrs Rashman going through the rigmarole of courtship – kissing, sitting about in City churchyards and so on. Provided they did not run into one another in the wine bar where the liaison had sprouted, she had no interest for him outside the context of the office.

Her obsession with groceries was a case in point. He was intrigued by the sheer volume of produce she accumulated on her shopping expeditions each lunch hour but he never wondered what she did with it all when it left the office. Her red canvas shopping bag crammed with special offers had a form, an entity, while it was perched at the side of her desk during office hours; it dematerialized, so far as Gryce was concerned, when its owner walked out of the lift in the evening. Mrs Rashman bought cat food, so it followed that she must own a cat: but since she never mentioned it, the cat had no existence. There would have had to be a blueprint for a cat, in the shape of a daily report on its doings, to give it any dimension, and even then it would exist only as an anecdotal facet of Mrs Rashman's own personality.

It was the same with Beazley's boys' club and its proposed new gymnasium, and Mr Hakim's brother who was a wholesale confectioner. They might be figments of the imagination for all Gryce cared, dreamed up to explain Beazley's raffle and Hakim's cutprice market in chocolates and sweets. They did not exist, because

Beazley and Hakim did not exist outside office hours. Neither did any of the others. Neither did Gryce himself, as he had long ago realized.

That he led any kind of life beyond the office he was fuzzily aware of, in a sleepwalking kind of way, only while he was leading it. He had found in all his previous billets that once he had hung up his mackintosh and got his feet firmly beneath his own desk, the outside world evaporated, like the waking memory of a dream. That was already beginning to happen at British Albion, even though the desk he occupied could not be called his own: it belonged to Vaart who was on holiday, and he could picture Vaart, even though he had never met him, more vividly than he could conjure up the face of the ticket collector at London Bridge or his local newsagent or even his own wife. Trying to remember what his wife looked like, he could only focus on an image of the tennis player Billie Jean King, whom she resembled when her hair was done in a certain way. All this was proof that he had found a billet which suited him very well.

His wife had only once impinged on his consciousness during his first week with British Albion, and even that intrusion had been to do with an office matter. In his elation at having landed the job, he had forgotten, when leaving the building after his interview with Lucas of Personnel, to hand over the Part Two of his appointment card to the three one-armed commissionaires. On the Sunday evening before taking up his appointment, while emptying the pockets of his business suit so that his wife could sponge and press it, he had discovered the crumpled document and asked her to remind him at all costs to take it with him. This, naturally, she had failed to do, and he had sailed off without it. Thinking the matter important, as it certainly was, his wife had tried to ring him at the office. She had found that British Albion was not on the telephone. At least, it was not in the book under B for British or A for Albion, and directory enquiries could not help her.

She had mentioned this curious fact to Gryce on the Monday evening, and he in turn mentioned it to Copeland on the Tuesday. The opportunity arose when he handed over the long-lost Part Two: he had done this on the advice of the three one-armed commissionaires who, after a long conference, had refused to accept it on the grounds that its absence had already been recorded in their occurrence book.

He found Copeland at his desk in his partitioned-off space by the filing cabinets, where he was meticulously smoothing out a toffee wrapper. Unlike the rest of the clientele of Mr Hakim's Friday morning market stall, Copeland did not buy his sweets for home consumption. He kept a large presentation tin of Sharpe's Toffee Assortment in a private drawer of one of the filing cabinets, and dipped into it often. Combined with ill-fitting teeth, his fondness for sucking toffees probably accounted for his occasional obscurities of speech.

Copeland's cubby-hole had no door and Gryce didn't think that knocking on the waist-high metal partition would be appropriate. He place himself in Copeland's line of vision and hung about until Copeland looked up and, with an encouraging 'Mm!', cordially beckoned him in. To Gryce's relief he showed little interest either in the Part Two or in Gryce's confused account of his adventures with it. To his further relief, Copeland did however agree to take possession of the wretched thing, and flung it into a filing tray.

Copeland seemed disposed towards conversation. He could not ask Gryce to sit down, since his status as departmental head did not rate a chair for visitors, but he did perform a vaguely agreeable hand-signal which Gryce recognized as equivalent to the 'Stand easy' wave of his Air Force days.

'Dialect wine,' said Copeland, after Gryce had told him, in the form of a little anecdote, about his wife having hell's own job in trying to find British Albion's number.

Effectively forestalling any attempt by Gryce to have this cryptic remark amplified, Copeland then rose abruptly, went to the filing cabinet that housed his private drawer, and swallowing the toffee that was already in his mouth extracted another one from a large tin bearing a picture of Windsor Castle. This was done quite openly, apparently without it crossing Copeland's mind that he ought to offer one to Gryce; but when it came to unwrapping the toffee and popping it into his mouth, some belated delicacy of feeling impelled him to turn his back and hunch his shoulders as if performing a minor private ablution.

At the conclusion of, to Gryce's mind, this farcical business, Copeland returned to his desk with the toffee wrapper concealed in his hand, insinuating it on top of the one that was already lying there in the clear hope of Gryce not noticing that there were now two wrappers on the desk instead of one. He then went on to smooth out the top wrapper as he had done the one beneath it. It seemed quite important to him to prove to his own satisfaction that the two toffee-papers, when smoothed out, were exactly the same size, and when next he spoke, to ask Gryce if he was finding his feet, it was in an abstracted sort of voice.

The question had already been asked of Gryce by several of his colleagues and he gave the same answer: that it was a little like finding one's way around an ocean liner. He had never been on an ocean liner but the simile seemed appropriate, bearing in mind the slightly nautical flavour of the phrase about finding his feet that everyone used. Copeland confessed that there were parts of the building he was himself still unfamiliar with, giving the piles suppository in haystack tree as an instance. Gryce thought he must mean the Files Depository in basement three. He said that he would have to find Gryce something to do, and Gryce said that he looked forward to it. And then, reverting to the subject of telephones as abruptly as he had departed from it, Copeland repeated:

'Yes, dialect wine.'

If, as Gryce now guessed, he was saying 'direct lines', it didn't go very far towards explaining the mystery. Gryce supposed if his wife had used a bit of initiative, she could have got him on the phone by unearthing his letter of appointment and ringing the direct line number quoted on it – except, come to think of it, that it would have been the direct line to Lucas of Personnel, so it wouldn't have helped her much. But that didn't explain why a big commercial concern like Perfidious Albion should choose to be ex-directory, and it didn't explain why the telephones on the seventh floor, direct line or not, never seemed to ring.

He was not going to raise these questions with a busy head of department, but Copeland, who was now engaged in folding down the four corners of his toffee-papers to form an octogram, evidently sensed his puzzlement. Carefully serrating one of the folds with a thumb-nail, Copeland explained:

'It saves clogging up the twitchboard with outside calls, so our masters the business efficiency wallahs assure us. Each department has its own dialect wine. So if your wife does want to reach you in an immersion, see, she can always get you at this number here.'

Copeland gestured, more of a flaccid gesture this time, in the direction of his own telephone. He had only slightly stressed 'immersion, see', but enough for Gryce to gather that he was saying 'emergency' and that outside calls were not encouraged. Sound policy. It would stop his wife, especially if she were never given Copeland's direct line number, from ringing up to ask if he was working late again.

'Of course,' added Copeland, 'there's nothing to prevent you from making your own cause outboard.' Calls outward, that would be. 'Just dial nine on your internal extension and that gives you an outside wine, provided you don't wish to ring Australia. But you can't get incoming calls.'

'Except presumably from other departments?' ventured Gryce, anxious to seem alert.

'Not encouraged,' said Copeland firmly. 'Verbal enquiries play the merry dickens with the cistern, such as it is. Our cistern is to get everything in writing. Memo in, memo out, that's the idea. Then we all know where we are.'

Sounds more like the civil service every day, thought Gryce. But that was how these big firms tended to conduct themselves these days. The business efficiency wallahs were the masters now, as Copeland had rightly said. Gryce wouldn't have been surprised to hear that they'd had one of those American teams of whizz-kids in.

Since Copeland had the quizzical look of one expecting further questions, Gryce was emboldened to ask: 'But isn't it unusual for a firm this size to go ex-directory?'

'Furiously enough, it's more common than you'd think. It does make cents, when you look at it from the business standpoint. Nine out of ten calls are from established clients who know what dialect wine to ring and whom they want to speak to. Your unsolicited calls – salesmen, dissatisfied customers and other pains in the nether regions – are eliminated completely. It cuts down on use of executive time enormously.'

Oh, yes, they'd had the American whizz-kids in all right, revamping the organization from top to bottom.

Gryce, who had been encouraged by the tone of the interview to lean familarly against Copeland's desk, straightened up. Thinking that Copeland might want to go back to the theme of how difficult it was to find one's way around a new billet, and perhaps express the hope that he had at least managed to find out where to draw his pay cheque, he did not immediately leave.

He was surprised when all Copeland said was, 'Does that add to your pension?' Gryce, with an inane grinning nod, withdrew. Not until he was back at his desk did he work out that Copeland had asked, 'Does that answer your question?', just as Seeds had done when asked what British Albion was in aid of.

5

As to work: perhaps because he had drawn attention to himself by going into Copeland and pestering him about one thing after another, he was that very afternoon assigned his duties. Gryce felt hard done by: he had been banking on a week's grace at least.

He had also begun to hope that when the axe did fall, he would be asked to take over Mrs Rashman's job. Given that his arrival in Stationery Supplies overlapped Mrs Rashman's departure to get married only by a few days, it followed that he must be her replacement. From the evidence of Gryce's own eyes, Mrs Rashman was employed solely to snap rubber bands around batches of documents before they went down to the Files Depository in basement three. It would have suited him admirably, and he would be intrigued to know who was going to take over Mrs Rashman's little sinecure. Perhaps young Thelma was due for promotion.

For himself, he was given more exacting work, which was flattering in a way. Under the tutelage of the Penney twins, he was instructed in a process known as 'calling-in'. This meant he would be responsible for encouraging the various departments of British Albion to return their stocks of obsolete office stationery, for example the weekly sick-leave record sheets which had now been simplified, and to apply for replacements. Issuing the replacements would not be Gryce's pigeon. As he understood it, an operation that had hitherto been handled solely by the Penney brothers was now being divided, amoeba-like: where they had once called-in old stocks and subsequently issued new supplies, they would now be responsible only for the second stage of the procedure after the first stage had been cleared by Gryce. It was probably a lead-up to the reorganization programme that Copeland had talked about, doubtless resulting from the visit of that American whizz-kid team.

'It does give us one advantage – ' began Hugh Penney.

' – a chance of catching-up,' finished Charles Penney. Gryce had noticed already that they distributed their sentences between themselves, so that each brother had an equal share of whatever had to be said. It was only rarely that either of them made a complete statement.

What he had not noticed, until they brought their chairs across and sat one on either side of him, was that the brothers suffered from joint halitosis.

The co-ordination they achieved in matters of dress, posture and so on did not extend to their diaphragms, so that while one brother was breathing in the other was breathing out. Gryce, as he put it to himself with unaccustomed crudeness, copped it both ways. He had had it in mind to spin out his indoctrination to last several days, but as wave after wave of fetid air assaulted his nostrils he determined to get the mysteries of 'calling-in' unravelled as quickly as possible. He did wish that Seeds, who had been inconvenienced slightly by having to move his chair in order to accommodate Hugh Penney on Gryce's left, would stop prolonging the proceedings with jocular interruptions such as: '*I* see. Three heads are better than one, eh?'

'So let me see. Taking it step by step, the first step is to send out the pink check-list – '

' – to all heads of departments.' Hugh Penney, probably from life-long habit, finished Gryce's sentence.

'That's only if they haven't sent back their white check-lists,' Charles Penney reminded him.

' – which the majority are doing automatically,' supplemented Hugh Penney.

So far, so good. The white check-list required heads of departments to make a return of their stocks of obsolescent items by ticking off a series of boxes. The pink check-list was a duplicate of the white check-list, plus an urgent reminder, underlined in red, that the request was mandatory. Contrary to what Hugh Penney had just told him, it was apparent to Gryce from the thin file of flimsies that the majority of heads of departments were not returning their white check-lists automatically, for the reason that they had never received them. But he had already privately decided to save himself labour by despatching pink check-lists willy-nilly.

'And in the event that the pink returns are not forthcoming?' he asked next. Despite the invisible cloud of pollution enveloping his desk, he was determined to familiarize himself with every stage of the procedure. He envisaged that there would be yet further check-lists, of varying hues and increasing degrees of urgency, that the Penney twins had not shown him yet.

'Ah,' said Charles Penney.

'*Personal representation!*' intoned Hugh Penney, mock-dramatically.

'You chase them up,' said Charles Penney.

Gryce had an instant and pleasing vision of himself drifting about the building during the long afternoons, pausing for chats and making new friends as he chased up his pink check-lists from department to department.

There was one snag he had better dispose of.

'According to the Big White Chief' – he nodded towards Copeland's cubby-hole – 'the direct approach is somewhat frowned on. "Memo in, memo out", if I quote his golden words correctly.'

The Penney twins simultaneously brought their heads closer to his, releasing a pot-pourri of noxious fumes.

'Brother Copeland,' murmured Charles, 'doesn't have our problems.'

'He *doesn't* have to deal with our friends on the *tenth floor*,' sighed Hugh.

' – who are not only still using holiday rosters et cetera et cetera that have been out-of-date since the year dot – '

' – but which,' concluded Hugh, losing his brother's syntactic thread, 'were superseded by a whole range of forms we're now calling in!'

'Pre-obsolescent obsolescence, eh? *Sha!* I like that!' joked Gryce. Carte blanche, then, to amble about the place as he wished, starting with the tenth floor. He was already savouring his new responsibilities.

'And from there on, working from the completed returns, I send out a requisition calling-in such obsolescent stocks as are held?'

'Broadly speaking, yes – '

' – and no.' The Penney twins spoke grudgingly. They seemed reluctant to concede that Gryce had mastered their joint skills in less than twenty minutes. Serve them right for having bad breath.

'You send out *two* requisitions, after consulting your master check-sheet – '

'Yes, I meant to say two requisitions, I understand all that,' said Gryce, a shade testily. They really should see a dentist, the pair of them.

Hugh Penney, taking up the baton from his brother, plodded on regardless.

'Requisition *A* directs the *bulk* of the material back to Stationery Stores for recycling into rough memo pads – '

' – but sensitive documents, such as obsolete pay slips, accident reports – '

' – anything that could be used unscrupulously, in other words – '

' – everything you see here marked with an asterisk – '

' – they come under Requisition B – '

They'd ploughed through all this already.

'Yes, I know.'

' – and must be consigned to the shredding machine.'

'Yes. Thank you. I've got that. And the final step is to notify you that, as it were, all has been safely gathered in?'

'You notify us – '

' – in writing – '

' – on a blue slip.'

'Until, that is, the fatal day arrives,' said Gryce, leaning back with a smile, 'when the blue slip itself is called in as obsolescent. *Sha!*' Another little joke of his, this one with a purpose to it. It was meant to indicate to the Penney twins that their business with Gryce was concluded, and that after a pleasantry or two they should feel free to return to their desks.

They showed no such inclination. Gryce was very much afraid that they had allocated the entire afternoon to showing him the ropes and didn't mean to be done out of it. After laughing at his sally – '*Haaark!*' they had cawed in unison, exposing twin sets of ulcerated gums – they began to shuffle through the specimen white check-lists, pink check-lists, requisition forms A and B and blue slips with the obvious intention of going doggedly through the whole gubbins for a third time.

To forestall them, Gryce cut in quickly with a question that had been puzzling him rather, not that it was any of his business.

'After I've called-in obsolete stocks say, for the sake of argument, from our antediluvian friends on the tenth floor, it's up to them to apply for, again for the sake of argument, say replacement holiday rosters?'

'Yes,' said Charles Penney.

'From us,' said Hugh Penney.

'It's not done automatically?'

'On the contrary – '

' – they have to make application.'

'Yes, I thought so,' said Gryce, thoughtfully. 'They make application on a stationery requirements form, correct me if I'm wrong?'

The Penney twins, who had suddenly begun to twitch and avoid one another's eyes as if suppressing giggles, both nodded vigorously.

'But surely the stationery requirements form is one of the items we're calling-in as obsolescent?' He'd noticed that when running his eyes down the white and pink check-lists. It was what had given him the idea for his joke about the fatal day coming when the blue slip would itself be obsolescent.

'You *could* say that, yes. The stationery requirements form has been revised – '

' – or modified.'

'Oh, would you say modified?' Charles Penney asked his brother in a waggish sort of voice, squinting at him over Gryce's shoulder. 'I'd have said revised, personally.'

'Let's say revised *and* modified,' Hugh Penney said, also with waggish undertones. They seemed as if they were trying out their hands at being some kind of double act.

'Then as I see it,' Gryce pursued, with the flicker of a smile to prove that he was enjoying this as much as they were, although he was blessed if he could see what was so amusing, 'they can't get replacement stationery of any kind until they've filled in a revised, modified, call it what you will stationery requirements form. And since the wretched stationery requirements form is *itself* an item of stationery – '

'Ah,' said Charles Penney, tapping his nose.

'Catch 22,' said Hugh Penney, folding his arms.

Composing their faces owlishly, both men winked at Gryce. At the same time – it was presumably something to do with the way the facial muscles interacted – they breathed out heavily through their nostrils, releasing a poisonous stench. Gryce wondered if Seeds had ever dubbed them the Two Bad Penneys.

Gryce had forgotten to ask the Penney twins who exactly were the pink check-list backsliders on the tenth floor, and now that he had managed to extract himself from their company (as members of a biscuit-eating school composed of themselves, Mrs Rashman and Mr Hakim they had repaired to their own desks during the afternoon tea break) he certainly didn't intend to retrace his footsteps. Mumbling something to Seeds about there being no time like the present and striking while irons were hot, Gryce had gulped down his tea and headed for the lifts.

The flimsy copy of the unreturned pink check-list which he had extracted from the files gave him no clue. The check-lists were addressed to heads of departments only by the coded abbreviation used in all internal correspondence – he begged its pardon, in-house mail. Thus Copeland, he had noticed, was S7 – seven presumably being the floor number and S standing for Stationery Supplies. The head of Traffic Control across the way would be T7, and so on.

All Gryce knew was that his errand was with C10. It could very well mean C for Catering – for he remembered, as he stepped out of the lift on the tenth floor and looked around for a directory sign that was not there, that Pam had said something about believing the offices dealing with supplementary subsistence tickets, or SSTs, to be on either the tenth or twelfth floor. It would turn out, though Gryce had difficulty in crediting it to begin with, that they were on the tenth, eleventh and twelfth.

The tenth floor was unlike the seventh and third, the only ones on which he was qualified to pass comment, in that it was not sub-divided into sections. One department, in other words, occupied the entire length of the building at this level. The fact of there being no partitioned aisles meant there was room for more desks: about a hundred all told, Gryce would have guessed, all three-drawers locking, front-courtesy panel B4A/00621 models from Comform. (One of Comform's salesmen had pulled off a coup all right; rum that Gryce had no recollection of so substantial an invoice.) Behind each desk sat a male clerk – no females in this department, worse luck for those who worked in it – and on the black composition top of each desk, as far as the eye could see, were piles of SSTs which were being stamped, numbered, checked, entered into ledgers or card-indexes, or processed in some way. It was either this extraordinary sight or the uncanny resemblance of the nearest of the clerks to Jack Lemmon which put Gryce in mind of *The Apartment*, or it might have been another film, where they had made a humorous point about office drudgery in just such a scene.

There was no cubby-hole like Copeland's where the head of department might be found, but the desk where the Jack Lemmon-looking individual sat was placed near the doorway at right angles to the others, so that it could reasonably be taken as an enquiry desk even though Jack Lemmon was doing the same work as everyone else.

Without looking up, and in a weary, hundredth-time-today voice, he sighed, 'Twelfth floor' at Gryce's approach.

'Come again?'

'If you want your SSTs, twelfth floor. Hatch next to the Cockpit.'

'Oh, I'm with you. No, I wanted a word with the head of department, actually.'

'Which department?'

'This department.'

The clerk now gave Gryce his full attention, though without any improvement in his manner. He looked like Jack Lemmon looking foxy.

'Yes, I *know* this department. But how do you know this is the department you're looking for?'

Overworked, that was his trouble, Gryce thought. So was everyone else on the tenth floor, by the look of things. Not a head had been raised at his entrance, not a pen or rubber stamp laid aside. You would have thought they'd have been glad of the diversion.

'I was looking for C10, in point of fact.'

Gryce produced his pink check-list flimsy. Instead of reaching out for it, as expected, Jack Lemmon made Gryce hold it out for his inspection for all the world as if he were a human lectern.

'You want C12. Twelfth floor. Hatch next to the Cockpit.'

Thank you for nothing, said Gryce to himself, and went out.

Rather than wait for the lift he decided to walk up the stairs to the twelfth floor. Give his legs a bit of exercise. Reaching the eleventh floor foyer, and noticing that like the tenth it had no directory sign to identify the department or departments accommodated at this level, he paused out of curiosity to glance through the glass swing doors, one of which was invitingly propped open.

From the thumping of rubber stamps and the clicking of numbering machines, it was as busy a beehive as the floor he had just left. Gryce took a few diffident steps nearer. An all-male cast again; no one looked up. Hovering inside the doorway, he could now take in the length and breadth of the eleventh floor. It was an exact replica of the tenth, with the same rows of clerks at the same rows of three-drawers locking, front-courtesy panel B4A/ 00621 desks all stamping or otherwise dealing with their stacks of SSTs. Except that the clerk nearest the door didn't look remotely like Jack Lemmon, Gryce might have been the victim of some trick of space that had led him out of the tenth floor, up a flight of stairs and back to his starting-point.

Gryce didn't know what to make of it at all. While he was not quite sure what the numerical strength of Perfidious Albion might be in an actual head-count, it didn't need a degree in mathematics to work out that in an office block of twelve storeys, approximately one sixth of the workforce was occupied in fiddling about with wretched subsidized luncheon tickets. He had heard of firms being hot on staff welfare, they found it paid off in terms of productivity, but this was ridiculous.

Of course, it didn't follow that the tenth and eleventh floor battalions were engaged on such comparatively futile chores for all time. Indeed, the pace at which they were tackling their stamping and numbering and so forth seemed to suggest they had a deadline to meet. That, on reflection, would be it. Pam had explained in detail how the subsidized meal entitlement was in a transition period between orthodox luncheon vouchers and company or in-house SSTs. Gryce would have caught them slap bang in the middle of the change-over process. The clerks on the tenth and eleventh floors, or a substantial number of them, would have been diverted from other duties for this one-off rush job. When the crisis was over they would go back to their routine work, whatever that might be.

Satisfied, for the time being, by this deduction, Gryce proceeded to the twelfth floor, which a sign in the foyer told him was the domain of Catering (Administration). Supplementary to the explanation he had just given himself, Gryce could now see that there was probably a spot of empire-building going on this neck of the woods. He had come across that sort of thing before: he had once worked in a billet where the publicity wallahs had started out as one man and a boy and had finished up occupying a specially built annexe with their own typing pool. You had to hand it to them, in a way.

At any rate, one small mystery was solved. It was C10 for Catering as he'd thought all along, though why they couldn't have called it C12 and saved him all this trouble he was blessed if he could say.

Catering (Administration) occupied only two thirds of the space available, the other third having been walled off, papered with simulated brick and equipped with heavy mahogany doors to form the Cockpit executive restaurant. The doors were open. Gryce had a glimpse of several women, waitresses they would be, who were sitting at the white-clothed tables smoking cigarettes and gossiping. You couldn't blame them: lunch had been over a good two hours and they plainly had nothing to do except idle the rest of the afternoon away. Saving their presence, he didn't see why jobs like theirs couldn't be done by part-time labour, as in all the other billets he'd known.

The Cockpit was on Gryce's left as he entered from the foyer. To his right, beyond the same kind of waist-high partition as separated Stationery Supplies from Traffic Control, was Catering (Administration), or rather the hub of the Catering (Administration) empire if it proved that the tenth and eleventh floors came permanently under the same umbrella. Although the familiar rows of clerks were hunched over the familiar rows of desks they were not, Gryce was relieved to say, engaged in any log-rolling with SSTs. Even so, their noses were kept to the grindstone as they busied themselves over files and ledgers. There was a martinet in charge of Catering (Administration) and no mistake.

Ahead of him, adjoining the Cockpit, was a kind of booth affair, constructed of hardboard, and featuring the famous hatch spoken of by Jack Lemmon downstairs. It was rather like a temporary booking office in a railway station – a closed, temporary booking office, as it happened, since the hatch was firmly shuttered. Feeling a bit of a fool under the collective gaze of the Catering (Administration) personnel, not that any one of them had so much as glanced up so far as he could tell, Gryce stepped forward and rapped on the shutter with his knuckles.

What followed was a bit of a pantomime in his humble opinion. One of the clerks rose from his desk, crossed directly behind Gryce, entered the Cockpit executive restaurant, disappeared smartly to the right, presumably opened a pass door leading into the hardboard booth affair, threw up the shutter, snapped 'Eleven till one!' and slammed it down again.

Gryce, keeping his head, waylaid him as he re-emerged through the mahogany doors of the Cockpit.

'Excuse me, I'm terribly sorry but I'm *not* after SSTs!'

Gryce consolidated this bold display of initiative by waving his flimsy copy of the pink check-list and explaining his mission as concisely as possible. The clerk, hissing through his teeth with the air of one who has had just about as much as he can take for one day, snatched the paper from Gryce's hands and once more disappeared into the Cockpit. In a moment he was back, minus the pink check-list flimsy, so that at least indicated some progress was being made.

'You'll have to wait.'

The clerk resumed his seat and, at once returning to his work, took no further notice of Gryce.

Gryce occupied himself at first in pacing to the doors of the Cockpit and back. His shoes squeaked slightly, and although no one looked up and glared at him a sixth sense told him he was distracting people who were trying to concentrate. He ceased his pacing and commenced to fork-lift himself up and down on the balls of his feet. But this too caused his shoes to squeak. Gryce abandoned the diversion and stood stock-still.

He waited a long time. The waitresses in the Cockpit were donning their cheap cloth coats and rummaging about with small packages, probably lard, sugar and so forth which came under the heading of perks from the kitchens. Gryce saw to his surprise that it was nearly on ten minutes to five. Down in Stationery Supplies, if yesterday evening had been representative of the week, there would be a slamming of drawers and a scraping of chairs as one after the other of his colleagues called it a day. Up here in Catering (Administration), and doubtless in the slave-galleys of the tenth and eleventh floors, they soldiered on.

Gryce, watching the red second-hand of the clock over the entrance doors sweep round, found himself in a quandary. If he left now, not only would he be relinquishing his file copy of a pink check-list that officially should never have been taken out of the department, but he would have the embarrassment of drawing attention to himself by approaching, in squeaking shoes, the clerk who had taken it from him and explaining that he would come back in the morning. But if he hung on, he would be late. Gryce was dashed if he could see why he should work overtime on only his second day in a new billet.

He was considering his position when the shutter of the hatch was suddenly flung up and the flimsy pink check-list landed at his feet in a crumpled ball. The fat, wobbling face that glared out at him was vermillion with rage, and so in sharp contrast to the gleaming white chef's hat that crowned it.

'Tell Copeland we've more to do up here than fill in his bloody stupid forms! If he wants to run this department he can come up here and run it, and bloody welcome! If not, he can stick that bumph where the monkey stuck the nuts!'

With that, the shutter was banged down with such force that papers blew off some of the nearby desks. Gryce was very conscious that all eyes were upon him. At least it proved that they were human.

Despite his confusion and concern as he bent to retrieve the despoiled flimsy – he supposed (he would have to consult the Penney twins on this) that a fresh pink check-sheet would have to be made out now and this one consigned to the wpb – he could not help but admire the head of department of Catering (Administration), if that was indeed whom he had just had dealings with. No nonsense here about delegating or buck-passing or being too preoccupied with bumph and paperwork to do the job he was paid to do. His brief was to run the catering operation smoothly and to the best of his abilities, and by heavens if that meant taking his jacket off and supervising the kitchens after a full day at his desk, then take off his jacket and supervise he jolly well would. He had prob- ably, Gryce surmised, been preparing the soup for tomor- row's lunch. And on top of that he had the change-over from luncheon vouchers to SSTs to cope with.

Gryce felt, as a matter of fact, enormous respect for

78

the whole department, although he was fervently glad not be a part of it. In his Air Force days, he had once been sent on a filing course to a camp in North Yorkshire which was also a transit depot. In the next hut there had been a bunch of sergeant fighter pilots who were awaiting posting to Germany or the Far East. They kept themselves to themselves and made it obvious that they felt a cut above the trainee pen-pushers who marched off every morning to learn their trade at school desks. And they were right: they were. They had been where the action was. Gryce did not envy them but he admired them, and that was how he felt about Catering (Administration).

Everyone had gone when Gryce got back to Stationery Supplies. Not surprisingly: it was two minutes past five. The lift had been a long time coming and a crush of people had got on at the ninth and eighth floors, pinning him against the back wall and forcing him to travel to ground level and then wait for the lift to go up again, which despite all his pressing of buttons it had been in no hurry to do.

Gryce was very annoyed. No one had bothered to clear his desk so there were all the papers the Penney twins had dumped on him to be put away somehow. God alone knew where. All the filing cabinets were locked and so was Vaart's desk of which Gryce was only the tenant. You would have thought the Penney twins would have realized that. You would have thought they could have shown a bit of consideration and taken all this bumph under their wing for one night at least, even though they had technically handed over the 'calling-in' side of things to Gryce. Or was that too much to ask?

Then there was the pink check-list flimsy dramatically rejected by the departmental head of Catering (Administration). Gryce had straightened it out a bit but it was badly torn and, being only a carbon in the first place, now practically illegible. But that too had to be put away. Gryce had all this to do before he could even dream of putting on his raincoat.

You tried to show a bit of initiative and at once you were taken advantage of.

As it just so happened, getting the appropriate filing cabinet open was no problem to Gryce. Like the desks, the filing cabinets – or storage cabinets as they were more properly called, to distinguish them from the multi-drawer flat-stacking unit – were all supplied by Comform. Catalogue No. B4B/04885, duo-grey metal, four deep drawers on telescopic rails, recessed handles, standard lock. There was a trick with that standard lock, as Gryce knew of old. By prodding at it with a ballpoint pen, you depressed the retractile mechanism which in nine cases out of ten released the lock-spring. Well: nowhere in the catalogue was any statement made about the B4B/04885 being burglarproof. Fireproof, yes.

But the Penney twins were not to know this little trade secret. Oh, no: for all they knew, Gryce could have been faffing about until six o'clock, trying to find a home for the bumph they had wished upon him. It really was a bit much being left to hold the fort like this, when he had barely been with the firm five minutes.

Gryce opened the filing cabinet without difficulty and dumped the assortment of papers in it without ceremony. He was blowed if he was going to sort them into their proper folders at this hour: that could wait until morning when, by looking tight-lipped and doing a certain amount of crashing and banging with the filing cabinet drawer, he would make jolly sure the Penney twins knew what he thought of them.

He was feeling sorry for himself by now. The long,

empty office with its harsh lights – left on, so he understood, for the army of night cleaners who would soon be descending on the seventh floor in great droves – had a forlorn air, reminding him of the North Circular Road. He wished he had had a chance to say good night to Pam. He wished, come to that, he had had a chance to say good night to all and sundry. The office was desolate now that they had all gone home, and he missed the camaraderie as keenly as any child kept in while its friends are playing in the street.

As always when in a self-pitying frame of mind, Gryce was getting peckish. After all, he had had nothing since lunch. A gulp of tea before setting off on his abortive expedition to Catering (Administration), yes. But nothing solid. There was a case, he had always felt, for having a biscuit in the afternoon tea break. When Mrs Rashman left in a few days, a vacancy would exist in the Penney twins/Hakim/Rashman biscuit-eating school. But then the question arose: who would look after the biscuits? At the moment the responsibility fell on Mrs Rashman, who clearly found it convenient to replenish supplies when buying in her vast stocks of groceries. Mr Hakim, with his connections in the wholesale confectionery business, might reasonably be expected to be next in line. But supposing the Penney twins asserted themselves? Gryce didn't know whether halitosis could transmit itself to a Huntley and Palmer's assortment in an air-tight tin but on balance he was not willing to take the risk. He would wait until he had got his knees brown, as they used to say in the Air Force, then start a little biscuit-eating school of his own, with probably Pam and Seeds as founder-members.

Pondering thus, all alone under the gently hissing, fluorescent strip-lights, Gryce was suddenly possessed by an overwhelming craving for one of Copeland's toffees.

Even the far distant rumbling of the lifts had stopped now. All was quiet. When exactly the night cleaners arrived on duty Gryce could not say, but he expected they would come barging along with vacuum cleaners and enormous waste-bins on squeaking wheels. He would get plenty of warning, God willing.

His own shoes squeaking ten to the blessed dozen he made his way, on tiptoe for no reason he could pin down, towards Copeland's personal filing cabinet in the partitioned-off space across the office. It certainly wasn't that Gryce felt guilty: more a bit of a devil, if anyone wanted to know. Anyway, if they wished him to work overtime, they could hardly expect him to do it on an empty stomach.

Even so, Gryce's pulse raced as he unclipped the ballpoint from his top pocket, and his hand trembled as he took aim like a darts-player, and pressed the pen home against the lock-face. Like a knife through butter, he told himself as the lock sprang open with a satisfactory click. If all else failed, he could always take up housebreaking.

He slid open the top drawer gently, gripping its sides to reduce the harsh scraping of the telescopic runners.

It was the lid of Copeland's Windsor Castle toffee tin that made more row than anything. Judging wrongly that it needed a good tug to get it open, Gryce pulled at it with a force that spun it clattering against the metal wall of the filing cabinet. What was more, the impetus had sent several toffees flying in all directions. If the noise had alerted anyone – how did he know the building wasn't crawling with security guards? – he would be in the soup now and no mistake.

Heart thumping, Gryce froze, his arms angled in such a grotesque position over the open filing-cabinet drawer that he could have been posing for a steel engraving of a body-snatcher desecrating a tomb. He counted ten. All clear.

He had better get himself organized. The first step was to select his toffee, call it two toffees for luck, making sure that the wrapper of the one to be consumed on the scene of the crime was placed in his pocket *and disposed of later*. The second step was to go methodically through the drawer and replace the four or five toffees that had been dislodged from their tin.

Gryce unwrapped what he hoped was a treacle brittle, found to his disappointment that it was fudge, wondered if he could re-wrap it expertly enough for Copeland not to notice, rejected this speculation as wild, popped the fudge in his mouth and the wrapper in his pocket, and abstracted a second toffee for future consumption. Then he set about eradicating traces of his visit.

It would, as luck would have it, be the work of only a moment. Besides the toffee tin, Copeland's personal drawer contained only a pair of string-backed driving gloves, the paperback novel *Airport*, a half-used packet of drinking straws for some reason – perhaps, taking his example from Mr Hakim, Copeland went on a 7-Up jag during summer coffee breaks – and a couple of what looked like instruction manuals, one white-covered, one black. The few scattered toffees were readily locatable among these sparse belongings.

Gryce recovered them, hesitated for a moment, then helped himself to an extra toffee and replaced the lid. He had already eaten his piece of fudge. He unwrapped the toffee in his hand and saw to his delight that it was butterscotch. Carefully pocketing the wrapper, Gryce sucked contentedly.

He wondered if the rest of Copeland's filing cabinet contained anything worth knowing about. Personal files, anything of that kind. He slid the middle drawer open: it was empty except for a teapot with a broken spout and a pair of braces. As for the bottom drawer, it was stacked with empty toffee tins, a dozen or fifteen of them there must have been. If Copeland were knocked down by the proverbial bus tomorrow, what a pathetic sight this little array would present to the bod detailed to clear out his cabinet.

Gryce returned to the top drawer. He had better make sure the toffee tin currently in use was exactly as he'd found it, that was to say, half-resting on the pair of driving gloves and tilting slightly. His eye fell on the two manuals. Sucking away at his butterscotch, he picked up the white-covered one. It was a dog-eared copy, probably badly out-of-date by now, of the guidelines leaflet summarized for him by Pam and Seeds. He flicked through it: not much there he didn't know already, except, on the last page, a list of the various firms of which British Albion was the parent company. About twenty of them all told: Binns Brothers, Rugby; Cobbs and Co., Harrow on the Hill; Fallowfield (Processing) Ltd, Slough. And so on and so forth. They meant nothing to Gryce.

The other manual, the black one, was a loose-leaf affair with pages of stiff card embellished with index tags, and if Gryce was not mistaken, it was an internal telephone directory. They were all much of a muchness, these things, presumably there was a firm that specialized in printing them. For no other reason than that he had not as yet finished his butterscotch, and didn't care to say goodnight to the three one-armed commissionaires, assuming they were still on duty, with it still in his mouth, Gryce picked up the internal telephone directory and idly turned its pages. Here it was then: the key to all those magic dialect wines explained at such length by Copeland.

Gryce looked up first the number of Stationery Supplies, then of Personnel, then the Buttery, the Cockpit,

Catering (Administration), Traffic Control, In-house Mail, and Main Door. Those were the only departments he could think of. He began to dip into the directory at random.

A slow frown etched into his forehead as he browsed on. After some time he turned back to the opening page and started to plough steadily through the volume from A for Accounts.

He had got to the letter F, and was wondering whether to rummage in Copeland's tin and fish out another butterscotch, when there was a sound so strange and unexpected that the hairs bristled on his neck.

It was a telephone ringing.

It was, to Gryce, like hearing the fog siren on an abandoned ship. The office was empty. Even when it was not, no telephone had rung at all during his two days with British Albion. Not encouraged, Copeland had said: memo in, memo out. Gryce's ears had already re-edited the familiar medley of background office noises so that the absence of the telephone no longer jarred. Now, it was its presence that jarred. In the silent, deserted aircraft hangar that the seventh floor in his fancy resembled, the ringing of the telephone sounded as raucous and urgent as a fire bell.

Gryce's first instinct was to get out of it. He slammed the filing cabinet shut, remembering with great presence of mind to push the lock home. He swallowed the sliver of butterscotch that lay on his tongue like a flat iron. The telephone went on ringing.

He had to get his raincoat.

Gryce had not much aural sense of direction and so he had no idea which of the seventh floor's sixty to eighty telephones had given him such a jolt. It was certainly not Copeland's, he knew that much. Trying to think rationally, he came up with the theory that someone was trying to get through to the departmental head of Traffic Control on his direct line. The direct lines did ring from time to time: Copeland had more or less said so.

Blundering across the office, however, Gryce realized that he was far off the mark. It was Seeds' phone that was ringing.

The discovery was at once calming and puzzling. It was a call for his own department, Stationery Supplies. Or, more likely at this hour, a personal call for Seeds from someone who probably thought the office closed at five-thirty or six instead of five. Gryce was on the premises for a legitimate reason: to file away documents that the Penney twins, in their wisdom, had washed their hands of. If a telephone rang, he was quite entitled to answer it. Indeed, since everyone else had cleared off and left him to it, he was the Joe Muggins who would *have* to answer it.

But departmental phones were not supposed to ring. Incoming calls were discouraged. And how would anyone know what number to call anyway, since the disc inside the dial where the extension number ought to be was blank?

It was probably a wrong number.

Gryce, compromising between acting positively and leaving well alone, gingerly lifted the receiver and listened.

There was the sound of a man breathing, such as he imagined his wife must have heard in a period when she was being plagued by obscene phone calls. Then a familiar voice, enunciating clearly as if dictating a telegram, said into Seeds' telephone:

'*He was a member of the Forest Hill Liberal Club for a year, but only for social reasons. No further political connections.*'

Gryce was so stunned at hearing this biographical

fragment about himself – it could only be about himself, it would be stretching the long arm of coincidence too far for it to be otherwise – that he reacted in what it later dawned on him was the most foolish manner possible.

He answered, in a faltering, puzzled voice, '*Hello?*' thus giving away his identity.

Lucas of Personnel, as it unquestionably was on the other end of Seeds' line, hung up.

Gryce grabbed his raincoat from its peg and ran for it.

6

'And what about you? Are you married?'

'Oh, very much so.'

They were in the Pressings wine bar, on the Friday evening. Gryce, sipping his second glass of Soave (he should have ordered a bottle and been done with it) congratulated himself again on the speed at which this first clandestine rendezvous had been arrived at. Nor was he in any doubt that clandestine was the right word: it was Pam, not he, who had headed for the discreet corner under the stairs.

He still couldn't believe it. Only four days, well, four and a half days, had gone by since that lunch they'd had with Seeds in the Buttery, yet here they were with their hands practically touching across a table made out of a sherry barrel, in a whitewashed cellar off the beaten track, discussing every subject under the sun. Including the fact that Pam had a husband called Peter who often worked far into the night, or laid claim to working far into the night more like, as an inspector of listed buildings for the Department of the Environment. Ideal.

It was even more unbelievable when you considered that things had not gone according to plan. His hopes of having another lunch with Pam on the excuse of returning her SSTs had come to nothing: friend Seeds had seen to that.

Gryce no longer knew what to make of Seeds since eavesdropping on that unnerving telephone message from Lucas of Personnel on Tuesday evening. He'd seemed pally enough on the face of it: they had had quite an invigorating discussion one afternoon about the route of the No. 73 bus after it reached Hammersmith. But he'd made no attempt to consolidate the easy-going acquaintanceship they had struck up on Gryce's first day: no further invitations to lunch, no offer to whistle up a copy of the guidelines booklet, no tips or wrinkles to make a newcomer feel more at home. On that level, it was not pitching it too strongly to say he'd been evasive.

It might well have happened, of course, that Seeds had had reports from Lucas of Personnel about Gryce intercepting his private phone calls. Gryce had fretted a good deal about that. He had thought of taking Seeds aside and explaining what he had been doing in the office at that hour, why he had answered the phone and what he had heard when he picked it up. But that might have put them both in an embarrassing position. Seeds might not have been able to tell him what was going on without breaching a confidence. He might have resorted to bluster and said something like, 'Well, you know what they say, old man. People with big ears never hear good of themselves.'

Not that Gryce had actually heard ill of himself: the reverse, when he thought about it. '*No further political connections*', Lucas had said. A clean bill of health, that sounded like. Thank the Lord he had never been a blessed Communist.

The phone call business had Gryce stumped. He had toyed with several theories, none of them entirely convincing. Perhaps Lucas had mis-dialled: instead of ringing Seeds he had meant to ring some high-up or other – the head of Security came to mind, there had been a Security Department listed in that internal telephone directory – who would have had a reasonable enough interest in Gryce's political affiliations. This wouldn't have been the first billet Gryce had heard of that took pretty good care it was not harbouring reds under the beds. There was, it was common knowledge, such a thing as industrial sabotage.

Or again, it could conceivably have had nothing at all to do with the office. It could have been a personal affair between Seeds and Lucas. Perhaps they themselves were reds under the beds – or, as seemed more probable, members of the National Front or some such. Perhaps Lucas was abusing his position in Personnel with its wealth of confidential records to seek out possible recruits. If so, he would get no change out of Gryce.

Bringing it down to a more mundane level, it could simply have been that Lucas had been doing a spot of checking-up for Seeds on the old-boy net. Seeds might have got the idea into his head that Gryce was a political extremist of some kind – perhaps he'd seen some Marxist or National Front demo on television and spotted someone who looked uncommonly like Gryce: such things, in Gryce's experience, did happen – and he'd tipped Lucas the wink.

There could be a hundred explanations. But it was all rather rum. So, if only Gryce could find a moment to settle his thoughts, was that curious business of the internal telephone directory in Copeland's filing cabinet. There was definitely a puzzle there to be got to the bottom of, one of these days.

Meanwhile, life had to go on. Come what may, Gryce had to eat; and furthermore he was blowed if he saw why he should eat at his own expense when there were heavily subsidized meals to be had for the asking. On the Tuesday, failing a second invitation to lunch from Seeds, and *failing* Pam keeping her promise to let him know where he could get his SSTs, he had been reduced to wandering about the streets until he found a shop that sold sandwiches wrapped in Cellophane. Hence the hunger that had caused him to dip into Copeland's toffees. It was an unsatisfactory meal and would have been a wretched one but for the chance that Mr Hakim was also taking a simple snack in the office from a variety of paper bags. Mr Hakim was departing on a fortnight's holiday in the Algarve at the end of the week and his lunch hours were very much taken up in seeing travel agents, getting currency from his bank and so on. They had a talk about the Algarve, where Gryce had never been. Gryce told Hakim something about Tenerife, advising him to try it one year, and then Mr Hakim departed to find out if he could buy espadrilles cheaper than in Portugal, from a cousin of his who imported fancy goods. Gryce spent the rest of the lunch hour going through his pockets and getting rid of old bus tickets.

On the Wednesday, however, using his new-found knowledge of the twelfth floor and its workings, he had gone up and signed for a supply of SSTs on his own initiative. He had returned to the seventh floor with every intention of inviting Pam to lunch only to find that Seeds had got there before him. In the Buttery, where he had the bad luck to fall in with the Penney twins who breathed with gusto all over his tongue salad, he could see them twittering like lovebirds at a neighbouring table. If he hadn't known they were arguing about the Albion Players he would have sworn they were in the throes of an affair like the long-suffering Cargill from Salary Accounts and the lady who was definitely not Mrs Cargill.

It had been the same on Thursday and today, Friday. On both occasions Pam and Seeds had waltzed off to the Buttery together without a glance in his direction, leaving him once again prey to the Penney twins. During the coffee break he had wandered across to Pam's desk and diffidently mentioned that he was now in a position to return the SSTs she had generously donated in his hour of need, but she had replied off handedly that it would do any time, meaning never.

All this would have been discouraging but for a parallel development in their acquaintanceship which unfolded in the lift.

Lifts, so Gryce had noticed in some of his previous billets, were very intimate places in their way. People behaved in them in a private, idiosyncratic manner not all that very far removed from pulling faces in the bathroom mirror. Beazley, as an example, was in the habit of jutting out his lower lip and blowing hard up his nostrils, while Grant-Peignton would make tocking noises as if in imitation of a grandfather clock. Neither would have dreamed of making such a public exhibition of himself outside the confines of the lift. Seeds, whenever he was a fellow passenger, was given to humming the opening bars of an obscure song called 'I'm Happy When I'm Hiking'; it was the only instance in which he evidenced an interest in music. Among other behaviour patterns noted by Gryce was that Copeland would sigh heavily as the lift stopped at each floor, swivelling up his eyeballs to invite collusion with his impatience from whoever was standing next to him; and Mrs Rashman, possibly in sympathy with Copeland, would bend slightly at the knees, while imploring, 'Come on, lift.'

For Gryce's own part, he was a bit out of touch with such rituals because at Comform he had worked on the ground floor of what was in any case a low-rise building. But quite quickly he managed to establish his own particular style. Riding to the seventh floor each morning and down again each evening, he took to levering himself up on the balls of his feet, at the same time sliding his back against the vinyl panelling of the lift and constricting his shoulder-blades so that they almost met. This seemed an acceptable enough arrangement to the other lift regulars, and Gryce was able to feel almost from the start that he was of their company. It was, he told himself, a bit like joining the freemasons.

So however discouraging – or anyway not actively encouraging, in fact quite cool really – Pam might have been in the relatively anonymous territory of the seventh floor, once within the vertical cloisters of the lift-shaft she was camaraderie itself. Gryce had not yet had the pleasure of travelling up with her in the morning – she was a notorious late-arriver, indeed it was a standing joke that Mrs Rashman would sing out, 'Here comes the early bird!' when she rolled in at ten past nine – but he seized with both hands the opportunity of travelling down with her in the evening. While Pam might be the last to arrive each day it could be said in her favour that she was also the last to leave. Gryce found that by loitering at the glass doors of the seventh floor foyer until he saw her gathering up her handbag, then summoning the lift and keeping his finger pressed on the 'Open' button, he had every chance of inducing her to run for it. This she did with the scuttering, crab-like movement common to all last-minute lift passengers. To recover her composure, as the lift descended to ground level and Gryce slid his shoulder-blades up and down against the vinyl panelling, Pam would peer into her handbag and ruminate: 'Now what have I forgotten?' Gryce took to saying: 'Door key? Purse? Season ticket? Adequate supply of the firm's ballpoint pens?' and thus a bond between them was forged.

Gryce shared the lift with Pam four times in his first working week: not bad going. It would have been five but for his over-zealousness on Tuesday when he had found himself stranded in Catering (Administration); he wondered if Pam had been disappointed not to see a certain familiar figure holding the lift doors open.

But they had made up for that. On one occasion – yesterday, Thursday, red-letter day – she had been so slow in clearing her desk that the building had just about emptied and they had had the lift to themselves. Gryce had been able to push the frontiers of their relationship forward a little by remarking, after they had enjoyed the familiar exchange about what Pam might have forgotten, 'You know, I'll swear these lifts are centrally-heated!' To which Pam had replied, 'It's air-conditioning, so-called. They pump in hot air all through the summer and cold air in winter.' Gryce had then made a great show of wiping imaginary beads of sweat from his brow. Pam had responded by puckering her lips and exhaling heavily – a genteel version of Beazley blowing up his nostrils – and making a fanning motion with her rolled-up *Evening Standard*. A cosy moment. It was going very well.

Gryce, however, was not one to run before he could walk and failing any luck on the Buttery front next week he was content to let their lift relationship blossom as slowly as might be necessary. He was, after all, in no hurry. It would be his first extra-marital affair, his first affair ever, actually, if you discounted his courtship of Peggy back at Docks and Inland Waterways, and he would just as soon take it slowly.

He was astonished when, as they reached ground level on this Friday evening, Pam called good night to one or two people and then turned back and asked him boldly which way he was going.

'What? Oh. East, usual, though I coo go west. I'm equidistal between two bus-sops.' In his surprise and delight Gryce slurred and tripped over his words like Copeland with a toffee in his mouth. He could feel himself going hot and hoped he wasn't blushing.

'I go west,' said Pam, with a smile as explicit as an engraved invitation card.

They walked – strolled, Gryce would have said: Pam seemed in no hurry and he certainly wasn't – along Gravechurch Street, talking of this and that. The chief topic was the gristly quality of the veal and ham pie which, as was quickly established, both had had at their separate tables in the Buttery that day. The coincidence gave Pam an opportunity, which she did not take, of apologizing for not having had lunch with Gryce. She probably felt too embarrassed.

Pam's bus-stop was only two hundred yards or so up the street. Gryce's was opposite, or so he pretended. In fact his bus didn't stop there at all and he would have to retrace his steps east to get the No. 13 for London Bridge. But it had been worth it.

The parting of the ways, then. Pam tagged on to the end of the longish queue and Gryce hovered by her side.

'Request stop, thirty-eight and one-seven-one,' he read aloud. 'Which is yours then, the thirty-eight or the one-seven-one?'

'Both. Either.'

'You live where? Islington, that way?'

'Islington, yes. I go as far as the Angel and then it's just three minutes' walk. I say the Angel, it's the next stop, actually.'

'So you're home in next to no time. What is it – seven pee, twelve pee?'

'Nineteen, if you don't mind! That's when they bother to stop!' retorted Pam as two thirty-eights, both crammed with standing passengers, sailed past.

Gryce wondered how long he ought to wait. This was all very pleasant but they were bang in the middle of the rush hour and there were a good twenty people ahead of Pam. He would be here all blessed night at this rate.

He was about to ask her if she had ever thought of walking east where she would have a better chance of getting a thirty-eight or a one-seven-one before they filled up, when she began to strip naked in front of him.

That, at any rate, was the sensation that came across to Gryce as he heard her saying, with studied airiness, 'When the seventy-three used to stop here, I always used to wait with Mrs Rashman. And I *knew* what she was going to say every night, before she even said it. "Oh, bubbles to it, let's go and have a drink."'

Although she was taking care to speak casually, Gryce thought he caught a tremor in her voice indicating the same excitement as he felt himself. Hoping, in vain, that his own voice would remain steady, he said thickly:

'I believe there's a wine bar in the vicinity.'

'Just round the corner. The Pressings. Do you know it?'

'I've passed it. I've never ventured over the threshold.'

'It's not much, but at least you can sit down.'

And so here they were, on their second glass of Soave, and she was asking him all kinds and manner of personal questions such as was he married? Gryce felt quite light-headed.

It was early days, probably, to confess that his wife didn't understand him but a hint or two in that direction wouldn't go amiss.

'Oh, very much so. More years than I care to remember. So of course, we don't live in one another's pockets any more. *But*' – a generous little sigh here – 'it's all very amicable.'

He hoped he was striking the right note.

'Does your wife work?'

'Part-time. For a local firm. She just looks in each afternoon, keeps the books straight. Gives her something to do.' He hoped it didn't reach Pam's ears that Peggy was working in a betting shop. Lucas of Personnel probably knew: he seemed to have familiarized himself very fully with Gryce's life story. And if Lucas knew, then it was very much on the cards that he had told Seeds. ('Yes, the wife joined the Liberal Club at the same time, but she's even less interested in politics than he is. Bit of a dimwit, between you, me and the gatepost. Yes, works in a betting shop of all places.') And Seeds, who did not seem averse to passing on bits of gossip, was well in with Pam.

Gryce wondered, not for the first time, exactly how well in with her Seeds really was. They would have to see. If the present tête-à-tête continued as promisingly as it had started, friend Seeds might end up with his nose being put severely out of joint.

'She works evenings quite often,' added Gryce recklessly, 'so we don't see all that much of each other. *And* I suppose we've – well, not drifted apart, but we do have different interests.'

'What are they?'

'Oh, she's very much involved in the – ' He was about to say 'local dramatic society'. Given what he hoped would be his own involvement in the Albion Players one of these fine days, that would never do. In the nick of time he substituted, 'local women's organizations type of thing.'

'I meant what are your interests?'

'Ah. Wrong end of stick. What are my interests? Well, let me see, there's lifting the elbow for one, as at present. Could you manage another glass of this Spanish-type grape juice, by the way?'

'Actually, it's not all that bad, considering.'

'Oh, no, we could have travelled further and fared worse. What do you think?'

'I don't mind. If you're having one.'

Gryce went up to the bar and got another two glasses

of Soave. In future he would definitely buy a bottle. He was paying way over the odds at this rate.

'*And* – what else?' he continued, after an observation about them not exactly believing in filling their glasses to the brim. 'I watch the box a good deal, as who doesn't? Did you see *Oh No It's Selwyn Froggitt* at all last night?'

Pam shook her head.

'*I like it!*' asserted Gryce as if he'd been challenged. 'I think they get some really good twists, whoever dreams it up.'

Pam was still shaking her head, but more slowly, suggesting mystification or total lack of interest rather than an acknowledgement of her sin of omission. He would be losing his audience at this rate.

'Actually I spend far too much time stuck in front of the box, it's only habit, I don't get out as much as I should, that's my trouble.'

'Where do you go when you do get out?'

'Well, that's it, isn't it? Where is there *to* go?' Gryce took the plunge. 'I really ought to join something. What was it you were saying the other day – the Albion Players, was it?'

'I thought you weren't interested.'

'Oh, on the contrary. Let's say *not uninterested*. I'd certainly like to come along one evening, have a look-see. You never know, I might finish up playing Hamlet!'

Pam smiled, but said nothing. Gryce added that assistant spear carrier was probably more in his line but she still didn't rise to the bait.

Instead, she changed the subject.

'What do you think of Perfidious Albion after your first week on the treadmill?'

But for the voice, that might have been Seeds talking. Gryce had heard of chameleon-like women who picked up the mannerisms of their lovers. He felt a pang in his chest which, though unfamiliar, he recognized as jealousy. That was absurd at his age. He would put it down to the acidity of the wine.

'What can I say? I find it highly congenial.'

'But not over-tiring?'

'I don't think anyone could accuse Perfidious Albion of running a sweatshop.'

'And it doesn't bother you?'

'How do you mean, bother me?'

'It's a straightforward question, does it *bother* you?'

For the first time it began to register with Gryce that Pam had an inquisitorial, some would say hectoring, way with her. He had noticed it during their lunch with Seeds the other day but had not really taken it in. It had to be admitted, in fact, that he had not given much thought to Pam's personality at all. He had simply decided that there was some ingredient missing from his life and that it was time he had an extra-marital flutter to give it that added bit of spice. His move to a new billet gave him the opportunity, since what his wife learned of his working pattern would be entirely up to him, and Pam looked the likeliest candidate. Whether he actually liked the woman was something he supposed he would have to consider sooner or later.

'I'm still not with you, I'm afraid.'

Pam sighed heavily, as if coping with someone of low intelligence. Quite a characteristic of hers, he was sorry to say.

'How can I put it, in words of one syllable? You've spent a whole week in Stationery Supplies. You must have noticed that we're not exactly over-employed. And believe me, it's like that *all the time*.'

'I'm relieved to hear it.' He could have added, since she seemed to take him for a half-wit, 'That's not all I've noticed, believe you me,' and mentioned something about

99

his recent browse through the internal telephone directory. But that would have meant confessing that he'd been dipping into Copeland's private filing cabinet. He decided not to pursue that one.

'So it *doesn't* bother you?'

'Why should it? Take the money and run, that's my motto.'

'It bothers some people, you know. Haven't you ever heard Mrs Rashman chuntering on, for instance?'

'I haven't noticed that Mrs Rashman is what you'd call over-burdened with work,' said Gryce, rather too sarcastically, considering that Mrs Rashman and Pam seemed to be friends, or anyway they were always gossiping in corners.

'No, but she gets quite incensed about it. I think that's why she'll be leaving when she gets married. She doesn't think she's earning her keep.'

'Who is, in this day and age?'

'Then there's our Mr Hakim, he's another. He was quite shocked when he first joined. He couldn't get over it – how little he has to do.'

'He's fortunate to have had a job to come to. As indeed who isn't?' Gryce added this rider quickly in case his retort smacked of racism. He was beginning to suspect Pam of leftish leanings.

'Well, that's one way of looking at it. But from the point of view of an outsider, you have to admit there's a lot of time being wasted, and you know what they say, time is money. *Someone* has to pay for it.'

Or perhaps right-wing leanings. Gryce shrugged. 'Joe Public, I suppose.' Although there were several aspects of British Albion he was mildly curious about, questions of ethics such as Pam was airing didn't interest him at all. He tried to think of something else to have a conversation

100

about: something rather more in tune with a third glass of Soave in a discreet little wine bar.

He could have saved himself the trouble, for Pam abruptly changed tack again, or seemed to.

'Tell me, are you what they'd call a political animal?'

What an odd question: or not an odd question, if she did have left- or right-wing leanings, and certainly not an odd question if she was in cahoots with Seeds and Seeds was in cahoots with Lucas who had troubled to check out his political affiliations, though goodness knew how he'd gone about it. But if that chain of communication did exist, she would know the answer already, so why was she asking?

'I was a member of the Forest Hill Liberal Club for exactly one year,' he replied carefully, reminding himself of a witness in front of the UnAmerican Activities Committee in an old film clip. 'I joined for social reasons. It was somewhere to go in the evenings. In fact I've no political convictions one way or the other.'

Whatever the reason for this interrogation, he could at least answer with a clear conscience. Gryce traditionally supported either the party that had last lowered his income tax or the one that promised to do so in future.

He had tried to end his brief statement with a 'But why do you ask?' inflection, and Pam obligingly responded.

'No, neither have I. You could call me the original floating voter.' (Gryce begged leave to doubt that.) 'But I did just wonder, because it is after all a political question when you get down to the basics.'

'What is?' She had completely lost him now. Having drunk what must have been a good half bottle of Soave, Gryce was beginning to feel, not drunk but certainly a bit foggy. He wouldn't be surprised if Pam was going the same way.

'This whole question of whatever you want to call it,

jobs for the boys. I mean, in an ideal world, is full employment an end in itself? I mean do you deliberately spread out the work to what's the word, accommodate all those who need jobs, or do you say right, it only needs two people to do this work so you, you, you and you can all go home?'

'I don't follow you,' said Gryce, in whom the phrase 'ideal world' had kindled something approaching horror. It was all getting too metaphysical for him.

'Let me spell it out, then,' said Pam, a shade garru-lously. Her glass was empty but he judged that if he gave her a fourth one he would have to carry her out. 'Supposing just for the sake of argument, that you're the chairman and managing of British Albion – '

Managing director, she should have said. The woman was as tight as a tick.

'Which mercifully I am not and never will be,' inter-jected Gryce.

'*Which* mercifully you're not but do *not* humour me. I know I've had three glasses wine but this is a *serious question*. You're the big boss of British Albion, right, and you pay a surprise visit to Stationery Supplies, right, and you see me doing the *Evening Standard* crossword, Rashman doing her knitting, our little friend Ranjab Hakim selling choccies and sweeties, you with your feet on the desk – '

'I could hardly see myself, now could I?'

'You know *exactly* what I mean, don't interrupt! The question is would you say right, this department is over-manned, we're getting rid of you, you and you, or would you say oh, well, they don't take up much room and they don't add all that much to the annual budget, and if they didn't work here where the hell *would* they work?'

The question, insofar as he understood it, was too close to home for Gryce's comfort. It was not all that long ago since he had been thrown on the street by just such a process as Pam had described in the first part of her postulation, and it was not in his view a subject for idle debate in wine bars.

He was beginning to notice that Pam wasn't half as attractive as he'd at first thought. Her skin was too sallow, olivey he'd call it: in fact, in the subdued lighting used in this kind of place and in contrast with the white walls, she looked positively unwashed. She had the faintest trace of a moustache. Nor was that her only masculine trait: when in argumentative mood, she expressed herself like a man. Too opinionated and bossy by half, if you asked Gryce.

'Well, I certainly couldn't bring myself to give anyone their marching orders, if that answers your question. I've been through that all too recently. It's no joke, I can assure you.'

'So you'd keep the whole gang of us in work, even though there wasn't any work for us to do?'

'Yes, I would. All other things being equal.' Gryce wasn't entirely sure what he meant by that qualification but it seemed to satisfy Pam. She seemed, thank goodness, sober again, perhaps she'd just got herself over-excited. But on the negative side, it had to be said that she suddenly appeared to lose all interest in Gryce.

Pushing her glass aside and gathering up her gloves and handbag, Pam said carelessly: 'That's all right then.' Their first, and it very much looked like their last, little get-together was clearly over. It seemed to Gryce, he could have been wrong, that Pam had manoeuvred him down here for a specific purpose. He had been sitting an examination. Whether he had passed, he was sure he could not say.

Rummaging through her handbag in silence – though the cue was there to be taken, Gryce did not feel friendly enough to ask if she was sure she had an adequate supply of the firm's ballpoint pens – Pam presently unearthed a grubby white pamphlet which, to Gryce's disgust, looked like a wretched manifesto or tract. She was probably about to try to enlist him in the Fabian movement.

'By the way, I dug this out for you. Let me have it back when you've read it, they're few and far between.'

It was, after all, the celebrated guidelines booklet. If she had offered it in the right spirit – as a little token gift, a special favour, an act of friendship – he could have been touched and grateful. As it was, she was behaving like a welfare officer.

'Many thanks indeed, it's very kind of you,' said Gryce with what he thought was a touch of haughtiness. 'But I've already had sight of it, courtesy of Copeland.'

He shouldn't have blurted that out. Now he would have to cover his tracks.

'It was lying about on top of his filing cabinet,' he added shiftily.

Pam, he couldn't think why unless she suspected him of doing what in fact he had been doing, namely helping himself to Copeland's toffees, was giving him a look that put him in mind of the glances she and Seeds had exchanged during their dust-up in the Buttery on Monday.

'*And* were you any the wiser?'

'Not significantly. To give you a for instance: although there's a list of subsidiary companies as long as your arm, nowhere are we told what it is they actually do, or what Perfidious Albion itself actually does.'

'I know,' said Pam – as intriguingly as, the other day, she had said, 'Well may you ask' when he had raised the same question.

But whereas on that occasion she had been silenced by Seeds with one of his looks, this time she did the job for herself. While throwing off this cryptic remark she had risen to her feet and was now heading for the stairs, leaving Gryce to follow or not as he thought fit.

On the half-landing, however, she paused, on the excuse of fiddling with her gloves, and after looking thoughtful for a moment came out with something quite provocative.

'Look, this may sound silly, and we've both had too much to drink, but I can't make my mind up whether you're an observant person or not. I mean in some ways you seem to be one and in other ways you don't.'

'I keep my eyes open,' said Gryce huffily, but with an interrogative lilt to show that he would like to hear what came next.

'If you hear or see anything strange,' said Pam, 'will you let me know? I mean, privately.'

'*Anything strange. Now how would you define strange?*'

That was what Gryce meant to answer, but he hadn't the time, for she was once more on the move, taking the rest of the stairs so quickly that she was out in the street before he caught up with her.

The evening air hit them both. Pam, despite those sessions with Mrs Rashman in the days when the seventy-three had departed from the same stop as the thirty-eight and the one-seven-one, was evidently no more used to three glasses of wine on an empty stomach than was Gryce himself.

'I feel queasy,' she muttered, swaying a little. 'Think go loo.'

'Not bad idea,' Gryce slurred.

The ladies' and the men's room were on opposite sides of the half-landing. When Gryce emerged, having to his surprise vomited rather a lot, the door to the ladies' was open. The street was quiet by now and he thought he heard the sound of retreating footsteps. Following them unsteadily, he was in time to see a thirty-eight pulling away from the now deserted bus-stop. Pam, or it might not have been her at all, since the windows were steamed up, did not wave.

It had been an unsatisfactory evening, taking it all round.

7

On the following Monday, just before all the department's furniture was moved out and a few days before it vanished altogether, Vaart returned from holiday and Gryce shifted to the desk vacated by Mr Hakim who would by now be sunning himself on the Algarve.

Vaart was not at all as Gryce had imagined him. He'd seen him as like that South African statesman, not Vorster, the other one. Instead, he looked like Mickey Rooney. Nor was he South African or Dutch, although it was probable that his father had been one or the other. He spoke with a strong cockney accent and was what Gryce called a knocker.

It was Gryce's experience that there was a knocker in every billet. Sometimes there would be two or three, but one would always rise naturally above the others, sometimes to the status of office 'character'. The knocker took an irreverent approach to the organization that employed him and could be relied on to comment on each and every example of inefficiency or red tape with some such rhetorical question as 'Would you believe it?' or 'Isn't it marvellous?' (in Vaart's case, 'Ennit marllous?'). But he was usually an unmalicious soul who, provided he didn't overdo it, performed a useful role as a safety-valve for the frustrations of office life.

Vaart, when introduced by Seeds, was amiability itself, and even helped Gryce carry all his paraphernalia – 'arse-wipe', as he inelegantly called it – across to Hakim's desk. He seemed in no hurry to get back in harness after his holiday, and after lighting a cigarette, which he held concealed in the palm of his hand between bunched fingers, like a workman, he assumed a loitering position with the plain intention of idling half the morning away.

Gryce had gathered that Vaart's duties, when he got round to performing them, were concerned with maintaining stock levels, including liaising with Stationery Stores and ordering bulk supplies of stationery from Central Buying on the fifth floor as and when necessary. While orders on such a scale would obviously have to be checked and countersigned by Copeland, it seemed a remarkably responsible job for one who, without being unkind, could barely pronounce his own name. Vaart was certainly not what you would call run-of-the-mill clerical material.

'Arja gerron wiv Cowpland, den? Gerrin on your tits, izze?'

'Seems all right,' shrugged Gryce, anxious neither to endorse any implicit criticism of his master nor to get off on the wrong foot with one who might be, for all he knew, Copeland's sworn enemy.

'Eezer bleedin washerwoman. Azze given you one of is toffees? One of is creamy assortmen? I bettee azzen! What? *Tuh!*'

Vaart's laugh, like most of his observations, had a positively derisive flavour. Gryce dutifully, but non-committally, responded: '*Sha!*'

It took him some little time to steer Vaart away from the dangerous area of personalities. Having disposed of Copeland, Vaart seemed inclined to go on, in none too modulated tones, to discuss the shortcomings of Seeds, Beazley and the Penney twins, whom he described as wankers. Only by asking him for what knowledge he might have of the forthcoming reorganization programme did Gryce manage to stem his good-humoured but nevertheless perhaps compromising flow of abuse.

'Starts amorrer, sposed to.'

'Tomorrow. And what does it entail, exactly?'

'Chrise knows. *Tuh!* Tellya one fing, all these desks aster to be moved, so you're wastin your time spreadin all that shit out like a bleedin greengrocry stall. *Tuh!* Loser bleedin lot, fore they've finished.'

'All that shit' was Gryce's stock of blank white and pink check-lists, requisition forms *A* and *B*, blue slips and so on which he had begun to display in neat piles about Hakim's desk. He began at once to gather them up again. He had fully intended to spend the morning submitting a new pink check-list to Catering (Administration), with probably a strongly worded memorandum stapled to it. That would have meant acquiring a stapling machine: he had that task earmarked for the afternoon. But now he could coast through the day with a clear conscience.

'At least after the holocaust I shall have a desk of my own. That's one thing.'

'Leave it out! Invoiced for one, avyer?'

'It's news to me that I had to.'

'Iss not gerna walk ere, izzit? You wanna slap inner ninvoice, sharpish. Take weeks. Monfs. Equipment Supplies, fif floor, nexer Cenral Buyin. Lorrer bleedin wankers. Worsan us, an that's sayin sumfin.'

'Equipment Supplies, fifth floor, thank you indeed. How do I invoice them, exactly?'

'Chrise knows.'

Vaart had the music-hall comedian's trick of retreating a few steps whenever he delivered anything that could remotely be called a punch-line. On 'Chrise knows' he got so far across the room, almost to his own desk in fact, that Gryce thought their conversation was over. He was mistaken. With a sly glance at such of his colleagues as caught his eye on the return journey, to show that what he had to say next was of a confidential nature, Vaart bounded back.

'Byva way, talkina desks, I ear you ad a query?'

'About acquiring a desk of my own?' asked Gryce hopefully. Vaart looked the kind of chap given to passing on tips and wrinkles on how to short-circuit the system.

'Naow!' Vaart's face momentarily disfigured itself into what seemed to be an expression of blind rage, but what was only, as Gryce would learn when he knew him better, mild impatience. 'Not *your* bleedin desk! *These* bleedin desks! I fought you was arskin Bollockchops over there ow they got ere.'

Following the elaborate jerk of Vaart's head, Gryce identified Bollockchops as Beazley. How very curious that Beazley should have troubled to remember a casual exchange of a week ago and then retail it to Vaart; and to do so, what was more, before Vaart had been back in the office five minutes.

'Yes, the subject did crop up, I can't remember in what context. I was only saying it was interesting that all our office furniture should turn out to have come from Comform. Considering I used to work for them.'

'Whereas they never ad no contrac wiv Bri'ish Albion, ri?'

'That did puzzle me, I must say.' What puzzled him even more was why Vaart was bent on making a song and dance about it. It was almost as if he had been deputed by someone to set Gryce's mind at rest.

'Ri. Now this wossicalled again, *Comform*, I betchew anyfin you like, I bet they gorra govmen contrac, ri?'

'Oh, indeed. A very big Government contract.'

'Oo they deal wiv, den? I meanersay, Minstry Vousing, Minstry Vealth, Minstry Veducation . . .'

'Ah. It's not done *quite like that*. You see there's a central buying agency on behalf of all Government

110

departments. What's known as the Property Services Agency. It used to be the Ministry of Works, in time gone – '

'Yeh, well nair mind all that crap. The point is, the point *eez*, worrisit that all govmen deparmens do? Above all else?'

Gryce looked mystified. Vaart's malleable Mickey Rooney face registered agony near to death.

'*Cahm* on! Work it out! Worrisit that all govmen deparmens do, what they do what nobody else does? Think abaht it. They over-buy, don they? Wivaht exception. Anyfin they want, they always get in twice as much as what they need. Known for it.'

'That's true enough. In fact when it comes to desks and so forth, the Property Services Agency does happen to be the biggest furniture buyer in the whole – '

'There you are den! Proves my point! An what they do when they gorral this stuff, they don know worrer do wiv it?'

'I've often wondered. Sell it, I suppose.'

'Course they do! Course they do! They auction it, don they? Bleedin govmen surplus auction! You've only gorrer open a noospaper! Ere's one every bleedin day! Gasmasks, tyewriters, you name it.'

'And presumably desks. So you're saying British Albion bought all this stuff at auction?'

'Gorrit in one, my old *son*!'

But that was absurd. Why should an important commercial concern like British Albion, which in any event could set depreciation of all its fixtures and fittings against tax, want to clutter up its prestige City offices with second-hand furniture?

Gryce put the query to Vaart.

'Cos they're a lorrer wankers,' was Vaart's reply.

Seemingly well pleased with this piece of repartee, he

did one of his little perambulations, giving Gryce time to digest the information that had just been passed on to him. When Vaart turned back, it was as if he had taken a crash-course in elocution, so precisely did he enunciate his parting sentence.

'Does that answer your question?'

All Gryce could think was that it must be an office catchphrase.

Whether Vaart's explanation was based on knowledge of the facts or guesswork remained to be seen: he was certainly a reliable source on when the reorganization programme was to commence. Gryce reached the seventh floor foyer the following morning to find it seething with workmen who were manhandling all the department's desks, chairs and filing cabinets out of the office and stacking them in any space they could find. They were not performing their task efficiently. They were already in violation of the fire regulations by blocking up the emergency stairs, and it looked as if it needed only one more desk to be trundled out for access from the lifts to be cut off. The confusion was added to by young Thelma who was crashing about among a nest of filing cabinets as she tried to locate her tray of cups and beakers for the morning coffee break.

Gryce threaded his way along the narrow passageway between the piles of furniture and through the glass swing doors, one of which had been smashed during the removal operation, into Stationery Supplies. There was quite a festive atmosphere about the old place. Except for the telephones, which although still connected to their floor-sockets were heaped in a corner like a miscellaneous lot in one of those Government surplus sales spoken of by Vaart, the department had been stripped bare, as if a dance were about to be held in it. Gryce's colleagues were either standing about the composition floor with their hands in their pockets or leaning against the waist-high metal partitions until asked to move by two young men in blue suits who were taking measurements with a retractable steel rule, noting their findings on a clipboard.

Enquiry from Seeds and Beazley, to whom Gryce attached himself as at a social gathering, revealed that the metal partitions were at the root of the reorganization. They were all going to be moved, hence the dumping of all the office furniture in the foyer. Copeland's cubby-hole, to begin with, was to be housed on the opposite side of the office by the outer wall, to afford him a window of his own. The banks of filing cabinets would be shifted along a bit, into the space presently occupied by Copeland, and would be screened off by some brand-new partitions that were even now being manipulated through the glass doors by two men in overalls. Why the partitions that were already there couldn't be left where they were, and the new partitions used to make Copeland's re-sited cubby-hole by the window, was a question no one could answer. Finally the main partition dividing Stationery Supplies from its neighbour Traffic Control was to be pushed back six inches, thus giving the department a strip of extra territory. On the past form of Design and Maintenance, who had been briefed by Traffic Control to undertake these structural changes, it would take three days.

Gryce remarked to Beazley that it was quite a rigmarole.

'Annual event,' barked Beazley. 'Give 'em something to do. They've nothing to complain about, considering they spend most of their time in their sub-basement, playing gin-rummy.'

That didn't surprise Gryce a bit. It was the British workman all over.

Feeling an obligation to circulate, as he would have done at a cocktail party, Gryce moved on. He would have liked to have talked to Pam, to see how she responded after Friday's jaunt to the Pressings, but she was doing one of her silly word games with the Penney twins and so he lighted upon Mrs Rashman, who was standing alone with her empty grocery bag crumpled at her feet. From her he learned that he himself was the catalyst, or if you liked the culprit, of the present upheaval.

'Oh yes, dear,' explained Mrs Rashman. 'It's all in your honour, most of it. You see they work it all out, now whether it's a health regulation or what it is I do not know, but there's got to be so many cubic feet of air per person. *Got* to be.'

Gryce had heard that there were such regulations but he could not remember a case of their being enforced with such thoroughness. It hardly seemed worth turning the office upside-down for the sake of an entirely notional increase in the volume of air available on an open-plan floor, and he said as much to Mrs Rashman.

Mrs Rashman laughed – *'Tchair!'*, a grating, sarcastic shriek. 'Don't tell me, dear, tell the Welfare Office. I agree with you. They've nothing better to do up there, if you ask me. No, it's all laid down so it's got to be done. Got to be Welfare set it all in motion, then Traffic Control next door get it all planned out, that gives *them* something to do, then Design and Maintenance come in and do the work. Supposed to. Look at them – I've seen tortoises moving faster.'

Gryce saw what Pam had meant when she'd said that Mrs Rashman got incensed about such matters. He wished she would get incensed in a rather lower key – the young men doing the measuring were easily within earshot.

'So my arrival adds a requirement of x cubic feet of air,

114

I can see that. But Traffic Control will be *losing* so many cubic feet.'

'That's their problem, if they want to cut their own throats let them get on with it, that's what I say. No: the thing is, dear, they've just had someone retire, so they've got that many cubic feet going begging. Of course, what they'll do when they get a replacement I *do* not know.'

'Shift the partition back in our direction, most likely.'

'Oh, they will do! You think you're joking, but they will do! And there'll be nothing Mr Copeland can do about it, because do you see I shall have gone by then, so we'll be back to our original strength.'

'Back to square one, in other words. But surely, Mrs Rashman, since your departure more or less coincides with my arrival, it would have made more sense to have left the partition where it was?'

'You'd think so, wouldn't you? *Tchair!* But you see, dear, according to *their way of thinking*, we overlap. We do, we overlap.'

'I suppose so, technically.'

'There's no technically about it in their eyes, dear. We overlap and that's that. Now if you'd arrived *after* I'd left, that would have been a different story altogether. But you didn't, do you see, you arrived before. So it all had to go through.' Mrs Rashman sighed deeply, shaking her head at the folly of it all. 'Oo, you wouldn't believe it, what goes on. As soon as you came in through those doors last Monday, there'll have been a memo sent down from that Welfare Office – he's got to have his so many cubic feet of air. And that's what those young men are measuring up – they've got a formula, do you see, so many cubic feet for each desk.'

'But I don't have a desk,' Gryce pointed out.

'You don't have now, but you will have, dear. We hope. Have you invoiced for one?'

'No, I gather I should.'

'Oo, you must! Must! I should get cracking on that as soon as poss. Equipment Supplies, they're the worst of the lot. It could take ages.'

'So Mr Vaart was saying.'

Strange how every conversation seemed to get round to the subject of desks. Or not so strange, when you considered how much of one's working life was spent at one.

Vaart himself, calling across to Pam that it was all go and to Beazley and Seeds that they were not to let it get them down, was heading towards them. Gryce was reminded of a thought that had struck him during their talk yesterday.

'Without wishing to tread on anyone's toes, Mrs Rashman, wouldn't it be far simpler if I conveniently forgot about invoicing and took over your desk after you'd gone?'

Vaart, as was plain from his expression of comic incredulity, had heard this as he homed in on Gryce and Mrs Rashman.

'*Tuh! Yew* don fink iss as easy as that, do you!'

'I was just telling him, dear,' said Mrs Rashman with a certain tartness at having her thunder stolen. 'We overlap.'

'Course you do! Course you do! Iss like that panomime wiv ol Norm!'

'Norman Ferrier, before your time, dear,' Mrs Rashman parenthesized for Gryce's information. 'Now *I* overlapped with *him*. I got here just a fortnight before he had to stop work, through ill-health.'

'Dicky ticker,' said Vaart.

Norman Ferrier, the name rang bells with Gryce. He remembered: Copeland, on his first day, had had a discussion with Seeds about the illness of someone he'd seemed to call Norwich Terrier. He was on the mend, from what Gryce had gathered.

'. . . but would they let me take over his desk? They would not!' Mrs Rashman was recounting. 'Back to stores it went, and I had to go through all the palaver of invoicing for a desk of my own.'

'Adter sirrin my lap for free monf, till it come froo, dincha darlin?'

'And when it *did* come through, blow me down if it wasn't the self-same desk they'd carted off to stores three months before. *Tchair!*'

'*Sha!*'

'*Tuh!* Marllous, ennit? We was just sayin – ' Vaart half-turned to bring Grant-Peignton into the conversation. Gryce had noticed him hovering there, like a new arrival who doesn't know any of his fellow-guests. Oh, yes, very much the party atmosphere. 'We was jus sayin, baht ol Norm. That cock-up over the desks.'

'Oh, yes, how is he these days, does anyone know?' asked Grant-Peignton, going off at rather a tangent in Gryce's opinion.

To Gryce's surprise, this innocuous question impelled Mrs Rashman and Vaart to exchange what he was beginning to think of as The Glance – the look he had caught in Seeds' and Pam's eyes when they had had that heated exchange in the Buttery about the Albion Players. Now how on earth did this what-was-his-name, not Norwich Terrier, Norman Ferrier, fit in with that, if at all?

'I had a card at Christmas, he didn't say anything,' Mrs Rashman replied, in what seemed to Gryce to be guarded tones. And why should he send her Christmas cards, when they'd only overlapped by a fortnight?

'Lives down in the West Country, somewhere down there, doesn't he?'

'Somewhere dahn that way,' Vaart replied, or you

117

might say hedged. He was even more guarded than Mrs Rashman. '*Eez* orl ri. It was *this* madouse gerrin on is wick. Sprised we don all ave bleedin art attacks.'

Grant-Peignton, perhaps because small-talk was not his long suit, seemed reluctant to leave the topic of their mutual friend.

'Pity he had to leave. He must have been our oldest inhabitant, just about. How long had he been here now – four years, five years?'

'Lemmy see, e lef eigheen monf ago, so eedabin ere four year. Tell you ow I know, we bof joineda same week. I come from Buckton's, that worrer prinnin works out at New Cross, and e come from wossicalled, the Pilgrim Press, that worrer prinnin works as well. Ammersmif. An they was bof taken over by Bri'ish Albion wivvin a monfa each ovver.'

Gryce ran his mind over the list of Perfidious Albion's subsidiary firms as featured in the guidelines booklet. He couldn't recall either a Buckton's or a Pilgrim Press. He told this to Vaart, adding that it was funny.

'*Tuh!* Course you avven erdovem, mate. They're bof oles inna grahnd by now, ent they?'

'Rationalized,' explained Grant-Peignton. 'They fell by the wayside.'

'Ass why I come to work here. They took fifteen of us on. Ol Duggie, onea the commissionaires, e was wiv Buckton's. Coupla blokes dahn inna Files Depostry, they was wiv Buckton's. Design an Mainnance, they took free of us. Bloke up in wossicalled, *e* was wiv . . .'

Gryce took the liberty of interrupting this roll-call by addressing himself to Grant-Peignton. Mrs Rashman had already drifted across to talk to Pam and Grant-Peignton showed signs of restlessness. Gryce didn't really want to be left to the tender mercies of Mr Vaart, thank you very much.

'You mentioned "oldest inhabitant". And yet your friend was only here for – what was it, four years? Surprising. I get the impression that British Albion is a relative newcomer to the scene?'

'The reverse. By no means. On the contrary. Not at all,' said Grant-Peignton with vigour. 'They've been around for donkey's years, under one name or another. *Now originally* – ' Grant-Peignton moistened his lips, as if about to launch on a long narrative. Vaart, with a broad wink at Gryce, departed hastily, and was to be heard advising the Penney twins that Grant-Peignton was off down Memory Lane again. You would have thought he could have shown a little more discretion, if not respect. When all was said and done, Grant-Peignton was second in seniority only to Copeland.

'*Now originally* they were printers, pure and simple. Commercial work, paper bags, handbills, cloakroom tickets. The Albion Printeries: that stretches back to the turn of the century at least. Then they started diversifying, buying up this and that company, and finally they went into property. And hey presto, that's how British Albion was born.'

'So it does have quite a pedigree?'

'Oh, as long as your arm. *Now admittedly*, as the company is structured today, it was very much started from scratch. Apart from one or two souls like Norman Ferrier and Jack,' – Jack presumably being Vaart, you wouldn't have thought Grant-Peignton was on first name terms with him – 'nearly all the present staff were recruited as and when this present building was completed. That's going back only – oh, barely four summers.'

'Jack – ' Gryce hoped he didn't sound over-familiar. 'Jack must have started in some previous building, then?'

'The original Albion Printeries. One of those rambling old Victorian dust-traps near London Bridge. Pulled down by now, of course. They got out of printing long ago.'

At least, thought Gryce, one was a bit nearer knowing from what branch of commerce one earned one's daily bread. Ex-printing, now property, plus various interests as listed in the guidelines booklet. Given that the subsidiary companies were self-supporting, that might also explain the puzzling business of the internal telephone directory.

Perhaps Grant-Peignton meant to reassure him on just those lines. Gryce waited for him to say, 'Does that answer your question?' but he didn't. What he did do, however, was to expand on the historical lecture he had just delivered, crossing the t's and dotting the i's to such a tedious degree that Gryce was relieved when Thelma interrupted the monologue by arriving with beakers of coffee.

The staff of Stationery Supplies converged on Thelma. She had not yet collected the money for the coffee and there was much joshing speculation as to whether the management was providing refreshment free as compensation for the inconvenience caused by the reorganization programme, or alternatively, whether Thelma had robbed a bank or was standing treat on account of it being her birthday. The mood was one of end-of-term gaiety, almost of subdued hysteria. While willing hands passed out the steaming beakers, others dug into pockets for tenpenny pieces; jovial voices urged that the least Vaart could do, by virtue of having been on holiday, was to pay for coffee all round; others warned Thelma to beware of his palming off foreign coins. The victim of this badinage took it in good part. Everyone was good-humoured: even Copeland, who had joined in the throng without in the least pulling rank, was to be seen enjoying a joke with Ardagh, of all lugubrious people. Copeland's laugh – a dribbling '*Keeesh!*' was infectious. Soon everyone was joking and

laughing. 'Coh!' 'Tuh!' 'Sha!' 'Haaark!' 'Tchair!'
'Keeesh!' It was like Christmas.

The next day could have been equally memorable for
Gryce had he not been too embarrassed to join in the
fun. Little or no progress had been made on the partition
front, rightly described by Vaart as a shambles from start
to finish, and again Gryce and his colleagues were reduced
to standing about in groups, talking about what they had
seen on television the night before. After yesterday's
excesses it might all have been something of an anti-
climax but for the fact that this was going to turn out to
be a real red-letter day, over and above the excitements
of the reorganization. Mrs Rashman was leaving. Officially, of course, she was supposed to work until the end
of the week but she did have two days of her compassionate leave concession owing, and taking that into consideration and the fact that there were no desks to work at,
Copeland had used his discretion to release her at lunch-
time. There was to be a presentation.
    Gryce found himself in a quandary. He had been asked
to add his signature to the giant-sized card – of a cartoon
elephant woozily imbibing a glass of champagne: not at
all suitable, considering Mrs Rashman's girth and her
well-known proclivity for wine bars – which Pam had
bought at one of the many greetings-cards shops near the
office. (It bore the caption 'Don't forget to write', which
at least could be said to justify the elephant motif, and
most of the signatories had touched on this theme in
their parting quips – 'If you have time!!!', 'After the
honeymoon natch!!!' etc. Gryce, not being on familiar
terms with the woman, had contented himself with a
chaste, 'Best wishes, C. Gryce.') But he had not been
asked to chip in to the collection which Beazley had

121

surreptitiously made under the pretext of selling supplementary raffle tickets. Quite right too: Gryce had been sweating on the top line on that one. But it did place him in the position of having to decide whether to attend the presentation ceremony or not. A fruit cake had been bought with the few shillings left over from the set of teak-handled steak knives that was to be Mrs Rashman's leaving present. If Thelma could find it again in the jumble of filing cabinets out in the foyer, it was to be sliced and consumed during coffee break when Copeland would make a speech. Could Gryce eat cake that he had not subscribed towards? Could he look suitably bashful, along with the others, when Copeland spoke of 'a little something to remember us all by'?

Much as Gryce enjoyed a good leaving thrash, he came to the reluctant conclusion that he would be better off out of it. Accordingly, when Thelma began whispering audibly to Pam about paper plates, he discreetly absented himself, pretending to be heading for the lavatory but instead wheeling off sharply into the furniture-infested foyer. It was not as if there was any work to be getting on with. No one would miss him.

It was mainly to kill time that Gryce set about exploring the British Albion offices from top to bottom. He had had it vaguely in mind to embark on such an expedition ever since stumbling across the internal telephone directory last Tuesday evening, but what Grant-Peignton had told him about the firm had somewhat taken the edge off his curiosity. However, there was no harm in having a look-see.

He already knew what went on at the tenth, eleventh and twelfth floor levels. No need to trouble the Catering (Administration) empire with his presence again; and besides, he didn't fancy another confrontation with the sharp-tongued individual who looked like Jack Lemmon. Gryce started at the ninth floor.

His policy was to check the directory signs in the foyer and then glance in through the glass doors to see what was going on. From what he was able to make out, precious little so far as this particular home from home was concerned. The ninth floor was graced by the administrative wing of Design and Maintenance (the hordes currently at work, or not at work, on the Stationery Supplies partitions would get their instructions from here, although as blue-collar workers they were housed among their lengths of hardboard and angle-brackets down in some sub-basement or other), and also by two inscrutable departments called Services C and D, which presumably had some connection with Services A and B next to Personnel on the third floor. A case of bad office planning here: Gryce could see the day when Design and Maintenance would be invited to swop places with Services B, or when Personnel was shifted up to the ninth and Services C or D were moved to the third. But that would still leave one services department out on a limb. He was glad that such decisions did not fall within his ken. Anyway, whatever Services C and D did for a living, they seemed to be having an easy time of it. So did Design and Maintenance, one of whose draughtsmen was inking in a poster to do with a residents' association hot-pot supper. The atmosphere on the ninth floor, it could be said, was relaxed.

Gryce, with the very beginnings of a nagging sensation in the back of his head, descended to the eighth. This again was divided into three sections. Where Stationery Supplies would have been, there was a walled-off structure with a number of grilled hatches, rather like the ticket-office affair up in Catering (Administration). The cashier's department, or Great Bank In The Sky as Seeds had called it when telling Gryce where he could draw his salary cheque. That was worth knowing about, if nothing else was. The next section was the Welfare Office, staffed almost entirely by middle-aged women: doubtless research had shown that female employees had more problems to be sorted out than men. Each of the familiar desks had a chair invitingly placed in front of it, where harassed cooks and bottle-washers from the Buttery or Cockpit could plonk themselves down and pour out the saga of their troubles with worthless husbands who appropriated their wages to spend on drink. The nearest of the middle-aged women, on the look-out for custom, smiled at Gryce. He hoped he didn't look as if he needed advice on how to cope with his alimony payments or anything of that sort. He smiled back, noted that the farthermost section was the Central Typing Pool, and withdrew.

Skipping the seventh floor, where Copeland by now would be making an incomprehensible speech urging Mrs Ash-can not to ferment her old collies in Stationery Surprise, Gryce continued his exploration.

He still had no particular plan in mind, save that of making himself scarce for a while, but the nagging sensation in the back of his head was working its way forward. By the time he had by-passed the third floor, well-known as the lair of Lucas of Personnel, the curiosity temporarily satisfied by his talk with Grant-Peignton had returned. He had the same feeling as he had had on his first day when he'd cocked his ear for all the background noises of the office, being puzzled at the time and only realizing later that it was the sound of the telephone that was missing; the same feeling he'd had when browsing through that internal directory. Something not here that should be here.

Perhaps the second floor would provide what he was

looking for. Gryce took the stairs, turned into the second floor foyer and found himself face to face with one of the one-armed commissionaires. Which of the three it was he couldn't say, they all looked alike to him, but the man was definitely barring his way, and furthermore looked as if he had been placed in position with that very object.

'Can I be of any assistance, sir?'

For 'sir', Gryce read 'Sunny Jim'. He felt, for all that he had never risen above the ranks in his conscript days, like a very junior subaltern being addressed by a very senior colour sergeant.

'Ah – it's all right, thank you.'

'*You* say it's all right, sir. We don't know whether it's all right or not. What are you on?'

'Ah – well you see, I'm a new boy here. As you know. *You* remember – that kerfuffle over my B.52 part two?'

The one-armed commissionaire plainly didn't remember any such thing. It occurred to Gryce that he might be a different one-armed commissionaire from the three he had already encountered. It was only his assumption that the same three were permanently on duty. After all, they had to go on holiday or sick leave some time, they would have duty rosters and tea breaks and so on and so forth. There might, for all he knew, be a dozen one-armed commissionaires. There was probably a fuggy basement rest-room crammed with them.

'I was just getting myself orientated,' he explained. The word did not seem to register with his inquisitor. He amended it. 'Finding the geography.'

'The toilets, sir? There's one on each floor.'

'Yes, I'm aware of that. The truth of the matter is – ' Gryce commenced a babbling explanation of how, in view of the fact that one of his colleagues was leaving to get married, he had decided to explore the building. It didn't make sense even to himself. The one-armed commissionaire, however, woodenly heard him out and indeed even allowed a sizeable pause for revision or retraction before continuing his interrogation.

'You in possession of a docket, sir?'

'A docket. You mean a B.52 part two. No, if you recall, I did try to hand it in downstairs but – '

'We're not talking about Bee Five Twos, sir, we're talking about dockets. I'm asking for sight of your docket.'

Gryce, patting his side-pockets in a futile gesture of co-operation, confessed that he did not have one.

'Ah, well there you are then. Before you can visit this floor, for whatever reason whatsoever, you've got to be in possession of a docket. Fact before you visit *any* floor,' pursued the one-armed commissionaire, after apparently giving this wider aspect of the matter some thought, 'you've got to be in possession of a docket. And that docket is issued and signed by your head of department. It's the fire regulations.'

Gryce didn't understand that at all but wasn't going to say so. The one-armed commissionaire, however, was not one to leave incomplete explanations hanging in the air.

'If you'd read your guidelines booklet, sir, you'd find it all laid down. See, in the event of fire, everyone has to be booked out of the building. By nominal roll, from each and every department. That entails knowing where everybody is at all times.'

Pull the other one, it's got bells on it, thought Gryce, but said nothing. The one-armed commissionaire scrutinized him for a time through narrowed eyes.

'What floor you on, sir?'

'Ah – seven. Stationery Supplies, in fact. Name of Gryce.'

The one-armed commissionaire's lips moved as he

transparently made a mental note. Gryce could just hear him asking his colleagues on the main door if they had a Gryce on the seventh floor listed. 'My advice to you, then, Mister Gryce, is to return from whence you came with all possible speed.'

Mercifully, there was a lift in position. Mumbling his thanks and apologies, Gryce stepped into it. As the doors rumbled gently to meet each other, they framed the one-armed commissionaire like a camera viewfinder, seeming, in the last fraction of a second, to zoom in on his unblinking, staring eyes behind their bottle-glass spectacles.

Arriving back at the haven of the seventh floor, Gryce was distressed to find Mrs Rashman's leaving ceremony still in full swing. They evidently made a meal of such events in this particular billet. He could not pretend to be going to the lavatory again, and he dare not skulk among the stacked-up office furniture out in the foyer where he might be asked for his docket. There was nothing for it but to tiptoe forward in his squeaking shoes and hover on the outskirts of the little cluster of colleagues who encircled Mrs Rashman as if she were 'it' in a game of piggy in the middle.

At least they had got the actual presentation over with, for Mrs Rashman, pink-faced and moist-eyed, was clutching her box of teak-handled steak knives and jumbo-sized greetings card, not to mention a bunch of wilting carnations that had appeared from Gryce knew not what source. Copeland then, thank goodness, would already have made his speech and with any luck Mrs Rashman her reply. The fruit cake, also thank goodness, had been distributed, as was evidenced from the crumb-laden paper plates clutched by most of those present. What Gryce seemed to have stumbled on was an unofficial and probably unscheduled postscript to the proceedings, which consisted of the Penney twins reading a long poem of their own composition. They took the verses in turn, to the accompaniment of many snorts of laughter and ribald interjections.

> We'll miss her happy, laughing face,
> It really is a blow,
> To think our Mrs Rashman
> Has really got to go.

> But when you've got to go, they say,
> Then go is what you must,
> But don't forget your tins of peas,
> Or they will surely rust.

A cleverly-worked-in reference, that, to Mrs Rashman's preoccupation with groceries. It brought the house down. Gryce fervently wished he'd brazened the party out from the beginning. He'd never known such merriment.

> And don't forget your cornflakes,
> They're special, threepence off,
> So take them home, no more to roam,
> Your husband will them scoff.

Synchronizing with Mrs Rashman's high-pitched '*Tchair-hair, tchair-hair!*' as she doubled up with mirth, a telephone started to ring for only the second time in Gryce's stay with British Albion.

The general reaction was interesting. You would have expected shouts of 'Oh, blow!' or 'Tell them we've all gone home', or even a sympathetic word for the Penney twins at this interruption of their efforts: 'It's Sir John Betjeman, wants to know who his rivals are!' – something on those lines. But everyone in Stationery Supplies fell silent.

Gryce noted the different responses of his colleagues.

128

Seeds looked shifty; Pam, he thought, nervous. The Penney twins looked guilty for some reason, not exasperated at being thrown off their stride as you might expect. Copeland, Beazley and Grant-Peignton looked studiously non-committal. Vaart was rolling his eyes and whistling under his breath, evidently with the aim of exonerating himself from any blame for the interruption. Ardagh, with whom Gryce had had little truck as yet, had a look that could not be defined. If asked to select a word, Gryce would have said paranoiac. Really, the man's resemblance to Hitler in appearance was quite remarkable. As for Mrs Rashman, she looked unhappy.

It was Seeds who moved. That didn't surprise Gryce: if he had been a gambling man, he would have taken bets on it. Seeds made his way to the pile of telephones that had been jumbled together in a corner by the workmen from Design and Maintenance, and picked up one receiver after another while the telephone went on ringing. Nobody spoke. Finally Seeds located the right instrument, presumably his own, and answered it.

'Yes? Yes . . . Yes . . . Right . . . Leave it with me.'

He replaced the receiver. 'Sorry about that, chaps.' Those who had been looking inquiringly at Seeds swivelled back to the Penney twins. Those who had been looking studiously at the floor – notably Pam – did the same. The Penney twins resumed their poem. But it seemed flat now: all the life had gone out of the party.

> We'll think of you each morning,
> And every afternoon,
> Particularly at tea breaks,
> When we want our macaroons . . .

Seeds did not resume his original place in the circle surrounding Mrs Rashman. He sidled round the outskirts of it until he was next to Pam. As applause, and to Gryce's ear somewhat forced laughter, greeted the end of the Penney brothers' doggerel, Seeds whispered something to Pam. Everyone saw him doing it, but pretended not to. Pam nodded imperceptibly.

The celebrations seemed to be over, the formal part of them anyway. The circle broke its ranks, some people converging on Mrs Rashman to wish her luck and admire her steak knives, others to congratulate the Penney twins on a really brilliant composition. In all the criss-crossing, Pam managed to insinuate herself next to Gryce without anyone except himself particularly noticing.

'Do you fancy another drink at the Pressings this evening?'

8

Gryce was disappointed, although not much surprised, to find Seeds sitting with Pam in what, with an element of wishful thinking, he had already begun to look upon as their usual corner in the Pressings wine bar. If there was nothing going on between those two then he was a Dutchman.

One good thing: Seeds had already got in a bottle of red plonk and three glasses. While Gryce was a white wine man if left to himself, it would at least save him the price of a round unless they were going to make a night of it. But he would have to remember that it was his shout next time, if there was a next time.

His attempts at conversational preliminaries – he had worked out a jocular set-piece on the theme of it making a nice change to be able to park one's posterior after standing up all day – were cut short by Pam, who seemed in a brass-tacks mood. So, for that matter, did Seeds, whose expression could only be called glowering.

'You were going to tell me if you saw anything strange,' said Pam without preamble, although Gryce had made no such promise. 'What have you found out?'

Gryce had no particular urge to hedge, it was just that he had an aversion to direct questions, they made him feel put-upon.

'Well now. It depends entirely what you'd call – '

'Just answer Pam's question,' Seeds butted in with offensive weariness. Really: the pair of them were carrying on like two French resistance workers interrogating a captured parachutist in a barn. The impression was heightened by the fact of Pam wearing a beret and a tightly-belted white raincoat. Take into account her black stockings, or black tights more likely, and the effect was what Gryce supposed was called sexy. He would have been quite dry-mouthed had Seeds not been present as resident gooseberry.

'You were on the prowl today,' said Pam. 'I'm asking what interesting discoveries you made.'

The only phrase that formed itself in Gryce's mind was 'It depends, entirely what you'd call interesting discoveries.' But he did not wish to risk another rebuff from Seeds, who was beginning to strike him as quite the Jekyll and Hyde: it was blow hot one minute and blow cold the next with this one.

Gryce didn't reply, but he resisted the impulse to lick his lips.

'We *know* you were on the prowl,' insisted Pam, 'because that phone call to Ron this morning was from the commissionaire who stopped you.'

'I don't *think*,' said Seeds, with one of the cautionary glances that seemed to be part of his stock-in-trade, 'we need go into that *at this stage*.'

'Oh, for heaven's sake, he's not stupid!' flared Pam. And in the same snapping voice, though what he had done to deserve it he did not know, she continued to Gryce: 'You were seen poking your nose into the eighth floor, and someone else saw you on the sixth.'

'Quite the little espionage network,' murmured Gryce.

'Yes. There is. Luckily it was our network and not theirs.'

'"Theirs"? Who's "theirs"?'

'Tell him,' said Pam to Seeds.

Seeds waggled his head about in a demurring sort of way. 'You're sure you're not putting the cart before the horse here?'

'Ron, he *knows*!'

'Yes, but *does* he know? That's the whole point, surely?'

Pam closed her eyes and breathed out forcibly, to demonstrate exasperation tempered with patience. She then put down her glass of wine and held up her hands in an ironic gesture of surrender. 'All right, *all right*, we'll go back to square one.' And then to Gryce, in deliberate zombie tones to show that she was fed up of asking the same question over and over again, although in truth she had asked it only once: 'You-set-off-today-to-scour-the-building-from-top-to-bottom-now-*why*?'

In the kind of bossy mood she was in, thought Gryce, she wouldn't want to listen to a long rigmarole about why he'd deemed it best to avoid Mrs Rashman's presentation ceremony. Anyway, unless he told the story properly, it might not reflect creditably upon himself.

'Well, I mentioned the other – the other *day* – ' He corrected himself delicately. To say 'the other night' in front of Seeds might compromise both Pam and himself ' – that I'd been leafing through the internal telephone directory.'

'No, you didn't tell me that at all,' said Pam sharply. 'You said you'd been looking at the guidelines booklet.'

'Which, from what I gather, was lying about on Copeland's filing cabinet,' put in Seeds. Pam must have given him a blow-by-blow account of their conversation. Gryce wondered if Seeds knew that it had taken place after office hours, at this very table, when he and Pam had come within an ace of touching hands.

Still, that was neither here nor there. The fact was that he had got himself in a bit of a pickle.

'I thought I had mentioned the directory,' he bluffed. 'It was with the guidelines booklet, on top of Copeland's filing cabinet.'

'*Was* it, indeed?' Seeds asked, more of Pam than of Gryce.

'Are you sure?' said Pam. 'It would be very out of character for Copeland to leave it lying about. It's supposed to be a classified document.'

Gryce was beginning to rue the day he'd ever set eyes on Copeland's wretched filing cabinet. As soon as Mr Hakim returned from holiday he would put in an order for a supply of toffees of his own, and that would keep him out of mischief in future. Meanwhile, the best form of defence was attack: he would counter question with question.

'In what way classified?'

'Secret. For heads of department only.'

'Why secret?'

'Because,' said Pam, 'it would give the game away.'

While Gryce was wondering if it would be over-egging the pudding to ask what game, Seeds intervened hurriedly.

'I still think we're running before we can walk, Pam. Why don't we let him tell us, *in his own words*, what it was he was looking for?'

'You mean when I came across the internal telephone directory?' asked Gryce in some trepidation. Perhaps they knew all about the toffees, and were just waiting for him to dig his own grave.

'I mean after you read it,' said Seeds testily.

'Ah. I can't claim to have *read* it, but I did go through it pretty thoroughly. The first thing that struck me was that unlike all the other billets I've ever worked for, there's no advertising department.'

'Is that so very remarkable?' asked Seeds blandly.

'Oh, I think you'll find it is. Even the Docks and Inland Waterways had its own advertising manager.'

'We don't advertise,' said Pam. 'We're not even in the *Yellow Pages*.'

'Nor in the phone directory proper,' said Gryce. 'I've noticed that. According to Copeland – '

'Yes, we've all heard Copeland's explanation. Every head of department has his own direct line, which is more efficient et cetera and so on. It also *just so happens* that every head of department can accept outside phone calls and no one else knows who it is that's ringing or what the call is about. Of course, if we had a central line, with extensions, there'd have to be a switchboard, and that would mean the operators could listen in.'

Gryce's mouth fell open. 'Do you mean to say there's no telephone switchboard?' Nor was there, come to think of it. But if he'd inspected the office from top to bottom ten times over, he would never have thought of that.

Seeds, who appeared to have cast himself in the role of chairman of this particular tribunal, had been impatiently tapping his glass with a finger-nail during these exchanges.

'Getting back to the internal directory. You've said there's no advertising department listed and we're all agreed there's nothing so very sinister about that. What else did you notice?'

'No sales structure,' said Gryce. 'No reps, no market research bods, no – '

'There wouldn't be,' Pam cut in drily. 'We don't sell anything.'

Seeds gave an old-womanish '*Tsk!*' of annoyance. 'You will keep *jumping the gun*, Pam! Let him tell his story *in his own way*!'

'There's not all that much to tell,' said Gryce truthfully.

'Saving your presence, that's for us to decide. Now you couldn't find anything in the internal directory to suggest a sales department in any way, shape or form. So you set out to look for it. Is that the size of it?'

'Not exactly. It did puzzle me for a while, I must confess, but then I chanced to have a little chat with Mr Grant-Peignton. He seems quite the historian, as regards Perfidious – '

'And what did *he* tell you?'

'That we'd diversified into property.'

Pam shocked Gryce by exclaiming '*Balls!*' Whether Seeds was likewise shocked Gryce was none too sure, but it certainly provoked one of his famous glances.

Since she showed no signs of enlarging on this expletive, Gryce continued. 'Well now, that did seem to explain a great deal. I'm not particularly au fait with the world of property but I'm quite sure it's not bought and sold out of sample cases like so many – '

'Whatever British Albion does,' said Pam, to Gryce's annoyance interrupting what he thought was a rather pleasing display of verbal pyrotechnics, 'it doesn't buy or sell property. That's already established.' In other words, Get on with it.

'But what did occur to me, and mark you I didn't get further than the second floor, working downwards,' concluded Gryce, 'was that you'd think a firm this size, whether it buys or sells property or whatever it does, would run to a computer. It's probably in the basement.'

'It isn't in the basement,' said Pam. 'There isn't a computer. And do you know why there isn't a computer?'

Seeds' warning glances were as obvious as if he'd swung a red lamp in front of Pam's nose. Nevertheless, she answered her own rhetorical question.

'There isn't a computer because if there *was* a computer, the people who operate it would know what's going on.'

She seemed to have this obsession about something 'going on'. Gryce would have quite liked to know himself what Perfidious Albion was up to but it didn't seem worth making a song and dance over. If property wasn't the answer, then it was his bet that it was something to do with high finance.

It was out of politeness, then, that he asked: 'What *is* going on, precisely?'

Seeds answered, if you could call it an answer. 'What do *you* think?'

'I don't know. I was hoping one of you would tell me.'

'With great respect, I don't think you've *quite* finished telling *us*. You've done very well so far, you've observed that there's no advertising department, no sales force, no telephone exchange, no computer, and you've been with the company barely a week. I can tell you, there's people who've been on the staff for months and years without tumbling to a quarter of that. Now. What else?'

Patronizing devil, thought Gryce. On the other hand, Seeds had very kindly credited him with noticing the absence of a telephone exchange, which strictly speaking was not his discovery at all.

Gryce racked his brains. He could think of nothing else worth mentioning, except that curious phone call from Lucas, which considering that Seeds himself was supposed to have been the recipient of it, would be hardly appropriate at this stage.

'That's about all, I think.'

Seeds and Pam exchanged a glance, but not their accustomed one. This one plainly said, 'The poor boob.'

'I *told* you he didn't know,' said Seeds. 'The penny hasn't dropped.'

'It's incredible,' said Pam. 'Shall I tell him?'

'Considering what you've told him already, you might as well.' Seeds leaned back and began idly swilling the wine about in his glass, to show that the proceedings were no longer within his control. If he wasn't going to drink himself, thought Gryce as he contemplated his own empty glass, he might at least notice that other people could do with topping up. There was still half a bottle left, untouched since Seeds had poured the original three glasses.

Pam looked at Gryce with an expression of suppressed amusement.

'Do you mean to say you started on the twelfth floor and worked your way as far down as the second, and you didn't even notice *they're all internal departments*?'

Gryce was now glad that his glass was indeed empty, otherwise he might have been in the act of raising it to his lips and it would certainly have fallen out of his hand at this point. Of course! It was blazingly obvious, when you thought about it.

'Internal mail, but no *ex*ternal mail?' Pam persisted, still with a note of humorous incredulity. 'Invoice clearance, but no invoice despatch? An accounts department that does nothing else besides pay our salaries? A buying department that buys only office desks and office paper?'

Yes, all right, she needn't rub it in. 'I *did* notice that,' said Gryce defensively, half-convincing himself that such was the case.

'He certainly *should* have noticed, if as he says he found the internal telephone directory lying about!' Seeds, still lounging back in his chair as if a neutral observer, threw this remark at Pam in such a way as to suggest that any doubt about Gryce telling the truth was in her mind, not his own. 'Why else go through all the palaver of keeping the thing under lock and key? To *stop* people noticing.'

A slightly quizzical flourish on 'under lock and key' told Gryce that he was being got at. He countered sulkily: 'In that event, why have an internal directory at all?'

'What's the alternative? There must be thirty or forty heads of department – they can hardly commit each other's numbers to memory, or jot them down in their pocket diaries.'

'But aren't internal calls discouraged, from what Copeland was telling me?'

'For the likes of us, yes. Otherwise we'd need access to the internal directory. Heads of department are another matter. You don't really suppose Copeland trundles all the way down to the third floor when he has one of his frequent chats with Lucas of Personnel, do you?'

No, my friend, and I don't suppose Lucas of Personnel trundles all the way up to the seventh when he has one of his frequent chats with you. That was what Gryce would have liked to have said, if he'd been able to see any point in going on the offensive. A second later he wished he had done.

'Besides,' went on Seeds with studied offhandedness, 'it would never have occurred to them that anyone would go to the lengths of breaking into a filing cabinet to consult what seems on the face of it a routine office document.'

Oh, really, and while on the subject of the lengths to which British Albion employees might or might not go, may I have the temerity to enquire what business it is of yours or Mister *Lucas's what political organizations I happen to –* No, it was too late for that now; and in any case Gryce was so badly shaken that he could not completely trust his syntax. Opting for brevity, he said as curtly as he dared: 'I did *not* break into Copeland's filing cabinet, if that's what you're implying, it was open already.'

'Then you've changed your story, because according to an earlier version the internal directory *and* the guidelines booklet were lying about on top of it!'

Seeds grinned nastily, there was no other word for it. Some sort of explanation would have to be forthcoming.

Luckily for Gryce, while he frantically tried to cobble one together, Pam came to his rescue. Or rather, to the rescue of her own patience, for she was plainly bored by the diversion which Seeds had introduced: but it came to the same thing.

'Does all this matter?'

'It does if we turn out to have a master cracksman in our midst, dear heart,' said Seeds, still well pleased with himself. 'We may need to avail ourselves of his talents.'

To Gryce's alarm, this seemed to interest Pam very much.

'Did you really break into Copeland's filing cabinet?'

As wretched a cleft stick as Gryce had ever encountered. If he confessed, God alone knew what compromising situation these two would talk him into. If he continued to flounder, they would get the truth out of him somehow. The longer he spun it out, the more shaming it would sound when they heard that behind all his face-saving was the measly theft of a handful of toffees.

'I *can* open his filing cabinet, yes. You see, for anyone who's ever served his time at Comform, there's a knack – '

'But why would you want to?'

'Probably helping himself to Copeland's toffees!' chortled Seeds. The notion seemed to amuse him greatly. Gryce didn't know whether to feel humiliation or relief, now that the cat was out of the bag. Since he was so miserably confused that there appeared to be a choice, he decided pragmatically on relief.

'Well, do you know, you're not as far off the mark as you might think! The plain fact is that I had some papers to put away, some calling-in forms that I didn't want to leave lying around. Now, granted, I *could* have opened any filing cabinet in the depart– '

140

'Yes, well that's the important thing, isn't it?' Pam cut him short just as he was about to glide very nicely into a wryly-put account of what had led him to choose Copeland's filing cabinet above all others. 'If we wanted to look at files, documents, papers, and we hit any snags, then we could count on you?'

Shades of Watergate, thought Gryce with extreme nervousness. Aloud he said cautiously: '"Count on me" in effect to commit an act of breaking and entering – or whatever the legal expression may be. It's a very tall order.'

'Yes, but will you do it?'

'A *very* tall order. And what would be the purpose of this nefarious activity?'

Pam gave one of her frequent sighs, analysed by Gryce as registering nine parts exasperation to one part contempt.

'Haven't you *any* sense of curiosity? I mean, I've *told* you that British Albion doesn't sell anything, doesn't make anything, you've seen for *yourself* that all the departments are internal. Or seem to be. Don't you *want* to know what's going on?'

Gryce rather wished he had some prop – spectacles to polish, a pipe to puff at – which he could use to indicate that what he was about to say was of a judicious nature. There was a danger that he might sound colourless, and he wouldn't want Pam to run away with that impression.

'Surely the key phrase is "*or seem to be*". It's self-evident that the organization is top-heavy with administration, but someone, somewhere, must be getting down to what passes for the nitty-gritty. For example, what do all those mysterious service departments do – Services A, B, and so on?'

'Mysterious,' said Pam grimly, 'is the right word.'

'Meaning you don't know?'

'Nobody knows. They don't know themselves. They analyse statistics, make abstracts, compare one year's figures with another, the kind of work that ought to be done by the computer we don't have. But nobody knows what the statistics are, or where they come from. And the department is fragmented into four – as you say, A, B, C and D – so that even if anyone did know what it was all in aid of, they wouldn't be able to get a complete picture.'

'Certainly the only picture discernible to me,' observed Gryce, venturing a mild joke, 'was one of masterly inactivity. But that could equally be said of every other department, with the notable exception of Catering (Administration).'

'You had a good look in there, did you?'

'Well. A fair peep. So far as I could see, the entire tenth and eleventh floors are feverishly engaged in processing SSTs.'

'So they claim,' said Pam cryptically. 'Did they chuck you out?'

Gryce, remembering his reception from the character who looked like Jack Lemmon, replied fervently: 'Did they not!' Pam nodded, in a knowing sort of way, and said bitterly: 'And you still wonder why we want to get at their files!' Then, with a gesture of throwing in the towel, she looked at Seeds, as if to say, '*You* try banging your head against a brick wall for a change!' Honestly, thought Gryce, if looks could kill, one would need as many lives as a cat.

Seeds certainly made the most of this implicit offer of a return to the limelight. Having slumped back in his chair upon delivering the shaft about Gryce probably helping himself to Copeland's toffees, he now straightened up once more, put his glass on the barrel-top table, placed Gryce's and Pam's empty glasses on either side of it to form a neat row, and then proceeded to pour out the remaining half-bottle of wine, making a very fussy business of measuring each glass's level against the others. The effect of all this was to build up an impressive silence that was plainly intended to leave Gryce agog.

'Sal#ut#é,' said Seeds at last, raising his glass. Feeling rather absurd, Gryce found himself participating in what onlookers, had there been any, would have taken for a solemn toast.

'In this building,' began Seeds, presumably referring to Perfidious Albion rather than the Pressings wine bar, 'there are two factions – Them and Us.'

This statement was followed by a dramatic pause. Too dramatic by half, thought Gryce. He abruptly revised his opinion that Seeds looked like Jeremy Thorpe. He looked, in fact, like that television actor, what was his name, who for years had played the part of the interfering neighbour in a situation comedy about a man who had married his teenage daughter's best friend, and who when the series was over had unexpectedly and incongruously turned up as Martin Luther in a historical drama. In other words, completely out of his own league.

Happily, the wind was taken out of Seeds' sails by Pam, who took advantage of the pause for effect by contradicting him.

'Actually, there's three – Them, Us and the Others.'

'Shall I tell this or shall you?' asked Seeds snappishly. Pam sardonically conceded him the floor. He continued.

'By Them, I mean mainly heads of department, certain key personnel – all those who, until they provide evidence to the contrary, can be assumed to be in the know. By We, I mean those of us who have started asking questions.'

'Whereas the Others,' chipped in Pam, 'are the great majority who either don't know there's anything untoward about British Albion, or more likely don't care, so long as they get their salaries in their hot little hands each month.'

Gryce, if they would give him any say in the matter, would have liked to have opted for the latter category. As it was, he seemed to have been brought under the 'Us' umbrella without a by-your-leave.

'Tell me.' Gryce edged into the silence occasioned by Seeds glowering at Pam for interrupting him again. 'How would you classify friend Lucas of Personnel?'

Though addressing himself to Pam, he squinted furtively at Seeds for a reaction. There was none: or you could say, such an absence of reaction that it spoke volumes. A case of the dog that did not bark in the night.

'He's one of Them, very actively so,' said Pam. 'Why do you ask?'

'He put some very odd questions when I came for my interview. He seemed, how shall I put it, very keen on establishing one's personality rather than one's qualifications for the job in hand.'

'Yes. He'd want to make sure you were the passive type.'

'Oh, really? Then how may one ask did *you* get through the net?' Gryce was blessed if he knew why he was bothering himself with gallantries, even of the barbed variety such as he fancied he had just delivered, when the woman had insulted him to his face. However, he was rewarded with a faint smile, and was surprised at how grateful he was for it.

There remained the impassiveness of Seeds. Gryce was blowed if he knew what to make of him. If Lucas was one of Them, and Seeds was one of Us – ah, but was he?

As had happened once or twice before, Seeds seemed to read his mind. As well he might, considering that he must have been tipped off about Gryce listening-in on his precious phone call from Lucas of Personnel.

'You may find Lucas playing what with no wish to be theatrical can only be described as a double agent role. Once he knows you're one of Us, he'll try to give you the impression he's on your side. Feed you various tit-bits of information, possibly: he's tried that more than once. But be warned. Anything you say to him will get right back.'

That, at a stretch, could be said to answer Gryce's question, he supposed. It would have to, for the time being. Meanwhile, there was another one to be asked.

'"Get right back." To whom?'

'If we knew that,' said Seeds, elaborately pressing the button of his digital watch, 'we wouldn't be sitting here when all our suppers are waiting in the oven. My supper anyway, I don't know about yours.'

Seeds rose and made a performance both of draining his glass and looking at Pam to prompt her to do the same.

'I'll give it a minute,' Pam said. Whether this was a code message to indicate that she wanted a private word with Gryce, or that the three of them had better not be seen leaving the Pressings together, was open to question. But Gryce, for all that there was a risk that she might continue haranguing him when Seeds had gone, felt quite pleased. He had seen friend Seeds off, of that there was no doubt. He would have to fork out for another round of drinks, and he would have to dream up some cock-and-bull yarn about the trains running late for his wife's benefit, but the way he looked at it, you were only young once.

He became aware that Seeds had asked him a question, though for the life of him he couldn't say what it was. Very probably, something on the lines of, 'Well, then,

145

are you for us or agin us? Speak now or forever hold your peace.' An answer seemed to be called for.

'Oh, indeed!' said Gryce as positively and un-passively as he could. It seemed to fit the bill, for Seeds nodded his satisfaction.

'*We'll be in touch*.' Since Seeds had expressed a wish not to be theatrical, you would have thought he could have selected a less melodramatic exit-line. However, on that note he departed.

Pam and Gryce sat on in silence: an uncomfortable one on his part, what seemed a relaxed one on hers. At length she chalked up quite a milestone by calling him by his first name.

'Poor Clem!'

It was so unexpected that Gryce looked involuntarily behind him to see if she was talking about someone else. Then he smiled wanly: it seemed to be the reaction she wanted.

'Have we given you a hard time?'

'Not in the least! It's all very intriguing, all very stimulating. Mark you, I still don't think I can quite fathom out these two camps of Them and – '

Pam, with a smile that could have been condescending or sympathetic or even sexy, take it as you would, raised the index finger of her right hand and placed it gently on his lips. It was a totally new experience for Gryce. Considering that she had just been holding a cold glass, her touch was remarkably warm.

'I think we've had enough shop-talk for one night, don't you reckon? I was hoping we'd have a drink by ourselves again, but Ron insisted on tagging along.'

That didn't entirely square with her aggressive demeanour at the beginning of the evening, not to mention her subsequent grimaces, asides and general snappishness, but Gryce was not going to argue the toss. He smiled again, somewhat crookedly since her finger was still on his lips. She lowered her hand slowly, and some instinct told him that if he rested his arm casually on the barrel-top table, in just such a position, then there was every chance that their fingers would meet. The possibility became a reality, for all the world as if they had planned it together.

9

Gryce would have been the first to admit that he was anxiety-prone: a real old worry-guts as a slip of a girl at one of his previous billets had once told him. That had been over the affair of the missing ballpoints. He had been fool enough to accept delivery of the things in his superior's absence, three dozen of them, supposed to last the department a whole month, and every blessed one had walked by tea-time. If there had been an enquiry into the matter, it would have been his signature they found on the docket.

Yes, he did worry, but only about affairs appertaining to the office. If, on the self-same morning, his wife were to say, 'I've had enough and I'm leaving you,' and a colleague were to tip him off, 'The area manager's after your blood personally,' it would be his impending interview with the Big Cheese that would preoccupy him the most. He was very sorry, but there it was.

Whether Pam came under the heading of affairs appertaining to the office was a moot point. An office *affair* one could certainly say, if in a punning mood. Oh, definitely. It was only a matter of time now, he was like a moth drawn to a candle. They had finished up kissing and cuddling last night, well kissing anyhow: she had put her arm through his when he'd walked her to the bus-stop, and pecked him on the cheek when he had taken his leave after agreeing with her that there was no sense in hanging about considering the time it might take for a thirty-eight or a one-seven-one to roll up.

Getting on for eight it had been when he had staggered

home half-tipsy: they'd had another two glasses of wine apiece and she had given him a character analysis of himself. 'I'd say you take a long time making your mind up, but once you do, nothing can change it.' That was true enough, very shrewd, right on the button. They were going to have an affair. Her husband might find out, his wife might find out, the whole office might find out, they could become the talk of the Buttery like Cargill from Salary Accounts and his lady-love. She might become pregnant – of course, that was counting one's chickens rather, there was a long way to go yet before monthly health bulletins became the norm. But that day would come. It was frightening, but at the same time exhilarating.

To Gryce's annoyance, though, Pam kept being jostled out of his mind by Seeds. Lying awake long into the night, he found his thoughts drifting back to that curious phone call from Lucas. If all that Pam and Seeds had said about the office was true, if there was something fishy going on, then there was no individual fishier than Master Seeds in Gryce's opinion for what it was worth. You had to look at it this way: just supposing that the two factions 'Them' and 'Us' were not figments of their imagination, that they were not, after all, a feverish invention of Seeds', embroidered on by Pam who was perhaps more gullible than an outsider would have taken her for. Supposing that British Albion were indeed Perfidious Albion, involved in some shady traffic in international finance that it didn't want the world and his wife to know about. Where did that leave Gryce? By involving himself with Pam he appeared willy-nilly to involve himself with Seeds. A harebrained plan to break into office filing cabinets had been mooted. What if Seeds, who spoke so glibly of Lucas being a double agent, proved to be a double agent himself? If everything said to Seeds 'got right back' in the phrase he had used? Gryce would have to tread this particular tightrope very carefully indeed.

When he fell asleep at last, Gryce dreamed that he and Pam and Seeds were rifling the filing cabinets of Catering (Administration) at dead of night, while all the telephones rang incessantly. They came across a drawer that slid open on its telescopic rails to reveal a camp bed, and there seemed to be a suggestion that he and Pam should perform, if that was the word, in front of Seeds. But when they threw back the blankets it was to reveal a waking one-armed commissionaire.

To add to Gryce's problems, when he reached the office the following morning – having signed the late-arrivals book, surely no one was going to hold a few extra minutes in bed against him when there was no work to do – he found, to his great indignation, that he was being held responsible for the disappearance of the furniture.

That it had by now completely vanished he did not at first realize. He saw that the seventh floor foyer was free from obstruction again and he assumed that the work of shifting the partitions was done at last and that the desks and chairs and so on would be back in position. 'Back to the old grindstone, eh?' he had remarked to Ardagh with whom he had travelled up in the lift (so he was not the only latecomer thank goodness). Ardagh had replied philosophically, 'Ah well, onwards and upwards.'

But when they turned into Stationery Supplies it was to find the by now familiar tableau of all their colleagues standing around as if in the lobby of some hotel where a sales conference was about to be held, and Copeland in a state of great agitation.

Still in his mackintosh, Copeland was brandishing a piece of paper at the Penney twins and haranguing them about a Casanova occupant, it sounded like to Gryce.

The Penney twins' policy of dividing their sentences between them meant that they could not get enough purchase on the discussion to stem Copeland's flow. It looked like an AI office row, of a vintage that Gryce had not come across since a high-spirited junior at his last billet but one had put half a banana in the shredding machine.

His colleagues, not to mention the workmen from Design and Maintenance who far from completing their task seemed to have gone back to square one with lengths of partition lying about all over the floor, clearly and callously regarded the dressing-down of the Penney twins as a spectator sport. Not that Gryce blamed them: it was a case of pull the ladder up at a time like this. He was about to cross the office as inconspicuously as possible, and stand casually though perhaps proprietorially next to Pam, just to give Seeds something to think about, when he heard his name called.

'Mr Christ!'

Without acknowledging a sympathetic 'The balloon's gone up, mate' grimace from Vaart, Gryce deflected his course and, having drawn a deep breath, stepped into the poisonous cloud in which the Penney brothers had enveloped their superior. The paper which Copeland had been waving about was now waved in his direction. It was a sheet of photo-copying paper covered in what looked to be an illiterate or hysterical pencilled scrawl.

'Mr Christ, why is the five and seventy Austria without a Casanova occupant?'

'The Fire and Safety Officer,' explained Hugh Penney.

'He's had all our furniture removed,' said Charles Penney. Both the Penney twins seemed well-pleased at Gryce's arrival. It was as plain as the nose on one's face that they expected him to get them off whatever hook they had been wriggling on.

151

'Without leaving a Casanova occupant, Mr Christ!'

'A handing-over document,' translated Hugh Penney.

Gryce could only surmise what a handing-over document might be when it was at home. It would be a chit or pro-forma that you would sign and hand over when taking temporary possession of property from another department – a typewriter for repair, say. Certainly if the Fire and Safety Officer had made off with all the office furniture, though why he should want to do such a thing heaven only knew, he would be expected to leave a receipt of some kind. But Gryce didn't see what business it was of his.

The Penney twins, however, were about to explain. They did so with what struck Gryce as a certain malevolence.

'Apparently his pad of handing-over documents has been called in – '

' – and he hasn't had any replacements.'

'He tried to scrounge one from Traffic Control or In-House Mail – '

' – but it was quite late, so everyone had gone home.'

'Not, of course, that he would have been able to – '

' – because theirs have been called-in too.'

'As far as we can remember, that is,' concluded Charles Penney, with the faintest trace of a smirk. Otherwise the pair of them were looking as if butter wouldn't melt in their mouths.

Copeland, meanwhile, was fuming to himself and impatiently fanning himself with his piece of paper. Or perhaps his motive was a hygienic one, and he was trying to fan away the odious fumes of the Penney brothers' breath.

'You realize what's taken place, don't you?' Gryce had not the foggiest notion what had taken place. The key to it was presumably contained in the paper which Copeland now thrust into his hand. It was so ill-written – really, you would have thought that a responsible post like Fire and Safety Officer would have legibility and a grasp of elementary punctuation among its minimum requirements – that Gryce could barely read it. However, with excited interjections from Copeland, plus disjointed translations and linking dialogue from the Penney twins, he was able to piece the story together.

It was a strange tale, though not an unlikely one for someone who had worked in as many billets as Gryce: there was always, he had long ago concluded, an office Hitler.

The Fire and Safety Officer, about to go on compassionate leave to Cumbria where it was his melancholy task to find an old people's home for his widowed mother, had decided the previous evening to make a final duty tour of the building. At 5.48 P.M. he had attempted to gain access to the seventh floor but had found his progress hindered by a large quantity of desks, chairs, filing cabinets and the remainder stacked in the foyer, where they constituted an obstruction and serious fire hazard. He would remind the head of the Stationery Supplies Dept that when structural alterations, decoration, cleansing operations etc., etc., required the displacement of furniture and equipment, such furniture and equipment was in every case to be removed to the Design and Maintenance Dept's bay in basement three, where ample storage facilities were available. It was the responsibility of the head of the department concerned, liaising with the Traffic Control Dept and the Design and Maintenance Dept, to ensure that this regulation was adhered to. Since it had not been adhered to, the Fire and Safety Officer had found it necessary to obviate the fire hazard forthwith by instructing the night cleaning personnel to remove the obstructing furniture to a safe place. The night cleaning

153

personnel had protested that this was no part of their duties and had threatened to withdraw their labour unless they were paid Removal Money. They had been advised to take the matter up with the management who in turn would no doubt take it up with the Stationery Supplies Dept, whose full responsibility it was.

The Fire and Safety Officer regretted his inability to append the customary handing-over document, duly signed, which would authorize the head of the Stationery Supplies Dept to recover the offending items in due course, but his supply of said documents had been called-in as obsolescent and replacements had not been forthcoming. He likewise regretted writing this memo on the only piece of paper he could find, owing to his supply of memo forms having been likewise called-in and replacements likewise not having been forthcoming. He would mention that the Fire and Safety Unit was now seriously run-down as to stocks of stationery, owing to requisition forms for replacements of same having been themselves called-in, and he intended taking this matter up with the management on his return from Cumbria. In the meantime, he would advise the head of the Stationery Supplies Dept to make his own approaches to the management in the event that he wanted to see his furniture again.

'Quite the fait accompli,' Gryce couldn't help observing when the saga had been told. He hoped the remark didn't sound too facetious in the circumstances. Even if it did, he could not see why he had been roped in on the affair. The serious run-down of the Fire and Safety Officer's stocks of stationery, which was plainly what had sparked off this act of bureaucratic victimization, should be laid at the Penney twins' door and nobody else's. Furthermore he meant to make as much clear to Copeland. He was

154

dashed if he was going to take the blame for other people's incompetence.

However, while Gryce was trying to draft a short statement that would exculpate himself without giving offence to the Penney twins, Copeland came in rather icily with: 'Well, Mr Christ, I'm afraid I must hold you reconnaissance.'

Responsible for what, pray? for the run-down of the Fire and Safety Officer's stationery? For the high-handed commandeering of the department's furniture? For the fact that Copeland was going to be in it up to here with the management?

'With all due respect, I quite fail to see – ' Gryce did not have the temerity to speak thus to Copeland. Rather he made a deliberate half-turn and addressed himself, in wounded fashion, to the Penney twins. It made no difference, for Copeland swept on as though he had never opened his mouth. He had noticed that many people had that tendency. It was the age one lived in, Gryce supposed. Good manners were at a premium.

'You've been put in sole charge of calling-in. I'm told you now have all the flies.' Files, that would be. Well, as to that, Gryce didn't have the files at all. The files were in the filing cabinets and the filing cabinets had been spirited away by the Fire and Safety Officer who was now roaming around Cumbria. 'If I may say so, Mr Christ, it was up to you to notice that his Casanova occupants had been called-in, and issue re playmates.'

'But I understood,' protested Gryce plaintively, 'that issuing replacements was the task of Mr Penney and – ' To repeat 'Mr Penney' would have sounded absurd, so he settled for tailing off and waving flaccidly to identify the second of the twins, hoping that Copeland would come to his rescue by continuing. If Copeland was going to make a hobby of interrupting his every sentence, you

155

would have thought here was a golden opportunity. Perversely, however, he took his time: possibly because he had made an error in his attack on Gryce and wished to think out how to cover himself.

'*I'm well aware* whose cask it is to issue re playmates, Mr Christ. The fact is they can't be issued until the person requiring them fills in a rat suspicion.'

'A requisition? Ah. *Quite so, Mr Copeland*. A stationery requirements form.' Just the opening Gryce had been waiting for. He had got them where he wanted them. 'But the whole onus for issuing new supplies of stationery, and that must include stationery requirements forms if they have been called-in, *falls on my colleagues here!*'

Upon this, Gryce pointed melodramatically at the Penney twins. But the gesture was lost on Copeland.

'*Not,*' he said with an exaggeration of patience, 'if the five and seventy Austria has no rat suspicion forms *at his disposal*, owing to the fact that they have been called-in. If his rat suspicion forms have been called-in, it rests on you to give him a re playmates issue. That's only common cents.'

It was common sense indeed, Gryce had to admit. It would have been even more common sense for the wretched Penney brothers to have realized that the whole calling-in process was leading the Stationery Supplies department up a blind alley, and to have bent the rules slightly by replacing obsolescent stationery requirements forms even when no one had had the wit to ask for them, not that anyone who did have the wit could have asked anyway, seeing that there was no machinery whatever to enable them to do so.

But Gryce was not going to say any of that to Copeland, it was not up to him to point out the flaws in the system. That was what executives were paid for.

'Allowing that the ball seems to have been placed in

my court,' he said mulishly, 'what is it that you wish me to do?'

'I really don't know,' confessed Copeland. Honestly! and he was supposed to be the head of a department! Weren't these people given any aptitude tests when they were recruited, to prove their ability to make decisions?

Copeland went on to outline his dilemma, or rather what he insisted was Gryce's dilemma. The office furniture had presumably been shifted to basement three, unless the Resign and Maypole-dance wallahs down there had refused to have anything to do with such an irregular transaction, in which case it could be anywhere. Whether the stuff was in the custody of Resign and Maypole-dance or the Man in the Moon, however, it would certainly not be released except on production of a Casanova occupant, signed by the Five and Seventy Austria. To place supplies of Casanova occupants in the Five and Seventy Austria's hands, it was technically necessary for him to fill out a rat suspicion form, which he also did not possess. That procedure could have been short-circuited by the department slipping him the odd Casanova occupant on an ad hoc basis or on the old-boy net, call it what you would, but the snag here was that it would involve Mr Fart indenting for fresh Casanova occupants from Stationery Stores on the department's own rat suspicion form. All the rat suspicion forms, however, were in the filing cabinets, and the filing cabinets had been impounded by the Five and Seventy Austria.

'Full purple,' concluded Copeland.

'Full circle indeed,' agreed Gryce. 'But given that the Fire and Safety Officer has taken himself off to Cumbria, he would still be in Cumbria even if we had all the handing-over documents in the world to offer him.'

'True,' Copeland conceded. Then he added significantly, '*But who is to know that?*'

157

During the summary he had just delivered, he had surreptitiously taken a toffee out of his pocket and had succeeded in unwrapping it behind his back, seen only by Grant-Peignton, Ardagh, Beazley, young Thelma, several workmen and half the staff of Traffic Control at the other side of their flattened partition. On 'But who is to know that?' he made an attempt to slip the toffee in his mouth without either Gryce or the Penney twins noticing. The fact of his speaking through a cupped hand heightened the conspiratorial effect of what he was saying.

Gryce was quite shocked. He really was beginning to ask himself what kind of billet he had landed himself up in here. Was there no unwritten code of conduct at Perfidious Albion? First it had been Seeds and Pam recommending the wholesale breaking-open of filing cabinets, and now it was the head of a department, if you pleased, calmly proposing an even more criminal act.

'Are you suggesting, Mr Copeland,' asked Gryce in a formal voice, his gaze embracing the Penney twins to inform them that they were witnesses to this whether they liked it or not, 'that I should forge the Fire and Safety Officer's signature?'

'What I'm suggesting, Mr Christ,' said Copeland, 'is that there must be a blank Casanova occupant lying about *somewhere*. Whose signature appears on that occupant is not my concern. What does concern me is that I want all desks, chairs and filing cabinets back in position the moment the Resign and Maypole-dance people have finished their work.'

At least, thought Gryce who believed in looking on the bright side, that would give one a breathing space. He had a horror of doing anything immediately, whether illegal or not. It looked as if it would be a good two or three days before the partitions were finally up. Anything could happen in that time. The Fire and Safety Officer

158

could return from Cumbria, and be unable to resist the temptation to come up and gloat over Copeland's predicament. Or Copeland could be hauled up by the management to explain why the night cleaning personnel were claiming Removal Money. One way or another, Gryce felt confident of his own assigned role in the affair being overtaken by events. He was certainly not going to be a party to forgery, although he was not averse to nosing about in basement three to see what had happened to the furniture.

A thought struck him about the pleasant expedition he had already begun to plan for himself.

'With the Fire and Safety Officer and his precious regulations *very much in mind*, I've been advised that it's necessary to have a docket before visiting other departments.'

Gryce caught a whiff of what smelled like rotten eggs and saw that the Penney twins were breathing out heavily and rolling their eyes, presumably to make the point that he was being pedantic. Let them. They had contributed practically nothing to the discussion in hand. It had been left to him, Gryce, to make sense of Copeland's ramblings, to marshal the facts and to summarize the difficulties that faced them. He hoped his initiation had not gone unnoticed by interested bystanders, particularly Pam.

'The only docket at my disposal, Mr Christ,' said Copeland with uncharacteristic jocularity, 'is this.' Whereupon, very much to Gryce's astonishment, he handed him the toffee-paper which he had been compulsively folding into an octogram. And then, speaking more to the office at large than to Gryce, he announced: 'There's nothing to be done here, I intend to wend my way homewards. If anyone wants me, I've got Ancient flu.'

* * *

Copeland's abrupt departure caused quite a stir. From all Gryce gathered, although sick leave on the thinnest of pretexts was one thing, sliding off in this barefaced manner was quite another. But it was generally agreed that Copeland was pursuing the wise course in making himself scarce before – as Vaart insisted on putting it – the shit hit the fan. Grant-Peignton was heard to say that if anyone thought he was going to carry the can back, they were very much mistaken.

There was also some agreement, though by no means general, that what was sauce for the goose was sauce for the gander. Vaart, the Penney twins and Ardagh all became very vocal on the silliness of remaining in the office when there was nothing to do, Ardagh making the point that if they only had somewhere to sit it might be different. These broad hints were thrown in the direction of Grant-Peignton, whose only response was a muttered, 'On your own heads be it.' As the alleged No. 2 to Copeland and head of the department in the latter's absence, he was displaying all the authority of a dead fish if anyone wanted Gryce's view on the matter. Beazley, on the other hand, huffily refused an invitation extended by Vaart to piss off out of it, saying that someone had to mind the store. Young Thelma, of course, had no option but to remain at her post. For her part, Pam looked as if she needed only a word from the right quarter to persuade her to put her coat on again: Gryce, heading towards her, meant to suggest an early lunch and an afternoon at the cinema. As for Seeds, he seemed uncertain what to do. A messenger from In-house Mail had just dumped an enormous bundle of letters into his arms – there was work piling up there and no mistake: Gryce shuddered to think how many white and pink check-lists there were in that little lot – and he had absolutely no means of getting rid of it save handing it to someone else, as in a game of

160

Pass the Parcel. It was as effective in its way, thought Gryce with an inward snigger, as a ball and chain.

'I thought you handled that very well,' said Pam gratifyingly, referring to what surely would have been the chief topic of conversation had not the mice elected to play now that the cat was away: namely the way in which Gryce had acquitted himself in front of Copeland.

'No thanks to the Terrible Twins,' said Gryce with a nod at the Penney brothers who were even now scurrying towards the foyer.

'Tweedledum and Tweedledee, as Ron calls them.' Gryce was not in the least interested in what Brother Seeds called them, or didn't call them. 'You know what we were saying about Us, Them and the Others last night? I'm convinced they fall into a category of their own. For whatever reason, they're happily dedicated to sabotaging the system.'

Nor was Gryce interested in dredging up all that office conspiracy stuff again, thank you very much. He had enough on his plate to be going on with. But he was bound to admit that Pam did have a point about Tweedledum and Tweedledee: the more he saw of that prize pair the more he was convinced that they shouldn't be left in charge of a whelk-stall.

The reference to last night gave him an opening. 'I suppose even if one walked very slowly, it would be too early for a drink at the Pressings?'

'What, at this hour?' Pam laughed coquettishly. 'We'd be under the table by lunch-time!'

Gryce thought of a risqué reply to this, censored it at once, and voiced his suggestion of an early lunch and a visit to the cinema.

'I'd like to, there's no sense in hanging on here,' said Pam with what might or might not have been simulated regret. 'But there's one or two things I want to get done.'

161

Oh, yes? Then since those one or two things would have had to wait in the event that Copeland had not skived off, why could they not wait now?

Gryce, however, perked up at once when Pam went on to say: 'Look, why don't we meet up later?'

'Why not indeed?'

'Do you still want to look at the Albion Players?'

Gryce's heart sank. He had not had that in mind at all. A cosy drink at the Pressings, just the two of them: now that would have been worth waiting on for, he could have gone to the pictures by himself and then had a quick snack to line his stomach before opening-time. But the prospect of an evening in some draughty hall, with friend Seeds throwing his weight about in his capacity of stage manager or chief dogsbody or whatever, held little appeal. They would get no time to themselves and he would be seriously late for his supper.

'I thought you were full up?'

'Oh, we're recruiting again. Why don't you give it a try? I think after our little get-together last night you might find it *quite worthwhile*.' Thelma had clomped towards them with her tray of coffee beakers and Pam was signalling that her words were to be taken as having more significance than would be apparent to their young eavesdropper. She could only mean that the Albion Players would give them an excuse for being seen about together. Discovered holding hands in the Pressings wine bar they would pretend to be rehearsing. And their affair would blossom.

'Yes, all right, I look forward to it,' said Gryce. Nothing to be gained from sounding negative or passive.

As Pam was about to utter some word of gratification, Thelma butted in with the raw directness of youth: 'Do you want coffee or not?'

'Just a minute, Thelma, we're *talking*!' snapped Pam.

A believer in keeping juniors in their place, Gryce had noticed. To him, in a softer voice, she continued: 'Six o'clock, at the St Jude's Institute in St Jude's Lane. Do you know it?'

'I'll find it.'

'There'll be some familiar faces there, so you won't feel out on a limb. In fact,' said Pam with an arch smile, 'you should feel quite at home.'

She moved away, shaking her head crossly at Thelma who was clanking her tray of beakers. Thelma, quite unabashed, continued to hover.

'Excuse me, Mr Gryce, did Mrs Fawce say they were taking new people on for the Albion Players?'

'I believe that's the case, Thelma.'

'Do you think they'd have me? Only I've been trying to get in for ages. I love acting, always have done.'

A case of whistling for the moon, Gryce thought. It was pathetic really: the girl had the grace of a pantomime cow.

Aloud, he said: 'I *think* you'd better have a word with Mrs Fawce.'

But when he turned to look for Pam, it was just in time to see her and Seeds, both of them in their outdoor coats, hurrying out of the office. The bundle of mail that Seeds had been happily saddled with was now in the possession of Beazley.

One or two things to get done, indeed. He would give her one or two things when next he saw her.

'I'm sure you'd be most welcome, Thelma,' said Gryce nastily. 'Why don't you come along with me?'

'Pardon? Oo, thank you, Mr Gryce. Thank you very much.'

Later Thelma rewarded him with extra sugar in his coffee. He hoped it was a one-off gesture, he knew he had a sweet tooth but you could have too much of a good thing.

10

Gryce was in a thoroughly foul mood as he hurried along St Jude's Lane with the clodhopping Thelma in tow. They were twenty minutes late. The stupid girl had waited until they were about to leave the office before deciding that she wanted to 'spend a penny'. She could have spent fifty pee in there, the time it took. And to cap it all, they'd taken a short cut and finished up on a building site. It was the last straw.

He had bitterly regretted inviting her along to the Albion Players the moment he'd opened his mouth. Not that he gave a hoot what Pam might say but it meant he was now committed to spending the entire day loafing about the office with only Beazley and Grant-Peignton for company, everyone else except the Design and Maintenance workmen having sensibly slung their hooks. To have slunk off to the pictures alone and then met Thelma later would have meant making complex arrangements that would have constricted his stomach muscles; to have taken her with him would have laid him open to charges of kidnapping. He could just imagine what the boisterous Vaart would make of a titbit of that kind. There was nothing for it but to sit it out, pacing up and down, jangling one's loose change, and avoiding the eyes of the workmen who, for all that they were like a blessed slow-motion film, could at least claim to be occupying themselves constructively.

To add insult to injury, Grant-Peignton had actually given him work to do. Beazley, having announced his firm intention of not coming back after lunch, had unloaded on

Grant-Peignton the burden of mail that Seeds in the first place had unloaded on him. Grant-Peignton, in turn, had palmed it off on Gryce, with instructions that he might as well make himself useful by getting it opened and sorted. Gryce had been reduced to squatting on the floor, tailor-fashion, slitting open envelopes with a pencil and surrounding himself with little heaps of bumph, much of it consisting of angry memoranda complaining of the shortage of stationery. Not that sorting it out did the slightest good, since he had finally and sullenly swept the whole cat and caboodle together and dumped it in the wire basket where Thelma kept her coffee beakers.

Making painful smalltalk with Thelma after Grant-Peignton himself had vamoosed at about four o'clock, Gryce had a sudden thought about that wire basket. It arose out of another thought which he had toyed with and then rejected, that now would be as good a time as any to start looking for the office furniture.

'Thelma, where do you keep your tea and coffee things as a rule?'

'Pardon? In one of the filing cabinets, Mr Gryce. Mr Copeland said it was all right.'

'I'm sure it is, but all our filing cabinets seem to have vanished into thin air, as you've no doubt noticed. Were you able to wave a magic wand?'

'Pardon?'

'Where did you find your tea and coffee things *this morning*?'

'Oh, I see. Well, you see, I sometimes get to work very early, because you see my dad, he has to go up to Birmingham sometimes and he drives a van, so you see he sometimes gives me a lift as far as – '

'Yes, I don't want your complete biography, Thelma. Where was the filing cabinet?'

'Pardon? Oh, I see. In the front entrance hall.'

'In the front entrance hall?'

'You know where they've got all those potted plants, just where you go in? There. Only I knew which filing cabinet it was, because it has a bit of red wool tied to the – '

'Never mind red wool, Thelma. What was your filing cabinet doing in the front entrance hall?'

'I don't know, Mr Gryce.'

Neither did Gryce. 'Well, it certainly isn't in the front entrance hall now.'

'No, Mr Gryce.'

He expected the night cleaners must have left it there on its journey to basement three or wherever. Though why they couldn't have taken it all the way down in the lift, Gryce could not fathom. He was certainly not going to worry his head about it, why should he? And if Copeland's telephone rang (as Grant-Peignton had been nervously expecting it to do all day) he was hanged if he was going to cover up for anybody. As for Thelma's wire basket now piled high with the day's correspondence, it could spend the night on the floor, and if the night cleaners slung it in the dustbin, it was no skin off Gryce's nose.

The workmen from Design and Maintenance, who one assumed needed an hour at the very least to change out of their overalls and clock off, had long since gone. As the last clerks departed from Traffic Control and In-house Mail, and Gryce was left alone on the seventh floor with Thelma, he felt increasingly fidgety. Some men, he supposed, would have felt honour bound to make a pass at the girl, dumpy as she was. Not Gryce. It was not his style. Indeed, as they restlessly prowled up and down the empty office, he was careful to keep a good six feet between them. Brush shoulders with some of the girls you got nowadays, and you were up on a rape charge.

All in all, what could have been a carefree day had turned into an ordeal.

'Come *along*, Thelma, for heaven's sake!'

But Gryce brightened as they turned the umpteenth winding corner of St Jude's Lane and saw the Victorian-looking edifice that was journey's end. There was a dark alley running alongside and very possibly around the back of it: just the job for snogging purposes, as his old RAF comrades used to say. Some thoughts that had swum unbidden into his mind back there on the seventh floor had quite put him in the mood for snogging: it was with an effort, though, that he eradicated the picture of young Thelma that had lodged there, and substituted Pam.

They passed through an arched doorway and mounted two flights of stone steps, Thelma's clog-like tread sending echoes through the old building. The St Jude's Institute reminded Gryce very strongly of his old Sunday school: he had no doubt that places like this had been thrown up by the thousand from architects' pattern-books. He knew, before even turning the bend to the second flight of steps, that they would lead into a dank lobby with a scruffy recess containing a stone sink, a greasy draining-board and possibly a rusting gas-ring where alleged refreshments were prepared, and which in turn would lead through frosted-glass swing doors into the hall proper. What he was by no means prepared for was the trestle table occupying most of the space available, at which sat three one-armed commissionaires, their cap-peaks and buttons gleaming in the harsh pool of light thrown by the naked electric bulb.

Gryce was by no means sure that they were the same three who had insisted on his signature in the late-arrivals book that morning. Certainly, as one of them stared fixedly at him and Thelma through bottle-glass lenses, and the other two made a great show of not noticing that anyone had arrived who might be requiring attention, Gryce was left in no doubt as to which organization they graced with their presence.

There was the customary wooden silence before the inquisitor snapped out: 'Cards!'

'Come again, excuse me?'

'All-mem'ship-cards-to-be-shown.'

For all that Thelma was a junior employee, Gryce shared with her a glance to high heaven at this prime example of red tape run riot. You would have thought they were making application to wander round the firm's strong-room. Presumably the Albion Players had the company's blessing, probably even got a grant of some sort, but there was such a thing as being on parade when you were on parade, and off parade when you were not.

'I'm not yet a member,' said Gryce frostily. 'I'm here at Mrs Fawce's invitation.'

'Name?'

They went through much the same palaver as Gryce had encountered on arriving for his interview with Lucas of Personnel, with the first commissionaire asking the other two if they had got a Gryce there, and all three of them running bony forefingers down dog-eared lists and registers to an accompaniment of grunts. 'Gryce, not Gibson,' one of them stated, rather than asked, at one point, but nothing else was said to indicate whether his name had been found or not. At length, however, the first commissionaire fixed his gimlet stare on Thelma.

'And what's this young lady on?'

'She's with me,' explained Gryce.

This was received with a long intake of breath and a slow, turtle-like shaking of the head.

'Not if she hasn't been ratified. Did she make representations to Mrs Fawce, as mem'ship secretary?' There was a good deal more of this. The burden of it was that while the commissionaires had had notification of a Gryce, they had had no notification whatsoever of a Thelma. He would be allowed access, but she would not.

Gryce supposed he could have made an issue of it, but he was already late enough. It was funny, he reflected, that whenever he was pressed for time there were always three one-armed commissionaires barring his way.

'Sorry about that, Thelma.'

The wretched girl looked as if she were going to stand there half the night, shrugging her shoulders and shuffling her feet and muttering, 'Ah well, can't be helped' and 'Ah, well, worth a try.' Eventually, however, she traipsed off down the steps and, in some relief at having got shot of her, Gryce was allowed to pass through the swing doors into the hall.

As he'd imagined, it was a gloomy, raftered chamber with a smell faintly reminiscent of school dinners. There was a platform at the far end, framed by a plywood proscenium arch of recent origin. Gryce hadn't known what else to expect, he was not up on amateur dramatics. He had had the vague idea that Pam, in a smock, would be discovered painting scenery or more likely supervising the painting of scenery, while other people went to and fro carrying objects made of papier-mâché and a homosexual producer or director or whatever he was called, hands on hips, urged his cast to put more pep into it. Instead, he seemed to have walked into a full-blown public dress rehearsal. The bulk of the Albion Players' supporters – a good eighty or ninety of them, he would estimate – comprised the audience, while on stage, what was presumably the crème de la crème of the Players were performing a costume drama immediately identifiable as that play by Oscar Wilde, where Edith Evans or was it Sybil Thorndike says, 'A handbag?' But there was no scenery. Far from painting the same, Pam was dressed to

169

the nines in some kind of Edwardian get-up, and she was informing Ardagh – plainly recognizable behind an excess of mutton-chop whiskers – that it had always been her ideal to love someone of the name of Ernest, there being something in that name that inspired absolute confidence. Evidently her preference for a production of *An Inspector Calls*, mentioned when Gryce had first heard of the Albion Players, had been over-ruled in committee. He was surprised that rehearsals were so well-advanced, although neither Pam nor Ardagh had yet abandoned their scripts and Ardagh had plainly not learned a single line. Perhaps it was policy to wear their stage clothes from the outset, to get them in the mood. Pam certainly looked fetching in hers, and she was as good an actress as Glynis Johns if anyone wanted Gryce's verdict. Ardagh, on the other hand, was simply making a fool of himself.

As Gryce took in the scene, he was approached by Seeds, who by the fact of hovering about at the back of the hall like a spare part was clearly no more than an usher. From his pontifications whenever the subject of the Albion Players was mentioned by Pam, you would have imagined he was the leading man at the very least.

His manner of receiving Gryce was peculiar. It was to lean backwards from the waist in mirthful fashion and point a quivering finger, at the same time delivering himself of a prolonged, hissing laugh, for all the world as if Gryce were the victim of a practical joke of his devising. 'I did tell you,' uttered Seeds in a chortling whisper, 'that we'd *be in touch*!'

Asking himself what one was supposed to make of that particular remark, Gryce followed Seeds along the central aisle to an almost empty row of seats close to the stage. With what seemed an excess of fussiness, considering there were plenty of vacant places, Seeds indicated precisely where he should sit. Gryce obediently shuffled along the row and took his place next to its only other occupant who, as he sat down, turned towards him, winked solemnly and observed hoarsely: 'Bleedin carry-on, ennit?'

Vaart was the very last person he would have expected to see at a gathering of this kind. Nothing higher in the cultural stakes than a costermongers' outing to Southend, would have been Gryce's guess. He wondered where Vaart had been all day long, and Ardagh too for that matter, not to mention Pam and Seeds. Gryce had a suspicion that the whole pack of them had been involved in some spree or expedition from which he'd been deliberately excluded.

The house-lights, as he believed they were called, had not been turned down, and Gryce was able to look about him and see who else was present. He recognized several faces from the Buttery and elsewhere. There was a man from Traffic Control who looked like George Formby, and a woman from In-house Mail who always reminded him of a friend of his late mother's, a Mrs Cuthbertson or Culbertson. Fred Astaire, whom he had seen sometimes in the lift, was there, as were the Prime Minister of Rhodesia, Flight-Sergeant Neddyman from the RAF training camp at Bridgnorth in Shropshire, David Niven, Mrs Barbara Castle, the secretary of one of the railwaymen's unions, the show-jumper Harvey Smith, the comedian Eric Morecambe, that TV meteorologist whose forecasts were always woefully wrong, a younger version of Lt-General Sir Brian Horrocks, an older version of the singer Petula Clark, and a woman often to be seen in commercials for Cadbury's chocolate. But there was no sign of anyone else from Stationery Supplies.

Gryce turned his attention back to the stage, where Ardagh was down on one knee and making a complete shambles of a proposal scene. He had lost his place in his script and in his efforts to find it could hardly keep his balance. Pam took advantage of the diversion to smile at Gryce and give him a little wave of welcome. He waved feebly back, embarrassed. Vaart dug him in the ribs and chuckled lewdly. 'You givin er one, den? *Git in dere Charlie!*' That was the kind of gauntlet you had to run if you flaunted your affections in public.

From the side of the stage – there were no wings, much less a door – there strutted forth a grotesquely attired figure in what Gryce would have said was lemon chiffon, with a huge padded bosom, a grey-tinted wig set several degrees askew beneath what looked like an old Salvation Army bonnet, and a good deal of rouge and lipstick visible even through a heavy veil. Gryce guffawed loudly, imagining that a slapstick Charley's Aunt effect was being aimed at. To his mortification nobody else laughed: the character, who must have made an entrance previously, was clearly meant to be taken seriously. If this was the best the Albion Players could do there was hope for Gryce yet.

In a voice that reminded Gryce of a drag-queen he had once seen after allowing himself to be inveigled into an office stag party, the newcomer trilled: 'Mr Worthing! Rise, sir, from this semi-recumbent posture. It is most indecorous.' Since Ardagh's efforts to keep his balance had failed, and he had toppled over on to his side, this comment did more than justice to the author's intention.

'Mama!' cried Pam, who really did get under the skin of her character in Gryce's judgement. 'I must beg you to retire. This is no place for you. Besides, Mr Worthing has not quite – all right? Thank you very much.'

These last few words were spoken, called, rather, in Pam's normal voice. She was addressing, it would appear, Seeds, who had stationed himself in front of the doors at the rear of the hall so that nobody else could get in.

Pam, no longer the Edwardian ingénue but the brisk membership secretary or whatever her title was, clapped her hands. From either side of the stage trooped the remainder of the cast, carrying cane chairs on which they seated themselves in a semi-circle. One of them, got up as a bishop or senior clergyman of some sort, was immediately identifiable as Beazley. The other faces were faintly familiar, no doubt Gryce had seen them around the office but he could not place them. The comic gardener, if that was what he was supposed to be, looked a bit like Sir Richard Attenborough, but that was probably the effect of clever make-up.

Chairs had been fetched for Pam and Ardagh and they too had sat down, but the buffoon playing Lady Bracknell took the centre of the stage. Throwing off bonnet, veil and wig, he revealed himself to be Grant-Peignton. Gryce's low opinion of his characterization was instantly revised. Although he had quickly latched on to the fact that Lady Bracknell was a man, he would never have known it was Grant-Peignton in a thousand years. And how sporting of Copeland's No. 2 to have taken on such a role.

Hitching up his lemon tea-gown to reveal the suede shoes that he wore about the office, Grant-Peignton addressed his audience. 'Ladies and gentlemen, welcome once again, our apologies for having detained you on this occasion but we have several newcomers here tonight and it appears that one or two of them' – here he seemed to glare in Gryce's direction – 'had difficulty in finding their way. For the benefit *of* newcomers, I should mention that in the event of interruptions by shall we say *unwelcome visitors*, a signal will be given by our friends the commissionaires and we shall at once resume our rehearsal of *The Importance of Being Earnest*. Should

173

that contingency arise, I would ask you to do your best to look like an invited audience at a dress rehearsal.'

'Bleedin pennermime, ennit!' observed Vaart with another of his broad winks. Gryce bared his teeth non-committally. A charade, certainly; but that was what he was beginning to expect from all connected with Perfidious Albion.

After adjusting one of his brassiere straps, Grant-Peignton resumed. 'The first business of the evening is the minutes, which I will ask Mr Ardagh to read. Again for the benefit of newcomers, it is customary for the names of proposers and seconders to be omitted from written records. Our principle, as you will quickly learn, is no names no pack drill!'

With this sally Grant-Peignton changed places with Ardagh, giving Vaart the opportunity to lean over to Gryce and murmur, none too softly. 'E looks a right twat in that gear.' Gryce did hope he was not going to keep up a running commentary. One was out of one's depth already, without these constant interruptions.

Ardagh began to read from what Gryce had taken to be his script – indeed it most likely *was* a script, with the minutes of the meeting cleverly interleaved – in the gabbling monotone of the practised committee secretary.

'Minutes of a meeting of the British Albion Investigation Committee, known as the Albion Players, on the fifteenth of this month. A quorum being present, the minutes were read and agreed to. On matters arising, members were furnished with a list of the board of directors of British Albion, and it was agreed that further enquiries should be made into the backgrounds of these gentlemen. It was reported that of the twenty-three subsidiary companies listed in the guidelines booklet, fifteen had so far been shown to have ceased trading. It was further reported that an investigation into the source of British Albion's domestic supplies and equipment had now been completed, and it had been established that all supplies and equipment, from carbon-paper to furniture, from electric light bulbs and fluorescent tubes to typewriters, copying machines and filing systems, emanated from suppliers with large Government contracts. No invoice or similar document from any such supplier has yet been traced.'

Vaart nudged Gryce heavily with his elbow and said in conversational tones, 'Ad yew there, din I? Ja blieve all that codswallop I give you abaht govmen surplus auctions? I bet chew did!'

With Ardagh pausing at the interruption and looking towards them in a pained manner, Gryce tried simultaneously to frown his disapproval and give a half-smile of acknowledgement.

'Din know you then, did I?' went on Vaart, unabashed. 'Coulda bin anybody, cun chew? Coulda bin onea dem wankers outa Personnel. Avter be careful.'

Grant-Peignton, adjusting his padded bosom, half-rose. 'Can we get on, gentlemen?'

'Sorry, mate. I was jus explainin – '

'Yes, I think we owe all our new members a word of explanation, Mr Vaart, but at the appropriate time. If you'll allow Mr Ardagh to continue the minutes.'

Throwing back his Hitler-like lock of hair, which contrasted strangely with his glued-on whiskers, Ardagh mumbled on.

'There was general discussion about the company's function and the consensus was reached that British Albion was probably a Government or quasi-Government agency, its elaborately organized structure being the module for some unspecified future role. Another view was that the agency was already operative, the activities of a small number of key personnel being masked or camouflaged by the innocuous routine work-pattern of the majority. Among theories advanced was that British Albion was the present or future agency for the compulsory repatriation of immigrants, the issuing of civilian identity cards in the event of a threat to the peace, the collation of mortality statistics relating to fall-out or contamination from nuclear waste, or the accumulation of data for a computer-bank file on all citizens of the United Kingdom. It was also suggested that when the climate of public opinion allows, British Albion may be revealed as an agency of the European Economic Community, with a variety of possible functions too numerous to mention.'

'Bleedin mad as atters, arfovem,' muttered Vaart. 'One geezer even trieder crack on it's the bleedin Russians what's running it. What as? Bleedin state-registered knockin shop? Bet e don read that one aht!'

'*Thank* you, Mr Vaart!' said Ardagh with an ironic bow. 'If you've quite finished your conversation . . .? Under any other business, there was general discussion on the advisability or otherwise of a membership drive. It was strongly represented that the membership should remain closed or at least be strictly limited, on the grounds that to widen the net would arouse speculation in management quarters. Against this it was argued by the membership secretary that from a security point of view, anyone known to be curious about the function of British Albion should be invited to join the British Albion Investigation Committee where any information they had could be co-ordinated, rather than leaving them to pursue private investigations that would arouse the suspicions of management. The matter was referred to the executive committee.'

Gryce, so frequently nudged by Vaart during these proceedings, felt like nudging him back. Aha, he might have said, at last we know why friend Seeds was at such loggerheads with Pam in the Buttery that day. Knowing that she had already taken a shine to a certain person, he was in a filthy jealous temper because he knew he was going to be over-ruled by the executive committee on the membership issue, and that that certain person would be admitted to the Albion Players, with all that it implied in the way of snogging up dark alleys.

Gryce did hope that Pam wouldn't expect him to be a leading light. The idea of sitting up there in a frock, like Grant-Peignton, or even in gaiters and dog-collar like Beazley, did not appeal to him at all. Besides, he still couldn't really see what they were all making such a fuss about. If British Albion did prove to be connected with the Government in some way, so what? With experience of the Docks and Inland Waterways under his belt, it would not be his first taste of a nationalized billet. There were worse ways of earning a living.

Ardagh, after summarizing a resolution (defeated) that the Albion Players should have their own tie or lapel badge, closed his minute-book-cum-script. Grant-Peignton, who had removed most of his rouge with a paper tissue and to Gryce's mind now looked every inch the chairman from the neck up, for all that he resembled Widow Twankey from the neck down, rose authoritatively.

'True record?'

There was a murmur of assent.

'Matters arising?'

Gryce saw several hands shoot up. A keen lot, evidently. It was the man who looked like George Formby, directly behind Gryce, who caught Grant-Peignton's eye.

'Mr Chairman, on the question of directors. I *can't claim* to have got much forrader on these gentlemen's antecedents, in fact I know no more than what we had read out to us at the last meeting, which I gather emanated mainly from the pages of *Who's Who*.'

'What is the matter arising?' snapped Grant-Peignton. Curious how he could keep order at a public meeting yet be as soft as putty when it came to preventing Vaart, Seeds and Co. from calmly taking a day off.

'The matter arising, Mr Chairman, is as follows. Several of our directors are either retired naval or army officers of high rank, or they are what you might call landed gentry with little or no experience in the commercial sector.'

'We know all that, Mr Aintree. What is the issue you wish to raise?'

'The issue I wish to raise, Mr Chairman, is this. Three of these gentlemen are known to be connected, or I should say known to have *been* connected, with certain para-military organizations known in the popular parlance as secret armies. General Parkes-Exley, to give you an instance, has received write-ups in the media as the sometime president of the LOL or League of Liberty.'

'We're going over old ground, Mr Aintree,' protested Grant-Peignton. (This was evidently so, for there was a backswell of mutterings and someone was urging the George Formby-looking speaker to put a sock in it.) 'Time is short and I must ask you to make your point, if you have a point to make.'

'I do have a point to make, Mr Chairman. I do have a point to make. The point I would make is this. Has this Committee considered that British Albion may be a front for some undercover organization with the aim of overthrowing our duly elected Parliament?'

From the groans and catcalls Gryce could guess that this suggestion, too, came under the heading of old ground. This time he really could not resist turning the

178

tables on Vaart. Poking his companion's arm, Gryce snickered:

'He should stick to playing his ukulele!'

Vaart, who couldn't have noticed the speaker's extra-ordinary resemblance to George Formby and so couldn't be expected to appreciate the joke, looked blank. 'Don know baht that, eez fuckin barmy!' said Vaart finally.

Over the interruptions, Grant-Peignton was saying firmly: '. . . really are going back on our tracks there, Mr Aintree. It has been agreed that British Albion is *not* a para-military organization, that in all likelihood it *is* a Government agency, all the evidence at our disposal points in that direction, and I really think we should go forward from there. Any other matters arising?'

Fred Astaire rose.

'What documentary proof have we got that we're working for the Government?'

'That is not a matter arising, it is a question.'

'Very well, then it's a question. What documentary proof have we got that we're working for the Government?'

Grant-Peignton wearily threw up his arms, so that in his yellow chiffon tea-gown with its full sleeves he fleetingly resembled a druid at worship.

'Mr Bellows, you of all people should know that our case rests not on the *existence* of documents but on their *non*-existence. You are, I believe, my opposite number in Central Buying?'

'For my sins, yes. As you know.'

'How do you go about buying, Mr Bellows – for example, if you're required to provide Stationery Stores with replenishment stocks of shall we say *typewriter ribbons*?'

Vaart, for once in his life, addressed himself directly to

the chair. ''E don do nuffin, that's what e does. We bin waiting for typwrier ribbons for free monf.'

'Let Mr Bellows answer the question, Mr Vaart, he has the floor and you're out of order. Mr Bellows.'

'You know very well what we do, Mr Grant-Peignton. A Purchases Order is drawn up and despatched to the Purchasing Director for authorization and processing.'

'Who is the Purchasing Director, Mr Bellows?'

'It's never been within my province to ask. A member of the board, I've always assumed.'

'Have you ever set eyes on the Purchasing Director, Mr Bellows?' (Grant-Peignton was quite the prosecuting counsel when he got going, thought Gryce admiringly. A pity he had selected, or been dragooned into, one of the female roles. An Edwardian morning coat would have been more fitting altogether.)

'No. I've never had occasion to seek him out.'

'Have you any reason for supposing that he even exists?'

'He must do, Mr Grant-Peignton, because in due course our typewriter ribbons arrive on the doorstep!'

('Where are the bleeders, den?')

'Exactly, Mr Bellows. The typewriter ribbons arrive on our doorstep. As everything "arrives on our doorstep"! And that, is it not, is the end of the transaction? Do you ever receive an invoice? You do not. Does our esteemed "Purchasing Director" receive an invoice? Come come, Mr Bellows. Can we really picture for example *General Parkes-Exley* sitting at the boardroom table and signing fiddling cheques for typewriter ribbons?'

Grant-Peignton, in between bouts of applause for this sustained piece of rhetoric, went on to ask the wretched Fred Astaire, or Bellows, whether he thought the type-writer ribbons were donated as an act of charity by Messrs Ryman's or W. H. Smith, whether alternatively they fell out of the sky, or whether there was any explanation other than that they were provided by the true employer of all British Albion personnel, which if it was not an eccentric billionaire could only be HM Government. Having brought the house down – even Vaart conceding that he was a bugger with the words – Grant-Peignton plucked at the folds of his dress, blew down his false cleavage to cool himself off, and was once more the impassive chairman.

'Any more matters arising *from the minutes*?'

'Mr Chair!'

Gryce recognized Seeds' voice. Turning round, he saw that Seeds was advancing, some would have said strutting, to a commanding position in the centre of the aisle.

'Yes, Mr Seeds?'

'On a point of information, Mr Chair. The number of fifteen subsidiary companies mentioned in the minutes as having been shown to have ceased trading should be amended to sixteen. This morning, Mrs Fawce and I travelled to Rugby, where British Albion is supposed to own a factory manufacturing we know not what but trading under the name of Binns Brothers.'

Gryce, in the pause for effect left by Seeds, who was certainly having his big moment, felt a twinge of jealousy. So that was where the two of them had got to. And no doubt they had enjoyed a pleasant lunch with a bottle of wine, either courtesy of British Rail or in some Midlands trattoria.

'Binns Brothers, Mr Chair, does not exist. There *was* a firm of that name, engaged so we're reliably informed in the reconditioning of diesel engines, but it ceased trading several years ago and the factory premises were demolished shortly afterwards, as part of a road-widening scheme.'

This, Gryce grudgingly had to admit, caused quite a

stir. He thought, though, that Seeds needn't sound quite so full of his own importance as he went on to demand: '*Is it the committee's wish* that we continue our survey of the remaining subsidiary companies?'

There were cries of 'By all means!' and 'Carry on with the good work!' Gryce was thankful when the focus of attention switched to Beazley, by dint of his rising and asking Grant-Peignton whether a brief comment would be in order. Until now Beazley had been sitting patiently enough with his gaitered legs crossed and his arms folded, like a rural dean at a public school prizegiving. But he had obviously been itching to speak: as president of a boys' club with considerable experience of this sort of thing it must have rankled with him that Grant-Peignton and not he was in charge of the meeting.

'Chairman,' began Beazley in his gruff way. 'I'm sure a vote of thanks is in order to Mr Seeds and Mrs Fawce for their efforts. Whether there's anything to be gained in pursuing these enquiries, when they might be exploring other avenues, is another matter. I think we have the general picture.'

'Would you agree with that, Mr Seeds?'

But it was Pam who answered. Quite right, too: Seeds had already had his fourpennyworth. 'If Mr Beazley is saying we're unlikely to find any subsidiary company that *is* operating, I'd go along with him. The pattern seems to be that they bought up firms that were either dead or dying, for two reasons. Originally, when they were still in the transitional stage from the old Albion Printeries to British Albion, they absorbed mainly printing companies . . .'

'S'right,' volunteered Vaart, bobbing up to address anyone who would listen. 'An then they do no more, they go an close em dahn.'

'The object there seems to have been to build up the

nucleus of a staff for British Albion without causing too much comment on the labour market. If anyone noticed they were closing down these plants as soon as they took them over, they could claim to be "rationalizing" – it was all the rage at that time.

'Then,' went on Pam, well in command of her audience: her bossy streak coming out, thought Gryce, 'as they started to expand – I mean expand in terms of recruitment – they began buying up these other shell companies. The only explanation we can think of is that it was a cosmetic operation: they wanted it to be thought that they were diversifying, because the more a large organization diversifies, the less anyone knows about what it is actually up to. I'm sure Mr Beazley is right and you can take it as read that all the firms listed in your guidelines booklet are merely names and addresses. They don't exist any more.'

The older version of Petula Clark, in the front row, got hesitantly to her feet. She looked nervous to Gryce: probably not used to public speaking but felt encouraged to have a crack by the example set by a member of her own sex.

'Excuse me, I don't know whether this has anything to do with it, but my brother-in-law, I should say my sister's brother-in-law, he lives in Aldershot.'

She paused as if this statement in itself was of significance.

'Yes?' said Grant-Peignton with an encouraging, others than Gryce might have said patronizing, smile.

'Only he goes into some of the army camps on account of his business, he's a dry cleaner. According to him, they've got a whole mock coal-mine down there, all hidden away. You go into a gymnasium, apparently, and some steps lead down from a trap-door, and when you get through this tunnel you're in a coal-mine.'

'Yes?' said Grant-Peignton again, as baffled as every-one else.

'Well you see, they're training them in case of an all-out miners' strike. Only what I'm wondering, all these firms that Mrs Fawce has been talking about, could they be doing the same thing? I mean they could be training for *anything* in these factories and that, couldn't they?'

'Madam,' replied Grant-Peignton, hitching up his skirts and bending in her direction to lend emphasis to his words, 'these factories *no longer exist*. They're simply *holes in the ground*. Our own parent company, the Albion Printeries, is a *hole in the ground*. What possible training use could be made of *holes in the ground*?'

As the older version of Petula Clark sat down, thoroughly rebuffed, Flight-Sergeant Neddyman from Gryce's RAF days was already on his feet.

'If they're all holes in the ground, why are some of them still on the phone?' Same face, different voice: the original Flight-Sergeant Neddyman had had a distinct Cornish burr.

'*Are* some of them still on the telephone?' asked Grant-Peignton.

'Cobbs and Co. of Harrow is,' replied Flight-Sergeant Neddyman, triumphantly brandishing what looked like a page torn from the telephone directory. 'Yet according to what we were told last week, they closed down over four years ago. Now I rang this number two days ago, Mr Chairman, and I was put through to a bloke who *said* he was the sales manager. That's of a firm which from what Mr Seeds tells us, doesn't exist.'

'Yes? And?'

'I gave him some cock-and-bull story about being interested in wallpaper, which is what they manufacture, and he said to write in, they couldn't deal with telephone enquiries and definitely no retail. I said what address,

184

and he said they were in process of moving premises but I could write to a Post Office box number.'

A murmur of interest went through the hall. Gryce looked towards Seeds, still standing in the aisle, in the hope of seeing him nonplussed. He did not: in fact he looked too dashed smug for Gryce's liking.

'Mr Seeds!' called Grant-Peignton. 'I'd like to get on to the business of the evening but we should really get this cleared up. We seem to have a situation whereby British Albion, where all of us are employed, is not in the telephone directory, while apparently its subsidiary companies, where *nobody* is employed, *are* in the telephone directory. Is there any explanation, briefly?'

'There is indeed, Mr Chair. I was coming to that when we were diverted to other matters.' Seeds now moved up the aisle until he was at the foot of the platform, where he turned to face the audience. He was certainly going to milk this particular opportunity for all it was worth; Gryce wondered why he didn't doll himself up as an Edwardian butler and climb up there with the rest of the gang, if he craved attention so desperately.

'It's perfectly true that Cobbs and Co. is still on the telephone. So are all the other firms. We certainly intended to acquaint you with this fact when our dossier was complete . . .'

'Dossier', indeed! Who did he think he was – MI5?

'Binns Brothers of Rugby is also on the telephone. I rang their number today. Now in each case, the procedure is the same. There is a clicking sound as the call is automatically transferred to another number, and then, as our friend rightly says, one is put through to "a bloke". Sometimes "the bloke" claims to be the sales director, sometimes the manager, sometimes he is even the official receiver. In each case, however, "the bloke" is the same

185

man. And that man, ladies and gentlemen, that "bloke", is *Mr Lucas of Personnel*.'

There would have been no use Gryce denying that this caused the biggest sensation of the evening so far. Nor had Seeds yet finished. Over the babble of exclamations and cries of '*Good – Lord!*' he was raising his voice to add, though only those nearest to him could hear, 'The reason – I say *the reason* for this charade is obvious. They want to know just how curious we are about these subsidiary companies and our curiosity is being monitored!'

Yes, thought Gryce darkly, it certainly is, and one wonders exactly who else is involved in this monitoring. He could see himself rising on a point of information. And is this Committee aware, he might ask, that Mr Seeds knows better than any of us what Mr Lucas's voice sounds like on the telephone, for the very simple reason that –

Too late. Grant-Peignton had called the meeting to order and, pointing at random into the forest of up-raised arms, had called upon someone near the back. This individual, so far as Gryce could see, did not resemble anyone.

'Mr Chairman, on a matter arising, why are all the SSTs printed in Belgium?'

The question was so absurdly inappropriate that it was greeted first with a puzzled silence and then with a volley of sniggering laughs. 'Tuh!' 'Cuh!' 'Cash!' 'Hurk!' 'Fau!' Gryce joined in. 'Sha!' Obviously the man had not the foggiest grasp of committee procedure.

Grant-Peignton, perhaps he was glad of a chance to relieve the tension after Seeds' disclosures, seemed to welcome the diversion. Indeed, he even went so far as to replace his grey-tinted wig at a jaunty angle, and strut backwards and forwards across the stage like a pantomime dame. This, as it was no doubt meant to, caused more merriment. If anyone wanted to canvass Gryce's opinion, it was that Grant-Peignton knew very well how to handle

186

an audience that had been in danger of becoming over-excited.

'How do we know that the SSTs *are* printed in Belgium, Mr Armstrong?' asked Grant-Peignton at last, with a straight face.

'Because it says so on the back cover. My question is, why don't we do this printing ourselves?'

Vaart, who was not amused, snarled loudly: 'Cos they've shut dahn all the prinnin works, avenn they?' To Gryce he added: '*Cunt!*' Not his usual sunny self by any means.

'Does that answer your question, Mr Armstrong?'

'No, sir, it does not! My question was of a rhetorical nature. They are printed outside this country for one reason and one reason only. If you will all examine your Supplementary Subsistence Tickets' – here he waved a specimen book of SSTs, rather like Mr Chamberlain waving his bit of paper on his return from Munich. (*That* was who the man looked like: Neville Chamberlain, without the moustache.) – 'you will see that they closely resemble the war-time ration book, except that they are designed for communal feeding rather than individual shopping requirements.'

'What are you suggesting, Mr Armstrong?'

'That Catering (Administration), which is processing these documents far in excess of the needs of employees, is engaged on a pilot scheme for mass feeding of the civilian population. Such a scheme to be put into effect in the event of any future war or uprising, probably the latter. Hence, Mr Chairman, the need for the utmost secrecy.'

This suggestion, perhaps because of its novelty value, caused almost as much commotion as Seeds' recent revelations about Lucas of Personnel, although Gryce noticed that there were some dissenting cries of, 'Oh, come off it' and 'A bit far-fetched, wouldn't you say?' On this occasion

Grant-Peignton ignored the clamour from the floor, favouring instead the executive committee on the platform.

'Any comments on that?'

'I suppose it's *possible* – ' began the comic gardener, speaking for the first time.

'But not probable,' said Beazley firmly, taking over with ease. 'On the other hand, it's noticeable that Catering (Administration) have never been represented at our meetings. One does begin to wonder whether they have something to hide.'

'Mrs Fawce? As membership secretary – ?'

'*As* membership secretary,' said Pam tartly, 'I've been trying *as you know* to broaden the basis of this Investigation Committee. Now that we've *finally* made a decision to do so' – she looked witheringly at Seeds, to Gryce's satisfaction – 'I certainly agree that someone from Catering (Administration) should be invited in.'

'Do any of us *know* anyone from Catering (Administration)?' asked Grant-Peignton, throwing the question to the floor. There was silence, not surprising to Gryce. The denizens of the tenth, eleventh and twelfth floors were notorious for keeping themselves to themselves.

He saw that Pam was smiling in his direction and nodding encouragingly. He couldn't imagine why: she knew perfectly well that he had been given what he believed was called the bum's rush when he made his exploratory foray into the department in question.

Perhaps she wanted him to do something 'for the cause'. Perhaps she wanted to demonstrate to Seeds that he was not the only one capable of pulling his weight, that just because she had accompanied him to Rugby it did not mean she was in his pocket. If so, the proposition was worth thinking about.

Gryce was not one to stand up to be counted but he was almost on the verge of shuffling to his feet when he heard Pam saying, rather mischievously he thought: 'I believe Mr Gryce knows one or two people up there.'

'Mr Gryce?'

Gryce, to the accompaniment of a leering wink from Vaart, rose a few inches from his seat in some confusion. 'Slightly.' He felt obliged to remain in this rather subservient crouching posture until Grant-Peignton had finished with him.

'Then perhaps we could ask you to make diplomatic approaches? Obviously you'd consult with Mrs Fawce on the best way of making representations. One has to be careful.'

Gryce sat down again, rewarded with a big smile from Pam. Grant-Peignton, having straightened his wig and made some adjustments to the bodice of his dress to show that he wished the proceedings to continue in a more business-like manner, stepped forward to face the audience at large and launched on what was evidently a set-piece.

'Thank you Mr Gryce. Ladies and gentlemen, Mr Gryce is one of our newcomers, both to British Albion and to this Committee of Investigation, the Albion Players as we prefer to call ourselves. It is to the newcomers, at this point, that I wish to address a few words of welcome and explanation. The rest of you, I know, will bear with me if – '

He got no further. There was a cry, more of a shout really, of 'Mr Chairman!' from the side of the hall. Gryce saw that a famous racing driver, seen often in road safety advertisements, was on his feet.

'On a point of order, Mr Chairman, there was someone looking in at the window!'

The resultant uproar was quelled by Grant-Peignton as abruptly as it had begun. 'Quiet! Ladies and gentlemen, nothing is to be gained by stampeding!' If Grant-Peignton had never seen service as an army officer, probably in quite a senior rank, then all Gryce could say was that it was the army's loss. He was a natural-born leader.

As all but the dozen or so who were trying to peer out of the grime-encrusted windows resumed their seats, and there was comparative quiet, Gryce thought he heard, and was then sure he could hear, the retreating sound of clomping feet on metal – the rungs of a fire escape, he would guess. Only one pair of feet he was acquainted with was capable of making such an almighty din. The silly, foolish girl!

'Mr Seeds. Ask the commissionaires to search round the back of the hall. Quickly! Mr Bellows. Take Mr Seeds' position at the doors. Mr Calloway – ' While Grant-Peignton, in his unruffled way, was barking orders, most of the cast of *The Importance of Being Earnest* were walking off the platform in an orderly manner, carrying their cane chairs. Obviously a set emergency procedure which, if Gryce was any judge, they had got down to a fine art: within seconds, only Grant-Peignton, Pam and Ardagh remained on stage.

'No need for alarm whatsoever!' called Grant-Peignton, securing his bonnet with a hat-pin. And then, without pause, he switched to the falsetto register as he turned to Pam and Ardagh.

'To lose one parent may be regarded as a misfortune . . . to lose both seems like carelessness. Who was your father? He was evidently a man of some wealth. Was he born in what the radical papers call the purple of commerce, or did he rise from the ranks of the aristocracy?'

He was word-perfect, a man of steel. Pam, her only sign of agitation being that she was fanning herself rapidly, waited for Ardagh to reply, but he couldn't find the place in his minute-book.

11

Copeland, fictitiously nursing his imaginary Asian flu, did not put in an appearance the next day. But all the partitions were suddenly, magically and unexpectedly in position. When Gryce got to the office – by common consent, there was not much point in turning up on the dot this morning, so he had rolled in at about eleven – the workmen had already been and gone. The two young men with the clipboards and retractable steel rules still lingered, but after measuring everything in sight in the evident hope of finding a partition out of true by a sixteenth of an inch so that they could dismantle the whole apparatus and start again, they too departed.

The view of Stationery Supplies was that it was remarkable how quickly the Design and Maintenance wallahs could get on with the job once it was Friday and the weekend beckoned.

Having inspected the new filing cabinet annexe and Copeland's re-sited cubby-hole by the window, with some derogatory remarks from Vaart about the head of the department now having the choice of two places for his afternoon zizz, they tested the partitions by leaning against them. The Penney twins, in skittish mood, were reminded of yokels leaning against a farmyard gate: they sang, in something approaching close harmony, a snatch of 'Old MacDonald had a farm, ee-i-ee-i-oh'. Others picked up this theme and made jokes of their own. 'Ideally,' cracked Seeds, 'we should all be chewing straws!' Badinage on these lines took them through the coffee break.

At length, however, Grant-Peignton said heavily: 'Well. *All we lack now* are our desks and chairs!' But he avoided Gryce's eye while saying it. It was very strange. The Grant-Peignton who had been in command of the Albion Players last night would have been very courteous in suggesting that the desk and chairs be found, but the suggestion would have been an order. The Grant-Peignton who was supposedly No. 2 to Copeland seemed incapable of saying boo to a goose. Perhaps it was not so strange after all: he was not being paid an executive's salary, so why should he shoulder the burden of an executive's responsibilities? Since the remark had been addressed to thin air, Gryce felt free to ignore it.

The Albion Players saga of the previous evening was not referred to by anybody, except obliquely by Beazley when he came round selling his raffle tickets – Beazley's Benefit. '*For the cause!*' he whispered with an almost Vaart-type wink as Gryce fished in his pocket for small silver. It dawned on Gryce that Beazley's boys' club gymnasium, like British Albion's subsidiary companies, was probably an elaborate fiction. But just as he was about to ask knowingly what cause he was really supporting, Beazley put a finger to his lips and moved on.

Discretion of that order made sense to Gryce. There were enemies at the door, or if not enemies then saboteurs as Pam had dubbed them, resident clowns as Gryce himself would have said. The Penney twins had been conspicuous by their absence from the meeting: one whiff of last night's proceedings and they would have it all round the office.

In the scheme of things, Beazley's Benefit was a day late: he should have done his rounds on Thursday, not Friday. But of course yesterday had been thoroughly disorganized. And it was not as if there were any other diversion to offer him competition: with Mr Hakim sunning himself in the Algarve, the Friday morning sweetstall was badly missed. It was a shame: as Ardagh suggested, in the absence of furniture Mr Hakim could have spread his wares out on the floor and brought a touch of the Eastern bazaar to Stationery Supplies.

There was a lively discussion about the dilemma faced by the department without Mr Hakim. It was agreed that it was too bad of him not to have reminded them last week that he was going on holiday. Grant-Peignton was committed to taking a box of chocolates home to his wife; Ardagh had a nephew's birthday coming up and had been relying on Mr Hakim to furnish him with a cut-price selection box left over from Christmas. Then there was the absent Copeland, who would never get through the week ahead without his supply of toffees.

It emerged that the Penney twins, for a change, had something constructive to contribute. They had been pretty thick with Mrs Rashman and had sometimes accompanied her on her lunch-time shopping expeditions. (Vaart said, 'Aye-aye' upon this being revealed.) They knew of a cut-price sweetstall in Leather Lane market. Although the discount by no means compared favourably with that offered by Mr Hakim, at least a worthwhile saving was there to be had. The suggestion was favourably received by all: a collection was made and Thelma was furnished with a list and instructed to take herself off to Leather Lane. The price of a tin of Copeland's favourite toffees was staked out of his raffle money by Beazley, who asked her to get a separate receipt.

After this excitement there was a lull. The question of the desks and chairs was raised again, this time by Ardagh who said that he could do with a sit-down and that they must be somewhere. Gryce began to feel, although it was probably his imagination, that his colleagues were looking at him reproachfully. But he stood his ground until the messenger from In-house Mail arrived with the morning's bundle of letters. They were signed for by Grant-Peignton who at once looked round in a speculative manner, quite obviously with the intention of repeating yesterday's farce of having the mail opened, sorted, and then dumped among the dirty coffee mugs in Thelma's filing tray. His eye fell on Gryce, who now wished that he had positioned himself over by the window out of harm's way, like Vaart, Ardagh and the Penney twins. Grant-Peignton, however, hesitated and then said pointedly: 'No, you already have your hands full, if we're ever to see our desks again' and turned instead to Seeds.

Mutinous rejoinders coursed through Gryce's head. 'Considering all that we heard last night,' he might have said, 'and the probability that we are working for a Government agency engaged in heaven knows what outlandish schemes, I would have thought that the absence of furniture was the least of our problems!' But he could just hear Grant-Peignton saying with good-humoured firmness, 'Mr Gryce, whether we are working for a Government agency or invaders from Mars, we would all like very much *to sit at our desks*!' Again: he could have pointed out the inadvisability of roaming about the building without a docket. But he had already tried that one on Copeland, and got short shrift.

With a martyred sigh, Gryce announced loudly: 'Well, assuming they haven't vanished into thin air . . .!' and headed for the foyer. Vaart shouted something ribald after him, he couldn't make out what, and there was a roar of laughter. Well: if he was stopped by one of the commissionaires again and asked what he was on, it would be Grant-Peignton who would have to answer for it.

As his luck would have it, after the lift had rumbled

194

down past ground level into the bowels of the building, and the doors had slid open to reveal the whitewashed brick walls of basement three, Gryce stepped straight into the arms of, or rather the one arm of, the same commissionaire who had detained him the other day. Or perhaps it was not the same one. Perhaps it was one of the three commissionaires who had been on duty at the St Jude's Institute last night, or one of the three different commissionaires – assuming they *were* different commissionaires – who when last seen had been staring vacantly into space in the entrance hall. Or perhaps the commissionaire who had detained him was a member of either or both of these groups. There was no way of knowing.

The unidentifiable commissionaire was consulting a sporting paper, expertly folded to accommodate to his disability, beneath a hanging sign that read: 'FILES DEPOSITORY. AUTHORIZED PERSONNEL ONLY'. Behind him was a desk strewn with the paraphernalia of his office: signing-in register, sheaf of what looked like authorization passes secured by a bulldog clip, ink pad and several rubber stamps. Beyond the desk, and at the other side of a metal-and-glass partition that ran the length of the basement leaving the narrowest of corridors on Gryce's side of it, were row upon row of filing cabinets. Many of them looked donkey's years old to Gryce. Those nearest to him were of the wooden variety, three drawers sliding but lacking telescopic runners, dimly remembered as No. A2A/0629 from a Comform catalogue long ago withdrawn. But there was also, in the middle distance, a fair number of the more up-to-date B4B/04885s, duo-grey metal, recessed handles. Thank goodness he didn't have to search for the Stationery Supplies filing cabinets among this lot, talk about needles and haystacks!

The commissionaire, again thank goodness, didn't ask

Gryce what he was on, or for his docket. He didn't say anything at all, merely lowering his newspaper and concentrating hard on Gryce's face as if focussing his thick lenses, like binoculars, by will-power.

'I'm *not sure* whether I'm on the right level, at all? Design and Maintenance bay?'

The commissionaire, after staring for some time at Gryce like an elementary school headmaster suspecting veiled impertinence from one of his charges, raised his surviving arm and, deploying his folded newspaper as an arrow, pointed along the corridor. This gesture was completed in silence, but was followed some seconds later by a brief verbal addendum.

'Straight on. All way round. Come to a sign that says Design and Maintenance.' He uttered the words as if debating whether Gryce would be better off having them written down on a sheet of paper.

'Thank you indeed.'

The Design and Maintenance bay, when he had followed the narrow corridor around two corners, proved to be a mirror image of the Files Depository occupying the back half of the basement. But here the rows of filing cabinets were new, unused, the very latest that Comform had to offer, with push-button drawer-retraction and 'At-a-Glance' concertina-action index system: they hadn't even been given a catalogue number when he'd left his last billet. Some department was going to be lucky. And besides the filing cabinets there were lines of new desks stretching apparently into infinity, their legs still sheathed in protective corrugated-cardboard cladding; and there were new free-standing coat-racks without number, new stacking chairs in stacks ten deep, executive padded armchairs and showroom or conference-room tables, glass-topped, pedestal, straight from the Comform warehouse. For anyone with an interest in office furniture, it was a veritable Aladdin's Cave.

The equivalent hanging sign to the one back in the Files Depository announced: 'DESIGN & MAINTENANCE/ EQUIPMENT SUPPLIES. AUTHORIZED PERSONNEL ONLY'. But to Gryce's relief, there was no equivalent commissionaire and no table where dockets would have to be shown. He passed through the grotto unchallenged until he reached, in the centre of it, a clearing some twelve feet square, fenced off by the same type of waist-high metal partition that was common throughout the building. Here, as divined by Beazley in a recent conversation, the workmen who had been such a feature of Stationery Supplies during the last few days were playing cards. At least, Gryce supposed they were the same workmen, they were like the commissionaires: interchangeable. One thing he did notice, that they had commandeered the most superior type of executive furnishings for their rest area.

He leaned ingratiatingly over the partition, waiting for attention. The game was brag and the pot a large one: Gryce had time to reflect that if anyone – Copeland – had had the wit to question the workmen about the whereabouts of the office furniture when they were per- forming their slow-motion antics up in Stationery Sup- plies, the department might by now be sitting comfort- ably at its desks again.

The dealer glanced in his direction – none of the other workmen, who were studying their playing-cards, so much as nodded – and Gryce stated his business as succinctly as he could. After the obligatory sharp intake of breath common to this class of person, the dealer said: 'Din fetch it dahn ere, mate. Inna foya, lass we saw.' Clearly he had been to the same finishing school as friend Vaart.

'Yes, I've just said – it was brought down by the night cleaners.'

'Cunna bin. Snot their job, shiftin furnisher. Sahr job.'

'Apparently there were special circumstances. Don't ask me, ask the Fire and Safety Officer.'

'Snorrupper me task nobody, mate. Gorrer nandin-over doc, avvyer?'

'A handing-over document *no*. Not with me.' That, Gryce had concluded on his way down to basement three, was no longer the insuperable problem it had once seemed. His plan was diabolically simple: identify the Stationery Supplies filing cabinets; force open the one containing his white and pink check-lists and abstract a goodly quantity of the same, if necessary concealing them under his pullover; send out check-lists to all departments at random until one rose to the bait and admitted holding stocks of obsolescent handing-over documents; follow this up with a requisition form calling-in such documents; get Copeland or Grant-Peignton in his absence to sign one such document *per pro* the excommunicado Fire and Safety Officer, and present it to the Design and Mainten-ance workmen as a fait accompli, trusting to luck that in their simple ignorance they would not realize an obsol-escent form had been palmed off on them. The scheme would take time, but it was as near foolproof as made no difference. It was certainly better than any idea Copeland had come up with.

The dealer, who seemed anxious to get back to his card-school, was as far as Gryce could make out telling him that even if the furniture had been brought to basement three, which it hadn't, he would need the required authorization to release it.

'I do realize that, it's in hand. Meanwhile have you any objection if I at least look around and see if the furniture can be located?'

'Bess fing *you* can do, mate, is inden for all new furnisher. Save yerseller lorrer bovver.'

Gryce, had he been in the mood for debating, could

have pointed out that without a requisition form to its name his department would be hard-pressed to indent for so much as a new coat-hook. He thought it more prudent, since the dealer plainly imagined himself to have delivered a devastating parting shot, to leave the matter there. The game of brag had resumed, and none of the workmen seemed to care whether he went, stayed, or set the place on fire.

As inconspicuously as he could, Gryce moved on. He now saw that beyond the workmen's rest area the Design and Maintenance bay took on a different character. Here the desks were old and broken, the chairs lopsided on their pedestal bases, the glass-topped tables cracked, the filing cabinets buckled and rusting where the gun-metal paint had flaked away. He was in an elephants' graveyard of office furniture.

Picking his way through a thicket of mildewing composition floor tiles, lengths of hardboard and plywood oddments, he was soon out of sight of the workmen. He came across a green glade of metal wastepaper bins, hundreds of them, nothing much wrong with them but presumably deemed too small since the ones now in use were bigger; and then, beyond a leaning stack of the familiar waist-high partitions, more filing cabinets. Some of them were newish, not really ready for the scrap heap yet if economy was any consideration in this establishment, which apparently it wasn't, and others of the old wooden type such as he had noticed in the Files Depository.

With a shock of apprehension Gryce realized that he had in fact strayed into the Files Depository. The two departments sharing the basement obviously converged, with no dividing wall, the junkyard of abandoned furniture and fittings serving as a no-man's-land between them.

All he could say was that security was definitely a hit-and-miss affair at British Albion. At the Albion Players' meeting last night, after the excitement caused by Thelma eavesdropping from the fire-escape – he was sure it had been Thelma, though the intruder hadn't been caught – there had been some discussion about no-go areas in the office and the Files Depository had been singled out for mention. He wondered if anybody, Lucas of Personnel to name but one, realized that you could walk into the place more or less off the street. He had better turn back.

Cursing his squeaking shoes, Gryce was about to retrace his steps – the neutral zone was fully five or six yards away, but by arching his toes so that they pressed up against the leather of his toecaps he could probably eliminate the squeak altogether – when he saw, jutting out from under the heavy base of one of the old wooden filing cabinets, the corner of a scuffed piece of paper, a bill or invoice or something of that sort that had worked its way loose from an over-full drawer. What encouraged him to pick it up was the old-fashioned lettering visible beneath the ingrained dust: –ION PRINTERIES.

It was indeed an invoice: Dr to THE ALBION PRINTERIES, Estb. 1891. Grain Yard, London Bridge SE1. A date of some four years ago, when as Grant-Peignton had recounted the place had been pulled down. And, in the badly-aligned lettering of some battered old typewriter of yore, a table of hieroglyphics recognizable only to some-one steeped in commerce: qty 12 grs rms 8093/1, qty 6 grs rms 7842/02, and so on. In the cash column was the item *as per quote* – as per agreed quotation, to the initiated.

Gryce had a head for numbers. There had been a standing joke at his last billet, that he ought to go on that television quiz programme *Mastermind* with Comform catalogue numbers as his chosen subject. The tattered invoice might have meant nothing to nine out of ten of his fellow-slaves at British Albion but to Gryce it was the Rosetta Stone. Quantity twelve gross reams 8093/1 – that was the code number of his own pink check-lists (the white ones were 8093, without the oblique digit). Quantity six gross reams 7842/02, they must be a long-obsolescent version of the holiday roster forms, the code number of the present series being 7842/14. Gryce always registered details of that kind: there was hardly a number on his master check-list that you could stump him with, wet behind the ears though he might be in terms of length of service.

What it came down to, then, was that he had stumbled across probably the very last invoice submitted by British Albion's parent company before it had been devoured by its own progeny. Gryce's first thought was that it would make a nice souvenir for Vaart, given that he was capable of appreciating such a gesture: he was, after all, one of only a handful of British Albion personnel who had worked for a time in the old building when his previous billet, Buckton's printing works wasn't it, had been absorbed in the early days of expansion. He would be able to frame it and hang it in his bathroom, always assuming there was a bathroom in whatever East End hovel he inhabited.

Gryce was about to tuck the invoice in his wallet when he noticed that the bottom portion of it was folded back. Turning it over revealed a boxed-off space for the recipient's address, designed to fit snugly into a window envelope. The recipient's address was typed in the same ill-aligned characters:

Special Supplies Division,
HM Stationery Office

– followed by an address in Slough, no doubt a Stationery Office depot of some kind.

What was it that some Doubting Thomas had asked at last night's meeting? 'What documentary proof have we got that we're working for the Government?' And Grant-Peignton had replied, had he not, 'Our case rests not on the *existence* of documents but on their *non*-existence.' Well, if that had been the case, it was the case no longer. Gryce recalled the sensation caused by Seeds when he had made certain revelations. It would be as nothing to the sensation caused by Gryce. In his mind's eye he could see himself walking up the aisle of the St Jude's Institute, turning, facing his audience, producing from his wallet the vital scrap of evidence. '. . . That documentary proof, however, ladies and gentlemen, has now to come to light . . .' Oh, yes, it would be someone's finest hour all right.

As he put the invoice carefully away in his wallet, between two pound notes, Gryce heard a footfall. It was a footfall in the literal sense, in that the foot had been raised some inches from the ground and then allowed to drop with a crash. It was followed by another. It could only be young Thelma.

'Mr Gryce!' This was in the loudest of stage-whispers. 'It's over here!'

'Thelma, you gave me the shock of my life, I thought you were supposed to be out buying sweets? And what's over where?'

He too thought it prudent to whisper. But his question was too lengthy to be comfortably sustained at such a level, and he felt ridiculous. Bubbles to it: if anyone came at least he had some semblance of an excuse, Thelma had none.

'Pardon? Oh, that filing cabinet that I keep my things in.'

Thelma's clodhopping steps led him back to the sanctuary of Design and Maintenance. Lying on its side among a clutter of old bulletin boards, fire extinguisher brackets, free-standing ash-trays and anglepoise desk lamps was a metal filing cabinet with a wisp of red wool tied to its top drawer handle.

'Well, that would appear to be Exhibit A, Thelma. Any sign of the rest of our belongings?'

'Pardon? No, there's only this, Mr Gryce.'

'How do you know?'

'They left it behind, Mr Gryce,' said Thelma mysteriously.

'"They". What do you mean, left it behind?'

'That's what the commissionaires said, Mr Gryce. They said it should have gone with the rest of the stuff and they weren't going to have it stuck in the entrance hall where everyone could see it. So they fetched it down here.'

'Meaning the commissionaires?'

'Yes, Mr Gryce.'

Yesterday morning, that must have been, before anyone except Thelma – the only one who had had sight of the blessed filing cabinet when it had been incongruously dumped among the potted plants in the entrance hall – had arrived at the office. An irrelevant image of three one-armed commissionaires manhandling a hefty metal filing cabinet flitted into Gryce's mind. They must have found a porter's trolley or barrow somewhere.

However, that was by no means the point at issue. Left behind? Should have gone with the rest of the stuff? Gone where?

'You seem privy to a good deal of information denied the rest of the staff, Thelma.'

'Pardon?'

'I'm asking how you know all this.'

'Oh, I see. I heard one of the commissionaires talking to my uncle.'

'Your uncle being – ?'

'He's one of the commissionaires.'

Gryce regarded Thelma's moonlike face. He could never decide whether it was a study in imbecility or whether blank expression concealed depths of intelligence or, what was probably nearer the mark, native cunning.

'One assumes, then, that your uncle was not among the commissionaires who denied you access to the Albion Players yesterday evening?'

'Pardon? No, Mr Gryce, he's in charge of the Files Depository.'

'Which is how you come to be prowling around here, instead of buying sweets in Leather Lane market as you were asked?'

'I was going to go in a minute, Mr Gryce.'

'I'm sure you were. Do you often come down here, Thelma?'

'Sometimes, if my uncle lets me. Depends if he's in a good mood.'

'Under what pretext?'

'Pardon?'

'The Files Depository is supposedly out of bounds except for authorized personnel. What possible excuse can you offer for being down here?'

Thelma shrugged her podgy shoulders and giggled. 'I just tell him I'm bored with nothing to do upstairs, so he lets me have a look round. See with me being just a school-leaver, nobody cares. They think I'm too young.'

'That suggests you've been having "a look round" as you put it in other departments?'

'Some of them.'

'Yes,' said Gryce, putting sternness into his voice – mock-sternness, he hoped it came out as, he didn't want to be hard on the girl but she really was going to get herself into trouble one of these days, for instance if he took it into his head to make a sudden pass at her there

204

was nothing she could do to prevent it. 'You had a good "look round" at the Albion Players' meeting last night, didn't you? Hm? You do realize you were nearly caught?'

Thelma shuffled her feet. Coming from anybody else, it would have been called stamping.

'Just wanted to know what was going on, Mr Gryce.'

'Did you, indeed? And what *is* "going on", in your considered opinion?'

'Don't know, Mr Gryce.'

Thelma giggled again, nervously this time, and then composed her features into an exaggeratedly sober expression. Looking this way and that through the petrified forest of abandoned furniture, to ensure they were not overheard, she added melodramatically: 'My dad says it's germ warfare.'

'Your dad,' said Gryce, 'is mistaken.' ('A fool', he'd nearly said there.) 'Now my advice to you, Thelma, is to get yourself off to Leather Lane at once, and don't concern yourself with what doesn't concern you.'

'Pardon? Yes, Mr Gryce.'

Waiting for the lift under the steely eye of Thelma's uncle, Gryce peered closely at his watch as if it were transmitting a lengthy telex message. It was well into the Stationery Supplies department's staggered lunch hour. He would go straight up to the Buttery, hoping that Pam would be keeping a place for him.

On last night's form, she should have eyes for nobody else at lunch-time. While the hoped-for snogging session in the dark alley next to the St Jude's Institute had not materialized, owing mainly to Gryce's having no idea how to suggest it, they had had a quick drink at the Pressings wine bar, to the exclusion, it was to be noted, of Seeds. Hand-holding had taken place and they had talked easily of making another assignation when time was less of the essence. Gryce had staggered home at ten with a cooked-up story about office stocktaking at the ready. Fortunately he had found his supper in the oven and his wife out at the pictures with a friend; how often he had seen that situation in newspaper cartoons, and now here it was in real life! That left him with the stocktaking excuse unused; he was thinking in terms of an early dinner in Soho.

But Pam was not in the Buttery. Nor was anyone else from Stationery Supplies. Standing with his plate of cold roast beef and ample portion of coleslaw, he had become quite a fan of the Salad Bowl, it really was good value, he recognized no one at all, save an unmistakable face from Catering (Administration).

The man who resembled Jack Lemmon was lunching alone, with a paperback novel propped up against the sugar bowl. He was wolfing his ham and egg pie as if his life depended on his getting through every last morsel by a certain time. Probably it did: noses were kept very much to the grindstone in his particular neck of the woods. He barely glanced up when asked whether he minded if Gryce joined him.

Gryce considered himself to have been well-briefed by Pam. 'Just work round to the Albion Players casually,' she had said. 'Quite a few people have a *pretty shrewd idea* what we're trying to do, so if they're at all interested, you can safely leave it to them to make the running once you've given them an opening.' More importantly she had added: 'Ron Seeds dearly wants to see what's in the Catering Admin files, that's why he was so taken with your safe-breaking capabilities! *I* think we're more likely to get whatever there is to be got straight from the horse's mouth.' Gryce heartily concurred.

By way of introducing himself he asked the Jack

Lemmon-looking person if he would mind if Gryce had the salt.

'We *have met*, by the by. I was the wretch who disturbed you at your labours while trying to unload some bumph on C10. In the event it turned out I wanted C12.'

Jack Lemmon grunted without looking up and turned a page. Then, as he must have judged his minimal response over-churlish even by his own standards, he supplemented the grunt with: 'Get any joy?'

'Not really. In fact, truth to tell, I got very short shrift indeed from presumably your head of department. Fellow in a chef's hat.'

'Hatch,' said Jack Lemmon succinctly.

'Yes, he did peer balefully out of a hatch. Somewhat reminiscent of a Punch and Judy show.'

'Hatch is *his name*! Clifford Hatch!' Although Jack Lemmon spoke with withering scorn, the clearing-up of this little misunderstanding well and truly broke the ice. He closed his paperback, a copy of *The Young Lions* by Irwin Shaw. This left the way open for Gryce to ask if he liked Irwin Shaw. Other authors could then be tossed into the conversation, and after that dramatists – Agatha Christie, Harold Pinter, Oscar Wilde. It would then be but a short step to mentioning the Albion Players.

'If you're going to ask me to join that knockabout minstrel troupe,' said Jack Lemmon before Gryce had a chance to put this process into effect, 'don't.'

Gryce could only describe himself as taken aback. He confessed as much to Jack Lemmon, saying that he must be a mind-reader.

'I was assuming that was what it was all about,' said the other modestly, unbending somewhat in the light of his small triumph. 'You're the third one today.'

'Oh? Really?' Gryce was keenly interested. 'Who were the other two, if it's not a rude question?'

'What's-her-name for one. Works in your department.'

'Pam Fawce.' Oh, charming. Ask someone to do a job for you and then do it yourself.

'That's her. She was sitting where you're sitting now, not five minutes ago.' Charming.

'Who was the other one?'

'Don't know his name, he grabbed me in the lift coming in this morning.'

'Did he look like Jeremy Thorpe, would you say? Passing resemblance?'

'I wouldn't say that. Tell you the truth, he looked a bit like you. Talks like you as well, you could be brothers.'

Seeds! Attempting to steal Gryce's thunder and ingratiate himself with Pam (with whom, by the way, a sharp word must be had). Well, they would see about that.

It would be rather a coup if Gryce could succeed where the other two had failed.

'Of course, when you say knockabout minstrel troupe, you're probably taking the Albion Players at their face value. Does it occur to you to wonder why three people in the space of a morning should canvass you to join?'

'It's obvious.' Jack Lemmon pushed aside his empty plate and reached for his dish of pear Melba, Gryce must try that one of these days, it looked very tempting. 'You want to know what's going on in Catering Admin.'

So much for Pam's 'Quite a few people have a pretty shrewd idea what we're trying to do.' The understatement of the year, that was. It was clearly all round the office exactly what the Albion Players were up to, they might as well print it on posters and pin them up on all the bulletin boards.

'There is,' admitted Gryce with pointless caution, 'a certain amount of curiosity in some quarters.'

'Yes, well you know what curiosity did, don't you?'

('Killed the cat,' Gryce replied to himself automatically.) 'If you lot want to get yourself fired, that's up to you, but leave me out of it. Because you are, you know, you're all going to finish up out on your ears.'

Privately, that was Gryce's opinion too. In all honesty, he couldn't argue against such a case.

Jack Lemmon had finished his pudding course with incredible speed and was picking up his paperback novel even as he dabbed strawberry syrup from his mouth with a serviette. 'And if anyone wants to know what we're doing up there, I can tell them what *I'm* doing, I'm doing my job. Listen, friend, I was out of work for eight months before I came to this place. I do my job, I work eight hours a day, I keep my head down, I draw my salary once a month and I don't ask questions. All right?'

These sentiments too were so close to what Gryce's would have been if left to himself that he could think of nothing to say. He had expected Jack Lemmon to rise and stalk off to the escalator, en route for an afternoon's grind in Catering (Adminstration). Instead, the man sat clutching his book and glowering. Perhaps he had another two minutes or so to kill before his lunch hour expired.

In the event it was Gryce who rose to leave first. A sensation of the floor vibrating told him that a person known to him had approached. True enough, Thelma was standing by his table. 'Excuse me, Mr Gryce, could I have a word with you, only I think it's important?'

Thelma, he didn't know what she thought she was playing at, she merely grinned inanely when he asked her questions, led him down the Buttery's stainless steel escalator to the first floor. 'It's through here, Mr Gryce.'

They were at the point where you either had to go down the stairs to the ground floor or up them to the second. Thelma seemed to want to get him into the foyer.

209

If she had a journey by lift in mind, he could tell her for nothing that the lifts did not function at this level.

Gryce followed her nonetheless, obediently. The first floor was new territory to him, his much discussed exploration of the premises having been mandatorily curtailed at the second. He noticed at once that there was something different about this floor, although he couldn't place what it was. The familiar glass doors led into the familiar open-plan offices – Auditing, Invoice Clearance and Data Processing according to the directory sign, though all concerned with these activities seemed to be at lunch – and, opposite, there were the three familiar sets of flush sliding doors of the lifts.

Each of the lifts had in front of it a little wooden barricade, like a novice-event showjumping fence, as a reminder that since the fuel crisis of whenever it was the lifts were no longer programmed to stop at the first floor. This was not the detail, however, that had glanced obliquely into Gryce's mind. He now saw what it was. There were not three lifts, there were four of them.

That didn't make any sense at all. British Albion was served by three lifts, it was a known fact. Yet here, sandwiched between them and the stairs, was an extra one. How could it possibly go anywhere, either up or down?

Like the other three conventional or established lifts, it had its individual call-button, to which Thelma applied her thumb. Even as Gryce opened his mouth to say, 'It's not the slightest use pressing that, Thelma, the lifts don't operate on the first floor and I beg leave to doubt if this particular specimen is a lift *at all*,' the doors slid open to reveal that this would not have been a correct appraisal.

Thelma had pulled aside the wooden barricade affair and stepped into the lift. Bearing in mind the discussion he had recently had about curiosity killing cats, Gryce now had to decide whether to follow her.

'It's all right, Mr Gryce, it only goes up one floor,' urged Thelma, as if she thought she was being reassuring. Gryce, he supposed he didn't want to lose face by appearing timid, joined her without enthusiasm.

Thelma was right, it only went up one floor, and an uncommonly long time it took about it too. More like a goods hoist than a lift. Gryce had plenty of time to notice another unusual feature: it had two sets of doors instead of one, the second lot being at right angles to the ones through which he had just reluctantly entered. He had seen lifts like this in old-fashioned department stores, where on one floor you stepped out in one particular direction and on the next floor in another.

It was this other pair of doors that slid open as the lift shuddered to a stop. Stretching before them was a narrow corridor, running parallel with the outer wall of the building in the direction of the extension housing the Buttery.

From the red-printed notices on the concrete-slab walls – 'Safety helmets to be worn', 'No naked lights' and the like, not to mention a framed copy of The Factories Act, Gryce judged that they were in a service area. This was the second floor and they were going towards the Buttery, although that was on the third. Gryce remembered what Seeds had told him about the notorious revolving mechanism by which the Buttery was supposed to turn full circle to catch the sun, although it had never done any such thing. That slab of useless machinery would be housed beneath the floor of the Buttery and it was obviously towards it that he and Thelma were heading.

So it proved. The corridor culminated in a thick steel fire-door, through which Thelma noisily led the way. Gryce did wish her parents had taught her the gentle art

211

of walking; if anyone heard her clattering footsteps there would be a great deal of explaining to do.

'Thelma, I hope you haven't dragged me all the way along here simply to – '

It was not at all like what Gryce had been expecting. Quite what he had been expecting he couldn't say: something, he supposed, on the lines of those cut-away diagrams of the clock-tower of Big Ben or the boiler-room of the Queen Mary that he remembered from the educational periodicals of his boyhood. He had half-imagined a circular structure, obviously it would be the same shape and dimensions as the Buttery, with an enormous cog-wheel thing that would be the actual revolving mechanism, plus all sorts of cranks, pistons and so on to make it go round, or not go round.

The reality was that he and Thelma were in quite a small chamber, of an irregular shape, barely fifteen feet across at its widest. Certainly there was some machinery here but it was housed in enamelled cabinets like freezers or washing machines and controlled, it would seem, by a dusty panel of buttons that didn't look as if they had been pressed for a considerable time. The age of auto-mation with all its failings.

The outer wall, what he could see of it, was indeed circular like the Buttery, and up there, let into the ceiling, was what must be the revolving mechanism. Not an enormous cog-wheel thing at all but simply what appeared to be an endless belt like the hand-rail of an escalator, a very streamlined piece of gadgetry it seemed to be. But only a few degrees of it were visible, for the rest of the chamber, a good three-quarters of it, was partitioned off up to the ceiling in what looked to be very good polished wood. Mahogany, probably.

Thelma, for all that she herself had been making enough racket to waken the dead, raised a finger to her lips and shushed Gryce loudly. Then she pointed to the mahogany-looking panelling. Gryce now saw, was just able to make out, that let into it was a door, absolutely flush with the surrounding woodwork and lacking a handle.

Gryce listened. No question: from the other side of the door could be heard the faintest murmur of voices.

Had he dared speak he would have said: 'Now look here, Thelma, I think it's high time you stopped making a hobby of poking your nose into what can't conceivably be any of your business!' He would then have turned on his heel and marched off, or hurriedly tiptoed off, leaving her to follow or not as she pleased.

Thelma was now pointing first at the battery of machinery units or whatever they were, and then up towards the ceiling, where Gryce could see that high up in the wood-panelled wall there was a ventilation grille. She wanted him to climb up and have a look through it.

Gryce shook his head vehemently. Thelma, with the kind of petulant face she probably put on when her parents told her she couldn't stay out late, began to lurch towards the tallest of the units, directly below the ventilation grille. Gryce grabbed her elbow in alarm. If she was going to clamber on the thing she might as well do a clog-dance on it and have done with it.

Hitching up his trousers he levered himself up and knelt on the enamelled top of the machinery cabinet. It gave out a hollow buckling sound that frightened him. He stayed where he was for a few seconds and then, very slowly, edged forward on his knees until he was able to stand up, which he did in gingerly fashion. Bracing his toes against the squeaking leather of his shoes, a trick it would seem necessary to dredge out of his repertoire every time Thelma was in the immediate vicinity, he raised himself on tiptoe, his face close to the grille of the ventilator.

He was looking down on what appeared to be the company boardroom. Its main feature, certainly the only one that interested Gryce, was a vast oblong conference table, around which sat some twenty or so distinguished individuals surrounded by all the impedimenta of their rank in the way of blotters, scratch-pads, agendas, individual pen-holders on onyx bases, carafes of water, well-used briefcases and the remainder. The chairman, as he presumably was, reclined judiciously in his leather boardroom chair (catalogue No. F/03777) with a gold pen balanced between his two index fingers, while the rest of them carried on a discussion. There was an air-conditioning-type sound coming from somewhere, the Buttery upstairs probably, and Gryce could not hear what any of them was saying. But he could see their faces clearly.

They were mainly military-looking people, they would be the General Parkes-Exley and other gallant souls spoken of at last night's meeting of the Albion Players. Several of them looked familiar: they had probably made appearances on television either in some hour of national crisis or to make appeals on behalf of a favourite charity.

One of the directors, as clearly they all were, looked a bit like President Carter, another looked like Dame Margaret Rutherford although he was in fact a man. An academic that one, by the look of him. A third, with his back to Gryce, momentarily half-turned to hand a paper to his companion, revealing a profile uncommonly like that of a high-ranking Cabinet minister, Gryce had never been sure of his function but he was forever in the news with his controversial speeches on this and that.

Gryce, continuing to peer through the ventilation grille, was now able to inspect this profile at greater length: apparently its owner had made a mistake and handed over the wrong paper; he seemed to be making a humorous apology as he recovered it and substituted the right one. On Gryce's part, however, there was no mistake: the man bore such an uncanny resemblance to that high-ranking Cabinet minister because, without any doubt at all, that was who he was.

Gryce had no time for further reflection. The heavy steel fire-door behind him had swung open on its not-very-well-oiled hinges: framed in its portal was a one-armed commissionaire.

Whether it was the same one who had stopped him on this very floor a few days ago, or Thelma's uncle from the Files Depository, or any permutation of the numerous other commissionaires observed both on and off the premises, Gryce did not wait to enquire. With an alacrity that in retrospect astonished him, he took a flying leap from his enamelled perch, landing by the fire-door just as the commissionaire stepped smartly forward to apprehend him. Heart thumping painfully he sprinted along the narrow corridor, desperately relieved to see that the lift doors at the end of it were open. Even in his panic Gryce was already concocting his story: that he had been quietly lunching when he had been approached by Thelma who had said that she had something to show him; he had followed her into the forbidden lift believing that there was nothing more sinister to be found than the revolving mechanism for the Buttery, which he had very much wanted to see because of a lifelong interest in anything to do with machinery.

12

Gryce's instinct was to return to the seventh floor and mingle with the rest of the gang from Stationery Supplies, the dreaded SS as they were jokingly known. But there was no gang to mingle with. In the continued absence of desks and chairs, an early start to the weekend must have been decided on by one and all.

Over and above an obscure feeling that there was safety in numbers, Gryce was particularly peeved not to find Pam. In the case of ructions, she might have proved an invaluable ally. Besides, he had much to tell her. Again, looking at it from the purely personal angle, one would have thought the woman could have put herself out a bit and waited around for a while, a visit to the cinema was very much on the agenda and they could have fitted it in very nicely this afternoon.

Gryce did not propose to spend the rest of the day propping up the partition and being gawped at by the time-servers of Traffic Control across the way. He would have dearly liked to have heard what account Thelma had to give of herself after her interrogation by the one-armed commissionaire and presumably his superiors, but there was no knowing when, or if, she would return to the seventh floor. She might have been given her marching orders for all Gryce knew. Perhaps Gryce's own marching orders were in preparation. It was not something he wanted hanging over him for a whole weekend, but on the other hand there was little to be gained from loafing about here and waiting for the axe to fall. He wished now that he had read what the guidelines booklet had to say about severance pay.

On the bus to London Bridge, Gryce tried to concoct a suitably plausible yarn for his wife about his unexpected afternoon off. If he could persuade her that he had been sent home early against the prospect of working very late indeed on say Monday or Tuesday, the projected dinner in Soho with Pam could become a reality. But he was unable to concentrate, his head was in a whirl. Every second person he saw looked like the Cabinet minister in the secret boardroom, or like the Home Secretary or the Prime Minister or whoever. The City, when he glanced out of the window as the bus paused at traffic lights, seemed to be seething with one-armed commissionaires. The conductor looked like Muhammad Ali, the woman on the opposite seat like Joan Baez the folk singer. The bus passed a wine bar: he thought he glimpsed Pam and Seeds going into it. A traffic warden on emergency points duty was Copeland, then a second later he was the actor Mervyn Johns. Crossing London Bridge, Gryce saw Mrs Rashman and Mr Hakim walking arm in arm in the direction of Southwark. He would have sworn it was them on a stack of bibles.

It was all too absurd. Mrs Rashman would be setting off on honeymoon within a day or two, she had more to do with her time than stroll across bridges with Mr Hakim, who in any case was at this moment sunning himself on the Algarve. Not that he had the simple courtesy to send his colleagues a postcard, perhaps it was not the done thing at British Albion. (Gryce would rather regret it if this were so. In previous billets, postcards from those on holiday had made a colourful display when Sellotaped to windows or the sides of filing cabinets. They had been quite a feature.)

But as the bus turned into the station forecourt after

being held up considerably on London Bridge by a brewer's dray, Gryce, clinging to the platform rail, saw them again, just crossing the road. Well, if it was not Mrs Rashman and Mr Hakim, it was their exact doubles. Such things, he well knew, did happen in life.

In the station, where the President of one of the African republics was waiting to inspect his season ticket, Gryce learned from a chalked notice on a blackboard that trains were subject to delay due to a signal failure at New Cross. He suddenly felt that he could do with a drink. He was not a drinking man by any manner of means, especially not at this hour of the day, but he had to admit that he had been getting a taste for the old vino lately. A glass of cold white wine, if pubs sold wine by the glass as he believed they did in this enlightened day and age, would steady his nerves. There was also a case to be made out for having a sausage or shepherd's pie style of thing, he had left most of his lunch untouched thanks to Thelma.

He found a Victorian-looking pub not a hundred yards from the station, quite pleasant really and they served a Scotch egg superior in every way to some of the mildewed golfballs encountered by Gryce during his lifetime. The wine was well chilled and the measure generous, by pub standards. Gryce was beginning to feel better. The fellow standing at the other side of the circular bar reminded him of someone or other, but he wasn't going to put himself to the trouble of trying to put a name to the face.

A television actor, would it be? Jephson, Jepson, some name like that? Had appeared years ago in, oh, what was it now, *Z Cars*, but was little seen these days, probably the victim of typecasting. Jefferson. No, that wasn't it either.

As Gryce tried to put the conundrum firmly out of his head he saw that the familiar-looking stranger was staring across the bar at him with the same kind of puzzled, in fact pained, expression as must have been evident on Gryce's own face. After a moment the expression turned to the relief of recognition. Picking up his half pint of lager, this Jephson or Jepson or Jefferson did a loping circuit around the bar and greeted Gryce warmly.

'Long time no see!'

'Long time no see!' echoed Gryce. In fact – it took him only a second, he never forgot a face – it had been barely a month. Of course! Parsloe, one of his partners in crime at his old billet, Comform! One of the famous Four Musketeers who had all got their redundancy notices on the same day!

There certainly was a resemblance to that *Z Cars* chap. Curious that Gryce had never noticed it in all the time he had known Parsloe.

'Funny,' said Parsloe, 'how you can see somebody you've known for I don't know how long, and your mind goes blank.'

'It's seeing them out of context,' said Gryce.

Parsloe agreed that this was so, backing up the theory with a story about giving a light to a man at a bus-stop and not realizing until later that it was his milkman. 'And I wouldn't mind betting,' said Gryce at the conclusion of this anecdote, 'that he didn't recognize you either!'

They began to gossip warmly, each one asking the other what brought him to this neck of the woods. It appeared that Parsloe, for his sins, was polishing his trouser seat at a billet known as United Products, one of those glass shoe-boxes somewhere off Borough High Street; the pub was one of his ports of call when the delights of the staff canteen palled. Parsloe had always had something of a reputation for elbow-lifting, it was what was supposed to have tipped the scales against him when the redundancies were being considered.

The news of their two other fellow-reprobates was good: one had wangled his way into local government complete with bullet-proof pension, apparently his father-in-law had been able to pull strings, and the other had taken the plunge and had emigrated, or anyway was about to emigrate when last heard of by Parsloe, to New Zealand.

Gryce did not particularly want a second glass of wine and positively not a third, but Parsloe had drained his half pint and whether Gryce bought him a drink or he bought one himself, a further round would then have to be got in by one or other of them to complete the sequence. It looked as if Gryce had let himself in for a lunch-time drinking session. He might as well relax and enjoy himself for a change.

'What happened,' he asked after he had ordered the drinks and Parsloe had thanked him and said that it was his first today, 'to that plan you had for starting up a what was it now, a *do-it-yourself shop*, was it?' Gryce in fact remembered very well what it was: Parsloe had talked of nothing else during their last days at Comform, he had become a bore on the subject. Goodness knew how much he had added to the company's telephone bill with his interminable calls to timber merchants and the like, as if they had nothing to do all day except discuss the price of materials with total strangers.

'Couldn't get the wood,' jested Parsloe. 'No, seriously, it was no joke. Whenever I found suitable premises it was a case of, oh, you'll need planning permission for change of use, and that's going to take six months at least; or the local authority hasn't yet decided whether to designate the area for future development, so come back in another ten years' time and we'll let you know. *And* to cap it all, the bank gave me back-word on the loan they'd promised, half-promised anyway, they don't want to know about the small businessman these days, simply do not want to know. In the end I gave up. I thought sod it.'

A likely story, was what Gryce thought. If you asked him, it was more a question of coming down to earth with a bang after discovering that one cannot live on pipedreams.

'So now you're with who is it again, United who?'

'Products. I was so cheesed off I just marched into the Job Centre and picked the first clerical post going. Pays the rent.'

Gryce decided against mentioning that he had done the self-same thing, Parsloe made it sound as if the Job Centre was the last resort of the damned. 'United Products, I don't *think* that rings any bells. What do you do, in a word?'

'As little as possible. No, seriously. If I told you I was in a department called Traffic Control, you'd get the wrong idea. Nothing to do with transport in any shape or form, it's supposed to be the nerve-centre of the office, keep it ticking over smoothly. Or so I'm reliably informed.'

'What I meant was,' pursued Gryce with a distinct feeling of déjà vu, 'was what does United Products do?'

'That's a very good question,' said Parsloe, setting down his glass. 'A very good question indeed.'

Gryce felt a need to breathe in deeply. He was conscious of an internal trembling which, he knew from past experience, would have an unfortunate vibrating effect on his voice. So his question, 'You mean you don't know?' did not get asked. Parsloe answered it, nonetheless.

'I can tell you what they *used* to do, if that's any help. Exports – packing, shipping, they had their own fleet, so I'm told. Then when the export market slackened off, they started to diversify. What into, I couldn't tell you.

High finance, who knows? I don't think any of us know. I very much doubt if they know themselves.'

Gryce now had better control of himself, although his forecast that he wouldn't want a third glass of wine had by now been sharply revised. He signalled the barmaid to fetch more drinks, hoping that when it came to poppying up Parsloe would remember it was his round.

'If I told you that for my sins I work in a department called Stationery Supplies,' asked Gryce, 'would that mean anything at all?'

'Good heavens small world!' exclaimed Parsloe. '*I* tried to get into Stationery Supplies at United Products, but there were no vacancies! It's on the same floor as Traffic Control!'

'The seventh, would that be?'

'What are you – psychic or something?'

'And on the other side of you is what?'

'Thingy. In-house Mail.'

'Snap,' said Gryce, adding 'Cheers!' as a broad hint to Parsloe that the barmaid was waiting for her money.

Over the next glass he and Parsloe compared notes: or rather, Gryce compared the notes that he managed to extract from Parsloe, whose interest seemed confined to the amazing coincidence that they both worked on the seventh floor of their respective offices. At Comform, Gryce recalled, he had never been noted for his intelligence.

United Products, it was clear before very long, was a replica of British Albion in all major respects, even down to its indeterminable quota of one-armed commissionaires. Design and Maintenance roamed the premises tearing down and re-siting partitions, enigmatic Services departments spent their days poring over inscrutable statistics, the Catering (Administration) floors were bureaucracy gone mad in Parsloe's opinion – yet he

222

saw nothing extraordinary about Gryce's billet being practically a facsimile of his own. 'It's the Great God Standardization' was Parsloe's view on this.

Gryce, as usual these days when he strayed from the straight and narrow, was beginning to feel drunk: he must be, or he wouldn't have ordered a fourth round of drinks. He didn't know how he was going to manage another glass, they really were generous measures.

He found that he was fighting an urge to tell Parsloe about what he had seen with Thelma in the secret chamber under the Buttery, not ninety minutes ago. He had better not, for one thing Parsloe wouldn't believe him. But he did very much want to tell him something. Even if Parsloe's hair could not be made to stand on end, at least it might be possible to shake him out of his complacency.

'Tell me, on the social front, does your billet go in for *amateur dramatics*, anything in that line?'

'Funny questions you do ask. Why, d'you think I've missed my vocation in life? *To be or not to be!* No, seriously: there's a social club of some kind, but what they get up to I've no idea. Not my style.'

'You haven't been invited to join?'

'Haven't *wished* to join, wouldn't join if they paid me! For one thing who wants to spend his evenings in a draughty church hall, and for another it's miles out of my way. Up your end, somewhere, other side of the river.'

'The St Jude's Institute?'

'Could be, not sure.'

Gryce, talking in what he hoped were measured, rational tones, furnished Parsloe with a brief outline of the Albion Players and their purpose. Perhaps he told it badly, it was difficult to marshal his thoughts with all this drink sloshing about inside him, but Parsloe didn't seem very impressed. In fact downright scathing was what Gryce would have said.

'The Goverment? You must be out of your tiny Chinese! What makes you think you're working for the Goverment?'

Gryce gulped down the last of his wine and suppressed the belch that would have surely brought it up again, thank God the bell had rung for 'Time'.

'It isn't a question of thinking, *it's a question of knowing*!' He hadn't wanted to show Parsloe his Albion Printeries invoice, you never knew who he might blab it out to, but there seemed no alternative. He unfolded it carefully, noticing that until he closed one eye the bigger words on it were out of focus.

'Grain Yard, London Bridge, SE1,' read out Parsloe woodenly. Instead of looking at what it said about HM Stationery Office, where Gryce was pointing, the fool was staring at the printed lettering of the billhead. He was probably as drunk as Gryce was. 'I know Grain Yard very well, curiously enough. I take a short cut along there when I go to the Crown Inn. As is sometimes my wont. Very nice riverside pub, you can drink on the patio.'

'Then,' said Gryce sulkily, taking the invoice back and folding it over so that Parsloe couldn't possibly miss what he wanted him to see, 'you'll be familiar with the hole in the ground that is all that remains of Albion Printeries. Assuming it hasn't been built on.'

'Hole in the ground?' echoed Parsloe. He was now looking at the Stationery Office address part, but simply not taking it in. 'What are you talking about, hole in the ground? It's still there!'

'Albion Printeries, we're talking about.' It was Gryce's turn to let his mouth fall open stupidly.

'Albion *Printeries*! Ramshackle place, broken windows, has a big wooden sign up. I've passed it many a time. It may be *falling* down,' said Parsloe, 'but it hasn't been *pulled* down. I can assure you. I can take you to it if you like!'

'I wouldn't want to take you out of your way,' said Gryce thickly, putting the invoice back in his wallet. He was feeling sick. Too much wine and too much excitement.

He excused himself abruptly and descended to the Gents'. When he returned it was in the expectation of Parsloe having gone, otherwise he would have taken care not to re-emerge dabbing sweat from his forehead with a piece of lavatory paper.

Parsloe, after saying that he should have been back hours ago, made the usual suggestion that he and Gryce must not lose touch but must have lunch sometime, he knew of a really good Japanese steak bar. One's former colleagues always made these overtures and they never came to anything, but Gryce felt that he should go through the motions and he said that he would give Parsloe a tinkle.

'Ah. By all means ring me at home but if you want to get me at the office it's *rather difficult*. Sounds ridiculous I know but they're not in the book. I gather all the best firms are ex-directory these days!'

Gryce fell asleep on the train home and went past his station. Quite a day. Had he kept a journal, he would have been hard-pressed to squash the morning's events in a single page, or third of a page as it was in his Lett's Businessman's Diary.

'Have you told anyone else?'

'No one.'

He was beginning to regret, in fact, having told even Pam. She had of course been gratifyingly fascinated by all that he had to report and had at once said that this

225

called for a special meeting of the Albion Players, just as soon as she had passed on his information to her executive committee. But now Gryce saw that his thunder had rather been stolen. It would be Grant-Peignton, it was to be supposed, who would break the news. Due credit would have to be given to Gryce and probably he might even be invited up on the platform, but that was not quite the same as making a world-shattering announcement of his own as he had dreamed of doing. He had even meant to introduce Thelma so that she could take her own little bow and, of course this really was wishful thinking, he had entertained hopes of inveigling Parsloe into coming along as a guest or visiting delegate, so that when the doubting Thomases began to scoff at what Gryce had to tell them about United Products, he could be pulled out of the hat like a convert at a revivalist meeting.

It was now Monday. It had been a funny old day so far. Gryce, not so fearful as he had been of the possible consequences of being caught red-handed in the secret room under the Buttery (perhaps he hadn't been recognized, perhaps Thelma hadn't given him away, perhaps the management would deem it politic to pretend that he hadn't seen what he had) was the first to arrive. Although he was itching to talk to Pam, he had a long time to wait. Office discipline had gone to pot in the last week and it was half-past ten before any of his fellow-toilers deigned to put in an appearance; then, of course, Grant-Peignton had to go and monopolize Pam's attention with a blow-by-blow description of a visit during the weekend to a new gardening centre in of all places Catford. This was in Gryce's home territory and Grant-Peignton tried to include him in the conversation on that account, but Gryce was not having any.

There were some noticeable absentees from the dreaded SS this morning. Copeland had still not seen fit to return, and Vaart and the Penney twins were also on the missing list. More significantly from Gryce's point of view, so was Thelma. She was given to spending up to forty minutes in the lavatory in the early part of the morning, so, while naturally anxious to see her and compare notes, he had not really noticed her absence until the others began to drift in and clamour for coffee.

It could be that she was ill, or pretending to be: office juniors could be expected to take off one day in ten so Gryce had observed, so Thelma was about due for one. Or, the fact had to be faced, she could have been sacked.

Her uncle down in the Files Depository would have knowledge of her movements if anyone did, anyway it was worth a try. Gryce was not at all keen on this approach: in the first place, what if it proved to be the same commissionaire who had caught him and Thelma where they had no right to be? Gryce's concern would then suggest that he was more deeply involved with the wretched child than was the case; in the second place, there was no way of knowing that the commissionaire now on duty would be Thelma's uncle at all, perhaps they divided their work up on a roster basis. That could get him into even deeper water.

But it had to be faced if Gryce was to get a moment's peace. Waiting until everyone's attention was seized by an illustrated catalogue which Grant-Peignton had brought from his precious gardening centre, he sidled off to the lifts and down to basement three.

There was no commissionaire at all on duty outside the Files Depository. Gryce, had he so wished, could have waltzed in and microfilmed every blessed document in sight. Monday Disease had obviously claimed another victim: from the number of absentees one could almost imagine it was a public holiday.

Back on the seventh floor, Gryce found his colleagues,

227

his *few remaining* colleagues he should say, getting increasingly restive about the non-appearance of Thelma. Ardagh was positively indignant. He said that for Copeland, Vaart and the Penney twins to take French leave was one thing, they were paid to perform certain duties and if those duties could not be performed it was no skin off anyone's nose whether they turned up or not. Thelma was in a different category, she was supposed to attend to the department's needs. After taking an hour to run a five-minute errand on Friday, she had been told that she might leave at lunch-time (here Ardagh looked accusingly at Grant-Peignton). She now clearly had the fixed impression that she could come and go as she pleased. It was too bad.

Pam, during this diatribe, had taken matters into her own hands and gone out to the vending machine in the foyer to fetch coffee for all. That, in Gryce's view, was uncommonly civil of her and it did not warrant the barrage of cat-calls and comments from the denizens of Traffic Control upon her return. 'Don't overstrain yourself' and 'Tell you what, you get our coffee and we'll lend you our chairs!' were among the remarks made. Barracking of this kind from the other side of the partition had become commonplace since the disappearance of the furniture. Even the Traffic Control junior, the African-looking girl, had been heard to say, 'All right for some' on more than one occasion.

Grant-Peignton, clearly stung both by Ardagh's innuendoes and by the chaff from Traffic Control, seemingly wished to take it out on Gryce. 'I suppose it goes without saying that our desks and chairs have yet to be traced?' Gryce, editing out all reference to Thelma, gave him a summary of his expedition to the Design and Maintenance bay on Friday morning.

'So no progress has been made?'

'I'm afraid that's about the size of it.'

'Then it seems there's nothing to be done until the return of either Mr Copeland or the Fire and Safety Officer, whichever be the sooner. This is a management matter now and completely out of my hands. If any of you wish to stay here twiddling your thumbs for the rest of the day, that's a matter for you. For myself, I have no intention of providing a free sideshow for our hardworking friends next door.'

Grant-Peignton said this quite loudly so that he could be heard in Traffic Control. There were one or two people in that department whom Gryce had recognized at the Albion Players' meeting and it was clear that their chairman's shaft had gone home, for they ceased their grinning and gawping at once.

After expressing the hope that it would not be too much to ask for his colleagues to turn up tomorrow, in case their head of department should choose to do the same, Grant-Peignton put on his coat and left. He was quickly followed by Ardagh, leaving only Pam, Seeds, Beazley and Gryce.

Before Seeds and Beazley could draw Pam into the inquest which they immediately began on Grant-Peignton's somewhat temperamental performance, Gryce touched her elbow and drew her to one side.

'*I have to talk to you as soon as possible. It's very urgent.*' As he whispered the words it occurred to him that it was the kind of thing she ought to be saying to him, not of course that she had yet been given cause to.

Pam nodded briefly, perhaps she had already guessed there was something in the wind, and turned casually to Seeds and Beazley to say that she was going with Gryce to Hatton Garden to choose an anniversary present for his wife. Pam could be very glib when she wanted: still, it

229

did mean she could be relied on to cope with a suspicious husband if, touch wood, the need arose.

Twenty minutes later they were sitting in a small Frenchified restaurant in Soho which Gryce had once or twice passed but never been in before. Glancing in through the net-curtained window at the tables for two with their chequered cloths it had seemed to him to be just the place to get an affair off the ground. It was a shame that Pam and he would be talking mainly shop.

He had rehearsed his material in chronological order: starting with the aperitif of what Thelma had overheard about the missing furniture – not much to go on there, but Pam might have a theory – he would produce (with a flourish) the Albion Printeries invoice, hinting that that was not the end of the story by a long chalk, and then digress to the hidden lift that served only one floor, the boardroom under the Buttery and the presence at its table of the important Cabinet minister; after that he would bring in Parsloe. The sting in the tail could be either United Products, that mirror-image of British Albion, or the not-pulled-down-after-all printing works in Grain Yard, he would have to play it by ear.

In the event, the restaurant service was so bad that he had to break off many times to have dishes they had not ordered sent back and to ask if there was any possible chance of the wine he had selected arriving before the dessert. A harassed waiter cleared away the Albion Printeries invoice along with their soup plates and Gryce had to retrieve it from the kitchens. He found himself backpedalling on his narrative and in the end it came out all in a jumble. But Pam listened intently, prompting him from time to time with intelligent questions, and finally congratulated him on his detective work.

'And you're absolutely sure you've told nobody?'

'Absolutely.' Gryce was emphatic. Perhaps he had told

Parsloe more than he ought to have done, he couldn't remember, but Parsloe didn't count.

'I'm *not sure* how much of this we ought to reveal at this stage,' Pam mused, after saying that she would have to get the executive committee together as soon as possible. 'If Thelma's been questioned, as she must have been, then obviously we're in one of those they-know-that-we-know and we-know-they-know-we-know situations. So it can't do much harm to call the Albion Players together and tell them about this boardroom business, it might lead to some interesting theories. As regards the rest of your fascinating saga, my *gut feeling* is that for the moment the executive committee ought to know and nobody else.'

'You think it might "get back", to quote Ron Seeds?'

'I'm quite sure it would. I can't prove it, who can, but I'm absolutely sure that someone's been planted on us to keep tabs on what we're doing. Everything gets back to Lucas, I'm convinced of it.'

'In effect a spy in the camp?'

'It sounds melodramatic, but there are spies all over the office. It would be very strange if we weren't harbouring at least one in the Albion Players.'

Gryce, despite the incompetent service which harassed him, was hugely enjoying himself. Pam was already considerably impressed by what he had had to tell her and unknown to her he had one more trick up his sleeve. He ordered coffee, or rather failed to order it since the waiter hurrying past ignored his signal, then said nonchalantly:

'There is of course always the possibility that the cuckoo in the nest is the very last person you'd suspect, in other words, truth is often stranger than fiction.'

'Someone on the executive committee, you mean? I

231

hope not. We've worked together a long time and we trust one another. You have to trust someone.'

'Not on the executive committee but someone you've worked with closely. Would it surprise you to hear, my dear Pam, that your spy is no other than our mutual friend *Mister Seeds*?' Gryce said this rather effectively he thought, making it sound like a throwaway remark.

'Don't be ridiculous,' said Pam. 'He's the most hard-working, loyal member we've got.'

'*Is he*, indeed?'

Gryce had read in detective novels how this or that character gives 'a hurried explanation' of some important clue. He tried to give Pam a hurried explanation of what he had heard on Seeds' telephone, on the evening he had picked it up and recognized the voice of Lucas of Personnel commenting on his own involvement with the Liberal Club in Forest Hill. He must have made the explanation too hurried, for Pam kept saying things like 'I'm sorry, you've lost me' and 'Just a minute – what time was this?' until he had completely lost his thread. In the end she had to take him through the story by a process of question and answer, and after all that she burst out laughing.

'You silly juggins, that call wasn't for Ron Seeds at all! It was for the foreman of the night cleaners, they come on duty as soon as we've gone home!'

'I fail to see,' said Gryce huffily, 'why the foreman of the night cleaners should be interested in my political affiliations.'

'Because he's one of Lucas's stooges, isn't he? Ask Jack Vaart. He went back one evening to pick up a raincoat or something and found him searching through all the desks with a bunch of master-keys – that was in the palmy days when we *had* desks. He pretended he'd been told to look for stolen property but of course we knew what he was after. Anything that we might have unearthed and had squat away – such as your invoice.'

Pam picked up the invoice, unexpectedly kissed it – a surrogate kiss for himself was how Gryce read it – and put it in her handbag.

'Don't look so woebegone, you've done splendidly. A large brandy is called for and then we'll go and stare at the Albion Printeries, I don't know what to make of that *at all*.'

'Nor can I. What I also don't understand is why Grant-Peignton should have made such a point of saying it had been pulled down years ago. You don't suppose *he's* the nigger in the – '

'No, I don't, you've got spies on the brain. He said that because he believed it. We all believed it, we believed it because we didn't check. What we want to know now is who put the story about in the first place. And why.'

They took a taxi to Grain Yard, why not, it was an occasion. And it gave Gryce the opportunity for holding Pam's hand which he did quite brazenly, without any accidentally-on-purpose brushing of sleeves. Must be the brandy.

Watching the clock tick up faster than he'd thought possible, they'd only gone fifty yards and he could already kiss goodbye to sixty pee, Gryce said: 'It may be only a side-aspect but I'm rather worried about young Thelma.'

'So am I.'

'Do you suppose she's been given the Order of the Boot?' He hoped his anxiety for himself on that score didn't transmit itself to Pam.

'It's very difficult to get fired from British Albion,' said Pam to Gryce's relief. 'All sorts of rigmaroles to be gone through, I don't think it's ever been done.'

'Then what can have happened to the girl? She can't have been kidnapped.'

233

'Let's hope not,' said Pam, in the mysterious way she sometimes had.

Gryce had already paid a brief visit to Grain Yard on his way to the office that morning, just to satisfy himself that what Parsloe had told him was true, he would have looked a bit of a fool if he'd dragged Pam all this way and then found a hole in the ground. It was a cobbled, mews-type thoroughfare in the form of a crescent, connecting two down-at-heel streets, more alleys really, near the river. It was an area of old warehouses, most of which had fallen into disuse, although here and there could be seen signs that a modest regeneration might be on the way, of the kind that had taken place in the vicinity of the Pressings wine bar. Grain Yard itself consisted mainly of small workshop-looking places, some of them long ago closed down, others seemingly on the verge of it, a few perhaps recently re-opened. The wide doors of one or two of the surviving premises were thrown open, or propped open since they seemed to be falling off their hinges, to reveal dumps of carboys or used tyres. Behind other splintering doors could be heard the sound of sawing and hammering or the whine of small machines, power-drills they sounded like.

Albion Printeries, as stated by Parsloe, was identifiable by a big wooden sign, its elaborately serifed lettering blistered almost into oblivion. The sign surmounted a squat single-storey building that reminded Gryce of the gate-lodge of the Victorian hospital, believed to have once been a workhouse, where his mother had died. A gate-lodge, indeed, was what it effectively was, for adjoining it was a high stone arch with iron gates secured by chains and a big rusted padlock. This led into an old brick-paved yard beyond which could be seen a corner of what must be the printing works proper.

'This would have been the despatch and delivery office,'

said Gryce. 'I expect many a horse-drawn van has drawn up here in days gone by.'

'Very romantic,' said Pam, rattling the gates. 'The question is, can we get in?'

Gryce, to his own satisfaction, already had the answer to that one. The gate-house affair's two windows were smashed and boarded up on the inside with planks, so there was no access there; but the door between them looked a better proposition. It was locked, of course, Gryce had already checked, but its paintwork had flaked away leaving it vulnerable to the weather, and the surrounding woodwork was spongy to the touch. One good shove, Gryce reckoned, would do it.

Prudently, he reminded Pam that on the other hand there was such a thing as breaking and entering.

'I don't see how we can break and enter a building that doesn't officially exist,' retorted Pam cheerfully, and to Gryce's distress put her shoulder to the door. If she hadn't been so impetuous he would have told her to take a good look up and down Grain Yard to see if anyone was coming. Another thing: breaking open doors was man's work.

They were in a square room with a linoleum-covered counter, the goods counter it would be, running at right angles from the door, which Gryce had hastily shut behind them. There were no other furnishings, but a good deal of debris. The planks at the broken windows were ill-fitting and pale shafts of light fell across piles of paper and old cardboard boxes strewn about the floor. There was another door in the blank wall opposite but it was more solid than the outer one and very firmly locked. It would lead, both Pam and Gryce supposed, into the brick-paved yard approaching the printing works.

'Nothing much here,' said Pam, picking up and discarding a handful of crumpled papers. Old-fashioned letter-heads they were mainly, some of them with engravings of factories or of the medallions won at trade fairs by the products advertised. No wonder the place had gone bust, thought Gryce, their concept of commercial stationery design had not budged one iota since the latter half of the nineteenth century.

Pam shook the unyielding inner door impatiently. 'What we want is a good bunch of skeleton keys.'

Gryce was feeling edgy. Having worried about breaking into enclosed premises he was now worrying about getting out of them unseen. He had just stood in some sticky black stuff, printer's ink it would probably be, grown tacky with age; he had a vision of leaving a trail of black footprints all the way along Grain Yard.

'At least we've established that the Albion Printeries is, or are, alive if not well, and living in Grain Yard,' he said with forced chirpiness. 'I don't *really* see what else there's to be done at this stage.'

'Don't you?' asked Pam on what Gryce was very much afraid was a husky note. She was very close to him: had, in fact, been close for most of the time but was now even closer. 'I didn't tell you in the restaurant but there's another reason why I don't want anyone else to know about this place just yet.'

Gryce could think of nothing at all to reply except, 'Really?' which he did with a nervous snigger.

'I know it isn't exactly the Ritz,' said Pam, putting her arms around his neck. 'But it does save us from signing in as Mr and Mrs Smith, doesn't it?'

It hadn't been all that brilliant, from Gryce's point of view, more of a two-minute scuffle really. Time and place were to blame: it was his first experience ever of sex before nightfall, and a nest of old cardboard was hardly one up on the conjugal bed he was accustomed to, not that it had been all that conjugal of late or indeed

236

ever. But Pam seemed to have enjoyed herself. She had thrashed about a lot and moaned rather more loudly than was advisable, considering that anyone could walk in from the street. Gryce nestled her in his arms, wondering if any of that printer's ink stuff had got on his clothes and trying to think what he would say to his wife if she found any trace of what had been going on. As always when in an office context he had difficulty in conjuring up his wife's face, in fact he couldn't conjure it up at all this time. What was even more unsettling, he couldn't even remember her name, try as he might. It had gone, completely. Did that mean he was in love with Pam?

'I think we'd better make ourselves respectable,' Gryce whispered, when he felt that the post-coital nestling period had been done full justice to. He scrambled to his feet and adjusted his clothing, noticing in the dim light a black mark on Pam's discarded knickers where his shoe had scuffed against them. Well, that was her problem rather than his, but it was only fair to warn her.

'I'm afraid I seem to have been treading what looks suspiciously like printer's ink all over the place . . .' He lifted up his foot to see how bad the damage was as regards himself. He had seen worse, it would wear off in time. What was interesting, though, was that stuck to the patch of black tarry stuff on the sole of his shoe was a small, octagonal wedge of paper, a folded-up toffee wrapper it looked like.

13

It was about four the next afternoon when Gryce paid his next visit to Grain Yard. No one knew he was going, not even Pam: if there was anything to be sniffed out he wanted to do the sniffing himself, and then present her with another fait accompli. 'Quite the little Sherlock Holmes,' he could hear her saying admiringly.

He was quite fagged out. Not only did his bones ache from yesterday's exertions on that pile of old cardboard, but it had been a long day of loitering about with absolutely nothing to do. Doing nothing, Gryce had found as he went through life, was very tiring.

He had reported for duty as fervently requested by Grant-Peignton, a little later admittedly, only to find Stationery Supplies utterly deserted. Not a soul there. The only sign that the entire department was not on permanent holiday was a Xeroxed notice which had appeared on the bulletin board: 'Albion Players. Extraordinary Meeting at Six pm. To Discuss Important Cast Changes. All Members Requested To Attend If Poss.' Signed: G. M. Ardagh, Secy.

One of the amused supernumeraries of Traffic Control volunteered the information that Pam, Seeds, Ardagh, Beazley and Grant-Peignton had arrived more or less on the dot, the rest of the crew being absent without leave as per usual. Seeds was somewhere about the place distributing the Albion Players notices, but the others had no sooner arrived than they had cleared off again. The Traffic Control supernumerary advised Gryce to do the same, adding that some people had all the luck.

Gryce was puzzled until he recalled that all the colleagues mentioned, with the exception of Seeds, were members of the Albion Players executive committee. What it boiled down to was that Pam would have carted the others off somewhere to brief them on everything she had heard from Gryce yesterday. He was, in a way, rather relieved not to see her this morning: after yesterday's little romp he was not sure how to conduct himself. Was one supposed to wink, smile knowingly, whisper a few sweet nothings or carry on as if nothing had happened?

On the Grain Yard question, Gryce was hazy as to whether Pam meant to tell the executive committee about the Albion Printeries or not. In the Soho restaurant she had said, 'My gut feeling is that for the moment the executive committee should know and nobody else,' but before they sank down on that pile of cardboard it had been a case of, 'There's another reason why I don't want anyone else to know about this place just yet,' followed by the remark about it not being exactly the Ritz. Perhaps she had been speaking in the heat of the moment. To play it safe, Gryce would assume that she was taking Grant-Peignton and Co. on a conducted tour of the Albion Printeries, or as much of it as could be seen, so he had better wait until they came back to the office before pursuing his enquiries. Gryce fingered the octagonal little wad of paper in his side pocket, still sticky from its coating of printer's ink. How Copeland fitted into the jigsaw he had not the slightest idea, but it would be a feather in his cap if he could find out something else that Pam and the others had missed. Mr Hawkeye in person, some of them would say.

Presently Seeds returned from his wanderings. To Gryce's satisfaction it was evident that Pam had kept him completely in the dark, for all that the pair of them were as thick as thieves. A murmured 'Apparently something's

239

in the wind,' with a discreet nod towards the Albion Players notice, was all Seeds had to offer.

Gryce, there was no point in not being civil and he did have the whole morning to kill, suggested that he and Seeds should go out and see if there was any establishment nearby that served coffee and digestive biscuits. But Seeds wouldn't hear of it. 'I promised Grant-Peignton I'd hold the fort. If the management start enquiring why the dreaded SS has ground to a halt in the past week, it's going to look *rather bad* if there's nobody here.'

'Who is or are the management exactly?' Gryce enquired. 'One keeps hearing that the management might do this and the management might do that, but so far as one can see there isn't any management in sight, unless you count heads of department. The office seems to run itself.'

Seeds frowned and jerked his head towards Traffic Control, indicating that this was Albion Players talk and that walls, or rather partitions, had ears. Gryce and he got themselves coffee at the vending machine and, choosing the window-ledge of Copeland's cubby-hole to lean on as being farthest away from the grinners and gawpers, began to talk on neutral subjects. Their shared interest in bus routes saw them through until lunch-time. They ate together in the Buttery where the conversation turned to Indian and Chinese food. After lunch they were prompted by a butter stain on Seeds' tie to compare notes about dry-cleaning establishments. They had nowhere near exhausted this subject when, at half-past three, Pam, Grant-Peignton and the rest trooped back, looking serious but smug. Gryce, after treating Pam to an intimate smile which he feared came out as more of a leer, promptly put on his raincoat, saying that he had to see a man about a dog before the Albion Players' meeting.

Now he was back in the gate-lodge or despatch office

or whatever one chose to call it in Grain Yard, with its linoleum-covered counter, its litter of old billheads and its nest of flattened cardboard. Squalid, it looked on renewed acquaintance. Sordid. The patch of tacky printer's ink was over here, by the inner door, not of course that it followed that the toffee-paper Gryce had found adhering to his foot had been in the same spot; once the ink was on his shoe he could have picked it up anywhere in the room. But the inner door was worth a closer examination than he had given it yesterday.

The door knob, as he had surmised, was shiny from recent use. With the outside door you couldn't tell one way or the other, it had a corroded iron handle that gave nothing away. But this one was brass, and gleaming where it should have been thick with dust. Pam, of course, had rattled it, but she hadn't got dust on her hand or she would have said something about it, she was fastidious about things like that if not about where she engaged in extra-marital relations. This room was frequently used as a passage to the printing works, was Gryce's guess, it would be less conspicuous than unchaining the gates. He tried the door knob as Pam had done, and this time the door opened.

Gryce found himself out in the worn brick-paved yard with an uninterrupted view of the printing works a few yards away, a soot-grimed old nonconformist chapel of a place with high arched windows. Those windows hadn't been in view when he and Pam had caught their glimpse of the building from outside the gates, so it was only now that he saw they were not shuttered and boarded-up as he'd expected, not one of them. He wouldn't swear it was new glass in all those windows, but it was certainly glass that had had a good clean.

Staring up at the roof, he didn't know what he hoped to see up there but he did note that some of the slates had been replaced, he heard a noise like one of the drayhorses that must have clattered over this brick-paved yard many a time. Gryce lowered his gaze to the church-porch-like entrance of the printing works. Thelma was loping towards him, a sly, silly grin on her face.

'Mr Copeland says would you like to come in for a minute, Mr Gryce.'

Before passing through the doorway and finding not a gutted factory but what looked like a fully-operational printing shop Gryce lowered his gaze to the church-porch-like entrance of said that Thelma was the last person he expected to find in the vicinity of Grain Yard. This assessment was quickly revised when he saw the Penney twins waving inanely from a gantry overlooking a sturdy Wharfedale press, its name embossed on an iron plaque such as Gryce had seen on the cabs of steam locomotives, that dominated all the bits and pieces of machinery surrounding it. The fact that the Penney twins were wearing identical workmen's dungarees made them look more like Tweedledum and Tweedledee than ever.

Three other men, all wearing brown dust-coats, were sorting out cases of type arranged in sloping cabinets like the newspaper racks in a public reading room. Two of them Gryce didn't recognize but the third, who looked far more at home in the garb of a warehouseman or shopfloor overseer than in his usual business suit, was Vaart. He too waved and called out a word of greeting that Gryce didn't quite catch – probably 'Wotcher, cock' if he knew his Vaart.

Moving a little further into the iron-girdered hall – Thelma, still simpering idiotically, seemed to be trying to edge him towards the big Wharfedale printing press – Gryce saw that there were yet another three men present, although only their heads were visible by reason of their being in a deep trench where they seemed to be laying or repairing electric cables. This work, while being expertly carried out by the look of it, was a three-handed operation rather than a six-handed one: for as Gryce looked down into the trench from the narrow plank traversing it, he saw that each stooping toiler sported an empty shirt-sleeve tucked into braided trousers. Neatly folded on the clay and rubble of the excavations were three uniform jackets, surmounted by three peaked hats.

Nor had he yet been waved to, or nodded at, or in the case of the three one-armed commissionaires ignored by, the Albion Printeries' full complement. Beyond a bank of what at a guess were Linotype machines, like old-fashioned dentists' chairs with all sorts of inky-looking devices attached, was a glass-partitioned area, presumably the works office. Moving about in it, they seemed to be assembling stacks of blank paper on shelves, could be observed the figures of Mrs Rashman and Mr Hakim. The sight of them was comparatively unsurprising to Gryce: if he had found someone to take his bet that he had seen them crossing London Bridge the other day, he could have been the better off by a large sum of money.

Copeland was not yet visible. Gryce was not sure what he would have to say to him when he did become visible. He hadn't expected to find all these people, he hadn't even expected to find Copeland himself – only evidence more substantial than a folded toffee wrapper, perhaps, that he had been here. Gryce's private theory, which he had not voiced even to Pam, had been that the old printing works was being used as a store for large quantities of secret documents, perhaps the millions of identity cards mooted in the minutes of the Albion Players the other night. If that were the case, it would make sense for the head of Stationery Supplies to be in charge of it. But it patently wasn't so. Although a majority of those present were from Stationery Supplies, they didn't look in the least secretive. What they did look was as if they were thoroughly enjoying themselves, like children turned loose on an enormous John Bull printing outfit. Gryce could see neither rhyme nor reason in it.

'It's Mr Gryce,' announced Thelma, addressing a pair of scuffed shoes that protruded from under the printing press. The owner of them was lying face upwards on a low-slung trolley affair, of the kind used by mechanics when inspecting the undersides of motor vehicles. Propelling himself into view with oil-stained palms, he revealed a pair of filthy, tattered dungarees and a countenance so smudged with ink and grease as to be unrecognizable to Gryce.

'Ah, Mr Christ. I'd better not shake hams, but allow me to bid you welcome to the Albumen Penises. Now let me see, I believe you know most of us . . .?'

As Copeland rose to his feet, wiping his hands on what looked to Gryce like an old vest, the Penney twins descended from their gantry and Vaart and the other two men in the brown dust-coats drew nearer, forming a semi-circle around their visitor, or unwelcome intruder, depending in which light they saw Gryce's arrival. Copeland, it had to be said, seemed friendly enough.

'I *don't think* you've met Norwich Terrier. Mr Terrier, Mr Christ.'

'How do you do?' Norwich Terrier, now known to be Norman Ferrier, and supposedly convalescing in the West Country after a heart attack or dicky ticker as Vaart had termed a condition clearly as fictitious as Copeland's Asian flu, gravely shook hands. He was what Gryce would have called a studious-looking man, stoop-shouldered, with some resemblance to the middle-aged Robert Donat in *Goodbye, Mr Chips*. A type more likely to be found behind the counter of a secondhand bookshop than in an office, not that he had set foot in the office for the last eighteen months, by all accounts.

'And Normal Service, our Five and Seventy Austria.'

'Ah, Mr Service, not in Cumbria after all!' Gryce couldn't help saying as their hands met.

'Norman Jervis, in fact,' said the Fire and Safety Officer. A commissionaireish sort of individual, he struck Gryce as, but of a senior rank and with all limbs intact. 'As you say, *not in Cumbria after all*! Fiff!' His laugh was so infectious that Gryce found himself sharing the general mirth. 'Keeesh!' 'Tuh!' 'Haark!' 'Sha!'

Introductions completed, Copeland suggested that they should all move into the office. They proceeded in single file, with Norman Ferrier explaining to Gryce the function of various machines en route, particularly a treadle contraption capable of turning out a thousand visiting cards an hour. Gryce, who had always craved a business card of his own in all the billets he had ever worked in, it was one of his few ambitions in life, found this of interest.

He was greeted effusively at the door of the office by Mrs Rashman, who cried, 'Hello stranger, bet you didn't expect to find us here!' and by Mr Hakim, who pumped his hand and chuckled: 'And I thought you were holding the fort while I was on holiday, if I had known you were going to sneak away like this I wouldn't have gone to the Algarve!' Everyone laughed again, a 'Tchair!' from Mrs Rashman and a 'Skork!' from Mr Hakim adding body to the chorus of amusement. There was another laugh, 'Parp!' that Gryce couldn't identify. He saw that a familiar-looking figure was doing some paperwork at a familiar-looking desk. The desk was familiar because it was the one he had sat at in his first week at British Albion, it was Vaart's desk with all its telltale marks and dents. The figure was familiar because he was the spitting image of the owner of the sweets and tobacco kiosk hard by Forest Hill Station where Gryce had bought many a Mars bar. 'And this is my fiancé, Mr Cooley from Stationery Stores,' said Mrs Rashman.

Rubbing his oil-smeared hands genially, so that he reminded Gryce less of Mervyn Johns and more of a Pickwickian coalman, Copeland said: 'No hope whatsoever of rustling up toffee, I suppose, Thelma?'

Or anyway, that was what Gryce thought he said, but Thelma took him to mean that there was no hope whatsoever of rustling up coffee.

'Pardon? Still haven't got any cups, Mr Copeland.' Without actually doing so she gave the impression of standing on one foot and twisting one ungainly leg around the other.

'Shoulda fetched er filin cabinet.' Vaart winked solemnly at Thelma to show he wasn't serious. 'Most importan fingada lot an we aster forgerrit.'

Gryce was having a good look around the partitioned-off area into which he had been led. Office, Copeland had called it, but it was really part office, part storeroom. The outer wall was fitted with broad wooden shelves stretching up as far as the high windows, and these were piled up with ream upon ream of paper of every size, boxes of business envelopes, blank postcards, gummed labels, newspaper wrappers, visiting cards enough to keep Norman Ferrier's treadle-operated press busy for a six-month. Where all that virgin stationery had come from Gryce did not care to guess, but he knew where the desks and chairs and filing cabinets had come from all right. It was as if British Albion's Stationery Supplies Department had been scooped up in a cyclone like the clapboard house of that girl played by Judy Garland in *The Wizard of Oz*, and had come to rest in a corner of this Victorian printing works, complete to the last detail including coat-stand, wastepaper bins and indeed most of the staff.

'Just like home, dear, isn't it?' said Mrs Rashman.

'Shuddavad all new furnisher if we'd gonner ri way abaht it,' chuntered Vaart. 'They wouldena missed it. Stackser the stuff dahn in that Design an Mainenance Bay, there is.'

'We did consider all the pros and cons of that, Mr Vaart,' said Jervis, a shade testily Gryce thought, or perhaps that was just the officious way of speaking he had got into. As Fire and Safety Officer, he would have need of projecting a certain authority. 'If we'd been seen loading new furniture into the van it would have been a clear case of theft.'

'See, they cracked on they were taking all our desks and that back to the factory for renovation,' confided Mrs Rashman. 'Or I should say, they would have done, if they'd been stopped.'

Mr Hakim, smiling broadly, had produced an expensive crocodile-skin wallet, doubtless he had got it wholesale from a relative, and taken from it an official-looking paper which he handed to Gryce. 'As you can see, all our documentation was in order. Quite a souvenir, in years to come!'

It was in the style of the various forms and documents that Gryce had familiarized himself with in Stationery Supplies, complete with the British Albion trademark. 'Renovation/Repairs Requisitions – Authorization for Removal' it was headed. A typed inventory of all the office furniture was signed on the dotted line by Copeland and countersigned by an indecipherable scribble, probably bogus if anyone asked Gryce.

He ran his mind's eye over his master check-list which, come to think of it, would be in one of those filing cabinets not ten feet away from him. Eerie, when you looked at it in that light. 'But there's no such form, surely,' he pointed out.

'Our friend Mr Copeland ran it off on the treadle press I just showed you,' said Norman Ferrier urbanely. 'Not a bad job for an apprentice, wouldn't you agree?'

Copeland beamed at the compliment and said modestly that it would have looked more convincing if they'd been able to use the wash-pail.

'The Wharfedale,' translated Ferrier. 'We had the expertise, Mr Gryce. Most of your colleagues here have been taking printing courses of one kind or another at various night schools, plus a little private tuition from Mr Vaart and myself. But of course we didn't have the power.'

'Do you see, they'd cut off the electric, dear,' said Mrs Rashman. 'Well I mean to say, they would have done, wouldn't they? But the boys have managed to connect us up to the main cable. Apparently.'

'Or so we ope and trust,' said Vaart. 'They bin at it long enough.'

The Penney twins, whose bad breath was for once deodorized by the not unpleasant mixture of industrial smells thrown off by Copeland's ragged dungarees, chimed in.

'They could easily have connected us with the paint depot two doors away – '

' – but someone might have started asking why their electricity bill was going up in leaps and bounds – '

' – so they finally got us hooked up to the Electricity Generating Station on the river – '

' – who presumably don't have to pay for it. Haaark!'

Gryce, who was seething with indignation and had been so ever since Mr Hakim had shown him the bogus renovation requisition, felt that they were all straying far from the point. He turned to Copeland.

'*Am I to understand* that your memorandum from the Fire and Safety Officer was a put-up job, and that when you instructed me to locate the missing furniture and get it returned to the department, you were deliberately sending me on a wild-goose chase?'

'*Very much afraid* that's the case,' admitted Copeland. 'We had to cover our claques.'

'And all the while, what you were in effect doing between you was stealing this quantity of desks, filing cabinets and so on?'

'Let's say commandeered,' said Jervis.

'Eyejacked,' amended Vaart.

They were all looking very well pleased with themselves: a genial rogues' gallery, Gryce would have said. Plainly they were hugging themselves in anticipation of the question it was inevitable he should ask sooner or later.

'May one ask why?'

Norman Ferrier moved forward in the darting sort of way that seemed to be a characteristic, Gryce noticing that it was with some respect that the others stood aside to let him past. He led Gryce across to his desk, or rather to what was not his desk at all but rightly Copeland's desk: slightly larger than the others, junior executive type, catalogue number B4B/00621 as against the standard B4A/00621. It was very busily furnished with pots crammed full of pencils, filing trays piled high with papers, engraving blocks used as paperweights, plans, blueprints, specimen type-charts, and a book-trough tightly packed with a higgledy-piggledy assortment of bruised-looking volumes. Gryce saw some of the titles: *The Authors' and Printers' Dictionary*, *Roget's Thesaurus*, the *Concise Oxford*, *Whitaker's Almanac*, and several tattered Penguins, some of them looked like poetry. Quite the intellectual.

Ferrier, tugging out one of the Penguins with undue haste so that several other books were dislodged and slithered to the floor, peered at Gryce over his spectacles as if taking his measure. He struck Gryce as a bundle of nervous energy, yet at the same time commanding a calm authority. Thelma, at any rate, had scuttled to pick up the fallen books without anyone telling her to do so, very unusual for her.

'Have you ever read any Arnold Bennett, Mr Gryce?' In the context of Ferrier's bookishness, the question did not sound at all out of the way to Gryce, who supposed he had probably started many a conversation with a reference to a favourite author.

Gryce had not read any Arnold Bennett, although he had seen one or two instalments of a television adaptation of *Clayhanger*. He saw that it was a dog-eared copy of that work, it looked as if it had been fished out of a dustbin, that Ferrier was handing to him.

'Just glance at the passage I've marked, would you?'

He took the book with grave mistrust. He had not enjoyed *Clayhanger*, too slow-moving by half had been his verdict. Besides, he detested people giving him something to read and then standing over him while he did so: he never knew whether he was supposed to laugh explosively, comment '*Honestly!*' or make indignant tutting noises.

He focussed on the paragraph that had been underscored in red ballpoint.

'. . . *The trickling, calm commerce of a provincial town was proceeding, bit being added to bit and item to item, until at the week's end a series of apparent nothings had swollen into the livelihood of near half a score of people. And nobody perceived how interesting it was, this interchange of activities, this ebb and flow of money, this sluggish rise and fall of reputations and fortunes, stretching out of one century into another and towards a third! Printing had been done at that corner, though not by steam, since the time of the French Revolution. Bibles and illustrated herbals had been laboriously produced by hand at that corner, and hawked on the backs of asses all over the county; and nobody heard romance in the puffing of the hidden steam-engine multiplying catalogues and billheads on the self-same spot at the rate of hundreds an hour.'*

It conveyed absolutely nothing to Gryce. Without comment he handed the book back, still open at the marked passage, in the assumption that Ferrier was about to point out a hidden joke or unfortunate misprint. Ferrier, however, closed the book and slipped it absently into the pocket of his dust-coat.

'Printing, Mr Gryce, is the lifeblood of commerce. Wherever you see a thriving business community, you'll find print shops somewhere. If the print shops move away or close down, you may be sure that business is failing. If on the other hand there is a district or neighbourhood that has already failed, where the factories are empty and boarded up, and a printer sets up his press in some back street or alley, that's a sign that things are on the move again. Printing makes commerce, Mr Gryce, it's at the very heart of commerce, it *is* commerce.'

A set speech, by the sound of it. Gryce saw that the others had quietly drawn near and had formed themselves in a group around Ferrier's desk and were listening respectfully. Copeland, who apparently was No. 2 rather than No. 1 in whatever set-up they had here, showed no resentment at being upstaged by one who must have been very much his junior when employed in Stationery Supplies. On the contrary he was hanging on to Ferrier's every word as if he were the saviour of mankind.

'The jobbing printer is like the old-time travelling apothecary, Mr Gryce, he can cure all ills, or anyway he'll make you think he can which often comes to the same thing. Is your business slack? He'll print your posters and handbills. Even a brochure if you want it: how many thriving companies have come into this world riding on a coloured brochure? He'll print the slogan you put in your window, the hours-of-business card you hang inside your door, the business calendar your customers hang on their walls. But do your customers know where to find you? You'll need letterheads. Do they have to come to you or will you send your goods out to them? That's mail order, that's print. Your catalogue, that's print. Attractive packaging, or common-or-garden paper bags, that's print. And most important, do your customers pay their bills? Well, they certainly won't if you don't have any billheads to send out to them. And if I were you, I'd also order a stock of those little printed labels: "May we draw your attention to the fact that this account is now considerably overdue. An early settlement would be appreciated." '

There were polite titters at this. Gryce wondered if Ferrier was possibly a part-time lecturer at one of those night-school printing courses he had mentioned. He certainly had the gift of the gab, he could make whatever it was he was talking about sound interesting.

'I don't know how much if anything you know about me, Mr Gryce. You must have heard something or you wouldn't have found us here. I've spent a lifetime in printing. I was trained at the Pilgrim Press in Hammersmith. It wasn't as grand as it sounds, dance invitations and raffle tickets rather than limited editions and Mr Bennett's illuminated herbals! But we had some out-of-the-way work from time to time: a community newspaper, a series of lithographs, a privately published book, I did the binding for that and tooled the leather, there was no job I couldn't do or didn't do. We were unionized but everyone pitched in, there was work to be done. Then we

252

were taken over by the Albion Printeries and here I came, into this very building. Not that I minded much, there was a dual carriageway scheme in the pipeline and we'd have had to close down anyway. But mark this: when that dual carriageway got under way and they started demolition, ninety per cent of our business was carried off by the bulldozer. So we brought nothing to Albion Printeries at all: they laid out much-needed capital and only weakened their own position.'

Fascinating, Gryce was quite sure, but he didn't see what possible concern it was of his. Was no one going to ask him what he was doing here? For all they knew he was going to march straight back to British Albion and report the whole bunch of them to Lucas of Personnel. Or at the very least, to Pam and her executive committee. Now that was a thought to be conjured with: how did this gang stand with the Albion Players; there was only one member here and that was Vaart? Whose side, if anybody's, were they really on?

Vaart, Albion Players or not, seemed very much in his element here and had ventured to interject a word of his own: 'Still, you gorrer admit, there was plennyer work ere in dem days. It was all go, mornin till nigh.'

'Oh, absolutely,' agreed Ferrier, but he continued to address himself directly to Gryce. 'I don't know whether you can imagine what this area was like a few years ago. All those lock-up workshops you see out in Grain Yard were occupied, by every kind of business, there was a waiting list for them. The big warehouses may have been empty, because the docks were finished, but there were all sorts of plans to turn them to other uses. They never came to anything, the plans weren't big enough I suppose: the council wanted to clear the whole district so they could rebuild from scratch, something grandiose. So when the workshop leases ran out they weren't renewed, one place after another closed down, the shops and back-street cafés went, the commerce died, and Albion Printer-ies died with it. At a stroke of a pen they turned us all into clerks and storemen: we sat crammed in this very office doing useless paperwork – inventories, stock-lists, filing bits of paper, more inventories – against the day they moved us across to British Albion. Needless to say, the grand new redevelopment never took place, they could just as well have left us scratching a living. As our friend Arnold Bennett says, "bit being added to bit and item to item, until at the week's end a series of apparent nothings had swollen into a livelihood".'

'Too bleedin true. You woulden chuckle.' This endorse-ment from Vaart seemed to have the effect of bringing Ferrier's discourse to a halt. No one else spoke. Gryce sensed that having given their explanation to him, not that he was quite sure he understood what they were up to, they now expected his explanation to them.

He cleared his throat, hoping that the little coughing noises he was making didn't make him sound nervous. 'I must say I was very surprised to discover the premises still standing, quite by chance. That's really why I thought I'd have a look around – I'd understood quite definitely from Grant-Peignton that the building had been demolished.'

'Our friend Fart's doing,' chuckled Copeland.

'Marllous what a little rumour'll do, ennit?' said Vaart, tapping the side of his nose in what Gryce thought was a vulgar manner. It would be cockney body-language, he supposed, for low cunning.

Ferrier, making it crystal clear that if there was any tale to be told he would be the one to do the telling, picked up the reins of his narrative with ease.

'As you know, Albion Printeries was absorbed by

British Albion and closed down as soon as that monstrosity in Gravechurch Street was completed. It *was* scheduled for demolition, I know that for a fact: the statutory notice was hung out there on the gates for months. I kept an eye on the place, only because there's a riverside pub nearby I'd grown fond of and I used to pop over at lunch-time rather than face that dreadful Buttery.'

Ah, yes: the Crown Inn that would be, as spoken of by Parsloe. Gryce wondered whether to mention that he'd heard it had a nice patio where one could drink outside. He decided that it would be an irrelevant interjection, as would any comment about the Buttery being not as bad as all that, speaking as one found, in fact quite good value.

'However, the demolition squad never arrived, that goes without saying. I asked one or two questions up and down Grain Yard, it turned out the council had dropped their redevelopment plans. Shortage of cash. So I waited for the building to be re-let, but that didn't happen either. By this time it was beginning to dawn on some of us who we were really working for over at *so-called* British Albion, and I began to wonder if they'd simply forgotten about this place. Just lost it in the books, such things do happen, especially when Government's involved. I got some keys made, had a look inside, and of course it was exactly as we'd left it. The Wharfedale, the Linotypes, binding machine, everything – thousands and thousands of pounds' worth of plant that could have been sold, just left to rust. That confirmed it: they *must* have forgotten. I'll tell you what it is, Mr Gryce. Every piece of paper to do with Albion Printeries is locked away in a big brown envelope in that basement Files Depository across the river, and no one's going to dig it out again in a million years.'

'So ere we are, ent we?' Vaart gave Gryce one of his winks, delighted either with his own succinct summing-up on the situation or with the situation itself.

'So here you are,' echoed Gryce. There seemed to be a need for him to add something to that so he said: 'Here indeed you *all* are.' Ferrier took that as a cue to continue.

'You can imagine how I felt, a printer working as a clerk, and all the tools of my trade lying idle in a building that nobody wanted. What would you have done, Mr Gryce?'

Gryce shook his head politely but did not answer. What he would have done would have been to make an anecdote of it, pointing at the incompetence of management. 'Would you credit it?' he would have gone round asking. But he knew that such a reply would not suit Ferrier.

'I talked to Jack Vaart and he felt the same way; so did Douglas, one of the commissionaires you see out there – although he'd only been an odd-job man here he had ink in his veins, he loved the smell of it. Then, very discreetly, over the months, we sounded out the others – I mean those who'd gone over to British Albion instead of taking redundancy. They weren't interested: they had a desk to sit behind or a broom to lean on and a pension to look forward to, they'd been craftsmen, some of them, but they'd lost interest. I suppose if they'd known the press was still here, aching to be used, they might have taken a different view, but we couldn't risk telling them. We began to look around in other directions, watching for those who were disgusted at what was happening at British Albion, and then mentioning vaguely that we were thinking of starting up a little printing business one of these days. Mr Copeland here was our first recruit.'

'The point is that I was already taking a prinking course three lights a week out of sheer boredom,' explained

Copeland with a convert's eagerness. 'I was sick to the back teeth of British Albumen and the chance of making a living out of what had been a hobby came as a cod's end.'

'We were all sick to the back teeth, dear,' put in Mrs Rashman. 'I'm telling you, as soon as Jack Vaart started dropping hints about this place I said count me in, dear, I don't care what I do, whether it's typing or cleaning out the lavs, just so long as it gets me out of this bloody British Albion, and that's swearing.'

In turn, like reformed alcoholics at a temperance rally, the others gave their testimony. Mr Cooley of Stationery Stores had always had a hankering to do something with his hands: his contact with Albion Printeries had also led him into contact with Mrs Rashman so he had been presented with a double bounty. He looked to Gryce as if he was about to kiss the hem of Ferrier's dust-coat. Mr Hakim had been signed on after asking Vaart's advice on how much he would require to set up an Urdu press in Leicester, from which he believed a fortune could be made. The three one-armed commissionaires, still toiling in their trench out on the works floor, did not give evidence but Gryce was told that Douglas had recruited Thelma's uncle from the Files Depository and his sick-leave and holiday relief, their joint belief being that British Albion was a scroungers' paradise. The Penney twins had joined originally for a lark; it was a toss-up for a while whether they threw in their lot with the Albion Printeries or the Albion Players.

'You chose well,' commented Ferrier. 'You'd quickly have become bored with that bunch of amateur detectives.'

'Lorrer wankers,' said Vaart, and made as if to spit on the floor.

'But you're a member,' Gryce felt justified in pointing out.

'Gorrer keep an eye on em, ent we? Don do no arm to know woss goin on. I'm tellinya, when I go to them borin meetins, thass my good deed for the day.'

Only Thelma had not so far spokèn. She was smirking at one speaker after the other as if they were telling jokes. Gryce occasionally wondered if the girl was all there.

Copeland must have caught his glance in her direction. 'Thelma,' he said, 'is by way of being our musket.' He would mean mascot, if he meant anything. 'She was a damson in distress and we rescued her from the dragon, did we not, Thelma?'

She giggled, going bright red while doing so.

'After what you and she saw at British Albion,' said Ferrier, letting Gryce know for the first time that he knew more about him than he'd so far let on, 'we didn't think it safe for her to remain there. Fortunately the commissionaire who caught her was our friend Douglas, otherwise who knows what might have happened? You've presumably told the Albion Players people about what you saw?'

'Yes, there's a special meeting this evening.'

'I shall be very interested to hear what transpires at it,' said Ferrier, speaking to Vaart, who nodded. 'The balloon has gone up, that's my opinion.'

For someone who had left British Albion eighteen months ago, Ferrier seemed very well-informed about its doings. But Gryce found that he trusted his judgement. 'What do you think will happen, at all?'

'I don't know. I can only guess what might have happened to Thelma. The last person who stumbled on anything of any magnitude about British Albion was a rather simple office boy from In-house Mail. He stole some letters: one of them was a secret memorandum from a certain Government department, let's say it came into my possession. The boy was arrested, charged, found unfit to plead and shoved into an institution where he remains. For myself, I staged a diplomatic heart attack and vanished. If that sounds melodramatic, Mr Gryce, let me assure you they'll go to extraordinary lengths to cover their tracks.'

'Then, if I may say so, aren't you taking a tremendous risk in being here?' asked Gryce. After what he had heard, he certainly felt at risk himself, for all that Thelma, still grinning gormlessly, seemed to have no appreciation of the danger she had led them both into.

'I don't think we are. Look at it from their point of view. We're not the ones who are trying to upset their applecart, it's your interfering Albion Players who are doing that. We have our own fish to fry.'

'So ere we are, then,' repeated Vaart. It seemed to be his catchphrase of the moment.

Gryce surveyed his colleagues, or former colleagues as he supposed they had now become through their actions. He couldn't help but admire their nerve. What they were doing was certainly criminal but they were as jolly and carefree as a seaside concert party. He was reminded of that film, *The Lavender Hill Mob*. Ferrier, he now saw, could easily be played by Sir Alec Guinness who was a master of disguise.

'The fact remains that you have simply walked into a printing factory that doesn't belong to you and appropriated it for yourselves.'

'Why not?' said Ferrier. 'It was here to be taken. The plant was here, it needed renovation but we've managed that over the months. We've repaired the roof, we've got our electricity although I'm not going to enquire too closely how, and we've acquired enough stocks of paper to last us a year. We're in business, as you can see.'

What Gryce could certainly see was that the stocks of paper referred to were very large indeed. They couldn't possibly have been left behind with the printing plant, there were no signs of damp or anything of that kind, it was brand new paper, it must have cost a fortune.

He saw that the Penney twins were grinning bashfully and looking slyly towards Copeland. If they were trying to will him to speak out on their behalf, they succeeded.

'The Brothers Penney,' said Copeland paternally, 'will enlighten you as to how we came by our socks of paper, if you're at all furious.'

Thus prompted, the Penney twins commenced the chortling narrative with which they clearly hoped to impress Gryce no end. Stitching their fragmented sentences together he was able to gather that the famous calling-in process – of which he had now been put in charge so some of the blame would as likely as not rub off on him if any of this got out – was the key to it all. They had worked in league with Vaart who was in charge of maintaining the levels of stationery stocks, and with Mrs Rashman's fiancé Mr Cooley, of Stationery Stores. The calling-in process was, it seemed, the Penney twins' own ingenious invention, its sole purpose being to stock up the Albion Printeries with paper.

First, through Vaart, they had requisitioned enormous quantities of blank stationery of every kind and distributed them among selected departments, making sure they had genuine signatures for each consignment in case anyone checked up. Then, claiming that the various paper and envelope sizes had been declared obsolescent, they had set the calling-in process in motion and got all the stationery back again, together with various printed forms that were no use to anybody – that, Gryce learned, was merely a smokescreen to hide their real purpose. Hundreds of parcels of quarto, foolscap, envelopes of all sizes, invoice blanks, display cards and crown paper sheets (put through the books as planning materials for Design and Maintenance) had been returned to Stationery Stores, where Mr Cooley had promptly put them into a plain van and shipped them across to the Albion Printeries. If anyone wanted to know where the stuff had got to, his records would show that it had been mistakenly codemarked as classified material and fed into the shredding machine.

'*Rather* neat,' concluded Charles Penney.

' – though we say it as shouldn't,' added Hugh Penney.

'Foolproof,' said Charles Penney, determined to have the last word.

'The ole fing's foolproof, carn find a flaw nowhere,' said Vaart.

Gryce was not so sure, his natural caution would not permit him to be sure. He could see that they were all waiting for him to say something, what they obviously wanted was a word of congratulation. They were not going to get it. There must be a snag somewhere, whatever Vaart said.

Gryce thought long and hard, then an involuntary smile crept across his face, he hoped he didn't look too malevolent.

'What about,' he asked triumphantly, '*the rates*?'

'Haaark!' 'Fiff!' 'Keeesh!' 'Tuh!' 'Tchair!' 'Skork!' 'Parp!' He'd put his foot in it. He'd said the wrong thing. They were laughing at him.

'Really, Mr Gryce!' exclaimed Ferrier patronizingly. (Better than what the others were saying, anyway. 'We weren't born yesterday, you know' and 'Sod me, is that all yew can bleedin say?' were among the medley of comments when the laughter had died down.) 'The rates,

I can assure you, are taken care of. I made discreet enquiries at the town hall. They're paid once a quarter by the Paymaster General's office in Crawley. The rates demand was obviously fed into the computer when British Albion absorbed us and it's never been taken out again. Nor can it be until someone gives the order, which of course they won't.'

'Any more objections, *Mister* Gryce?' asked Mr Hakim in what Gryce thought was an unwarrantably sneering voice, considering that he was only a guest in this country.

'None at all,' said Gryce stiffly. 'I wish you all luck.'

'We shall need something more practical than luck,' said Ferrier. 'We need help. We're very few in number, although there are more of us than you see here today. There are twenty-four of us altogether, the others are waiting for the appropriate moment to slip away from British Albion, it wouldn't do to make a mass exit. But there's not enough of us. The Clarion Press is going to be very busy and we shall be on the lookout for willing labour right from the start.'

Gryce, with his usual attention to irrelevant detail, missed the main burden of Ferrier's remarks. 'The Clarion Press?'

From among the mass of papers on his desk Ferrier extracted several white sheets with a printed heading in good clean type. It was, Gryce conceded, a very good example of letterhead design, bold without being brash, uncluttered without being ultra-modernistic. It was only a layman's view but he would say that Ferrier knew his onions when it came to typography.

'Some of us thought it had unfortunate Fabian overtones but we had to call it something. The new signboard goes up in Grain Yard tomorrow and the last evidence that the Albion Printeries ever existed will have gone. If anyone is curious about us we are journeymen apothecaries, come to set up our stall. This area is about to thrive again, Mr Gryce, they'll need printing. Did you look about you when you came here today? You probably wouldn't have noticed but something is stirring. There are little workshops appearing in ramshackle buildings that have been closed down for years, one-man businesses taking their chance with short-term leases. It's like watching people creeping up from the deep shelters after all the bombs have fallen. The odds are still stacked against them but they want to have one last try, even though all the powers in the land conspire against them. "*And nobody perceived how interesting it was, this interchange of activities, this ebb and flow of money, this sluggish rise and fall of reputations and fortunes.*" There are reputations and fortunes to be made in and about Grain Yard, Mr Gryce. Very small reputations and tiny fortunes, but we're going to help to make them and we intend to make our own. The question is, will you join us?'

'I?' Gryce was flattered, not to say thrilled, by the proposal. It was the first time he had ever had the offer of a new billet, he had always had to make application for an actual or rumoured vacancy.

'Nuffin to lose, cock, avyer?' said Vaart encouragingly. 'Sides, oo wants to go back to *that* wankers' palace?' He cocked a thumb in the general direction of British Albion.

As Gryce considered his position, he was conscious of a great lightening of the spirits. This altogether foreign sensation had been with him to some extent ever since he had set foot in the Albion Printeries, although it had been masked by pragmatic anxieties about his own possible involvement in the merry conspiracy that had been unfolded. But Vaart had hit the nail on the head, he did not want to go back to the wankers' palace, he had served twenty-five years before the mast in wankers' palaces, and where had it got him? He wanted to be one of these good companions, he wanted to sit at Ferrier's feet and drink in his absurd visions of an England stirring again. He wanted to work the little treadle printing press that could turn out a thousand visiting cards an hour including one for himself, C. GRYCE, REPRESENTATIVE, THE CLARION PRESS. He wanted to start a new life altogether, to become a new person, to buy a new suit, possibly a cream one like Mr Hakim's, he wanted to pluck the hair out of his nostrils. He wanted to stop committing small acts of meanness like counting his money in the lavatory at home and hiding some of it away in case his wife thought there was cash to spare. He wanted to be able to remember his wife's face, to discuss his work in the evenings, to have a happier marriage, with perhaps children, they had never even discussed the matter in all these years. He wanted to spend his lunch-times in wine bars or in pubs on the river, and to dine in Japanese steak houses. He wanted, as Vaart had so graphically put it while nudging him at the Albion Players' meeting, to give one to Pam – well, he had already given one to Pam, but he wanted to give her another one. Gryce wanted to live.

'I'd like to think about it, certainly,' said Gryce.

'What is there to *think* about?' exploded Ferrier with what sounded uncomfortably like scorn. 'All you have to decide is whether you'd rather be paid for producing *something* than for producing bugger-all!'

'That's what concerns me rather,' said Gryce defensively, his prudence enveloping him again like a mackintosh. 'I'd be happier in my mind if I knew what it was we were really supposed to be doing over at British Albion.'

It was Copeland who replied, very softly: 'Don't you know, Mr Christ? Of course you know. We all know.'

'Tellya what I'll do wivya,' cried Vaart, slapping his

hands briskly like a market trader offering a bargain. 'Iss gerrin on for ar par five. Izzatt wankers' meetin at six? Ri. Whyn't you an me go acrost there, see woss goin on, then you can make your mind up?'

Gryce had forgotten all about the Albion Players' meeting. It brought back to the forefront of his mind a problem that he had been trying to push to the back of it.

'There's one thing I should mention,' he blurted out. 'The Albion Players know about this place. Or rather, at least one member of their executive committee knows about it: that the building hasn't been demolished, that is to say.'

This had something of a bombshell effect. Although nobody spoke, everyone except the serenely beaming Thelma reacted with varying shades of alarm. Even Ferrier showed signs of consternation.

'Which one?' he asked sharply.

Even more uncomfortably, Gryce hedged: 'It's a matter of some confidence, I'm afraid.' He could imagine Vaart's leer the moment he mentioned bringing Pam to the cardboard-strewn room across the brick-paved yard. If they were going to learn about that particular assignation they would have to drag it out of him.

'Did you bring that person to Grain Yard, or did that person bring you?'

'We came together, in point of fact.' Gryce told Ferrier – he found he had a kind of loyal compulsion to do so – about the invoice he'd found down in the Files Depository and about his encounter with Parsloe.

'That puts matters in a new light,' said Ferrier gravely. 'We'd been assuming all along that you'd followed Mrs Rashman and Mr Hakim here. They saw you at London Bridge Station on Friday, you know, so it seemed likely when you turned up today that you'd seen them too and found out where they were going. Now this person from the executive committee: has he or she told anyone else?'

'I don't know,' said Gryce wretchedly. 'But I'm bound to tell you there's another complication. If the Albion Players at large do get to hear about it, although I'm assured that for the moment they won't, it's generally believed there's in effect a spy in their midst who will see that it gets back to Lucas of Personnel.'

Mrs Rashman, a catty smile on her lips, was looking beyond Gryce to the glass partition separating the office from the works floor.

'Now that's something we *do* know already, dear. In fact she's right behind you.'

Gryce, along with everyone else who was facing in the same direction as him, turned just as Pam reached the doorway. She stood perfectly still at the threshold, frozen in mid-step, very fetching in her belted raincoat and beret and black tights as they had proved to be rather than black stockings. It was possible to see a succession of expressions cross her face like slides passed through a magic lantern: surprise, triumph, suspicion, fear, panic. She backed away and was about to run, but standing behind her were the three one-armed commissionaires in their uniforms and peaked hats again, but each holding the implement he had been working with in the trench outside – a pickaxe, a shovel and a pair of heavy-duty pliers.

14

The executive committee, rather to Gryce's disappointment, were in mufti. Although he and Vaart were late,
they had hit the blessed rush hour on London Bridge, the
meeting had not yet started. Grant-Peignton, Ardagh and
Co. were sitting up on the platform like tailors' dummies,
legs crossed, arms folded. And not a script between them,
not a wig or false moustache or what Gryce believed was
technically known as a prop. An intruder would have
taken them for a public tribunal or planning inquiry
instead of the cast of *The Importance of Being Earnest*.

One chair was vacant: Pam's.

'Shun't worry, she'll foller on in er own good time,'
Vaart had assured him as their bus crawled through the
City.

'I'd far sooner have waited for her,' Gryce had said
uneasily. 'I'm sure she wouldn't give anything away at
the meeting.'

'Snot what she's gonner tell them wankers I'm bovvered
abaht, iss what she's gonner tell er bosses.'

'How can you stop her? What's going to happen to
her?'

'You keep rabbitin on abaht it, doncha? They jus
wanner asker few questions, thass all. An after that she'll
avter swear blind she's gonner forget all abaht Albion
Prinneries.'

'What if she won't?'

'You don know Norman Ferrier, mate. Got the gifter
the gab, e as, could talk the ind leg offer donkey. E'll
purrit on the line. E'll say, "Look, sweetart, you forget

abaht what you bleedin know and we'll forget abaht what we bleedin know, fair enough?" She'll swallow it. Got to.'

Gryce didn't know how he felt about Pam at this moment. He supposed he could be feeling hurt, but he was not familiar enough with the sensation to recognize its symptoms. Certainly he had reason to be: she had been using him all along. She had been using him even when they had bedded down on their nest of cardboard boxes, all that groaning and moaning must have been simulated. She'd just wanted to make sure that he didn't let any cats out of the bag before she was able to let them out herself.

Against that, his admittedly limited knowledge of female physiology told him that it couldn't have been all that simulated. Assuming that the woman wasn't plainly and simply a raving nymphomaniac, Vaart and the rest of them could be jumping to the wrong conclusion.

'I still can't credit it. Have you any actual proof against her?'

'Course we got bleedin proof! *Course* we got bleedin proof! Ask old Muvver Rashman! From the day she said she was leavin, Pam Fawce wunt geroff er back, would she? "Wot you wanner leave for?" "To get married." "Well why can't you still work ere after your bleedin oneymoon?" "Coss I'm sicker the bleedin place, that's why." "Wotchew mean, you're sicker the place, ave you fahnd sumfin out?" "No, course I ain't fahnd nuffin out, I've just ad a bellyful." "You know sumfin, doncha?" "I don know bleedin nuffin." "You muss do, else why would you wanner leave a cushy job like this?" "Cos isser pain in the arse." "Thass no reason for leavin, you've fahnd summink out, encha?" On an on she went, wunt leave er alone. Then she ropes in Ron Seeds, er bleedin sidekick e is, does what she tells im . . .'

(Better a sidekick than a mug, reflected Gryce with some bitterness. And the question arose: had Seeds been rewarded on a nest of cardboard somewhere?)

'. . . An *e* as a go. "Wotchew wanner leave for?" "To get married." "Well I'm bleedin married as well," says e, "but I still bleedin work ere." An that goes on an on, day after day, till she tells em bof to piss off.'

Gryce remembered how Pam and Seeds had exchanged that curious glance of theirs when the subject of Mrs Rashman's departure had cropped up on his first visit to the Buttery. They had both seemed agitated, but he had never been able to fathom out why.

'I don't see what that proves.'

'Wossit prove, wodyew fink it proves? Why should she give a monkey's wevver anyone leaves or not? I'll tell you why, cos she's wettin erself in case they goes some-where else an starts blabbin out what goes on at Bri'ish Albion.'

'But that's still conjecture, surely? Purely guesswork,' amended Gryce, unsure of the extent of Vaart's vocabulary.

'It *was* guesswork, granted! It *was* guesswork. Till I follered er.'

'You followed Pam?'

'Too bleedin true. Stuck to er like a bleedin leech. Know where she went one nigh, after knockin off time? I'll tellya. Down bleedin White-all, wassen it?'

'Nothing strange about that, she probably went to meet her husband. He's in the Department of the Environment.'

'Thass what she tells bleedin *yew*, son. E ain't in no Deparmen of no bleedin Environmen, it ain't even *in* bleedin White-all. E's in the same govmen office as what she works for. An she stayed in that office, lissen because I'm tellinya, she stayed in that office for over an hour,

269

tellin em all what goes on at these wankers' meetins we go to, bleedin Albion Players.'

'How can you possibly know that, after all you weren't a fly on the wall? And *which* office in Whitehall?'

'Don avver name, does it? Iss jusser number.'

'Then how do you know it's a Government office?'

'If Ten bleedin Downin Street ain't a govmen office,' retorted Vaart, savouring the moment, 'I'm a bleedin Chinaman.'

Three one-armed commissionaires, who might have been transported by time-machine from standing guard over Pam across at Albion Printeries, so interchangeable were they all, took the usual unconscionable time studying Vaart's and Gryce's credentials. Seeds, once again, was on duty at the doors. He became involved in a slight altercation with Vaart, who did not wish to sit where Seeds wanted to put him. While Vaart was telling Seeds that he was a washerwoman and that the job of glorified usherette was just about his mark, Gryce, keeping out of it, looked about the hall. He recognized many of what he supposed could be termed the old regulars: George Formby, Fred Astaire, the Prime Minister of Rhodesia, Flight-Sergeant Neddyman and the rest of the gang.

Eventually Vaart won the day and indicated to Gryce that they should sit in the back row. Gryce bared his teeth obsequiously to Seeds, to apologize for having taken the matter of seating out of his hands. Taking his place, he noticed two newcomers across the aisle: the Jack Lemmon-looking individual from Catering (Administration), and another man whose flushed, angry face also rang a bell. Gryce was pleased that he had made a convert of Jack Lemmon after all, he must have been more persuasive than he'd thought when they'd had that little chat in the Buttery; but he was blowed if he could place his companion who resembled no personality of stage or screen whether living or dead. He began to run through his mental card-index and, by the time Grant-Peignton rose to open the meeting, had the man placed. Of course! If he'd been wearing a chef's hat Gryce would have got him one, you had to think of people in their context. It was the head of Catering (Administration) with whom he had had that altercation, Hatch as his name had turned out to be after an amusing misunderstanding with Jack Lemmon. So Gryce had made a convert of Jack Lemmon and Jack Lemmon had made a convert of Hatch, it was a case of casting one's bread upon the waters.

Grant-Peignton began to speak, somewhat inaudibly. It was funny, reflected Gryce, that without his lemon tea-gown, his padded bosom and his wig, he lacked the presence he had displayed the other night, he was more like the waffling and ineffectual No. 2 who in Copeland's absence had failed to maintain any kind of discipline in Stationery Supplies. Perhaps he needed to don women's clothing before he could begin to assert himself; only a head-shrinker would know the answer to that one.

'. . . dispense with the usual minutes in the case of an extraordinary meeting,' Grant-Peignton was saying, or mumbling. He looked very nervous to Gryce, on edge he would have said if asked. 'Certain matters having come to light . . . felt it advisable . . . committee soon as possible . . .'

'Speak up, carn earya!' yelled Vaart with gusto, cupping his hands to his mouth like the costermonger he had very probably been at some stage in his career. Grant-Peignton, glaring back at Vaart, seemed to make an effort to pull himself together. He continued in a less shaky but only imperceptibly louder voice.

'Certain matters having come to light, I say, it was *felt*

advisable to bring them to the notice of this Committee, that's to say the British Albion Investigation Committee as a whole and not only the executive committee on this platform, as soon as would be practicable. The facts, speaking without a note – '(he could have done with one, thought Gryce)' – are these. Within the past twenty-four hours, one of our members has reported two discoveries of the utmost importance to the future of all here this evening and indeed to the future of British Albion. The first of these discoveries hinges on irrefutable evidence of the involvement of Government in our affairs – no less than the presence of one of Her Majesty's Secretaries of State at a meeting of the company's directors – '

The fact that Grant-Peignton could still not be heard at the back of the hall produced a ragged reaction. While there was a hubbub of excitement from the front rows, those behind were crying, 'Speak up! Can't hear you at the back, Mr Chairman!' Grant-Peignton tried raising his voice and repeating himself, but by now those who had heard him the first time were buzzing animatedly among themselves, so that he was inaudible to all. Only when Ardagh took it upon himself to bob up and appeal for the chairman to be given a chance was order partly restored.

'Thank you, Mr Ardagh. The second discovery, I say the second discovery if you will bear with me for a moment, is of the existence in the City of a company known as United Products which to all intents and purposes is an exact copy, I should say replica, of British Albion . . .'

Absolutely blooming typical, thought Gryce bitterly. Not only did the man give no credit whatsoever to the person who had furnished this all-important intelligence, but he had simply no idea how to project his material dramatically and in any case could not be heard by half the audience. Gryce now fervently wished that he had hugged the information to himself and presented it from the floor as Seeds had presented his the other night. It could have been his finest hour.

'. . . In view of these disclosures,' Grant-Peignton was doggedly resuming, after Ardagh had once more called for silence, 'your executive committee has been instructed to take certain steps . . .'

'Wossee ramblin on abaht, "bin instructed"? Oo by?' muttered Vaart.

'Heaven knows, I can hardly hear him,' grumbled Gryce, still smarting. 'Terrible chairman in my view.'

'. . . accordingly this will be the final, winding-up meeting of the British Albion Investigation Committee, or Albion Players. And now without further ado, and so that you will not be kept in the dark any longer than necessary, allow me to introduce . . .'

'Lars meetin, did e say?'

'I believe so, that's what it sounded like.'

'Wossee mean, lars meetin?'

Dealing with Vaart's tiresome interruptions, Gryce quite missed who it was that Grant-Peignton was introducing without further ado. He thought he heard the name 'Lucas' but it couldn't have been. It was only as Lucas of Personnel walked on to the platform that he realized that it must have been.

The noise from the floor swelled up and then subsided completely. One could, as Gryce expressed it to himself, have heard a pin drop. Lucas of Personnel bowed formally to Grant-Peignton and indicated courteously that he should seat himself. Then he walked forward to the edge of the platform where, in jocular fashion, he blew into a cupped hand as if testing a microphone. Several of those on the platform squirmed in embarrassment, clearly sharing Gryce's view that whatever he might be doing here, he was getting off on the wrong foot.

Lucas of Personnel spoke at last.

'*Surprise surprise!*'

Nobody laughed. Nobody murmured. Lucas, however, did not seem to feel that his opening shaft had fallen flat. He was thoroughly relaxed, that would be Gryce's impression in retrospect when he was able to pull his confused thoughts together. Also very well used to handling an audience.

'Mr Chairman, ladies and gentlemen, a very famous author was asked by a young man for advice on how he should write a story. The celebrity appeared to give the question his consideration, and then he replied, "Start at the beginning. Say what you have to say. And then stop." I propose to take that excellent advice this evening. I would appreciate it, ladies and gentlemen, if you would hear me out to the end. Many of you will have questions but if you will be patient, you will find that most of them have been answered by the time we adjourn.'

'*Turnup forrer book, ennit?*' whispered Vaart, at last finding voice again. Gryce, for once, felt emboldened to round on him and hiss fiercely, 'Sssh!' He didn't want to miss a word of this.

'Ladies and gentlemen, why are you all here? What attribute do you possess in common? I've asked for the indulgence of your complete attention so I will hasten to answer my own rhetorical question. You possess in common, ladies and gentlemen, the attribute of curiosity. All of you were curious, *are* curious, about British Albion.

'Please don't misunderstand me when I say that curiosity is not a quality that your company seeks out when engaging staff. Most of you will recall that when you were interviewed by me I laid great stress on the absence of initiative required in the post you would be filling. You were deliberately chosen for your compliancy, let me say even your complacency. Nothing to be ashamed

274

of there: the loyal, if you will *acquiescent* employee, the "company man" as he's sometimes dubbed, is among the most valuable assets that a healthy business concern can possess. Anyone who doubts that need look no further than some of the great corporations of the United States.

'But it was inevitable, without sophisticated personality tests, that some of you would turn out not to fit into that mould. The great majority of our personnel did fit into the mould – I shouldn't have retained my position for long if they hadn't – but you, ladies and gentlemen, you chosen few, did not. That's to your credit: it would be a dull world if we were all the same.'

Gryce thought he sensed a ripple of pride go through the audience. He certainly felt a ripple of pride go through himself. 'You chosen few.' That would be why he had been singled out by Norman Ferrier to join that band of outlaws across the river.

'You who are here this evening began asking questions. About British Albion's function, about the secrecy surrounding some of our departments, about such matters as why the internal telephone directory should be a classified document and indeed the absence of a telephone switchboard. I've heard many ingenious theories put forward about that, by the way! The real answer of course is that if we did have a switchboard it would be noticeable at once to the operators that nobody ever rings us up! I would have thought that some of you might have stumbled on that one by now.'

Vaart, who had maintained silence following Gryce's rebuke, now joined in the rhubarb chorus of mutterings. 'Tell us summink we don't know, cock!' Well: Gryce hadn't known, for one.

'Now there's no reason in a free country why you *shouldn't* ask questions, it would be a dull world as I say if everyone simply did as he was told. I think you'll agree, looking back, that we did our best to answer them. Heads of department and senior personnel, some of whom may well have been more senior than their nominal titles or positions suggested, were briefed to set your minds at rest as best they could. Where they succeeded, well and good. Where they did not, it was time for the Albion Players to step into the breach.'

Another chorus of murmurings, puzzled ones this time. '*Wossee drivin at?*' asked Vaart in aggrieved tones.

'If we listen,' said Gryce sourly as Lucas held up a hand for silence, 'we might possibly learn!'

'Each of you will have been approached, adopted if you like, by a member of the executive committee, or by someone closely associated with that committee, who in effect will have tested you.' Yes, indeed: that first evening with Pam had been like sitting an examination; the subsequent evening with her and Seeds could be compared to the third-degree in a New York police station, if anyone asked Gryce. 'They will have formed a view about what you had already learned about the workings of British Albion, about your political connections or sympathies if any, about your desire or otherwise to get to the bottom of who was paying your salary and why. If in their judgement your shall we say *thirst for knowledge* presented any threat to the security of the company, then and only then were you taken safely under the wing of the Albion Players.'

'*Jesus Chrise all-bleedin-mighty!*' Gryce saw rather than heard what Vaart was mouthing, for the excited babble of voices was deafening. Several chairs clattered back as half a dozen members sprang to their feet. On the platform, Ardagh and Grant-Peignton responded by jumping to theirs. It was Ardagh, Gryce noted, who tried to do something constructive about getting a modicum of hush, while Grant-Peignton ineffectually flapped his arms.

'Gentlemen! No questions at this juncture! Please!'

'Mr Chairman!'

'I am not the chairman, sir, and you are out of order! I am asking you to sit down!'

'If you are not the chairman, you have no authority to ask me to sit down!' The speaker, or shouter, was the Fred Astaire-looking character who had tried to make difficulties at the last meeting. '*I* am asking, *through* the chair, if Mr Lucas is telling us that your executive committee is no more than the tool of management?'

'What I am telling you, if you will allow me to continue,' said Lucas with great courtesy, 'is that your executive committee *is* the management.'

It was a pity, thought Gryce as Vaart passed a remark that he simply couldn't hear in all the surrounding racket, that Grant-Peignton was not wearing his frock. They would have got on much faster.

Order, not without some difficulty, had been restored, Lucas of Personnel taking advantage of the stunned silence that followed to cover a good deal of ground.

The history of the Albion Players was briefly related. The executive committee had started life as a clandestine management committee, charged with keeping up morale, deflecting awkward questions and pacifying awkward customers, and ensuring that the system ran flawlessly. (This would mean, if Gryce had got hold of the right end of the stick, that Pam, Ardagh and Grant-Peignton were all in fact senior to Copeland, no wonder he'd become sick to the back teeth if he'd known what the score was.) At the appropriate time they had brought the Albion Players or British Albion Investigation Committee into being, with the sole purpose of providing a channel where rumours and conjectures could be disposed of, mainly by creating counter-rumours and counter-conjectures. Such notions as that the company was secretly processing ration books or identity cards, or that it was an undercover headquarters for some future coup, had all been cleverly insinuated into the minds of the membership by Mrs Pamela Fawce, who was by way of being the company's senior manager. Lucas regretted that Mrs Fawce was not yet present, his conjecture being that she was in consultation with her masters.

There had been one more impassioned interruption, surprisingly enough from Seeds. White-faced, he had stalked down the body of the hall to face Lucas.

'No, I will not be silent, Mr Ardagh! I think Mr Lucas should be made aware that I have been spending an average of fifteen hours a week on Albion Players business. Not only have I attended every single meeting but I have had many ex officio meetings with Mrs Fawce, usually *in my own time*. I have been responsible for the selection and screening of new members, again *in my own time*. I have travelled both to the outermost suburbs and as far afield as Rugby *at my own expense*, in company with Mrs Fawce who in passing allowed me to *pay for her lunch*, in order to report back on what could be ascertained about the subsidiary companies. Now you have the brass nerve to tell me that all this work, all this sacrifice of time and money, was to no purpose, and that Mrs Fawce was quite deliberately leading me up the garden!'

Gryce could well understand Seeds letting off steam in this way. It was what he had felt like doing himself upon learning that the scene with Copeland and the Penney twins over the missing furniture had been calculatedly staged to throw everyone off the scent.

'I'm afraid that's the case, Mr Seeds,' replied Lucas. 'Any out of pocket expenses will, in due course, be refunded.'

'You can stick them up your jacksey!' shouted Seeds uncharacteristically. He turned on his heel and marched back up the aisle. Gryce fully expected him to barge out of the hall, banging the swing doors behind him. Instead he resumed his accustomed position at the back, and after fuming for a moment took out a pocket diary and began scribbling in it furiously. He would, concluded Gryce, be working out his expenses.

'I'm afraid,' continued Lucas, 'that we owe an apology not only to Mr Seeds but to a great many of you, who have given of your time freely when you might profitably have been doing other things. All I can say in mitigation is that the charade was necessary. Incidentally, I owe Mr Seeds a further apology. If I was unnecessarily curt when he rang the telephone number of Binns Brothers of Rugby the other day and was put through to the "export manager", that was only because I feared he was beginning to recognize my voice.' The object of monitoring calls to those moribund factories, let me assure you, was not to keep tabs on anyone present here tonight, but simply as a double-check that enquiries were not being pursued by any other person or persons. As you can imagine, we rather frown on individual endeavour!

'I was saying the charade was necessary. How long it could have continued I know not. Probably it was inevitable that sooner or later we should so to speak have had to *bring down the curtain* on the Albion Players. As you know, however, events have rather conspired to force our hand. Is Mr Gryce present?'

The question, or request to make himself known as he took it to be, caught Gryce on the hop. Confused and, he was very much afraid, blushing, he shambled to his feet, despite Vaart's curt advice: 'Tellimer piss off!' He was painfully yet pleasurably aware of a sea of faces turned in his direction.

'I must congratulate you, Mr Gryce, on some very astute detective work. As one of British Albion's new boys, let it never be said that you allowed the grass to grow beneath your feet!'

'Thank you indeed!' stammered Gryce, bobbing absurdly, and wondering why this handsome tribute was not taken as the cue for a round of applause. Vaart tugged at the hem of his jacket. 'Siddarn, silly sod!' Gryce did so reluctantly, feeling that his moment of glory had been an uncommonly muted one.

'The observant Mr Gryce, as your chairman has just informed you, has stumbled upon the existence of a company known as United Products. I don't know whether Mr Gryce's curiosity led him to set foot in United Products House, but in the event that he got past the commissionaires he would have found a more or less exact duplicate edition of Albion House. That having become common knowledge, it would be only a matter of time before you compared notes with your colleagues at United Products, as colleagues they indeed are, and began to make further discoveries. You would learn, almost certainly, of the existence of other organizations, all of them to a greater or lesser extent replicas of British Albion and United Products. How many of them there are I am not at liberty to divulge, but there are several more of them in London and they exist in all our great cities such as Birmingham, Liverpool and Manchester. Each one, I may say, has its equivalent of the Albion Players, so if Mr Seeds feels he has been hoodwinked, he is not alone.

'You would also have learned, ladies and gentlemen, that the boards of directors of all the companies in this network are one and the same – and may I say at this juncture that there is nothing sinister or conspiratorial about your directors. They are public-spirited men with a strong sense of duty, responding, as they will always respond, to a call from Government to perform a service for their country. If, as our eagle-eyed friend Mr Gryce has observed, they meet in bizarre surroundings, that has less to do with considerations of secrecy than with the pragmatic fact of their having nowhere else to go, the architect having quite forgotten to include a boardroom in his final blueprint. That, of course, was the least of our construction problems!'

This oblique reference to the Buttery's notorious non-working revolving mechanism, and probably to other structural cock-ups that Gryce hadn't heard about, got Lucas his first ragged laugh of the evening. He certainly knew how to hold an audience. Or anyway, how to hold most of it: for the man who looked like George Formby was on his feet and asking a long rambling question that was inaudible to Gryce and, it would seem, to Lucas also.

'I'm sorry, Mr Aintree, I didn't catch all of that.'

'I was merely asking if the architectural shortcomings of the establishment are relevant, and whether you are being entirely frank about the board meetings not being secret, bearing in mind – '

' – that they are occasionally attended by the Secretary of State for Employment, yes,' completed Lucas, cutting short the waffle. Gryce, to the surprise of Vaart, raised an arm, brought it down again in an extravagant swoop, at the same time snapping his fingers in a gesture of exasperated triumph. He had been trying to remember all along who the important minister was. He knew the name, knew the face, had seen him many a time on the television news but just couldn't place his Cabinet appointment, the present Government chopped and changed about so much. When he had given the man's name to Pam he hadn't liked to parade his ignorance by asking which minister he was when he was at home, and she of course would have assumed that he knew already, so she hadn't enlightened him.

The Secretary of State for Employment. It was beginning to make sense.

'On the first point,' Lucas was saying, 'I was only trying to underline what I was about to go on to say: that the Board very much have the interests of all British Albion personnel at heart. They could of course meet anywhere in London, but they have all along insisted, not only in our case but in the case of all the other equivalent companies, on holding their deliberations in-house, on the premises, where any problems that arise can be immediately dealt with. Think of them if you will rather like the governors of one's school on their annual inspection.

'On the second point, no of course we didn't shout it from the rooftops when the Secretary of State insisted on visiting what he was pleased to call "the front-line trenches". If you ask me *why* we didn't shout it from the rooftops, then we arrive at my purpose in standing on this platform and addressing you this evening. The plain truth, as of course you will have gathered from shall we say our reticence in other directions, is that we do not want the public at large to know what we are doing at British Albion and elsewhere; because if the public *did* know, then it would bring the Government down.'

Lucas allowed himself a pause to let this sink in. He changed his stance, leaning slightly forward to stress the importance of what he was about to say and looking rather as if he would have liked a lectern or reading-desk to support him.

'What do we do at British Albion, ladies and gentlemen? I think many of you, perhaps most of you, already know the answer, although you have perhaps not wished to look it in the face. We do not do anything at British Albion. The office in Gravechurch Street, like similar establishments up and down the country, exists to provide employment. It has no other function.'

'*Don't you know, Mr Christ?*' Copeland had said. '*Of course you know. We all know.*' And Gryce had known, for some time now, but he had never wanted to admit it. He didn't want to admit it even now.

Evidently that was the general reaction, for as Lucas paused again there was an uncomfortable silence, almost an ashamed silence Gryce would have said. The only sound was of shuffling as members of the audience examined their feet, or in some cases straddled the backs of their chairs, with affected airiness and looked up at the ceiling or at the walls: anything but look at one another, or at the speaker.

'You all read your newspapers, or if you don't, it's certainly not for the want of leisure to do so in most cases! You know about the economic difficulties that have to be faced, by the Western world in general and by this country in particular. You know the unemployment figures and you know that they are moving in an upward rather than a downward direction. What you may not know is that if our unemployment statistics were to be calculated in real terms, that is to say if we were to add the numbers of people who are technically employed but who are not engaged in productive or useful work, the figure would be so astronomically high that any remaining confidence in our prospects for recovery would be dealt a mortal blow.

'That is one reason why institutions like British Albion are maintained. Another is the strictly practical one that it costs marginally less to keep you employed than it would to keep you unemployed. In the first place, your salaries cost the taxpayer little more than would have to be found in unemployment benefits, bearing in mind that you are still paying income tax and national insurance contributions; and on top of that, you are in effect servicing your own welfare. Imagine the army of social security officials who would have to attend to your financial and other needs if your jobs at British Albion had not been created for you! So to that extent, ladies and gentlemen, you are self-sufficient and a burden to none. I'd like you to think about that, if you will.

'That being said, I don't want you to run away with the notion that the Government set up British Albion and similar companies with the premeditated intention of creating a honeycomb of sinecures. That wasn't the original idea at all. The original idea was to assist smaller firms that were in difficulties for one reason or another. They were to be given Government support. In fact, not to beat about the bush, they were to be acquired by Government as going concerns – call it backdoor nationalization if you like. Indeed you could go further and call it clandestine nationalization, for the essence of the scheme was that no one should know the State had anything to do with it. To Joe Public, it would look as if these ailing companies had been taken over by a bigger company that had mushroomed up from nowhere and was anxious to diversify its interests. It made sound commercial sense: these small firms would now reap the benefit of centralized resources. Instead of buying their materials individually in small quantities, they could rely on one big buying department to do their shopping for them. Instead of a dozen or twenty small fleets of broken-down vans and lorries, there'd be a streamlined, up-to-date transport pool. Accounting would be centralized: look at the saving there. And there'd be a powerful sales division, with export contacts far beyond the reach of a tiny family-run business out in Rugby or Harrow-on-the-Hill.

'Now I know what some of you are thinking – that Government was ducking its responsibilities. If the scheme failed, no one could point a finger at policies of State intervention because no one would know that the State had been in any way involved. That's fair enough, the point is there to be made. But supposing the scheme had succeeded! What a shot in the arm for business confidence! And the private sector would have been given all the credit, since all and sundry would believe that British Albion was a part of the private sector. So really, your Government was hiding its light under a bushel.

'In the event, British Albion as it was originally conceived never got off the ground. Nor did any of the analogous concerns such as United Products. The rescue operation came too late. All those small firms, those "subsidiary companies" of ours so assiduously investigated by Mr Seeds, had simply had their day. They had gone to the wall even before Albion House opened for business. Even more regrettably, the company from which British Albion so to speak acquired its credentials, namely the Albion Printeries, had also collapsed, as had the various export firms and so on from which British Albion's companion companies likewise took their antecedents. We now believe that this was the wrong way of going about it, that these firms couldn't possibly have survived the burden of reorganization and expansion that was thrust upon them. It was a management failure from which we have learned much.'

Gryce heard a smacking sound. It was Vaart repeatedly ramming his right fist into the palm of his left hand. The knuckles were white.

'What to do? Leave all these shining new office blocks empty? A fine shop window that would have been for British industry! Besides, ladies and gentlemen, there was another problem. With business continuing to contract, there was an immense shake-out of labour, particularly clerical labour, as one firm after another embarked on a ruthless programme of rationalization. But of course you know that only too well, for you were the ones who were shaken out.

'Should we leave you to stand in the dole queue or should we take you in out of the cold? That was the question. The answer was to create British Albion as we know it today.

'You had to be given work, but there was no work for you to do. No point in having a sales division now, we had nothing to sell; no buying department, we had nothing to buy; no transport pool, we had nothing to transport; the subsidiary companies we were meant to service had been reduced to heaps of rubble.

'Well, then: if there was no work to do, it had to be invented. Once the problem was faced, it was not a problem at all. Most large offices, even in the commercial sector, devote most of their resources to taking in their own washing, if I may use the phrase. Eighty per cent of the average office workforce exists only to service the other twenty per cent – to type and post their letters, file their documents, buy their stationery and other items, prepare their salary cheques, re-arrange their furniture, cook their lunches, man their lifts, empty their waste-paper baskets and so on and so forth. So it was easy enough to copy the standard office structure. Added to that we decided on frequent reorganization programmes: any department that could be reorganized from time to time was reorganized. That too is common enough in most large offices, so we were able to maintain the illusion of operating a conventional City company.

'As recruiting continued, and British Albion grew, it did become slightly more difficult to invent more tasks. Catering Admin was expanded rather more than it should have been, as were the various Service departments. Touching on the Service departments, by the way, there has been a good deal of speculation about the purpose of all those statistics they're so energetically processing. I *don't think* there's any great mystery: they're engaged in comparing all the numbers from the 1967 Manhattan telephone directory against those from the 1973 edition. The two sets of numbers aren't in the same order, and of course they lack the subscribers' names that would make checking easier, so it's quite a long task. On the other hand, I'm informed it's a rather exhausting way of occupying one's time, so if anyone can suggest anything more congenial I'd be glad to hear it!'

All this had been listened to attentively. Gryce, in particular, was enthralled, his only regret being that he didn't have a toffee to suck. What a pity that that human cornucopia of toffees Copeland was not sitting next to him instead of Vaart; particularly as Vaart was hunching his shoulders belligerently and looking as if he were on the verge of making an exhibition of himself.

'*Woss wrong wivver few bleedin treadmills?*'

Yes: he was bound to have made trouble sooner or later. Lucas, however, looked only momentarily put out.

'I'm sorry – would you repeat the question and identify yourself?'

Vaart, somewhat sheepishly it seemed to Gryce, jack-knifed himself to his feet but did not otherwise identify himself and did not repeat the question.

'It's Mr Vaart, isn't it?'

Vaart, perhaps sullen was the word rather than sheep-ish, didn't reply. Say something even if it's only good night, thought Gryce, embarrassed.

'Aren't I correct in thinking you had a career in the printing industry, Mr Vaart?'

'Thass ri. Afore your bleedin mob got their ands on it.'
Ah: so friend Vaart did have a tongue after all.

'And would you agree with me, Mr Vaart, that printing, I don't say the particular branch you worked in but certainly Fleet Street, is perhaps the most over-manned industry in Britain?'

'Iss no more over-manned than Bri'ish bleedin Albion, is it?' flashed Vaart. Unable to perform his usual trick of affecting to walk away after this robust sally, he contented himself with glaring with comic fierceness at those who had turned round to have a look at him. The performance was rewarded by a few nervous sniggers.

For the first time Lucas of Personnel showed signs of losing his cool, as Gryce believed the expression was. Really nasty, he looked.

'I'd like to ask this of you, Mr Vaart. I'd like to ask it of all of you. I don't really want to single out printing as the villain of the piece; over-manning is endemic to many industries, indeed it goes through trade and commerce in general. How many of you hand on heart can say that you used to do a full day's work before you came to British Albion?' (Not Gryce, for one.) 'Now will you tell me this. What is the moral difference between being carried as a passenger on a cargo boat and being carried as a passenger on a pleasure cruise? There *is* no difference! You remain passengers, whether those around you are working or not! If it's morally proper, and seemingly it is, that newspapers and car factories and local government offices should employ large numbers of people who do little or nothing, but who create industrial unrest when their non-existent jobs are threatened, surely the logical development is to get them all together under one roof where they can do little or nothing in comfort and not get in the way of those with real work to do! So don't talk to me about treadmills, Mr Vaart!'

Evidently he had not failed to hear Vaart's original question after all, but had chosen to wait until he could use it as a peg for what Gryce considered a rather fanciful piece of rhetoric.

Vaart, chuntering something about wankers, had long ago sat down, but now someone else was on his feet. It was the angry-looking head of department of Catering (Administration). He looked angrier than ever if that were possible, all Gryce could say was that he wouldn't like to meet him up a dark alley.

Talking of dark alleys: where was Pam?

'Yes? I believe Mr Hatch has a question?'

'I do not have a question, Mr Lucas, I have an invitation. I take the greatest exception to the snide remarks you have been pleased to let drop about the department of which I have the honour to be in charge, and I invite you to withdraw them.'

Lucas looked puzzled, as well he might in Gryce's opinion. It was becoming crystal-clear that the head of Catering (Administration) was a crackpot who should be given a good long rest.

'I don't think I mentioned your department, Mr Hatch, except in passing when I said it had perhaps been over-expanded. If you find anything offensive about that, then of course I apologize.'

'You have bracketed us with other departments, Mr Lucas! You have tarred us with the same brush! "Doing little or no work", "Being carried as a passenger" – those are the phrases you have been using this evening, yes they are! Now let me inform you, sir, that whatever other departments may or may not do, my staff in Catering (Administration) are the most hardworking, most con-scientious body of men you could meet in a day's march. They are hard at it from morning till night and if everyone

289

slogged his guts out as I have seen those boys do, this country wouldn't be in the state it is in today!'

Jack Lemmon, sitting next to Hatch, was nodding solemnly. There was a murmur of sympathy from the audience. It was good stirring stuff, perhaps he wasn't a crackpot after all: Gryce went back to his earlier conclusion that a comparison could be made with fighter pilots he'd known in his RAF days.

'*But you don't produce anything, Mr Hatch!*' said Lucas, with an air of wonderment for some reason.

Hatch, the relief map of veins on his forehead looking as if it were dramatically about to change its contours, held up a podgy hand to show that he was not finished yet, while he bent down for a hurried consultation with Jack Lemmon.

'You say we don't produce anything, Mr Lucas. Putting to one side the upwards of eight hundred hot and cold luncheons prepared five days a week, would it interest you to know how many books of SSTs have been processed by my department since the new meals subsidy scheme came into being?'

'Enough to last us till the year two thousand eighty,' said Lucas promptly. 'That doesn't alter the fact, Mr Hatch, that the galley-slaves of Catering Admin don't add a halfpenny piece to the wealth of this country.'

Hatch's rather slobbery mouth dropped open and he seemed at a loss for words. Again he tried to arrest the proceedings while he conferred with Jack Lemmon. But this time Lucas, having made a telling point, was not disposed to wait for him, and eventually the head of Catering (Administration) slid back into his seat, muttering.

'Now I'd like to get away from the ethics of work, ladies and gentlemen, otherwise we'll still be arguing the toss at midnight and I think even Mr Hatch will agree that we've certainly done our whack of overtime this evening! What we have to decide, what *you* have to decide, is where we go from here. You now know all that there is to know about British Albion. It rests with you whether we continue in business.

'Obviously the danger has always been there that a security leak could blow what we're doing sky-high. For myself, and this is a personal view, I always thought the danger was over-stated and that the establishment of the Albion Players as a safety-valve would be counter-productive – I certainly beg leave to doubt that certain of your members would have been so inquisitive if left to their own devices.'

Was that supposed to be a dig at Gryce? If so, then *he* begged leave to inform Lucas of Personnel that anything he might have stumbled upon hinged less on the Albion Players than on the disappearance of the office furniture. If Lucas had been more concerned with security than was apparently the case, he would have been well advised to have put a guard on the main door.

'After all, what *was* the danger? That people would talk? But people always talk, about any organization they work for. Fortunately it's a convention in this country that when you ask someone what he does for a living he'll reply, "As little as possible" or "Run round in ever-decreasing circles" or "Sweet Francis Adams". So any theory that British Albion *did* do Sweet Francis Adams would always be discounted as exaggeration. Then again, there's the media. Well: they *have* shown an interest from time to time, but experience shows that the media are highly co-operative on matters of national security, especially if someone waves a D-notice under their noses.

'However, there we are. The damage has been done. We could still, and this is my considered view, continue to fool all of the people all of the time, but only with the co-operation of those "some of the people" who are now in the know. Any one of you could close down British Albion tomorrow, simply by revealing what he knows in the right quarter. The Press, of course, would make a field day of it: they don't like being fooled.

'I mentioned national security. Now national security *is* at stake here, although not in the way some sections of the media may have been led to believe. We're *not* secretly preparing ration books, we're *not* secretly processing identity cards, we're *not* secretly engaged on a repatriation programme for immigrants, but what we *are* secretly doing is pretending to the world that this nation has more people in gainful work than is in reality the case. You can imagine the harm that such a revelation would cause. As I said at the beginning it would bring the Government down: and now it is my duty to warn you that it would bring all of you down too.

'I asked what you have in common. Curiosity, was the answer. But you have something else in common, and that is that you are unemployable. Nobody wants you. Your skills, those of you who had any, have been superseded. The trades and industries that once employed you no longer need you: in many cases they don't need anybody, because they don't exist any more. Jobwise, ladies and gentlemen, the world is getting smaller and smaller. I'm sorry to be brutal but it is for the best. British Albion was your last chance, it was your only chance. Now you have to decide whether you mean to throw it away.'

Lucas, on that to Gryce's mind ringing note, turned to Grant-Peignton and bowed. Grant-Peignton, rising at once, started to bring his hands together as if about to lead the audience in applause, then thought better of it and froze them in mid-air, so that he looked like an angler demonstrating the measurements of a fish. In the

292

silence, Gryce glanced at Vaart. His face was a caricature of scorn and contempt.

'I don't know whether you wish me to withdraw at this stage, Mr Chairman – ?'

Lucas took a tentative step towards the edge of the platform, presumably as a token indication of his good-will, since he plainly had no intention of going anywhere. He and Grant-Peignton were joined by Ardagh in a huddled conference, then Lucas sat in the chair that had been reserved for Pam, and Grant-Peignton stepped forward to address the meeting.

'Ladies and gentlemen, I'm sure we're all very grateful indeed to Mr Lucas of Personnel for sparing the time to come here this evening and give us such an interesting talk.'

While Gryce thought a little less banality would have been in order there, he did have the impression that Grant-Peignton had recovered some of the authority that had gone with his blue-rinsed wig and chiffon tea-gown. Doubtless the chairman had been feeling very nervous about how the evening would go and was mightily relieved that the worst was now over.

'I'm equally sure that you would all wish me to thank Mr Lucas on your behalf for spelling out the position so clearly and so frankly.' There being no indication at all that this was the wish of the meeting, Grant-Peignton hurried on. 'Now time is running short and we have to be out of the hall by eight, which gives us rather less than forty minutes for a brief discussion before the main resolution of the evening. Mr Lucas has kindly offered to withdraw during our deliberations, but both your Secretary and I feel it would assist us all in reaching a decision if he were to remain and keep himself available for any points that may come up. I don't know what the feeling of the meeting is about that – perhaps someone would propose it as a motion?'

George Formby rose immediately.

'Are you proposing, Mr Aintree?'

'Point of information, Mr Chairman. Just what is the "main resolution" mentioned by you?'

Grant-Peignton turned to Lucas. Lucas, shifting in his chair, turned to Ardagh. Ardagh, fishing a slip of paper from his inside pocket, rose.

'"That before formally dissolving the British Albion Investigation Committee, all members of that committee should sign the Official Secrets Act."'

Ardagh read out the words defiantly, and in a voice that rose in volume as he got to the end, as if he expected a repetition of the earlier uproar. But there was only a whispering murmur: consternation rather than anger, was how Gryce interpreted it. He could well understand the reaction: he personally had always been very wary about signing his life away on insurance documents and such.

Several members were on their feet. Grant-Peignton, unwisely in Gryce's judgement, selected the woman who looked like Petula Clark, the one who had treated the last meeting to a rambling discourse about mock coal-mines down in Aldershot. It could only be that as an impartial chairman, Grant-Peignton felt it was high time the ladies had a look in.

'Yes? Are you proposing the motion?'

'What – about the Official Secrets Act?'

'No, no, that has yet to be debated. The motion I'm looking for is that Mr Lucas do be invited to remain on the platform during our discussion.'

'Oh, I see. Well, I will propose that, most certainly, if someone else will second it. By all means. Only what I really wanted to ask is, why can't we do something for the blind?'

Like her reference the other evening to a brother-in-law with a dry-cleaning business, this had Grant-Peignton completely mystified. Looking as if he vividly remembered that particular moment, he said without much hope: 'Do you think you could clarify that a little?'

'Well, I mean to say where Mr Lucas was saying we don't really do anything, like to earn our keep. I know *I* don't for one, all I do is cancel SST coupons after they've been clipped out of the books, and they don't really need cancelling because they're not supposed to be valid once they've been – '

'Could you make your point, please, as time is short?'

'I just wanted to ask Mr Lucas why can't we do something constructive, like for the blind? Or for the old folk, *they* need a break if anybody does. Or the kiddies. I mean to say for the sake of an example we could visit hospitals and infirmaries – '

'I don't *quite* see what we could be doing for the old, *or* the blind,' cut in Grant-Peignton as some of his colleagues on the platform began to smirk. 'In any case, that does come under the heading of discussion. First of all we must have the proposal that Mr Lucas do remain. Are you proposing that motion, yea or nay?'

'Oh, definitely.'

'Then do I have a seconder?'

'Seconded,' cried several voices, with the affected weariness of seasoned committee workhorses.

'Show of hands?'

As some arms shot up and others held back while their owners assessed which way the cat was going to jump, Vaart attracted Gryce's attention in his usual manner, by nudging him with his elbow.

'Bleedin wankers. Cahm on, less gerrardovit!'

Gryce had brought up his right arm to a hovering

position, and so the blow caught him rather painfully in the kidneys.

'Are we allowed to, would you say?'

'Anyone stops us, mate, kickem in the goolies.'

Shoulders hunched and knees bent, so as not to attract attention, Gryce scuttled after Vaart. There was a short difference of opinion at the doors where Seeds confirmed Gryce's belief that they were not allowed to leave until the meeting was over. While Vaart was asking nastily how he proposed to stop them, Gryce, anxious not to be drawn into the scene, faced the body of the hall where he saw that Flight-Sergeant Neddyman was standing on a chair to make himself seen above the forest of hands.

'We are voting at the moment!' responded Grant-Peignton. 'Are you raising a point of procedure?'

'I don't know what you'd call it,' called Flight-Sergeant Neddyman. 'I just want to ask Mr Lucas this. Instead of providing jobs to keep us in work, why doesn't the Government provide us with work to keep us in jobs?'

While Gryce was trying to puzzle this one out, Vaart tapped him on the shoulder to let him know that the argument had been won and that they should be on their merry way.

'That, sir,' Lucas was replying with the bleakest of smiles, so that he looked like the civil servant he probably really was, 'is outside my province.'

15

It was dark when they got back to Grain Yard. There was no street lighting in the cobbled crescent but some of the surviving or re-opened workshops had not yet closed for the evening, so Gryce and Vaart were able to zig-zag from one puddle of light to the next until they reached the rotting front door of the Albion Printeries gate-house. The Clarion Press gate-house, as Gryce had better start calling it.

Across the brick-paved yard the high windows were tall oblongs of bright yellow. Very cheerful it all looked to Gryce, quite like a Christmas card.

'The bleedin lectric works, then,' observed Vaart as they crossed the yard. 'Abaht bleedin time, iss bin costin a fortune in bleedin candles.'

Gryce had expected to find Norman Ferrier and perhaps Copeland still on the premises, as senior personnel they would be the last to leave and were perhaps accustomed to having a chin-wag before wending their way home. He was surprised to discover that no one had knocked off at all, late though it was. In fact, there were now far more people here than when he and Vaart had departed for the Albion Players' meeting at getting on for six, he supposed they would be the others spoken of by Ferrier, the ones who were going to detach themselves from British Albion as and when the opportunity arose. They presumably had a quick cup of tea and a scone after finishing work at Perfidious Albion, and then put in an evening shift in the printing works. Gryce called that keen.

There was an air, if Gryce was any judge, of anticipation. On his earlier visit all the activity had had a repair and maintenance look about it, but now it seemed they had left that stage behind and were ready for business. Copeland was meticulously polishing the brass button that presumably set the Wharfedale press in motion, he was doing it with a finishing-touch flourish that suggested a sense of occasion. Perhaps Ferrier would be making a short speech and smashing a bottle of cheap champagne against some appropriate part of the machine where fragments of glass would not get into the works.

The Linotypes were manned, although their keyboards had not commenced to clatter. At the long metal bench which according to Ferrier was where the type was made-up into pages, the Penney twins and three other men were fiddling with lengths of wood and metal, Gryce did hope the newcomers didn't have delicate nostrils. Mr Hakim, Mrs Rashman and Mr Cooley, all holding bales of poster-looking paper, were clustered in the doorway of the office, quite still, as if posing for a photograph, while Thelma, standing nearby and gawping across at them, looked as if she had been told to get out of the way while the photograph was taken. By the typeracks, and by various items of machinery whose function had not yet been explained to him, stood a fair cross-section of his colleagues from British Albion, In-house Mail being perhaps more over-represented than any other department with the exception of Stationery Supplies. It was quite a tableau. They all seemed to be awaiting a signal from Ferrier, who was watching Copeland polish the brass button of the Wharfedale press. Only the three one-armed commissionaires were actually working. The long trench, that source of purloined electricity, had been filled in again, and they were cementing the cracked old floor-tiles back in position.

There was no sign of Pam.

'We were going to start up the Wharfedale but we thought we'd hang on and give you the honour,' said Ferrier to Vaart. 'How did it go? What did you learn?'

Vaart gave a résumé of the evening's proceedings that was incomprehensible to Gryce, and made even more so by occasional questions from Copeland. But Ferrier, who began to look grave, seemed to follow his drift.

'I didn't realize that,' he said at length. 'I didn't realize they were all in it. I really thought the Albion Players was a genuine – a genuine what? I don't know.'

'Ganger wankers,' suggested Vaart.

'I was going to say *resistance movement*. That's how some of the rank and file must have seen themselves, anyway. They must feel badly let down.'

'What – them bleedin wankers?' Gryce really did wish Vaart would extend his vocabulary a little. 'I'm tellinya, they was shit-scared. All they're worried abaht is wevver they've gorra job to go back to tomorrer. Dangle a wage-packet in fronter their noses an they'll sign their own bleedin deaf-warrants, nair mind the Official bleedin Secrets Act. Issa good fing we din truss none of em, thass all I can say.'

'But did we *mis*-trust them enough? We didn't trust Pam Fawce, but we didn't know that Grant-Peignton and the rest were in league with her. I wish she'd told us that when she showed up here this evening.'

'Why, what diffrence would itta made?'

'We might have handled her differently. Still, it's too late now. The important thing is can we be sure she hasn't told anyone about *our* activities?'

'Niney-nine percen certain!' asserted Vaart aggressively. 'I ad a real go at Lucas, deliberate, gorrim proper narked I did, an e ad a right go back at me. Started rabbittin on abaht the print, ow it was over-manned an that. I'm tellinya, if e'd know anyfin, the ole bleeding lot woulda come out, cos I was really gerrin up his nose. Ent that ri?'

The question was to Gryce, who nodded non-committally, he had barely heard what Vaart had been saying. It was on Ferrier's phrase, 'We might have handled her differently' that he'd begun to feel the hairs bristling on the nape of his neck. And then Ferrier had added, 'Still, it's too late now.' What had they done with her?

'Whether she told Glucose or not,' volunteered Copeland, giving a final rub to the Wharfedale's brass button and cocking his head to admire his handiwork, 'I don't see that they can do anything. I believe she realized that.'

While it was always hard to follow what Copeland was saying, Gryce had no difficulty in gathering that he was talking about Pam in the past tense.

'Where *is* Pam, by the by?' he asked in what he wanted to be a light sort of voice, but it came out thick and strangulated.

He saw Ferrier and Copeland both catch Vaart's eye, their glance harnessing his and guiding it to the filled-in trench where the three one-armed commissionaires had nearly finished replacing the worn tiles. Despite their joint infirmity, they had made a good job of it, soon you would not be able to tell that any trench had been there.

'Jesus God!' whispered Vaart.

'It was an accident, I promise you,' said Ferrier in a low, urgent voice.

'We have a dozen witlesses,' murmured Copeland. Gryce could see that the Penney twins, Mr Hakim, Mrs Rashman and Mr Cooley, the three commissionaires and even Thelma all knew what was being talked about, but were pretending not to hear, if hear they could.

'Christ on bleedin crutches! What appened?'

'She panicked.' Ferrier put one arm around Vaart's

shoulders and the other one around Gryce's and drew them together, as if already confident of their complicity. Gryce wasn't sure he cared for that. But Ferrier spoke convincingly and reassuringly, he would make a good impression in the witness box if it came to it. While Gryce thanked his lucky stars that he had been well off the premises when it happened, it did truly sound like an accident.

Mrs Rashman, it would seem, had been the catalyst. She and Pam had lost their tempers with one another and Mrs Rashman had gone for her with her handbag. It had all started low-key enough with Pam cottoning on at once to what was going on and warning Ferrier that they couldn't possibly hope to get away with it. She had gone on to suggest that they were rocking the boat, that British Albion, together with similar 'units' as she'd called them, was the last hope of keeping the economy on an even keel, and that the only alternative was a drift into anarchy. Ferrier had taken her up on this and Gryce could just imagine the lively debate that must have followed: Pam's bossy dogmatism versus Ferrier's quiet reason, Ferrier's vision and wisdom against all Pam's play-it-by-the-book pettiness. Gryce wondered why he'd never realized before how limited her horizons really were. Ferrier must have won hands down.

But then Mrs Rashman had barged into the argument, accusing Pam for some strange reason of being frigid, the one epithet which Gryce knew from experience could not be aimed at her. She had countered with the irrelevant charge that Mrs Rashman had a reputation for chasing men, it being common knowledge according to Pam that she had only set her cap at Mr Cooley after being spurned by Seeds, Beazley and both the Penney twins. There was also a suggestion that she was still chasing Mr Hakim, with a view to having a bit on the side. Mrs Rashman had lost her rag at this and, calling Pam a stuck-up frigid squint-eyed bitch, had lunged at her with her handbag, a very heavy and bulky object it was, more of a hold-all really, Gryce had often seen it crammed with tinned sardines and drinking chocolate when her shopping bag was full. Pam had tried to take evasive action but one of the commissionaires had grabbed her arm, thinking only to stop her running out into Grain Yard in the mood she was in. She had torn herself free, run blindly across the works floor, slipped on a patch of oil and banged her head very heavily against some part of the Wharfedale printing press, apparently known as the platen. It was an accident.

Gryce felt for Pam no more and no less what he would have felt for any colleague who had died unexpectedly: there had been several such cases in various of his billets, heart attacks mainly, and his reaction, if the truth be known, had invariably been one of pleasurable shock. It gave one something to talk about, that was the size of it, it passed a morning. Just as, he supposed, his brief affair with Pam had passed an afternoon. It was ancient history now, something he could put down to experience. Next time, if there was a next time, he would pick someone in his own league. From what he had just heard, Mrs Rashman could be a distinct possibility, his initial instinct had proved to be unerring.

'Reckon they'll come lookin forrer?' Vaart asked as Ferrier came to the end of his narrative.

'I don't see why they should, if we're right in thinking she told no one she was coming here. If you're sure Lucas doesn't know about us, then she was probably hugging it to herself: she didn't know what she was going to find here but whatever it was, it was going to be a feather in her own cap. They won't connect her with us.'

Gryce, for all that the affair was none of his concern,

his hands were clean, felt a duty to tell Ferrier that he was being recklessly optimistic.

'I don't want to be a wet blanket, but are you confident on that point? Pam's disappearance is bound to be linked in some way with the disappearance of two-thirds of her colleagues in Stationery Supplies, together with all the furniture. Surely enquiries will be made?'

'Of course enquiries will be made. They'll find that there was a conspiracy to carry out large-scale thefts from Stationery Supplies and Stationery Stores. That kind of thing is common enough in every kind of business of any size. But why should those enquiries lead anyone here? And if they do come here, what do they propose to do? Arrest us? Put us on trial? What a case it would be, Mr Gryce!'

'Iss like that twat Lucas was sayin,' said Vaart. 'It'd bring the bleedin govmen dahn.'

'More than that,' said Ferrier with great seriousness. 'It would bring England down.' Then, making an obvious effort to lighten the mood, he raised his arms and brought them slapping down against the pockets of his dust-coat. 'Well now! I did have some notes here but I think we've had enough speechifying for one evening! Are you going to press that button, Jack, or shall I spark off our first demarcation dispute by doing it myself?'

Vaart jerked his head towards Gryce. 'Worrerbaht Charlie-boy?'

'Clem, actually,' corrected Gryce, after the split-second that it always took him to remember his own name.

'We have our first order, Mr Christ!' beamed Copeland. 'Fyfe humbug ply coasters for a raffle Asian of two beers reformation!'

'Five hundred fly-posters for a travel agent of dubious reputation,' translated Ferrier with a smile. 'And more work to come. Can we count on you, Mr Gryce?'

303

'Looker it this way, son, you don av much option,' said Vaart.

Coming from anyone else that could have sounded sinister, but coming from Vaart it sounded like the cheeriest of invitations, for all that it had only just sunk in with Gryce that Vaart had not left his side since the moment he had set foot in the Albion Printeries, he begged its pardon, Clarion Press.

The same wave of euphoria that he had felt when he'd first met Norman Ferrier came over him again. He breathed in deeply, savouring the smell of ink. He was hours late for his supper but bubbles to it, or to employ the phraseology of Vaart, sod it. 'Yes yes yes!' he wanted to cry, but something more formal seemed appropriate.

'May I say this,' began Gryce. He had heard politicians use that preamble to effect. 'It has been a long day for me. I was very much persuaded by your arguments earlier, but when I listened to Lucas of Personnel on the subject of British Albion I was swayed by him also. Perhaps I am easily influenced, but now that I am back here, I feel on balance that there is a better future on this side of the river than on the other one, all other things being equal.'

Although he'd been listened to courteously, apart from a sigh from Vaart that was patently meant to be taken as a silent groan, Gryce wished he'd made less heavy weather of it and that he hadn't said 'all other things being equal' which sounded too cautious by half. He decided to finish on an up-beat note, he'd give them a joke, an in-joke as he hoped it would be to most of those present, he did hope they would get it.

'Does that answer your question?'

But he had muffed it. Gryce had paused too long and his joke was drowned by the roar of the Wharfedale press as Vaart pressed the shining brass button.

304